DEADLY CONTACT

"Blood," she whispered. "Lots of blood."

They used their penlights and stepped cautiously into the room. The small lights revealed a nightmare of blood: splatters and drops, stains across the wall, smears along the floor. On the dining room table they found what was left of a man. The fingers on his right hand had been cut off, his left arm amputated, a bloody ax on the floor beside it. A hundred slices and cuts crisscrossed his body. His throat had been slashed.

"Our contact," Wade said.

A moment later, the windows in the room exploded in a shower of glass as bullets jolted through them.

Someone kicked in the front door and a deadly spray of hot lead spewed from an automatic weapon ripping into the table.

They were trapped and it would take nothing short of a miracle—or every skill they'd ever learned executed to perfection—to get out of that damned room alive!

THE
SPECIALISTS

NUKE DOWN

Chet Cunningham

BANTAM BOOKS
New York Toronto London Sydney Auckland

THE SPECIALISTS: Nuke Down

A Bantam Book/February 2001

All rights reserved.
Copyright © 2001 by Chet Cunningham
Cover art copyright © 2001 by Alan Ayers
No part of this book may be reproduced or transmitted in any form
or by any means, electronic or mechanical, including photocopying,
recording, or by any information storage and retrieval system,
without permission in writing from the publisher.
For information address: Bantam Books.

ISBN 0-553-58077-9

Published simultaneously in the United States and Canada

Bantam Books are published by Bantam Books, a division of Random
House, Inc. Its trademark, consisting of the words "Bantam Books" and
the portrayal of a rooster, is Registered in U.S. Patent and Trademark
Office and in other countries. Marca Registrada. Bantam Books, 1540
Broadway, New York, New York 10036.

PRINTED IN THE UNITED STATES OF AMERICA

OPM   10   9   8   7   6   5   4   3   2   1

Dedicated to those real-
life men and women who do
the tough, dirty, and always covert
jobs of sniffing out and tracking
down terrorists worldwide
who try to destroy world
order and justice

✫ THE PLAYERS ✫

WADE THORNE, thirty-eight, the Specialists' team leader. He's six-two, 195 pounds, ex-CIA who quit to raise horses in Idaho. Eight years as a CIA field agent. He left the Agency when a Russian agent killed his wife and daughter. He can fly anything with wings or rotors. He's a master with weapons of all types, in hand-to-hand fighting, stalking, silent movement, camouflage, and surprise attacks. He's also a class-four chess player, Formula One licensed race-car driver, skier, loves to cook Italian food. Interested in Egyptology and has spent time there. Speaks Arabic, Italian, and French.

KATHERINE "KAT" KILLINGER, thirty-two, five-eight, slender, half Hawaiian and half English. She is second in command. A triathlon winner in Hawaii, a lawyer who has passed the bar in seven states, and an ex-FBI field agent. She has long, dark hair, a delicious golden coloring. She's gorgeous. Married at eighteen, divorced at nineteen, no children. Good with weapons, especially an automatic pistol. She has a sharp lawyer's mind, thinks well on her feet, uses karate, and has a historic Barbie doll collection. She's an expert on fifteenth-century Flemish painters, and speaks German, Polish, and Spanish. She volunteers at a school in London tutoring students in reading.

ICHI YAMAGATA, twenty-four, six feet, 175 pounds. A Japanese-American from Seattle. He's the arms expert for the team. He can repair, rebuild, customize, or create almost any small arm. He's a serious student of the Japanese Samurai warriors and a fantastic knife and short sword fighter. He is the silent killing expert for the Specialists. Had been a weapons expert for the FBI before being recruited for the team. Single, two years of college. A martial-arts expert. To relax he flies exotic kites. He speaks Japanese and Mandarin Chinese.

ROGER JOHNSON, twenty-four, six-three, 210 pounds. An African-American from the projects of New York. Kept out of trouble by playing basketball. Not quite good enough to be college-recruited, so he joined the Navy. Made it into the

SEALs. Caught Mr. Marshall's attention and received a "special circumstances" discharge from the Navy by order of the Chief of Naval Operations so he could join the Specialists. Knows various African languages such as Chichewa, Swahili, and Akan. Top demolitions expert for the team. Handles all explosives, timers, and bombs. He's the team's underwater expert.

HERSHEL LEVINE, thirty-one, five-nine, 145 pounds. Former Israeli Mossad agent who knew Mr. Marshall from the CIA. He's a computer whiz. Can program, hack into almost any system, rebuild, and repair computer hardware. Fantastic touch in researching on the World Wide Web. His young wife was killed in an Arab attack in Israel six years ago. Still has strong ties to Israel. Keeps some contacts with former coworkers on the Internet. Quietly efficient, an expert on all small arms. Speaks Hebrew, English, Arabic, Kurdish, and Persian (Farsi).

DUNCAN BANCROFT, thirty-four, six-two, 165 pounds, blond, clean-shaven, soft-spoken, former English MI-6 agent who used to work with Mr. Marshall through the CIA. A team player. Top intelligence man. Knows everyone, has contacts and friends in most nations. Can help procure weapons in countries where they can't take in their own. A bit of a loner off duty. Has a Ph.D. in English literature from Cambridge. Loves to sail his boat. Is a competition pistol marksman. Is divorced with two girls in Scotland. Speaks Russian, Danish, French, and German.

⋆ THE SPECIALISTS ⋆
NUKE DOWN

★ ONE ★

LEBANESE COAST

Wade Thorne looked over the rail of the weather-beaten freighter as it steamed southward at fourteen knots through the placid Mediterranean Sea. He couldn't see the lights of Lebanon to the east, but he knew they were there. Wade leaned his six-foot two-inch and 195-pound frame against the rail. He squinted from light green eyes into the pale darkness and soon saw a forty-foot fishing boat angling toward them, materializing out of the wispy fog, birthed by the uncertain moonlight.

Right on time. He liked that.

The ex-CIA agent checked his gear. He had only a light backpack and two weapons slung over his shoulders. Beside him a woman stirred.

"Is that our pickup boat?" Kat Killinger asked. She was five feet eight, slender, and dressed as the man was in black pants and shirt; blotches of dark makeup camouflaged her pretty face. She also had a black backpack and an H & K MP-5 9mm submachine gun slung over her shoulder. Her long dark hair had been braided, coiled, pinned, and concealed under a black floppy hat.

"Yes, this should be our friends," Wade said. The fishing boat powered along thirty yards off the side of the freighter. Three quick flashes of light stabbed toward the Specialists.

Wade sent two flashes back from a penlight, and both the figures at the rail relaxed a little.

"It could still be a trap," Kat said. "They would be delighted to grab a couple of U.S. spies on their turf."

"That's why we lock and load," Wade said. He pivoted down the weapons one at a time, chambered a round, pushed on the safety, and swung it back. He heard Kat do the same, and then they watched the boat come alongside.

"I finally got used to the freighter's sickening diesel exhaust smell combined with the dampness," Kat said. "What is this little boat going to smell like?"

"Fish," Wade said with a grin. "Live, dead, and rotting fish. Fish scales, fish guts, fish fillets, and lots of fish bait. Don't worry, we won't be on board long."

They had a simple assignment. Wade reviewed it as they waited for the boats to latch together. They had firm information that one of the terrorists involved in the Marine Corps headquarters bombing in Beirut in 1983 had surfaced in the southern Lebanese city of Sur, and was continuing to plan terrorist activities. They had a contact in Sur who would meet the Specialists and direct them to the terrorist's house.

The code name of the terrorist was the Hammer. Six different countries wanted him for murder, arson, bombing, and mayhem. Mr. Marshall had instructed the Specialists to go in and bring out the Hammer for trial in England.

The Specialists were a group of counterterrorists, privately funded, and made up of the best men and women in the world at putting down terror and crime. They were assembled two years ago by J. August Marshall, a highly motivated industrial multibillionaire who also had been the U.S. CIA director for ten years. He had his headquarters in England, offices in twenty capitals around the world, and divided his time between running his dozens of conglomerates and tracking terrorists. He was seventy-two years old, had a full head of white hair, and always wore a suit with a red carnation in his coat buttonhole.

His lead man in the group was Wade Thorne, ex-CIA agent and horse rancher from Idaho, who was tops in the field of detection and enforcement in the antiterrorists arena. After eight years doing fieldwork for the CIA he was an expert on the international crime scene. Wade's partner on this mission was Kat Killinger, ex-FBI agent and a lawyer who ran the triathlon in her native Hawaii. She was the team's logic guru and evaluator, and could carry her weight with any of a dozen hand and shoulder weapons.

The fishing craft bumped against the side of the freighter and gunned its engine to match the speed of the larger ship. A crewman dropped down a line fastened to a cleat on the freighter. It was caught below and tied to a fitting at the bow. The big ship continued its forward speed. Two heavy bumpers along the side of the fishing boat cushioned the steel-against-steel contact. Another crewman lowered a rope ladder.

"Let's choggie out of here," Wade said. The two moved to the freighter's rail. Wade went down first. The ropes swayed and slammed against the side of the freighter with the movement of the big ship. It reminded him of the times he had gone down a rope landing net from a fifty-foot training tower. He hit the bottom of the ladder, stepped onto the fishing boat rail, and jumped to the sloping deck. He skidded on a fillet fish carcass, then steadied. He swung his MP-5 up, clicked off the safety, and covered the three men who stood on the other side of the boat.

Wade snapped off two phrases in Arabic.

The correct answers came back at once in the same tongue. Wade gave the ladder two jerks. Kat crawled over the rail, and climbed down as if she did this sort of exercise every day. Twice the rope and her body swung away from the big ship, then slammed back into the side of the freighter. She remembered to let go of the rope at the instant of contact, then grabbed it again quickly. She soon stepped over the rail and onto the fishing boat.

One of the three Lebanese held his hat over his chest and nodded. Wade could smell the results of the day's work of catching, cleaning, and icing down the fish. The

Lebanese man's face showed plainly in the weak lights on the craft and Wade saw that the wind and water-reflected sun had turned the fisherman's skin into the shade of old leather. Wade figured the man at about forty. He had small brown eyes peering from under heavy brows and a bushy, black mustache.

"Welcome. We are on time, no?" the captain asked in English.

"You are on time. Good. How long to the dock?" Wade asked.

"My English is good, yes? We are about an hour to the dock or another place if you want."

"We need a safe landing, where no one will see us," Kat said.

The captain turned to her, his eyes flashing. "Oh, a woman. A most brave and courageous woman. I congratulate you. In my country women are not as . . . as free, can't dress . . ." He stopped. "Now, we must leave."

One of the men untied the line from the fishing boat's bow and threw off the rope ladder. At once the big ship surged away from the smaller one. The second man had moved to the cabin and the fishing boat turned and slanted toward the east at full cruising speed. Wade watched the glowing green phosphorescence of the wake. By the action of the water he figured they were making about ten knots. Good.

The captain with the wind-burned face and probing eyes rubbed one hand through his thick, dark hair. "We wish you well. We come to same dock at dusk each day for three days. Yes?"

"Yes," Wade said. "Half the pay when we land, the other half when we get back to the freighter."

"Yes, yes. We can do it. We fish only a little. My family thanks you. We wish to help."

"You have children?" Kat asked.

The captain beamed. "Oh, yes, six. Three of each. All so bright and happy. It takes much money these days just to feed so many."

Kat took a pair of small but powerful binoculars from

her pack and watched to the east. They sat on a hold cover and Kat kept telling herself to forget the smell of fish. It was everywhere. So far she had beaten down two surges of bile. She would not throw up. She would not. It was enough she would smell like fish for a week.

A half hour later, they saw the coastline.

The town where they would land was Sur, the ancient Phoenician port of Tyre, that was a bustling trade center as early as 3000 B.C. Wade wondered if there would be anything left from those early days nearly five thousand years ago? Some stone wharves? A stone dock?

"More lights than I expected," Kat said. "This is not a huge town."

Wade motioned for the captain to come over.

"How big is the town of Sur?"

"About fifty thousand. Many fishing boats."

"Can we get in without being seen?"

The Lebanese frowned, preened his mustache, and then rubbed his face with his right hand. "We go to a small wharf away from big docks, no?"

"Yes," Kat said.

The captain looked up quickly, then smiled. "I am not used to . . ." He stopped. "I have a friend repairs boats. He has dock away from big ships. We go there in dark. No one see. Yes. It is good."

As the boat approached the harbor, the two Specialists went into the cabin so they wouldn't be seen. Both sat on the floor and put on their G-16s, their improved, short-distance, person-to-person radios. The belt unit was the size of a beeper, and had wires that went under the wearer's clothes to the back of the neck where a wire went into the ear with a small earpiece. Another wire wrapped around the neck with a throat mike. The throat mike was not as sensitive as a lip mike, but much easier to wear and not as prone to being knocked off. They checked the radios by tapping the mikes, then left them on and waited. Wade could see lights now and the sides of tall ships beside them as they worked into the port. He knelt and looked out the forward window.

Dozens of ships of all sizes seemed jammed into the port. Then a waterway opened to the left and they veered that direction away from the rest of the ships. Ahead he saw only blackness.

Three or four minutes later Wade felt the ship nudge against a dock and come to a stop. The captain stepped into the wheelhouse and smiled in the soft light.

"We are here. The dock is empty. Go in safety."

Wade handed him an envelope with highly prized U.S. bank notes and repeated the instructions.

"Here at dusk. Next three days."

"As you say, so it shall be," the captain said.

They crept out of the wheelhouse to the deck and then to the rail. The fishing boat was tied to a stone wharf. Wade saw that this dock was moss-covered and did seem to be five thousand years old. Kat looked over the rail and scanned the narrow dock that fronted an equally narrow street. A hill climbed into the darkness just off the road.

She quartered off the area and checked each grid. After two minutes she lowered her binoculars and nodded.

"Nobody out there unless they are top-notch professionals."

"Let's go," Wade said and they stepped over the rail onto the ancient stones and hurried toward the road.

Both moved quickly along the street that wound around a small hill, then slanted down into a half-commercial, half-residential section. They saw only three streetlights ahead over several blocks. The buildings were a wild mixture of modern concrete block structures beside stone and mortar houses and buildings that looked a thousand years old. The street here was dirt with no sidewalks. Wade could see no telephone poles or light poles. Only an occasional building had any lights on inside.

Both of them had memorized the maps and instructions. But looking at a map and seeing the real town was a lot different. The town of Sur was larger than they expected. A quarter of a mile down the road they found a landmark in their instructions. There were few street signs.

They found a three-story building made of stone with a sign on top.

Most of the town here was still dark with a streetlight only every four blocks. The time was a little after 1:00 A.M.

A pair of headlights bathed the street ahead of them and they darted into the doorway of a building and let the rig roll past. It was a police van with two men in it.

They turned down the street by the tall building. The map said to go two hundred yards until they came to a large rock house with a dry fountain in front of it. The man they were to meet lived three houses farther and on the same side of the street. House numbers would have made it easier.

They worked ahead slowly until they found the large rock house with the dry fountain. It was across the street from them. They had seen only three men on the street. There were few cars or trucks. They looked at the target house. It seemed quiet, no lights. The place was small, maybe four rooms, Wade figured. Built of stone on the outside, probably brick or stone walls inside. There were two windows on the front and the side.

This was the home of their contact who would lead them to the terrorist. The two watched the place for five minutes, and saw no activity. No one went up or down the street. They heard one vehicle far off.

Both Specialists walked across the dirt street and up to the house, then turned in sharply and hurried to the back door they had been told to use. Kat tried the door. It was unlocked. She looked at Wade, then she jerked open the door and rushed inside with Wade right behind her. There was no reaction. Both used penlights and cleared the first room, a kitchen. They moved to a door leading into another room.

Quickly Wade and Kat cleared two more rooms, and found no one there. Wade wondered where their contact was. Kat opened the door into the front room. Her nose quivered.

"Blood," she whispered. "Lots of blood." They used their penlights and stepped cautiously into the room. The small lights revealed a nightmare of red: splatters and drops, stains across a wall, smears along the floor. On the dining-room table they found what was left of a man. The fingers on his right hand had been cut off, his left arm chopped off with a bloody ax on the floor. A hundred slices and cuts crisscrossed his body. His throat had been slashed.

Kat found his left arm on the floor. She picked it up and put it on the table, and shone her flash on the wrist. The numbers 1289 were tattooed into the flesh.

"Our contact," Wade said.

A moment later, windows in the room exploded in a shower of glass as bullets jolted through them. Wade and Kat dropped to the floor. Before they could react, they heard slugs hitting the wooden front door. Then more bullets slammed through the broken windows and dug small grooves in the stone and plastered inside walls.

Someone kicked in the front door and a deadly spray of hot lead spewed from an automatic weapon, ripping into the table.

Kat had her MP-5 up and fired a six-round burst into the spot a foot above the muzzle flashes of the weapon at the door. They heard a grunt, then a scream. Kat and Wade crawled to the front wall to avoid the new angle of fire. So far no one had pushed a weapon in the broken-out windows.

At once more rounds poured through the door and front windows. Kat moved to the corner.

She tapped her throat mike twice for the "okay here" signal. She heard two taps in response, then a whisper in her earpiece.

"Flash-bang, on three." There was a pause. Then her radio spoke again. "One, two, three."

Kat closed her eyes and put her face to the wall, then held her hands over her ears. The nonlethal weapon bounced once outside the front door, then went off with a series of six skull-splitting explosive sounds that drilled through the brain and rendered anyone nearby deaf for two to three minutes, followed by six intensely brilliant strobes of light that penetrated eyelids and blinded the terrorists around the front of the house.

Kat felt the thundering pulsations of sound and "saw" the strobes of light through her hands. Wade charged out the front door as soon as the last strobe died and gunned down two men he found writhing on the ground. Another man rushed toward the front of the house and Wade sent a six-round burst at him.

Two weapons at the rear of the house continued to fire. Wade stepped back into the front room, then slid toward the door into the middle room, crawled through to the kitchen where he could see out the back door. One muzzle flash appeared twenty yards away in the backyard near a trash pile. He sent a dozen 9mm rounds at the area and saw the weapon lift up and the man fire off three rounds in a death spasm before he fell.

Wade listened to the silence, and heard a man running down the street.

He went back to the second room where Kat was looking through the things that hadn't been trashed.

"Should be an address or a hint where the terr lives around here somewhere," Kat said.

Wade used his pencil flash and joined in the search.

"If this guy was any kind of a professional, he wouldn't have written down the address," Wade said. They continued to look for any clue but couldn't stay much longer. Either the police or terrorist reinforcements would be there soon. Then Kat had an idea.

She went back to the body and looked at the man's face. It was unmarked. She used both hands and pried his teeth apart. But there was nothing inside his mouth. He must have screamed a lot while they tortured him.

They looked in the last room. It had only a table with a pallet, oils, and brushes on it. A small unfinished painting stood on an easel.

Wade looked at it, then grinned. "Our contact was an artist. He told us he would leave a painting of the terr's house in case something went wrong. This must be it. See the large tower with a light on top? Four houses down a shaft of sunlight shines on one house. That has to be where the terr lives. Let's go find that tower."

They eased cautiously out the back door. In the distance they heard sirens. Wade replaced his MP-5 magazine with a full one from his backpack. His second weapon, a Colt Commando carbine, the Army's M-4A1, was tied over his back with a rubber cord. Kat put in a new magazine.

"That tower must be a landmark of some kind," Kat said. "I hope the light stays on all night."

They looked around just outside the house.

"We need a small hill so we can see more of the town," Wade said.

"Maybe we can see a hill from the street."

They walked to the front of the house and began to look around when suddenly bullets began screaming over their heads as an automatic weapon opened up on them from the killing range of less than thirty yards.

★ TWO ★

When the first shots came, Kat dove left, Wade dove right, and both rolled while bringing up their MP-5s. They each returned fire and rolled, fired and rolled. After the pair had fired three times, the guns across the street went silent.

The G-16 came on in Kat's ear.

"We put them down or scared them off. I'm okay. You?"

"Got a small nick in the pants leg but no blood. We still heading to the left?"

Wade lifted up and ran to where she was and Kat came to her feet and they hurried up the unlighted street between houses two steps up from the slum level. They sprinted for two blocks, slowed, and took a quick look behind them. No pursuit.

Both had changed magazines and had their safeties off on the submachine guns.

"They were waiting for us," Kat said.

"Yeah, and a damn poor job of closing the file. They had to be terrs, and down several notches on talent."

"How do we find the Hammer?" Kat asked.

"We try for some hill, a tall tree, something so we can see more of this town. It must be three miles across."

Kat pointed. "That string of four streetlights looks like they go up a hill."

"We're moving." They jogged forward along the dirt street for three blocks, then saw the rise. Five minutes later they had passed three of the four streetlights and paused to take a look. Half of the town spread out below them. Most of it was dark. Here and there an island of light showed, then more blackness.

From long habit, Kat began to section off the area and examine each square. She found it on the third one.

"There. Just this side of that large blob of lights. See that one light that's higher than the rest of the area. At least from here it looks higher."

"Let's give it a try," Wade said.

The light was to the right and partway back the way they had come. They picked another street and jogged along it. More of the same kind of houses, some stone, some newer ones that looked to be concrete blocks and plaster. Again there were no sidewalks and no paved streets.

After a ten-minute jog they slowed. They were in a section of better houses, and here and there part of the street was blacktop. Wade had been thinking about the timing.

"If those were the Hammer's terrs we ran off, they will be at his place long before we can make it, so they'll be waiting for us."

Kat glanced over at him. "Oh, yeah, and we'll be ready for them."

Wade chuckled at her remark and they jogged again. Ahead half a block, a pale streetlight sent down a cone of light onto the blacktop street.

"Around it," Wade said. They ran through two front yards and came out on the street again. Kat held up her hand. They stopped and listened. They heard an engine moving toward them. There were almost no cars on the streets, very few sitting at the curbs. They stepped behind a pair of trees in the front yard of a house and waited. A sedan drove forward slowly without any lights. Two men with what looked like long guns stood with head, arms, and shoulders out a sunroof, one seemingly watching each side of the street.

"Let them pass if they don't spot us," Wade whispered into his mike. He got two taps back in his earpiece. The sedan slowed opposite them and stopped. The men stared all around, then the sedan turned and headed back the way it had come.

"How far up this street?" Kat asked on the radio.

"Looks like another quarter mile if that's the right light on the right tower."

"Let's hope the car keeps on moving that way," Kat said. They came from the trees and continued up the street. Wade had used some of the time to take out a pair of NVGs, night vision goggles, from his pack. He slipped them on and watched ahead as the pale green landscape came into focus. No cars, no people, not even a stray dog.

Two cars with lights on drove across the street ahead of them. It seemed to be a major avenue.

"This the one we want?" Kat asked.

It wasn't. They crossed it when no cars were coming and took a left turn at the next street. The tower seemed to be in that direction.

Two blocks later they could see the three-story tower plainly. They paused near a streetlight and checked it again.

"Yes, it matches," Kat said. "That's the building. No houses this side, so it must be the other way."

They moved ahead slowly, watching for any movement. Wade saw nothing he hadn't seen for the last half hour along these deserted streets. The two passed the large building and saw that it held a group of small stores. They were just beyond it and looking for the fourth house, when a pair of headlights snapped on fifty yards in front of them.

A moment later two cars behind them turned on lights. The Specialists were boxed in and lit up for the kill. Wade jerked down the NVGs, momentarily blinded by the headlights.

Before they could take cover, shots barked from in front of them and hot lead whistled past. There was no cover in the street. Kat sprinted to the left, and Wade had enough vision left to pound to the right slamming past the edge of a concrete block house and stopping. He edged his MP-5 around the corner and kicked off a three-round burst. He still couldn't see much except the pinpoints of the muzzle flashes. Without the silencer on the weapon it had enough range for the cars ahead. He waited for muzzle flashes and silenced one of them with a three-round burst and picked off a second man as he leaned around the side of one of the cars. The third man cut and ran for the fourth house down from the tower.

Wade led him with a three-round burst and got lucky with one hit in the man's back. He stumbled and went down before he made it to the house. Wade looked the other way. The cars with the lights on had gone dark, as they backed slowly away from the confrontation. He sent two six-round greetings into the cars to hurry them on their way.

"Kat, looks like we've moved them. Are you okay?" He used the radio throat mike.

"Not the best. Caught one in my arm below the elbow. An in and out, so no big bother. I could use a bandage. Mine isn't all that effective."

"Stay there, I'm coming over." He sprinted across the street and drew no fire. Wade found her at the corner of the building, her MP-5 up and ready. She relaxed when she saw him.

"Sorry. I was in the wrong place."

He pulled up her shirtsleeve and found the wound.

"Yes, a scratch here." He pulled a bandage from his rear pocket and wrapped it around a handkerchief she had folded over the entrance and exit holes. Then he tightened the white cloth and wrapped it again. He taped the bandage and nodded. She pulled down the sleeve and flexed her arm.

"Going to hurt like hell in about an hour," he said. "Let's see if we can wrap this up before then." She nodded. They ran through the backyard of three houses, then both charged across the street toward the target house. The two

Specialists had automatically spread five yards apart as they ran, so no lucky burst would get more than one.

Firing came from the front door of the house but it was only a pistol from the sound and out of range. Wade blasted six rounds through the door from his sub gun and silenced the weapon. They both charged forward and slammed against the front wall of the house. Kat moved toward the door that had swung outward a foot.

As soon as Kat headed for the door, Wade pulled back to the side of the house and ran toward the rear. It was a stone structure with windows along the side. No lights showed inside. The rear door had a porch that had been covered and screened in. He watched it with the NVGs but saw no movement. It could be a death trap.

They had agreed to use tear gas grenades if the place looked buttoned up. It did. He took a tear gas canister from his backpack and pulled out the safety pin, then threw it hard against the screen. The thin plastic screening ripped apart, the grenade broke through, and fell inside the porch where it went off with a pop. He saw the whitish gas spilling out, filling the porch, then drifting through the hole and the screen.

Moments later he heard a strange cry of pain and anger and a man stormed out the porch door, rubbing his eyes with one hand and holding an automatic rifle in the other. He ran straight for Wade but didn't know he was there. Wade stood from where he had been crouching and butt stroked the terr in the head with his carbine. The terr went down hard, mumbled something, then passed out.

Wade almost shot him, but instead bound his hands and ankles with riot cuffs and put a gag around his mouth.

Wade watched the porch clear of the caustic fumes. Another few minutes. Then he lifted his weapon as a form came running out the porch. At the same time the radio warned him.

"Kat coming out the rear, don't shoot."

He lowered his weapon and called softly and she ran to him sliding to the ground.

"Just one body inside. No one else. Where the hell do we go from here?"

Wade handed her his MP-5 and stood, lifting the small terr over his shoulder. "Down this side street in a dark place for a conference," he said.

Two blocks down the row of houses, they stopped under a tree. Wade put the terr on the ground and slapped his face to bring him around. He groaned, screeched at them in Arabic. Wade screeched right back at him and surprised the Arab. They talked in Arabic.

"You killed my friend."

"He tried to kill us. We were better than he was. Where is the Hammer?"

"Who?"

Wade hit him in the side of the face with his hard right fist. The man fell to the ground. They lifted him back to a sitting position, and he spit out blood.

"We could start by cutting off your fingers one at a time," Wade said. "The way your people did to our man in his home tonight."

"Not me, I wasn't there."

"Where is the Hammer?"

"They would kill me."

"We'll torture you, then kill you if you don't. You tell us and vanish. They'd have to catch you first. We already have caught you. You have five minutes to live."

"Allah protect me!" he screamed. "Show me the way."

"He has. Protect your own life, vanish. They will never find you."

He hesitated. Kat slapped him with a full right-handed swing. He toppled to the ground again. They sat him up.

The terrorist sagged, his face worked, tears seeped from his eyes. Slowly he shook his head. "Let me think a minute."

Wade put the MP-5's muzzle into the man's mouth and eased his finger on the trigger.

"Take all the time you need. You have five seconds. Then I'm pulling the trigger."

The terrorist's eyes went wide, then as Wade showed him three fingers, he nodded. The muzzle came free.

"Yes. I know where he is. His most secure quarters. Out of town ten kilometers. I can take you there. I have a car. Promise me my life and I won't betray you or mislead you. Agreed?"

Kat looked at Wade. She shone her flash on the terr's face and let small worry lines form around her eyes.

"After we chop off three of your fingers, you'll be begging to tell us where the Hammer is," Kat said. "It is the safest way for us."

The terr's face showed lines of sweat coming down from his forehead to his eyes and dripping off his nose.

"Wait. You can trust me. I'd have to kill myself to warn my friends."

Wade nodded. "Where's your car?"

A few minutes later, they drove along a deserted country road ten kilometers outside of Sur. They saw few houses, only an occasional farm, and the road turned into a dirt track. They came around a corner.

"It's just ahead," the terr said.

"Lights, you use headlights as a signal?" Wade asked.

"Yes. On, off. On, off. Then leave on."

"Do it," Kat said. She sat beside the terr in the front seat, the muzzle of her sub gun in his side. "One wrong move and you're dead. We won't use the grenade. You'll stay tied and gagged in the car while we visit the Hammer."

"Where do you usually park?" Wade asked.

"In back, out of sight. The usual place."

"Do it."

The car slowed, the lights snapped off, and it came around the house toward an old shed and a rusting Citroen of some ancient vintage. The terr turned off the motor and told them to lie down below the windows of the car when it stopped. A sudden light stabbed through the darkness shining on the car and the terr. He stayed still for a moment, then turned and waved at the light. It snapped off. He opened the door.

"Stay," Wade said in Arabic. Kat cinched up the plastic riot cuffs on his hands, then put another around one arm to the steering wheel. Wade slid out the door on the off side of the car from the house. The way the car was parked, Kat was also away from the residence. She opened the door and eased out.

A voice barked from the shadows of the building.

"A minute," the terr shouted from the car. "I have some things to carry."

Wade heard the Arabic and nodded. Then he used the MP-5 with the sound suppressor and fired six rounds at where he figured the talker stood near the shadow of the back door. He heard a grunt, then something hit the ground and a weapon clattered on the dirt.

"Now," Wade whispered into his throat mike. He and Kat raced for the rear of the house. Wade almost stumbled over the body but missed it and eased against the wall next to the door.

Just then someone opened the door. A shaft of yellow light stabbed into the darkness outside as the panel swung away from Wade.

"What's taking you so long?" a guttural voice asked in Arabic. Wade slammed the heavy sound suppressor on the MP-5 down on the back of the tall, thin Arab's neck, and he crumbled to the ground like he was head-shot. He carried no weapon. Kat bent and put on a gag, cuffed his hands behind his back and his ankles together.

Wade used hand signals in the dim moonlight to indicate he would go to the front door. The rear one gaped open. Someone else would be coming soon, so she edged back out of the light and held her sub gun aimed at the opening.

A minute later nothing had happened. She braced herself and then heard the sound in her earpiece. "Let's shoot through the doors, then charge inside. Now."

She heard the firing from the front and her finger pulled the trigger three times, sending nine rounds into the area beyond the back door. Then she jolted inside into the light. It was a utility area and storeroom. A door in the middle was open a foot, swinging to the outside. She leaped across it and kicked it open so it moved away from her.

Six rounds slammed through the opening before she could move toward it. She held her sub gun around the doorway and sprayed in six rounds of her own. There was no response. She took a quick look around the door at knee level. A man lay on the floor across the lighted room. An automatic rifle trailed from one lifeless hand. His face showed three bullet wounds.

She jolted through the door and cleared the room, then ran to the door on the far wall.

"Clear two rooms in back. One more terr down."

Wade confirmed her report with two taps on the throat mike.

She heard firing from the other room but she wasn't sure who originated it. "Should I come through the door?" she asked.

"No," the one word sounded in her ear.

More firing. This time she recognized the chatter of the MP-5.

"Front room in control," Wade said on his radio. Kat pushed the door open slowly, looked inside. Wade stood beside an overturned sofa; his weapon aimed at someone on the floor. He had blood on his arm and one leg. Two lights burned in the room. Kat hurried in and kicked away the weapon, then looked at the man.

The Hammer. She confirmed it from photos they had of him ten years ago, and one from two months ago. They knew he spoke English.

"Hammer, we've come to take you back to England to stand trial," Wade said.

The man lying on the floor laughed. The laugh turned into a cough. "I'll never stand trial. I have told everyone that."

"Those wounds in your leg and arm won't kill you."

The Hammer laughed. "Quite right. You Americans are becoming more adept at playing the terror game. But you lose this one as well. The bullets won't kill me. But all I have to do is roll over three inches, and we all die."

"He's holding a grenade," Kat said.

The Hammer looked up and smiled. "You're a woman? They send a mere woman to bring me in? How terribly American. I might have known."

The Hammer moved an inch and Kat saw something sticking out an inch from his thigh. It was the round, smooth shape of a U.S. Army high-explosive grenade.

Wade dove on top of the Arab terrorist so he couldn't move.

"Excellent, excellent," the Hammer said. "But just what the hell are you going to do now so all three of us don't die in one quick high-explosive blast?"

★ THREE ★

"What can I do now?" Wade asked. "First I shoot you dead, then reach under you, hold the spoon, and take the grenade out and throw it out the window."

"Problem with that," the Hammer said in perfect English, "then how do you take me back alive for trial?"

"No problem for us," Kat said. "The trial wasn't our idea. We'd rather see you splattered all over the floor the way you killed our man tonight on that table in Sur."

"Yes, that one. Stupid peasant didn't know how to cooperate."

Kat pushed the muzzle of her MP-5 against the Hammer's head, "Good-bye you murdering bastard."

"You Americans. You send a beautiful woman to do a man's job. You should all be shot. A woman has no place in this business. We keep our females in the kitchen and naked in bed where they belong."

"Go ahead, shoot the bloody terrorist," Wade said. He watched her. They had agreed that they would bring him out alive if at all possible, and they had the drugs and the needles to do the job.

"Too bad though," Kat said. "I'd like to see him face the hundreds of relatives of those two hundred and fifty-eight Marines he killed."

"Yes, the Marine barracks. One of my better days."

Kat fired.

The Hammer screeched in pain where he lay on the wooden floor. The round had slammed through his ear chopping off the lower inch and buried itself in the floor. Blood splattered and then dripped from the wound.

"Sorry, I missed."

"Try again," Wade said.

The Hammer's eye looking up at Wade flared for a second. "Now if you're getting serious, let's talk this thing over. Cash money, gold, or diamonds. Whichever suits your fancy. No agent is ever wealthy. Let's say five million dollars for each of you. All you have to do is let me go, pick up your payoff, and be in Buenos Aires or the south of France living the life of luxury. Doesn't that sound better than working and risking your lives at every turn?"

"Sounds fine except you're too late," Wade said. "I have more money than I can spend now. I tried luxury living. Bored me out of my gourd."

The Hammer laughed low and mean. "American, you don't have the slightest idea what you're touching the far edges of here. You're too late anyway. The biggest, finest, most destructive strike against you is already in motion. It will set the Great Evil back twenty years. It will make your government change the way it conducts world affairs, and make you recognize the strength and power of the Arab world to rule itself."

Wade stared at the Arab terrorist, a frown edging onto his face.

"What do you mean a destructive strike is already in motion?"

"It is the Big One, the monster, and the giant strike that we all have been working for and hoping for now these many years."

"Already in motion?"

The Hammer smiled, then chuckled with delight. "Yes, yes, I know it has begun. Much work remains to be done."

"Who is leading this huge destructive strike?"

The Hammer shook his head. "I will never tell you who is the new leader of the Arab Freedom Strike Forces."

"We call you terrorists, killers of young women and babies," Kat said. "You are slaughter experts who blow up car bombs in markets, and bomb innocent government workers in their offices and murder their children in the nursery."

"Acts of war often have civilian casualties," the Hammer said from where he still lay on the floor on his stomach. Wade lay across his back, pinning him to the boards.

"The new leader of the Arab terrorists," Wade said. "That could be Osama bin Laden?"

"Could be."

"Or the men who blew up the passenger liner over Scotland?"

"Possible that it's them."

"Or someone new we know nothing about."

"Again, it could be."

"Enough of this game, Hammer. You lay perfectly still or I'll shoot you. Kat is going to take the grenade out from under you, and she'll keep the arming spoon in place. She's done it dozens of times. Go, Kat."

Kat knelt beside them. Wade was flat across the back of the smaller man pinning him in place. The terr's hips were visible, as was the ugly black metal of the bottom of the grenade. Kat felt a trickle of sweat seep down her forehead as she pushed her right hand under the grenade. She worked her hand farther in but could feel no arming spoon. Slowly she worked her hand from the bottom to the top and pressed upward on the Hammer's thigh. It gave a little but his muscles tensed. She pushed harder and felt the sweat track down past her eye.

Once more she pressed upward and moved her hand over the top of the grenade. Yes. Kat felt the spoon interrupt the smooth side of the lethal bomb. She pressed upward again, then closed her hand around the fragmentation grenade and the spoon.

"Now," she said, and Wade lifted off the Hammer and Kat jerked the bomb free of him and stood.

"Check him," Kat said. She searched her pants pockets

with her left hand but could find nothing to insert in the hole where the safety ring had been. She pulled out a riot cuff and looped it around the grenade, arming spoon and all, and cinched it up tightly. The small hand bomb was secure.

Kat put the grenade on the floor, then lifted her H & K MP-5 and trained it on the terrorist. Wade checked his legs, took away a hideout automatic, then found a six-inch knife on his left arm. Just as he rolled the terr over, the Hammer lifted up and slashed at Wade's throat with a second knife blade.

Kat fired. The three rounds went over Wade's shoulder, two slammed into the terr's right wrist dumping the knife from his hand. The third lead slug hit his neck, jolting him back to the floor.

"Damn close," Wade said, sending a silent thank you to Kat. He checked the prisoner. The throat wound pulsated with rich red blood spurting from the carotid artery. Wade pressed his hand over the flow, but shook his head.

Kat dropped to her knees beside the prisoner. "I'm sorry, Wade. I let it climb on me. It all happened so fucking fast."

He turned, his face serious, then he nodded. "Don't worry about it. No way in hell we could get him out of here alive. At least two of his men escaped. That means they'll be coming back as soon as they can with reinforcements. We'll be lucky to get out of here with our own skins intact. Not a chance we could lead a drugged Hammer out of here and get him to the coast."

The terrorist blinked, then his eyes stayed open. "You fucking bitch, you shot me. A damn stupid-assed woman killed me. Don't turn out the lights. No." He shook his head and sighed as the blood rushing away from his brain began to turn off the nerve functions. He coughed once, then he simply stopped breathing.

Kat had dug into her backpack and took out a new, specially made Polaroid camera. It was compact, little larger than a pack of cigarettes, but turned out high-quality photos two inches square. She shot six flash pictures of the

Hammer, concentrating on his face from different angles. She put the pictures and camera back in her pack.

"We search this place like we own it," Wade said. "If this was his main digs, he might have some records or plans or targets listed somewhere."

They spent fifteen minutes checking a bookcase, then a small desk, and a shelf that had stacks of paper. Wade found a book that had dozens of names in it with addresses and international phone numbers. He took it.

Kat sorted through papers on the desk. "Hey, look at this," she said halfway through a pile. It was a single typed sheet that had at the top "USA." Then it showed a list in Arabic. "What does it say?" Kat asked.

"Looks like a list of American targets for terrorists. Some have already been hit. The Beirut Marine barracks is listed." He folded the paper and pushed it inside his shirt. They kept hunting. Kat found some more papers that looked interesting and she bundled them together and pushed them into her backpack.

Wade heard it first. A car came to a stop somewhere outside and two doors slammed. "Damned sloppy of somebody," Wade said. "That's our signal to get the hell out of here." He turned off both lights in the room and they headed for the back door. As they did, a machine gun chattered from the front of the house and large caliber rounds slammed through doors and windows. The two Specialists hit the floor and crawled toward the back door.

Rifle fire cracked to the rear of the house and rounds jolted through a window and blew the swinging door open.

"Company," Wade said. They both listened to the firing.

"Two weapons, one automatic rifle and one pistol," Kat said.

Wade crawled to the rear door and held it in the open position, then swung it against the inside wall. He peered around the door at floor level as six more rounds hit the house. Muzzle flashes outside showed where the two attackers were. He brought around his MP-5 and waited. When the rifle fired again, he returned with twelve rounds in and around the muzzle flash position. The weapon stopped.

As Wade fired, Kat moved to the one window in the rear room and watched out the lowermost portion. Seeing that the rifle was silenced, she fired at the slower flash, probably the pistol. Kat used six rounds of the 9mm. She heard a cry, then the weapon fell silent.

"Let's move," Wade said softly into his throat mike. They paused on each side of the rear door. She on the right, he on the left. They would go out as usual, splitting hard to each side, then driving forward and joining up near the car they had come in.

That's the way it started. Wade was closest to where the rifleman had been hiding behind a low stone wall and just as he jumped it he eyed movement to his left. He swung the sub gun that way and drilled six rounds into a dark shadow. The terrorist cried out in pain, then slammed to the side and lay still.

Wade missed only one step, then ran again down past an old car behind the house and toward the car they had come in. He heard firing at the front of the house again.

Wade clicked his throat mike, "I'm behind the house close to our car." A click came back in his earpiece.

"I'm to the left of the car. I'll meet you there."

Wade hurried up to the rig and cut lose the Arab man they had bound to the steering wheel.

"Get this thing started, we're ready to move."

Kat ran up and climbed in the front seat beside the driver.

"Let's go, move it," Wade barked. "We'll hose down the other car and anyone we see. Roll down your window."

They came around the house to gunfire. Kat knocked out one submachine gun with a ten-round burst and put fifteen rounds into the other car near the front door. Wade sprayed the rest of his magazine at two shooters on his side and then they were past the gunfire and slamming down the road. The car had taken more than a dozen hits. The windshield was starred and the side and back windows had been shot out.

"Made it," Wade said. "How's that arm?"

"Thanks, I'd forgotten about it. Now it hurts."

"Take us to the docks," Wade told the driver. "You know where some of the fishing boats tie up?"

"Some of them. They use three piers."

"We need the one with the old stone pier."

"That one I know. My cousin has a boat in there."

An hour later they nosed the car around a corner and were a block from the same wharf where they had landed.

"We'll walk from here," Wade told the driver. "Now get out of town, lay low, and try to stay alive." They stepped out of the shot-up car and waited until it drove back the way they had come.

"But what about the fisherman?" Kat asked. "He won't be expecting us until dusk tomorrow evening."

"Maybe we can catch him working on the boat or on his nets. We might get lucky for a change."

The two Specialists took their weapons off safety and faded into the shadows. Kat checked her watch.

"A little before three A.M. Place should be deserted."

They moved ahead, staying in the shadows of a house, then a store until they could see the boat. It was in the same place. Wade touched her shoulder and they waited.

Five minutes later, Wade hadn't seen anything to make him suspicious. No movement, no noise.

Then someone near the boat coughed. They were only thirty yards from the craft but there was no mistaking where the sound came from.

Wade found a fist-sized rock and threw it hard at the shack next to the boat. It hit the wooden side of the place making a crashing sound in the dark silence.

Wade spotted a figure on the fishing boat move to the rail and look at the shack. It could be the fisherman. He put Kat behind the wide trunk of an ancient tree, and then he slipped a dozen feet the other way and called out in Arabic.

"What time we heading out?"

There was more movement on the boat. He spotted

another man in the stern. The voice that came back was tinged with surprise.

"Not fishing today. Told you."

Wade had wedged in behind the corner of a building. "All right. Didn't tell me." As he said it he heard the weapons. Both men fired at the sound of his voice. He edged farther behind the building and let the lead go past.

Kat came in on cue with four three-round bursts from her silent MP-5. They heard one screech of pain, then silence.

"Come out with your hands up and you live another day," Wade said in Arabic. He heard some whispers on the boat, then one figure stepped to the wharf with his hands up and walked away from Wade. The second man came off running and firing toward Wade's voice. The second man then headed away from Wade who cut him down with two three-round bursts from the silenced MP-5.

They waited. There were no more sounds from the boat. Wade hit his throat mike. "I'm going to take a look."

"Cover you," Kat replied.

Wade sprinted to a pile of nets halfway to the boat. He drew no fire. Next he dropped low and ran past a stack of lumber on the wharf. At the end of it he peered into the boat. No one on the small deck or near the hold.

He ran to the boat, vaulted over the rail, and with his pencil flash cleared the little cabin and the below deck area. No one. He tapped the mike twice and felt the boat move as Kat dropped on board.

He looked below again. Something hadn't seemed quite right. This time he checked the bunks. On the lower one under a blanket, he found the captain. His intense brown eyes were open and glassy. His throat had been cut.

It was nearly four in the morning before they had all the arrangements made. Wade had carried the captain to the dock and put the blanket over him. In his waist, under his shirt he had left the envelope with the other half of the payment.

Wade had checked the boat's fuel tanks, more than half full of diesel. The boat was basic. He looked over the small control panel again and was sure he could drive it. He started the engine at 4:15 A.M. and Kat cast off the lines. No one had stirred around the dock.

He worked his way out of the inlet and into the harbor. Now he saw other small fishing boats like this one moving out. Fishermen always went to their favorite spots early. Soon there were twenty boats moving out of the small harbor and across a sand bar and into the Mediterranean Sea. At once the small craft took different routes, many going north, some south. Only two continued due west from the port. He settled in at ten knots and checked the time.

"How long until we reach the ten-mile marker?" Kat asked.

"By five-thirty we should be on station."

"Let's hope that the captain of that freighter has his ears on this morning," Kat said. "He was supposed to listen for our radio call twenty-four hours a day until he heard it, right?"

"Right, and he was to stay within ten miles either way of Sur. Let's hope he did."

Kat took the radio transceiver out of her backpack, turned it on, and listened. For a time they picked up fishing crews talking with each other. There was a good catch going on to the south. Some of the boats would rush that way to get in on the bounty.

Just before five o'clock, Kat made her first transmission: "Elizabeth R, this is One Waiting calling. Do you read me, Elizabeth R?"

There was no response. She tried every two minutes until it was 5:20, then a whispery voice with static came over the speaker.

"One Waiting. This is Elizabeth R. At the end of our rope here and changing course. Your position?"

"We're on station, Elizabeth R. Your ETA our position?"

"About an hour, One Waiting. Take care. See you then."

•   •   •

An hour and twenty minutes later, Kat and Wade were both on board the freighter. Wade had aimed the unmanned fishing boat due east, tied down the wheel, set the throttle on cruise, and swung onto the freighter's rope ladder. The fishing craft powered away from the big ship. It would motor almost to shore before it ran out of fuel. Then some friendly fisherman who knew the boat would board her and tow her into port.

The freighter captain welcomed them. He would continue his trip to Haifa, Israel, where he would discharge cargo. Wade and Kat would fly out of Haifa in the Marshall corporate jet and be in London in six hours.

Later Kat winced when the attendant on the jet checked her arm wound and rebandaged it. For a few hours, she had forgotten that she had been shot.

Wade sat in the luxury seat looking over the list of what he decided must be some terrorist's wish list of targets to bomb in the United States. He was sure of most of them. Their Arabic expert would give them a final translation. The small book of names was not of as much interest, but they'd know for sure in London. Wade settled back in the seat. He had eaten lunch, had a cup of coffee, and now all he wanted was a short nap.

Beside him, Kat Killinger moved her arm to a more comfortable position. She winced. She didn't like being shot.

✶ FOUR ✶

J. A. Marshall Export/Import offices had moved after they were compromised on the last mission. Now they had digs deeper into the industrial section of London. There was a ground-floor office with two secretaries and a receptionist. They did just enough import/export business to make them look legitimate.

The second and third floors were filled with offices for each of the Specialists, storage, weapons, special projects, and research. In back of the offices they had hollowed out an area to bring in their vehicles. They had two armored sedans that could take anything up to a 20mm round with impunity. A full-size land mine might tip over the armored car, but it wouldn't penetrate the armor. With a special engine and oversize transmission the rig could do eighty miles an hour, and guzzled gasoline at the rate of one gallon every seven miles.

There were other specialty vehicles: four by four rigs, luxury cars, two fancy BMWs, pastel sedans for stakeouts, and two BMW motorcycles. Around London the Specialists drove the pastels.

Mr. Marshall had his office on the third floor. He had his primary corporate office in New York and another in a downtown London high-rise, but this one was where he spent most of his time these days.

J. August Marshall owned several international conglomerates that dealt with construction, oil drilling, gold mining, shipping, airlines, and a dozen other businesses. Most of his corporate work was now done by trusted employees and one of his sons out of New York. He had over forty-five thousand employees worldwide. He was seventy-two years old now, had a white mane of hair, and stood five feet nine inches tall. He had a tight-skinned, wrinkle-free face, green eyes, and a stern jawline that dominated his face.

Two years ago Mr. Marshall decided something must be done about the wave of international terrorism. He set up this office and began gathering experts in every field he needed to fight these terrorists. Wade Thorne, a former CIA agent and talented man in many fields, was chosen as leader of the Specialists, and he helped choose the other team members.

Now in their second year, the team had blended into one cohesive fighting machine. In a hostile fire situation, each person on the team knew instinctively how the others would react and how to support and enhance that action. So far they had suffered wounds, but none of the members had been killed.

Kat and Wade were met at Heathrow Airport by a company driver and returned to the headquarters. Now on the third-floor office of J. August Marshall, they gave their report to him and turned over the photos of the Hammer, clearly dead, and the book and list and papers they had brought back.

"The list of U.S. targets is the most interesting piece of paper that we've found," Wade said. "It could be vital in our fight against terrorism, or it could be somebody's dream list. Maybe our Arabic expert could take a look at it."

Mr. Marshall scanned the list. "Some of these I can recognize. We'll have it translated and researched. Kat, how is the arm?"

"Fine, sir. No real damage. In two weeks I won't even know I was shot. One other thing bothers me. Before he died, the Hammer said something we think is tremendously important. He said we haven't seen anything yet. He told us to wait for the 'Big One' that's coming. He said it will be larger and more destructive than anything that the soldiers of Allah had ever tried before."

"The Big One," Mr. Marshall said. "That does sound ominous. Did you ask him if it had anything to do with Osama bin Laden?"

"The Hammer said it could be bin Laden. We asked him if it was the men who blew up the passenger liner over Scotland. And he only smiled and said again that it could be."

"I'll talk to our other contacts in the Arab world and see what the talk is of this Big One," Mr. Marshall said. "I am saddened that we lost our fisherman. He has been productive for us in the past. I'll see that his family is taken care of." Mr. Marshall stood and went to the window. He stared outside a moment, then came back. "Nothing new on the scene right now that needs our attention. Several things cooking that could flare up and need some action. For now take a few days and do some training. Wade, no race-car driving. I know you say it relaxes you, but we don't want you smashed all over a track somewhere. Thanks for stopping by."

Kat returned to her room and took a long luxuriously hot shower, not bothering to take off the bandage on her arm. The doctor could do that. She dressed for the street and soon had a call that the doctor would see her in their small clinic downstairs. It was set up like a doctor's office but not with all of the tools of the trade.

Dr. Hocking mumbled when he saw the twin wounds.

"Small caliber, you were lucky. Even missed the bone. I'll put some ointment on the wound and give you a good shot of antibiotics and tetanus. It should heal in two weeks. No pushups or strenuous exercise with the arm for a week."

"Yes, sir," Kat said. She smiled. "You're as grouchy

as ever. What happened to the glorious English bedside manner?"

"It got drained out of me working for MI-6. But you didn't hear me say that." He bent and kissed her cheek. "You be a sweet girl now and don't get shot up any more."

Kat laughed softly and waved to him as she left. She had kept her just-dried hair long around her shoulders. It was black on black courtesy of her Hawaiian mother. She had inherited her five-nine size from her tall English father. Now at thirty-two years old, she had joined the FBI right out of law school. Now she gloried in her work with the Specialists.

Kat knew she needed to get in her miles. She tried to run five miles a day when she wasn't on assignment. That and swimming a mile a day kept her in fighting trim. Kat would have to do special training if she wanted to do the Hawaiian triathlon this year. She wanted to go. The only female Specialist had won the women's division several years ago. It depended on her schedule.

It was almost ten o'clock. Kat checked her appearance, then hurried out the door. She would just have time to get to school.

Kat walked down a corridor, used a key, and went into another small building, then in the back door of a medium-sized department store. There were six ways to leave the Specialists' complex. She tried never to use the same one twice in the same week.

After a short cab ride, Kat came to the school just before recess. She found the room where Miss Janette held forth with the third grade and exchanged hugs.

"So 'appy to 'ave you come again, love," the teacher said. She was short and heavy and wore dresses too tight because she didn't want to admit to another larger size.

"Glad to come, Janette. How is little Wally doing?"

Janette frowned. "Not the best, and I don't 'ave time to spend with the love. He misses you. Today he'll be delighted."

The twenty third-graders trooped into the room and Kat heard a yelp of delight, then a small boy with thick glasses and less than perfect coordination ran to her and hugged her about her waist. He looked up at her, blond hair falling into his eyes.

"Glad you come, Miss Kat. Glad you come."

He stepped back, caught her hand, and led her to his seat where he picked up a reading book and went to the back of the class where two chairs stood side by side. He jumped on one of the chairs and waited for her to sit down.

"Miss Janette says I got me to work hard on me readin'."

"That's what we're going to do. Where were we in the book, Wally?"

He showed her and frowned, squinting at the pages through the thick lenses.

"The wee lad . . ." He stopped and looked up at her.

"Paid, Wally. He paid for the candy. That's P,A,I,D. Paid. Try and remember that one."

They continued for an hour until the bell rang and the students scurried for their lunch sacks.

Janette came over, touching her hair. " 'Ow's me boy doing today, missy?"

"Better. I wish I could come every day. I should be able to for the next week or so. That will help."

"Miss Kat, you hurt your arm?"

"Yes, nothing serious. Dropped a knife and cut it I'm afraid. Janette, do you have time for lunch across the street?"

"Oh, my no. But thanks. I'm on lunch duty so I better run. Thanks so much for helping with Wally."

"Be here tomorrow if I can make it."

Kat had a salad and a cup of tea at the small shop across from the school, then hurried back to the office. Mr. Marshall had called a meeting for 1:30.

·   ·   ·   ·

Everyone was there. Ichi Yamagata brought along a new pistol he was field-stripping on the table. He'd never seen one like it before.

Roger Johnson was thumbing through a copy of *Soldier of Fortune* magazine. "Sometimes they have something new on weapons in here," he said.

Hershel Levine had a copy of *Computer World,* and made no excuses as he read an article before Mr. Marshall came.

Duncan Bancroft, the former English MI-6 agent, asked Kat about how the hit went in Lebanon. Wade came in with Mr. Marshall and the meeting began.

"Good, everyone is here. Nothing earth-shaking today. But Kat and Wade brought back from Lebanon a document that we're working on. I've made copies of it for each of you. This is the translation from the Arabic, which we believe to be accurate. It looks to be a hit list of desired targets for attacks within the United States."

Wade passed out the sheets of paper. The Specialists read the list and it brought some gasps and a whistle or two.

"Somebody has big plans," Ichi said.

"How authentic is this?" Duncan asked. "Is this from one of the top terrorists or is it just the wishing list of some Arab sapper with nothing else to do?"

"I wish we knew, Duncan," Mr. Marshall said. "Wade and Kat took it from the home of the Hammer, the Beirut Marine barracks bomber. Oh, you can cross him off our list of most wanted. He didn't make it through the firefight at his place. But, as for the list, we're just not sure how authentic it is or how high the someone who wrote it down is on the terrorist hierarchy.

"Right now, we just don't know but the list is frightening: the Hoover Dam, San Francisco sports stadium, the Washington Monument, the Prudhoe Bay oil fields, the United Nations Building, the Empire State Building, and the others. We'll just have to wait and see how we can confirm any of this."

Mr. Marshall watched his team. "There is nothing critical right now. We'll continue training tomorrow at the castle. Uganda is flaming up again, but it's mostly a civil war. There may be some problem with terrorists in the Philippines, but we're not sure.

"We have word that Osama bin Laden has left Afghanistan and is reported to be back in the Sudan but no one knows for sure. A dozen countries continue to track him as the number one wanted terrorist." Mr. Marshall told the rest of the Specialists about the idea of the Big One that Kat and Wade brought back.

"This Big One sounds like something that bin Laden could do the funding on. We'll keep tabs on him if we can. The Scimitar is still our number two wanted man. No one knows much about him. There are no pictures and little description, even his age is a mystery. But he is the driving force behind several terrorist attacks in Europe and the Middle East. We want him.

"The third terrorist we're researching is Abdel Salim, from Iran. We're not sure where his headquarters are. In the past he has specialized in terror bombs in crowded areas. Some reports are that he leads the raids himself and carries one of the bombs to the target. There are rumors around that he is working on a new project but we don't know how big it might be. We'll keep digging into his activities.

"Some of our experts wonder if this list could have come from one of these three. At least one target on the list has been hit. It's a matter of watch and wait. Now I'll turn the meeting over to Wade."

Wade looked over the group. "We're scheduled for live fire training the next two days. We'll leave in the minibus in two hours and have an information session tonight at seven on the whole idea of the fuel-air-explosive bomb, and the one in the U.S. arsenal, the two-thousand-pound BLU-96 HADES FAE. See you all in two hours."

★ FIVE ★

MOUNTAIN HOME, IDAHO

Charlie Harris had been in Mountain Home for a week. In that time he had adjusted to his blue contact lenses and his light brown hair. He had polished and refined his American English, drawing on his time at UCLA several years ago. He had a furnished apartment and had set himself up as a writer of children's stories.

The big stationery store clerks knew him. He had a good relationship with the apartment manager and explained that he would be paying in cash until he found a bank he liked where he would open an account. Cash was fine the manager said. He paid a month's rent in advance and the deposit and cleaning fee.

Charlie had spent a week in Boise getting his hair done and his contacts fitted. At the same time he bought American clothes so he would look like the other American men turning thirty.

In his apartment, Charlie set up his computer and signed on with OLC to get on the Web. The first night he sent an E-mail to uk@Gtrade27.com.

"Project progressing. Established in MH. Contacts to be made soon. On schedule." He signed it "Charlie." It went out under his own new E-mail address: Itype@OLC.com.

Charlie relaxed. Yes, it was going well. Taller than the

average Iraqi, he stood five feet eleven inches and weighed a trim 175 pounds. He was in excellent shape and did his six-mile run every morning and worked out three times a week at a serious gym.

He had dreamed of an assignment like this. When Osama bin Laden had recruited him to go to America to take two years of college and perfect his English and to become thoroughly Americanized, he'd had a goal. He wanted a tremendously important undercover job in the United States to prove how valuable he could be to the cause and to bin Laden.

He had studied English for six years in Iraq. Then spent a summer in England, but it didn't feel right. Then he had been accepted at UCLA as a freshman and had traveled there with his sights set on becoming as American as possible. After his two years in college, which bin Laden paid for, he returned to Iraq, then to the Sudan. There he took all the training that he could get with the bin Laden specialists in bomb making, infantry tactics, use of a crowd in demonstrations and panic situations, and bomb construction and planting.

His UCLA American experience and his English had moved him up quickly in the ranks of the terrorist organization. No longer was he simply Chay Sarihah. Now he was Charlie Harris, and he could fake an accent from any section of the United States. He went on small bombing assignments, graduated to bigger jobs, but always he was held back due to his special American saturation training.

He became an expert in firing all hand weapons, submachine guns, rifles, and shoulder-mounted rockets. He knew two kinds of martial arts and was an expert knife fighter. He had been more than ready for an American assignment.

When he was given this assignment three months ago he had trained and studied, come up to speed on current American slang and Air Force pilot's lingo, and now he was in a position to work his first important mission. He was ready. He would get it started in earnest tonight.

That evening Charlie went to a bar located just outside

the Mountain Home Air Force Base. It was called the Windsock and had been pointed out to him as the favorite watering hole for many of the pilots who flew jet fighters out of the base. He had thought of picking up a woman at another bar to tag along with him to this one but soon saw that most of the men were alone. Two booths were rocking with pitchers of beer and wild flying talk.

He decided on the half-drunk direct approach. He bought two pitchers of beer from the bar and carried them over to the second booth with the flyers. Five men sat there, all still in uniform and with three dead pitchers of beer in front of them. He set down the two pitchers spilling just a little.

The spill brought a wail of protest.

"Don't spill the good stuff," one officer called.

He swayed just a little. "My compliments to our boys in blue." He stopped and lifted his brows. "Or khaki as the case may be. Got to take care of our flyboys. Drink up." He gave a sloppy salute and backed off and just made it to the bar before he stumbled. He sat on the stool and waited.

Not over two minutes after his exit, one of the pilots came over and slid onto the stool beside him. He held out his hand.

"I'm Will. Wanted to thank you for the beer. Most of the guys are leaving. You want to join what's left? You a pilot?"

"Oh, yeah, a pilot. But little stuff." He slurred the words just enough but not so he sounded too drunk. "Join you? No shit?"

"Yeah, come on, tell us about your flying."

Charlie let the pilot hold his arm as they wound over to the booth and he sat down with infinite care. There were only two other pilots in the booth. Both working on full glasses of beer from the pitcher.

"I'm Charlie," he said, holding out his hand. The others shook and gave their names. He memorized them at once. Horace Grabowski and Marvin Clooney, both captains. The third man who had brought him over was Will

Clariadge, a first lieutenant. One of the men poured him a glass of beer.

"So, what do you fly, Charlie?" Clooney asked.

"What? I fly? Just little stuff. Twin engine Piper."

"Yeah, nice little crates," Grabowski said. "Going to get me one to play with when I get out of the service."

"Yeah, in another twenty years," Clariadge said. "Grabowski here is gung ho for the Air Force. A damn captain already and he's pushing for major. He'll make it too."

"What do you guys fly?" Charlie asked, sounding a little less drunk.

"Eagles," Clooney said. "The F-15, a jet strike fighter. We're in the 366 Wing here at the base, fighters."

"Fast I bet," Charlie said.

"Compared to a twin engine Piper," Grabowski said. They all laughed.

"Yeah, maxes out at sixteen hundred and fifty mph," Clooney said. "That's a little over Mach two point five."

Charlie shook his head in disbelief. "Hell of a lot faster than a hundred and ten. Jessssssssssssssssssssss. Really Mach two and a half?"

"That's at altitude," Clooney said. "At sea level lucky to get nine hundred out of her."

"Oh, man," Charlie said, flipped out. "Wow, that's still moving. Lot more than a hundred and twelve, even." They all laughed again.

"You guys probably got fly things to talk about. You mind if I just sit here and listen in? You know, kind of like I'm a bump on a log or another empty pitcher."

Captain Clooney shrugged. "Help yourself. We're about all talked out. Had a bitch of a training run today. One of the guys almost blacked out. We came damn close to losing him."

The talk swirled then about inside turns, diving to the deck, getting above and shooting down through a formation. Charlie listened intently. He knew most of it. He had studied the F-15 for a week before he recommended that it was the plane they needed.

He knew the air speed, the fuel consumption, the range, the flight characteristics. He was a bloody walking encyclopedia on the F-15. Clooney seemed to be the brightest one of the three. Clooney slid toward the front of the booth.

"Hell, past time I was getting home. Wife and girls gonna be bitching their heads off at me."

Charlie let him out of the booth and shook hands with him.

"Thanks for letting me sit in. Big thrill for me, no lie. I always wanted to fly one of them jets. Just never made the grade."

"Hey, we all do what we can do. You probably do several things I couldn't get it up for. Just be happy with what you're doing. That's what I always say. Now I'm off. Might see you again in here." He waved and walked out the front door.

The party broke up then. They had finished the beer, wiped their mouths, and moved outside. The fresh air seemed to revive Charlie and he assured Grabowski that he could drive, thank you very much.

That had been the first thing he did when he arrived in town. He rented a car using the stolen Bank Americard he had. It would be weeks before anyone noticed that his signature didn't match the one on the card. He went to his car, a year-old Ford, and drove back to his apartment.

Charlie was satisfied. He'd made the first contact with his victim. Captain Marvin Clooney would be the one. The wife and two kids had sealed the deal. Charlie grinned and sent an E-mail to his contact with the good news that a subject for the experiment had been located.

The next night he went back to the Windsock bar and claimed the same booth they had been in the night before. Promptly at 5:30 the pilots came in. Grabowski saw him first. As soon as three of the pilots sat down, the waitress brought three pitchers of beer and six glasses the way she had been paid to do.

Three of the same pilots were there as the night before, but not Captain Clooney. Charlie had about written it off as a bad investment when Clooney flew in a half hour behind the others.

"A short talk with the colonel," was the only explanation he gave. Then they were jet washed into airfoil and fly talk again and Charlie ate up every word. Before they broke up that night they started talking about the weekly poker party at the apartment of one of the pilots. Three of the men couldn't make it.

"Hey, you can't have a good poker game with just three people," Clooney said. He shook his head. "Guess we should cancel."

"I could come," Charlie said.

They looked at him.

"Cost two hundred bucks to buy in," Clooney said. "Table stakes. No new cash. Just the two hundred. Then nobody loses much."

"Hey, fine with me. I can afford to lose two hundred. Call it the price of admission." They all laughed.

"So where is it and how do I get there?" Charlie asked.

It was at Grabowski's apartment. His wife didn't mind. Sometimes she sat in for a hand or two. Grabowski drew him a map on a napkin. "Seven-thirty to midnight. We knock off at midnight because usually we're flying the next morning."

Charlie nodded and said he would be there with some new cash for the game. Clooney said he would be there. He was over fifty bucks a loser and wanted a big winner.

Captain Marvin Clooney was a career man. He was thirty-one years of age and had been in the Air Force for nine of those years. He graduated from high school when he was eighteen with special work in physics and math. He applied at once for admission to the Air Force Academy at Colorado Springs and with a recommendation by his U.S. Senator, he was admitted.

Four years later he graduated from the Academy and went at once into flight training for fighters. He married the love of his life, an Iowa corn-fed farm girl with long blond hair and a sleek, slender body. They soon had two daughters, and Clooney was promoted to captain. He was twenty-six years old at the time.

Clooney came out of a middle-class Iowa family. His father was a pharmacist and his mother had been a nurse, then when he was out of high school, his mother went back to work in the hospital in the small town. He played football and basketball in high school, but gave it up when he went to the Academy. He said it was to concentrate on his studies, but he knew he wasn't good enough at either sport to play college-level ball.

He had been a churchgoer in high school, but faded away from it, and soon realized that he simply didn't believe in the heaven and hell idea. That a loving personal God was a superstition and that all religions were founded in fear and fueled by hope and blind faith.

He built up an ironclad sense of loyalty that couldn't be challenged. He was suspended for a week in high school because he wouldn't tell which of two boys had stolen money from the athletic fund.

In flight training, he quickly picked up the nickname of Loony Clooney and it stuck. He was a one-woman man and had never cheated on his wife. He lived for his family, and he knew that he was in the Air Force to protect his country, and also his wife and girls.

KETTERING, ENGLAND
A. J. MARSHALL CASTLE ESTATE

Sixty-five miles north of London is a small village called Kettering. Seven miles beyond that is the twelfth-century Castle Baldemare, now the country estate of A. J. Marshall. The castle itself was attacked and captured in the early days and then looted twice more over the next two hundred years. It had been rebuilt four times, but as little as four years ago it again was in serious disrepair.

That's when Mr. Marshall bought it and the surrounding twenty-five hundred acres of woods, streams, and some farmland. Mr. Marshall spent a fortune rebuilding the castle, closely following the drawings and specifications of the original structure put up first in 1130 by the first count John Baldemare.

The new look changed the inside from solid but cold stone and drafty corridors to a more modern look. The inside had deep carpets, solid oak floors, air conditioning and central heating, some lowered ceilings and a communications room with the latest in satellite television and radio, faxes and E-mail.

There was a two-mile lane off the road to get to the main buildings. They were set in the center of the estate. Here the Specialists could train and test their weapons without any hue and cry from neighbors. The thick woods and distance meant no one ever heard the weapons firing.

The castle was complete with a grand assembly hall that would seat two hundred and had thirty-two more rooms. There were two complete kitchens. Mr. Marshall's den was on the third floor. A seventy-two-inch flat TV screen hung on the wall opposite his desk.

That afternoon at the castle, the Specialists had a grounding in the BLU-96 HADES FAE. Duncan Bancroft gave the information from two fact sheets.

"The FAE is short for Fuel-Air-Explosive. This is nearly a doomsday bomb that comes in several sizes. One is two thousand pounds and called the BLU-96 HADES. A big bomber can carry four of these canisters that contain three hundred gallons of explosive gasolinelike liquid that quickly vaporizes over the target. They are toss-released at ten thousand feet elevation. They descend rapidly to a thousand feet where they are programmed to burst open. The petroleum vaporizes on contact with the air and disperses into a large white cloud of volatile vapor. Quickly the vapor from each canister balloons to five hundred feet in diameter. When the heavier-than-air gas settles to six hundred feet, preprogrammed sodium detonators packed in each of the canisters and now dispersed in the cloud detonate.

"The resulting explosion is greater than the force of a twenty-thousand-pound bomb, creating a mushroom cloud and a fireball that can stretch across water or land for a mile. If set off over water, the water is churned into a boiling caldron for two miles in each direction. On land the explosion of just one of these canisters can melt cars into a pile of molten metal, burn down buildings in a flash, destroy everything for a mile from ground zero, and knock down buildings and troops two miles away.

"They are awesome weapons and so far the United States has tested them, but never had a need to use them in a battle. One heavy bomber carrying four of these canisters and releasing them in sequence can wipe out a division of troops in an instant."

Duncan looked up. "Questions?"

"Are these weapons in the field?" Kat asked.

"That's classified and they didn't tell us. My feeling is that they are kept in highly secure installations available for air shipment anywhere in the world on two hours notice."

"Would there have to be some authorization to use the FAE?" Hershel asked.

"Bet my last bloomers on that," Duncan said. "Informally I've heard that the President has to sign off on any use of the FAE. They are treated almost the same as atomic weapons in that sense."

"Does any other country have operational weapons such as this?" Wade asked.

"Our intelligence people say no. Our scientific community says why not? The principle is so simple it's like trying to deny anyone but Bayer from making aspirin."

Mr. Marshall thanked Duncan for the data and held up some papers. "I've been busy. I faxed this list to three friends, all experts in the Arab world who speak and read Arabic. They have some interesting conclusions about the list.

One suggested that we send the list at once to the Counter Terrorism Center in Langley. Both the CIA and the FBI will work together on this project. I faxed the list to the head man there an hour ago.

"Let's take a look at the top three terrorists that we know the most about and who could have originated the list. Bin Laden is on the top of the heap and we know the most about him. Right now he seems to be lost somewhere in Sudan or in the mountains of Afghanistan. He has a powerful worldwide association that is said to number over three thousand followers, some hardened professionals and some mere amateurs. He's been tied to a number of major terrorism projects over the past five years.

"The second man on the list is Abdel Salim, believed to be an Iranian who has been in on a number of major terrorism strikes, including three against Israel, two against U.S. servicemen in Germany, and another one an abortive barracks bombing in Kosovo. He is known as the Muslim Assassin, and is a flamboyant show-off who always leaves his mark on one of his terrorist strikes. He claims like the rest to be a soldier of Allah, fighting against the Great Evil. We've tracked him from time to time. The CTC in Langley thinks he has his headquarters in Tehran, but they are not positive.

"The third terrorist we think can be considered a factor here is known as Scimitar. He's from Iraq but not living there now. He tends to move around a lot. Wade has more. Tell us your second experience with him."

Wade remained seated and nodded. "I don't have many facts about him. I think I saw him three years ago when I was working with the CIA on a case in London. A barracks there was under threat and we moved in with massive force and prevented the bombing and almost caught all of the terrs. Two escaped and we think one of them was the Scimitar. My description of him at the time was that he was six-two, a hundred and eighty pounds, on the slender side. I never saw his face. He ran like a trained athlete.

"Since that time we've been hunting him. We have no photo, no fingerprints, no good description. We don't even know where he hangs his hat. He might have a headquarters in Jordan or the Sudan, or he could be in the U.S.

or even here in England. We do know that he likes his creature comforts. He's not the type to hide out in a drafty cave somewhere in the wilderness. Oh, one last bit of information. One of our sources says he never looks the same twice. He uses makeup and disguises and is also something of an actor so he can take on a role and be convincing at it. That's about it."

"Anything else?" Mr. Marshall asked.

"Yeah. We going to be doing some live firing tomorrow?" Roger Johnson asked.

"That's the plan," Mr. Marshall said.

"We have any luck getting our hands on those new army rifles the defense department is working on, the Bull Pup I think somebody called them? The 20mm exploding round fired from the top barrel and the 5.56 barrel below."

"Yes, Roger. I'm glad you mentioned that. I had to pull a dozen strings but I finally got one of them in working order. I could only get twenty rounds for the 20mm barrel. We'll give that a try tomorrow as well." Mr. Marshall looked around. "That's it, then. Breakfast will be served in the small kitchen from five-thirty to six. We're on the range by six-thirty. Good afternoon."

The next morning they took a four-by-four pickup truck three miles to the firing range. Another pickup came behind with the balance of their weapons and ammunition. First workout was in the death house. It was a mock-up of a close-quarters battle house. It had walls made to absorb bullets, three rooms, no roof, and a variety of pop-up targets, some terrs, some hostages. Some called this a kill house.

It was a copy of a CQB training house that the British SAS used. Every quick combat group in the world trained in a building much like this one.

They went into the house by pairs. Wade and Kat went first. They had been there before, but the pop-up targets would be different. The computer had over fifty combinations to spring on them every time.

Wade and Kat paused twenty yards from the door behind a log barricade.

"First team, go," Mr. Marshall said.

Wade and Kat raced for the door. Wade kicked it open and Kat dove through the door angling to the right. Wade went in and took the left side. Today they ran the exercise in the daylight. They also did it at night with NVGs.

Kat rolled once and came to her stomach, her MP-5 up and ready. At once two figures popped up in front of her. One was a terr with a gun, the other a hostage with a blindfold. Kat drilled a three-round burst into the terr, then watched the rest of the right side of the room. A hand lifted up to throw a grenade. Kat drilled the arm and then fired past a bale of straw where more terrs popped up.

As she fired she heard Wade working the other side of the room. Three terrs jolted upward. One held a hostage in front of his body. Wade blasted the two without protection, then slowed and aimed at half a head of the terr sticking around the side of the hostage and fired. The terr fell away, the hostage was safe. No more targets showed.

"Clear right," Kat said.

"Clear left," Wade said.

They both hurried to the wall next to an open door, one on each side. This time Wade went through first angling to the left. Kat did the same to the right.

No terrorists appeared for a moment. Then four sprang up on each side of the room. Both Specialists blasted with the MP-5s on full auto. Kat emptied her magazine. Wade eased up and kept rounds for any new targets. Kat quickly changed magazines. No more targets showed.

"Room two clear right," Kat said.

"Room two clear left," Wade said.

They ran for the back door and out into the sunshine. The other four Specialists went through the kill house shooting at the exact same targets. They had never seen this combination of targets before. One of the surprises was a late surfacing terr who won the score by shooting first and killing Duncan. He yelled foul, but they all learned not to judge a clear situation too quickly.

They moved from there to a regulation pistol and rifle range. Not all of the people were familiar with the McMillan .50 caliber sniper rifle with a five- or ten-round magazine.

"How far will it carry?" Kat asked.

"It's good with only a little elevation for a mile," Wade said. "We can use it for targets too far away for our machine guns." They aimed the big weapon on its bipod at a sturdy oak snag just under a mile away across a small valley. Wade put two rounds into the snag trunk.

"Yeah, both hits," Ichi Yamagata said, leaning back from the twenty-power scope they used with the long-range gun.

The spotter called out after each shot where it hit. Everyone fired until they hit the tree trunk once.

"We have two experimental weapons," Ichi told them. "I've fired both of these and neither one exploded so I guess they're safe to give a test. The first is a Yugoslav machine pistol. Not bad. Fires 9mm parabellum. See what you think."

Roger Johnson tried it on the short range. "Climbs like a billy goat," Roger said. "Takes a lot of concentration to hold it on target for even three rounds. I'd pass on it."

The rest of them tried it and gave the same verdict.

"This next weapon is the Carl Gustav .45 from Sweden. Some of you may have fired it before. A highly modified version of this with an integral silencer replacing the usual barrel was used by our Special Forces in Vietnam.

"It has a retractable wire stock that cuts its length down to twenty-two inches. It can be fired with one hand. The 9mm parabellum rounds jet out at six hundred rounds a minute on full auto. It carries a standard thirty-six-round magazine and is in use by four nations around the world and is a top favorite of many terrorists. Give it a try."

Duncan fired it first with the stock out into his shoulder, then with it retracted, with one hand. He had to hold it with two hands to keep it straight and level.

"I like it as a second weapon," Duncan said. "Get me one."

The rest fired the weapon and only Kat liked it beside Duncan, but she said she still preferred her H & K MP-5 for her automatic.

They wrapped up the live firing and looked for the noon meal. Today it was MREs from the U.S. Army.

"Do us good to get a taste of what we might have to use for some time on an extended operation," Mr. Marshall said. He had watched the workout. He smiled as he offered each of them the plastic pouches, then settled down by a tree and opened one himself.

"Oh, we won't be entirely primitive. We can have a fire to heat the entrée and make ourselves some hot coffee."

After they ate, Mr. Marshall brought out the Bull Pup. It was about the size of the Colt carbine. He showed them the 20mm round barrel on the top.

"It has a six-shot magazine. Each round costs thirty dollars. This weapon also has a video camera that works with a laser range finder. The laser beams back the range, which is set on the proximity fuse with the number of revolutions the bullet will take to get to the target. At that point the proximity fuse explodes the round. Devastating for air burst over dug-in troops or terrs, or those hiding behind buildings or under trees.

"Below that barrel is the more conventional 5.56 barrel with a thirty-round magazine. This air burst isn't magic. You have to laser your target or you have an ordinary impact round. It will reach out for a thousand yards. Let's try our favorite thousand-yard target."

Ichi, as the weapons specialist, fired first. He lasered the snag and had an air burst directly over it. He sat there shaking his head in amazement. "This weapon will change the way ground warfare is fought forever. This is a quantum jump in fighting for the dogface. I'm wildly enthusiastic. We should get a dozen of these as soon as we can."

As they fired the new weapon, the other Specialists agreed with Ichi. It was a fantastic weapon.

Wade sat there and patted it fondly. "I want one for Christmas," he said.

Mr. Marshall chuckled. "Figured you'd all like it. They won't be in production for five years yet. But I'll do some more fancy footwork and get five more. H & K makes the basic weapon frame. We have good contacts with them.

"Now, Wade has promised to lead us on a five-mile run. That was an editorial 'us.' I'm heading back to the castle to get some work done. See you for supper."

Wade waved good-bye and smiled at the troops. "Okay, guys, let's get moving. Why do you suppose that you're getting paid the big bucks?"

✶ SIX ✶

BAGHDAD, IRAQ

Much of current Baghdad is a modern city with more than four and a half million people. Yet some areas look as if they had come directly from the fourteenth century. In a small street well off the main modern boulevards huddled a two-story building made of stone, bricks, some concrete blocks, and lots of plaster.

El Ali Khatami sat behind a battered desk near the back of the third room. A loaded Ingram 9mm parabellum submachine gun lay on the desk close to his right hand. Today he wore a Western business suit that had come from one of the best tailors in London. His cream-colored shirt and blazing tie made him look like a well-to-do businessman with many contacts in the West.

The man frowned now and stared at a group of papers on the desk. He glanced up at his local chief of operations.

"Is this all you have on the project? We need much more. I want the background on the major players. The home life, what they drive to work every day, the route they take. If they have had any contact with any of the protection services now available to businesses in the United States. Get it all, then come back to me. We won't start a project this way."

The man nodded and hurried away. Beads of sweat had

popped on his forehead and now one rivulet raced down his dark cheek into his full beard.

For a moment Khatami stared out the window into the street below. It was a conglomerate of present-day Iraq. Faces of several shades and colors, half a dozen different languages spoken, and now and then the whirl of a Western woman in clothing shocking and displeasing to the traditionalists.

He signaled to a man at the door who left. A moment later he came back with a bottle of whiskey on a tray with two glasses and a canister of ice cubes. Even as the servant put down the tray, El Ali could see the tinges of condemnation on the man's face. With the tray safely on the desk, El Ali lifted up, grabbed the servant's white shirt, and yanked him forward.

"You disapprove?" El Ali roared at the servant.

"Oh, no, no. I for a moment thought of my wife and her habit of adopting some Western ways. That displeases me greatly."

"Good," El Ali said. "I have traveled the world. I know that there are pleasures for a man not outlined in the fundamentalist's doctrines." He took a deep breath and let the man's shirt go and waved him out of the room.

El Ali poured a splash of the whiskey over three ice cubes in the tall glass and tasted the welcome bite of the alcohol. Then he filled the glass and set it on his desk beside a briefing from America.

He had found a liking for whiskey on his first trip to England twenty years ago. There was the thrill of doing something the leaders back home would not like. Then he liked the taste and the surge of energy it seemed to give him. He had sampled the delights of some of the best whiskies the world had to offer ever since. He took another pull at the glass, then put it down.

The America briefings. Things were starting to move. Good. The target had been on the list for several years. It was past time. A successful hit would also be a boon to the economy of the Arab world. He thought about it a moment, took a sip of the drink, and smiled.

El Ali Khatami was a tall, slender man, almost six-three and pencil thin at 175 pounds. His skin was a soft brown weathered in his early days by wind and sun, but now mellowing a little as he reached his forty-sixth birthday. He had a heavy head of black hair and wore it long around his ears to complement his thick mustache that drooped slightly on the sides. His eyes were burnt umber brown, always on the move, watching everyone, everything.

Early in life, he had learned to look out for himself. He came from a family that was in the middle of the economic strata in Iraq. His father ran two tailor shops and another business selling brass ware. But his father's passion was working with any terrorist group he could find. At last he located one that was productive and active, and he began devoting more and more time to it. Twice he had taken his fourteen-year-old son along on bombing missions. Twice the young El Ali Khatami had tasted the thrill of watching a building crumble and hear the screams of the enemies of Allah inside who were injured and dying.

He learned the elements of bomb making, how to set up timers, and how to use radio-controlled detonators. Soon he was leading raids where he captured enemy explosives and weapons. By the time he was twenty-one he was leading a small band of his own.

Now it was different. Now he had a wife and two sons hidden away where no one could find them. He needed to provide for them, and to set aside enough money for his old age, so he did not die alone and broken up, living on the charity of his neighbors. He had seen three of his heroes live their last pitiful days that way and had vowed such an ending would not come for him.

He considered the American operation again. It was time. Too often he felt like he had a stable filled with prancing, eager-to-run horses, but there was no race. He had the trained men, but the American project was several days away, perhaps weeks, depending on one key man.

Before then he had a small matter to handle. Lately he had shied away from bombing trains, ships, and airplanes. The worldwide denunciation and hand wringing diluted the political effort of the bombings. Now he was more direct, more explicit, and at times he even left notes or made statements through third parties detailing the political ramifications of one of his attacks.

The project in hand was much simpler. The Arab oil cartel that oversaw oil production had determined that oil prices were too low and they would direct a production cutback for OPEC members. The figures were handed down two months ago, and most of the producers were in compliance. One notable exception. Iran's oil minister had not overtly refused to cut production, but there was no sign of fewer barrels being pumped.

Usually he didn't bother with small problems such as this, but the OPEC council had utilized his talents before, and he made an exception. The half-million-dollar fee would hardly cover his expenses.

He and two associates left by air later that morning and arrived in Tehran, Iran, a sprawling metropolis of almost seven million people. His men had arranged by telephone to meet the Iranian oil minister, Jajarm Ardakan, and two of his staff at a small hotel where identities could be kept quiet.

The six men met in a modest conference room. They had only exchanged names when the door burst open and two men propelled a third into the room. The prisoner had been beaten savagely about the face. One eye was swollen shut. Blood dribbled from the corner of the man's mouth, one ear had been half torn off, and his left arm hung as if broken.

El Ali looked up surprised and troubled.

"I told you that we would take care of that matter after this meeting," he said sharply in Arabic.

The men stopped. Then one said in Farsi so the Iranians could understand: "Khash, the thief, demanded to see you, to show you that he is still loyal and to put his future in your hands."

El Ali stood and paced a moment, then looked at the man. The Iranians watched with curiosity and a bit of awe.

"So you have admitted that you stole from me, is that right?"

Khash nodded. "Yes, sir."

"You have repaid all of the goods and money and the ten percent fine."

"Yes, sir, every rial has been repaid."

"Do you desire to continue working for me?"

"Yes, sir. I now know the price of loyalty. I will serve you to my death."

El Ali paced again. Then he signaled and a block of wood a foot square and a foot thick was brought forward and placed on the table. Beside it another man put a foot-long meat cleaver.

"The sentence is one," El Ali said. At once Khash was thrust forward, his left hand placed on the block and all fingers doubled over and held back except the small finger. The Iranians gasped.

El Ali stepped forward, picked up the cleaver, and as his men held Khash's hand fast on the block, drove the cleaver down sharply severing the small finger below the middle knuckle. Khash let out a scream, which he quickly swallowed. He was then led away but the blood and the block and the half a finger were left beside the red-stained cleaver on the table.

El Ali turned back to the Iranian oil minister and his two assistants.

"Please forgive me the small incident here of theft. As I'm sure you agree, theft must be punished. Now, we were to talk about the problem of the Iranian oil production that has not been curtailed the way OPEC directed. As members in good standing in OPEC, you are obligated to make these cuts.

"Mr. Ardakan, can you explain why such cuts in production have not been made here in Iran?"

Ardakan had nearly fainted when the finger was chopped off. Only now was he regaining his color. He blinked several times, and then his eyebrows came together as he frowned.

"I assure you, Mr. Khatami, that Iran is following the orders from OPEC. Even now our pumps and pipelines are scaling back. It takes time to get orders to every small well and pipeline and oil tanker. As I am sure the gentleman from Iraq knows, we are soon to be in compliance."

"Mr. Ardakan, you are lying and you are a thief. Do you think OPEC would send us here to talk to you if we did not have proof that not one oil well in your nation has slowed production. Not one pipeline has been shut off or the flow curtailed. That means that you are selling oil, and causing other OPEC nations to lose business. You are a thief."

Two of El Ali's men caught Ardakan from behind, lifted him from the chair, and carried him around the table to the chopping block. One took the Iranian's right hand and extended the first finger over the block. Then he folded back the rest of the oil minister's fingers and thumb and held them.

"Now, Mr. Ardakan, do you still say that Iran has curtailed production as ordered?"

The man's face had faded from a healthy brown to ashen gray. He could barely stand. He stared down at his finger, then at the bloody edge of the meat cleaver.

"You have stolen from other OPEC members, Mr. Ardakan. Do you now admit that?"

There was a sudden stench in the room as the oil minister's bowels voided and he shook with embarrassment.

"We did not steal . . ." Ardakan stopped.

Scimitar stepped to the table, picked up the cleaver, and lifted it shoulder high.

"Do you wish to repeat that, Mr. Ardakan?"

"We have not stolen anything from . . ." The meat cleaver jolted through the air and plunged into the chopping block, missing the end of the minister's finger by half an inch.

Ardakan fainted and at the same time his bladder emptied in his pants.

The next day in his office in Baghdad El Ali read in the official Iranian newspaper about a new oil minister. He announced that Iran would cooperate fully with OPEC and that oil production had been reallocated to meet the reduced figure OPEC suggested.

El Ali smiled, smoothed back his mustache, and looked again at his next project. His current client had agreed to pay fifteen million dollars once the job was done. He had asked for and was given two million dollars for expenses. In case something went wrong, the advance was nonrefundable. Nothing would go wrong. He had done eight jobs now in his international career and not one had failed.

That's why he was the highest paid terrorist in the world. At those prices he worked mostly for governments who could afford him. He had never done a job for a non-Arab nation, and he was sure that he never would. He was still an Arab, worshiped Allah and was loyal to him.

MOUNTAIN HOME, IDAHO

Charlie settled into the poker game at Captain Grabowski's home with ease. He started by peeling off two one-hundred-dollar bills from a money clip and giving them to the banker for his chips.

"Oh, yeah, that's what we like," Captain Clooney said. "Fresh money in the game. Always a good sign."

They played mostly straight five-card draw, but as the evening wound on, they came up with some stud, some horrendous low ball, and a game called seven-toed Pete that turned out to be seven-card stud. No draw, bet after every card.

By ten o'clock, Charlie was down to twenty dollars. It was his deal. He dealt a straight poker hand, five-card draw. It was the easiest game to cheat at and he did. He slipped a pair of aces into his hand and came up with aces over sixes to win fifty dollars. After that he lost again, often on purpose, throwing in a hand that would beat the others.

By eleven o'clock he was broke. That cut the game to three players.

"Come on, guys, let's keep the game going," Captain

Clooney said. "We'll each give Charlie here ten bucks to keep him playing until midnight, well, make it fifteen." They agreed and the game went on.

Charlie dealt again. He worked his magic on the cards and gave himself two eights and two kings. He drew one card and Clooney scowled.

"The civvie here is going for a full house. I bet he doesn't get it. I'll take two cards." Grabowski had opened and called to his wife to bring in another round of beers and some sandwiches.

So Grabowski had a pair of jacks or better. Charlie watched the others. He figured three of a kind in one hand and the other one had to be two pairs and hunting. He fumbled the deck just a moment as he dealt the draw cards and slid his third king out of the deck and dealt it to himself.

The men studied their cards. Grabowski swore and threw in his hand when Clooney upped the opening ten dollars to twenty bucks. The fourth man at the table, Lieutenant Anderson, stayed for one round, but dropped out when Charlie saw the twenty and jumped it five more.

Captain Clooney looked over the top of his spread hand and frowned at Charlie. "You wouldn't be bluffing just a little bit here, would you, old friend?"

"Bluffing? That's one element of the game I never learned to do well. But I can't tell you that, now, can I?"

Clooney saw the five and jumped it another twenty. Charlie matched the bet and called the captain.

"Let's see that great hand, Clooney," Charlie said. The captain laid down three aces and an eight and a six.

"Three of a kind, old friend. Can you beat that?"

"Take a look." He laid down his two eights, then one at a time he spread out his three kings.

"Be damned. Thought sure you were bluffing. Way it goes. My deal."

Charlie played conservatively after that but lost six hands in a row. Three of them he threw in his hand after two rounds of betting. Twice he was sure he had the winning hand, but threw them in so he would lose. It was all carefully planned. By then it was almost midnight. On the last hand he tried a bluff and lost and wound up losing his last borrowed money.

Clooney was fifty dollars ahead and pleased.

"Hey, guys, I need a ride home. Wife has the car to go to some kind of a sorority deal."

"I can take you home," Charlie said. "Hey, you bought the ride with that fifteen bucks. Can I pay you guys back now?"

"Hell, no," Grabowski said. "That wasn't a loan it was a gift, so you can't pay it back. Our two hundred dollar rule. Shit, we want you back next Friday night so we can clean your whistle again for another two hundred."

They all laughed, but Charlie had an idea they meant it.

In the car Clooney was still in a good mood. "Hey, you never said what you do for a living. It isn't flying."

"Nope, I'm a freelance writer. Right now I'm working on a contract to do a children's book set in Idaho, so I'm here gathering some local material."

"Sounds interesting. Me, I can't even write a letter, and my after mission reports are known for their brevity."

They talked about the weather and the job and flying and then they were at Captain Clooney's place. It was in a new subdivision and all the houses looked the same.

"Thanks, buddy," Captain Clooney said as he stepped out of the Ford. "Maybe we'll see you again. You take care now."

"Might at that. Thanks, Captain, for the poker lesson."

"Any Friday night, Charlie. You're welcome."

Charlie read the house number and the street name. He had them memorized before he had driven a block. He would be back to this address more than once in the coming week or two. It just depended how long it took to work his magic on Captain Clooney. Charlie remembered seeing two small bicycles in the front yard of the Clooney home. Yes, perfect, as a last-ditch effort, perfect.

★ SEVEN ★

The Specialists gathered around the conference table in Mr. Marshall's large office on the second floor of the London headquarters. Mr. Marshall tapped a file folder on the tabletop and looked at his team.

"This is the one we've been waiting a long time for. We have verifiable information that two of the top planners involved in the *Achille Lauro* passenger liner hijacking more than fifteen years ago have been spotted. During that hijacking an elderly American man in a wheelchair was killed. Two of the planners of that operation have been on our wanted list since we began.

"We have the addresses of the two men in Tehran, Iran. We can't risk compromising our contact in Tehran, so we'll have to go in without an inside agent.

"Wade and I have talked over the mission, and we have assigned Mr. Levine to the project because he speaks Farsi, and going with him will be Mr. Johnson and Mr. Yamagata. It will be an HAHO parachuting operation with exfiltration through Russia. Your final briefing will be this afternoon and you'll leave here by our aircraft at three P.M. for a flight to Turkey."

That afternoon they heard the final details from Wade.

"You'll fly into one of our Air Force bases in Turkey.

Mr. Marshall has persuaded one of his Air Force friends to make a training flight partway into Iran. The last twenty miles will be on your long parachute glide down from thirty thousand feet. That way we hope to avoid any air response."

"Yeah, and we'll freeze our damned noses off up that high," Ichi said.

"We'll thaw you out on the ground," Hershel said. "How close will that put us to Tehran?"

"Depends how much air activity Iran puts up. If they don't come up to see who the overflight is, we might get you within sight of the big city. Otherwise we air you as close as we can and then you'll have to borrow a car from some native and go in the rest of the way in style.

"You'll have native clothes on so you won't stand out. Your faces and hands will be browned out a little, except for you, Roger."

"I'm going to stand out," Roger said. "Not a hell of a lot of blacks in Tehran."

"We'll work at night," Ichi said.

Mr. Marshall continued, "We don't have an in-country contact we can use, but we do have two reliable addresses. If the targets are not there, you'll need to search the quarters for another address. You will bring out one or both of the men for trial if at all possible. We know that usually these men are heavily protected, and most will never surrender or be taken alive.

"Exfiltration will be to the north to the Caspian Sea, and then to the lower edge of Azerbaijan at Baku."

Ichi scowled. "Hey, if I remember right, Tehran is over three hundred and fifty miles from the Turkish border. We going to violate that much air space without their getting uptight?"

"That's part of the unknown. You might have two hundred miles to go by car to get to Tehran, that's why you'll have to play this one as it comes. My guess is that the plane will go into the northern no-fly zone in Iraq which will put you about a hundred miles closer to Tehran. Depends how the pilots plan the route."

"Whatever works," Roger said. "We get our choice of weapons?"

"As usual, Roger. I might suggest that you consider the Ingram. Small and easy to hide in a canvas traveling bag."

"Sounds good to me," Hershel said. "We have a change of clothes, and weapons and a radio signaler. What else do we need? Some Gatorade, maybe."

"That and a million and a half in rials," Wade said. "The current exchange rate is three thousand rials to a dollar, so that's only five hundred dollars' worth. You'll also each have five hundred dollars in U.S. currency for harder bargaining." Wade looked at them. "Any other questions?"

"If these gents don't want to come out with us?" Ichi asked.

"You have the right drugs to use to help them cooperate but not knock them out," Mr. Marshall said. "Use your best judgment. We want them off our list one way or the other."

"Yeah, I agree," Roger said. "Now let's get moving. We only have an hour to get to the airport."

SOMEWHERE IN TURKEY

Hershel had no idea where they were. "Somewhere in Turkey," was all the Marshall pilot of the sleek nine-passenger business jet would tell him. They had been met well out from the airbase by a pair of F-18 fighters and escorted into a smooth landing on the U.S. airbase in Turkey.

It was dusk when they landed. Hershel knew they had been on the way for almost a whole day, counting layovers in two airports and waiting for clearances to overfly certain countries. They were met on the tarmac and taken directly to a C-130 Air Force transport. The ship was huge compared to the jet in which they had arrived. Hershel knew the C-130 could carry ninety-two combat troops or spread sixty-four paratroopers into the sky. For this trip, the big bird had just three passengers.

Inside the huge hold of the ship, they were given a quick meal courtesy of the Air Force. It was a hot turkey dinner with all the trimmings served on military mess trays.

"Feels like this is the last meal of a dead man walking," Roger said.

Hershel had looked at the plane and guessed it was the J model, the latest one off the assembly line back in '94. This one was painted all black, had no insignias on it whatsoever. Hershel heard that some of these had special radar-absorbing material on the nose and fuselage so the radar return made it look like a much smaller aircraft. He hoped this one had that.

They took off just after dark. The pilot said they would overfly part of Iraq in the northern no-fly zone and would be high enough to avoid any antiaircraft fire. The Iraqi fighters had been cautious lately.

"Then we swing out over Iran straight for Tehran," the pilot, an Air Force captain, said. "That probably will get some response from Iran. We just don't know what. We've been over this way before and usually we get a hundred miles inside Iran, maybe fifty more before the Iranian planes get too thick and we turn back. Just before that you guys walk down the ramp and take a sail as far east as you can get."

Hershel thanked him and told Roger and Ichi what the captain said.

Ichi gave a quick nod and went back to honing the six-inch blade he carried in a sheath on his right leg. Hershel knew how good Ichi was with a knife and sometimes thought that Ichi was a throwback to the Samurai warriors. He had throwing knives as well, three of them that he kept on his left leg under the pale blue pants that were supposed to be Iranian.

They checked weapons again. Each had an Ingram submachine gun with a thirty-round magazine that dropped straight down from the receiver, three magazines, and five hundred more rounds ready to load in the 9mm parabellum size.

"How long?" Roger asked the pilot.

"About forty-five minutes from takeoff. If we're lucky we'll get into Iran a hundred miles and then take a hike."

Roger looked at his watch. "Twenty minutes to go. Which means we should be over Iran by now. Wish to hell we could see out of this bitch."

"First time we see out we'll be taking that long first step," Hershel said. "Let's check each other's chutes and equipment. Get those canvas bags tied around your legs in back and just below your chute. Let's do a check on the G-16s to see that they work right."

He tapped his throat mike twice. He got two taps back, then two more in his earpiece.

"Radio check is okay. Soon as we hit dirt we bury the chutes, join up, and hunt a road heading for Iran. Maybe we'll get lucky and won't have to walk all the way."

They checked their oxygen masks and the small oxygen tanks strapped to their chests. The bottles were good for twenty minutes and throwaways. The masks around their mouths and noses were held firmly in place by elastic straps so the air blast of the jump wouldn't blow them off.

They put on the masks, leaving them ajar so they could breathe. The masks were under the wool face masks. The temperature outside would be around thirty below zero for the first few thousand feet.

"We'll turn on the oxygen and be sure the masks work three minutes before we jump," Roger said. "Another safety check."

Ten minutes later the loadmaster came into the cargo hold and waved.

"We've had some Iranian jet interest. Captain says you hike out of here in five. I'll open the rear hatch in three. Everyone okay?"

They all nodded.

"Orders are we hitch you up to the rail for the automatic opening. You've got gloves. Time now to put on the gloves and those wool masks over your face. Gonna be frigging cold out there."

"Let's get the oxygen masks working, too," Roger said. They fastened them in place, put on the face masks, and turned on the gas. They all nodded, the oxygen was working fine.

Three minutes later they ran down the ramp and took the last step into nothing but thirty thousand feet of extremely thin air. The cold hit them like a bucket of ice water.

Hershel felt the air rushing past him as he tumbled once, waved his arms to try to get upright before the jolting shock of the wide chute straps under his legs slowed him down with a snap.

Then he felt the cold. It rushed at him, tingeing his eyes with pain and filtered through the wool mask numbing his cheeks in an instant. He put his right-hand fingers on the throat mike.

"Night walkers, give a yell."

"Fine here," Roger said, sounding a little strained.

"Up and running," Ichi said. "I don't see the glow sticks. You guys got them out?"

"Forgot," both said. They took out the plastic tubes and bent them, mixing the chemicals and making them glow. Hershel saw one to his left and used the guidelines on the squared-off chute to move that way.

It took them five minutes to team up, all in a row, then they checked their illuminated wrist compasses and made sure they were moving east with the prevailing wind.

Hershel had to grip his teeth together to keep them from chattering. This wasn't his first high altitude jump with high opening, but he didn't think he'd ever get used to them.

A slight mist below kept them from seeing the ground.

At last it was getting warmer. Hershel checked his wrist altimeter. They were going down fast.

"Ten thousand feet now," he said on the radio. "Another six or seven minutes."

They broke through the misty, moist clouds and saw the ground. In the distance they saw a small town, then a larger city, but it was too close to where they jumped for it to be Tehran. They would have to steal a car or a small truck.

Five minutes later they all chose a grassy field to land in and in the bright moonlight they came down together within fifty yards of each other. They found a small ditch and piled the chutes in it and kicked dirt down from both sides to cover up the black parachute material.

They came together on a small rise and looked around. Nowhere could they see a light, a road, or any headlights.

"Listen," Ichi said. They were quiet and he turned and pointed to the north. "Cars or trucks, our meat."

They walked for over two miles before they found the road. It was a secondary one, but paved, and Hershel found two signs that pointed east toward Tehran.

The sign read 170 kilometers.

"How many miles is that?" Roger asked.

"A hundred and ten miles," Ichi said. "Too damn far to walk. Let's find some transport."

They lay in some brush next to the highway for ten minutes. So far they had seen one highway tractor-trailer, two loaded farm trucks, three motorcars, and one pickup.

"The next sedan," Hershel said. "I'll be the injured body just at the side of the road."

Five minutes later a single car came. Hershel was on his hands and knees as the headlights hit him. He sprawled out on the gravel at the side of the paving. The car slowed, slowed some more, then sped away.

"One more time," Hershel said.

The next car that came slowed and stopped. An older man eased from the car and went over to Hershel and asked him if he was ill or hurt.

The old man was alone in the car. Hershel told him they wouldn't hurt him but they tied his ankles and put him in the backseat with Ichi.

"My friend," Hershel said to the car's owner in Farsi, "we are only using your car for a short time. I am not stealing it. I will pay you well for the petrol we use. We will give you thirty thousand rials. Will that please you?"

The old man nodded. "Yes, that is fair. Why did you trick me? I would have given anyone in need a ride."

"We didn't know, grandfather. We had to make sure."

The road was not the best. Hershel found that he could

make about sixty-five kilometers per hour. That would be about forty miles per hour.

The traffic was light, almost nil this early in the morning. By 4:00 A.M. they came to a rather large city called Hamadam. It was past the range of mountains they had climbed during the night. The old man said he had to stop there.

"We're going to Tehran, old man," Hershel said in Farsi. "When we get there, we'll give you back your car and your money and you will be a happy man."

They drove through the town slowly. There were enough signs for Hershel to follow to get them out of the place and still be headed for Tehran.

They were ten miles down the road and with twenty more to go to get to Tehran when they saw a cluster of lights ahead. It turned out to be four vehicles with lights on, showing a bar roadblock.

Hershel slowed when he saw the barrier a hundred yards ahead.

"How many of them?" Ichi asked.

"Four jeeps, a staff car, and maybe six men I can see."

Roger reached for his Ingram. "We slow down, almost stop, then blast ahead through the barrier. As we get there, Ichi and I will blast the tires and engines on the car and jeeps as we go by. Make it hard for them to chase us.

"Ichi, get on the other side. You take the rigs over there; I have the passenger-side vehicles. Ready now, we're still fifty yards from them. Do them tires good."

Hershel approved the plan. He slowed as if he were going to stop. The three soldiers with weapons slung relaxed and waited. When the Specialists were twenty feet from the vehicles and the thin wooden barrier, Hershel tromped on the gas pedal and the car slammed forward.

At the same time Ichi and Roger opened fire with the Ingrams on full automatic. Both weapons stuttered with five- or six-round bursts. The 9mm parabellum rounds riddled tires, blasted through windshields, and chopped up wiring on the engines.

Hershel ducked as they hit the wooden arm. It splintered

then came in half and they were through. There hadn't been a single shot in retaliation. They were almost a hundred yards away before the first rifle shots came. The first two missed, and the third went through the rear window shattering it.

More shots sounded, but Hershel began weaving back and forth across the road. Far back they saw one rig pull onto the road with lights blazing as it followed them.

"Shit, here they come with their rifles and we don't have a single long gun," Roger said.

"Maybe we can outrun them," Hershel said. He pushed down on the gas pedal and they raced down the blacktop road trying to miss the largest potholes.

Five minutes later Hershel made the decision. "They're gaining on us. We don't have space enough to get into the Tehran traffic before they catch us. We have time enough to pull off somewhere and surprise them. Roger?"

"Yeah, old SEAL trick. We pretend to hide the rig to the side in some trees, but make sure they see it. When they get close enough we riddle the jeep and put it dead in the water."

"Like old times for you, Roger?" Ichi asked.

"No. In those days we would concentrate on the driver and passengers. Kill them and the rig stops. Now we work the other way around. Lower body count."

Hershel found the spot, a small turnoff on the road and some trees a short way. He edged into the trees and turned off the lights but the rig was plainly visible from the road.

Three minutes later the jeep took the bait and jolted over the small ruts to the turnoff. Now all they had to do, Hershel thought, was to beat these guys to the punch with a few well-placed rounds.

"Shoot," Roger yelled. "We have to shoot before they do."

★ EIGHT ★

SOMEWHERE IN AFGHANISTAN

Osama bin Laden put the AK-74 rifle with a curved thirty-round magazine down on the edge of his large desk and leaned back in the leather chair in his study. Behind him the wall was crowded with floor-to-ceiling shelves of books. A tray of food at his elbow had been quickly attacked with surprising vigor for a man who had just turned fifty years old.

Osama bin Laden enjoyed the good life. No longer would he live in a cave or a tent. Far behind him were the days of organizing waves of young Arab fighters to do battle with the Soviet Union's army that had invaded Afghanistan. In 1986 he had led many of the men he recruited into battle and found he had an ability as a combat leader.

Then he began turning his talents and his wealth toward attacking other targets. He was furious with the Western nations and their rape of his homeland and his Arab neighbors of their oil. Osama bin Laden held a total hatred of Israel and its cancer in the side of the Arab states. He became active in planning and financing bombings and other raids on the Great Evil and other Western nations' facilities in Arab nations.

Bin Laden had the cash to support this lifestyle. He was a devout Muslim and came from an important family in

Saudi Arabia where he trained at King Abdul Aziz University as a civil engineer. His father became wealthy through construction projects, and Osama had more than fifty siblings by his father's many wives.

He inherited three hundred million dollars and began spending it on what the West called terrorist attacks. In 1989 he returned to his native Saudi Arabia where he was hailed a Muslim hero for his help in fighting the Soviets in Afghanistan. However he was expelled from the country in 1992 and went to Sudan. In 1996 he was expelled from Sudan and returned to Afghanistan where he set up training camps for terrorists and continued to export his teams to spread terrorist activities. About this time Osama issued a fatwa against all Americans and Jews. This fatwa is a religious order against any American who paid taxes to the government. Those persons were Muslim targets because they were helping the American war machine fight the Muslim nation.

The U.S. and other Western countries pressed Afghanistan to honor warrants for Osama's arrest but in 2000 he vanished. Afghanistan authorities say they don't know where he is and are not even sure that he is still in their country.

Osama settled back in his chair and considered the paper on his desk. He was not a large man, and wore a traditional white burnoose and a full beard and mustache. The beard was showing faint hints of gray and was now four inches below his chin.

He smiled as he remembered the glory days when he led his Afghanistan fighters and wounded and at last defeated the Soviet Red Bear. Yes, now there were new glories to create.

He read the brief outline on the page and nodded. Yes, it would work. It was his project and would be larger and more destructive than anything he had dealt to the Great Evil before. It would shock and wound them. It would be a new Muslim glory.

Al Qaeda was ready. His umbrella organization covered more than twenty Islamic extremist groups, and all controlled by Osama. Al Qaeda had been described by the West as an all-powerful globe-spanning conspiracy to promote terrorism with over three thousand operatives in nations such as Pakistan, Sudan, Somalia, Kenya, and Bosnia.

Osama motioned to a man at the door and Fazul Abdullah Mohammad came in.

"*Al hamdo lillah,*" Fazul said. The words meant "all thanks and praise to the Almighty."

Osama repeated the phrase and the two men stared down at the blueprint.

"It will work, we are getting people in position," Fazul said. "It will take some time yet, but all the parts are coming together."

"We have enough people inside the Great Evil?" Osama asked.

"Yes, four of our key players are there now establishing themselves, working into the community, getting jobs, creating airtight alibis."

"The materials they will need?"

"We are still working on that. Getting them into the country or obtaining them there is a big problem. Either one is risky, but we are used to taking risks for Allah."

"So, in good time we will be ready and it will happen in the Great Evil."

"Yes. Today is when we will strike a small blow at the hated Israeli Jews. It should happen in Haifa today."

HAIFA, ISRAEL

Mahmud Refai shook his head at the girl sitting beside him in the battered old Volvo sedan. He was twenty-three and Thuraia was just twenty-one a week ago.

"We have tried three times to park near the market. Each time the policeman has waved us on our way. Time is slipping away. We'll have to follow the backup plan."

Thuraia's eyes flared with terror. She reached over and hugged him tightly, then kissed his cheek. "No, you can't. It isn't worth it."

"We are fighting for the glory of Allah, Thuraia. It will be fine. I'll leave the car. We can't just park and walk away. I'll drop you off two blocks from the market, then drive back right up to the policeman at the very edge of the market. I'll turn off the engine, and get out before he can yell at me. Then I'll run."

"The policeman has a submachine gun," Thuraia said. "He'll shoot you when you run. We weren't supposed to get hurt doing this one. You planned it that way."

"Things don't always go the way . . ."

Thuraia stopped him by kissing his lips. "Mahmud, I don't want to lose you. I know, I know, it's for the glory of Allah, but not if you die in the process. We'll just drive away and forget about it for today."

"No. I had orders directly from Fazul Abdullah himself. It's all part of a bigger picture. It must be done today, and we have only fifteen minutes left." He pointed to the door. "Out. Get out and I'll come back and meet you here and we'll go to a café and have a good meal, then go home and make love again."

Tears streamed down her soft cheeks. "I can't let you go. If you die, then I might as well die, too. I'll go with you."

"No," he shouted it. "Thuraia, get out of the car, now. It is your duty. If I don't come back, you must work twice as hard for Al Qaeda as we have before. Now get out." He kissed her once more, then pushed her to the door and unlatched it.

Thuraia stepped out and he pulled the door closed. Mahmud looked at her one last time, then put the car into gear and drove slowly toward the market that was overflowing with shoppers.

The Israeli policeman on this side of the market was looking the other way, talking to a woman. Mahmud drove up within ten feet of the officer. He shut off the motor and eased open the door. The policeman turned.

Mahmud jolted out of the door, left it open, and ran away from the market. He held in his hand the electronic detonator, and before he heard the policeman's first shots, he pushed the button on the black hand piece.

In a fraction of a second he heard the roaring thunder of the thousand pounds of TNT exploding behind him. The blast came from the Volvo and threw the policeman twenty feet down the street. His shots just before the blast found their mark. Four of the slugs ripped into Mahmud's back as he ran, one severing his spinal cord and spinning him to the ground.

The grinding, roaring blast of the bomb shattered half a block of tents and temporary shelters of the open market, slamming goods and sheds and people fifty feet away. Sirens wailed as the sound of the blast faded. Screams and cries of pain came from the injured and dying in the destroyed market.

A man staggered out of the wreckage holding his arm that had been shattered. His shirtsleeve was gone and a white jagged bone stuck out from his blood-drenched forearm. He took another step and then fell to the pavement screaming until he passed out a moment later.

Ambulances rushed to the scene, police arrived looking grim and determined.

Thuraia watched from the slight hill two blocks away. She had seen it all happen. Seen the car drive up and Mahmud get out and then rush away. She saw the policeman turn and lift his weapon and fire just before the horrendous blast shook the whole area. Windows in a house behind her blew inward.

Thuraia saw Mahmud fall. He didn't move again and she was sure that he was dead.

She had dropped to her knees when the blast came, and now she stood slowly. She had her orders. Now she must fight twice as hard and twice as long for Al Qaeda. Her mission was just and pure and for the glory of Allah and it was only now beginning.

Later that day in Afghanistan, Osama bin Laden and Fazul watched the report on television.

"Over forty people were killed by the blast, mostly residents of Hadera, but also twelve tourists from Germany who were on a walking tour. Police are not sure who set off the blast but one Arab man was shot by a policeman just before it went off. Witnesses say the Arab man, who has not been identified, was seen running away from the car that blew up. The policeman who shot him was one of the casualties of the blast. More details later when we have been promised a complete account of the dead and injured."

⋆ NINE ⋆

Before the men in the jeep could shoot, Ichi and Roger both fired their Ingrams. The thirty-yard range helped and enough of the spraying bullets found the tires to flatten both on the near side. The men kept firing to keep the soldiers' heads down as the sedan raced out of the trees and through a small ditch and back on the road.

Three rifle shots hit the speeding sedan as it pulled away from the dead jeep. One grazed the old Iranian but did little damage. The other two hit the rear of the sedan but did not penetrate inside.

"Yeah, we left them in the dust," Ichi said, looking through the blown-out back window. "They won't bother us anymore unless they radioed ahead."

"Would the soldiers back there have radios?" Hershel asked the Iranian in his own language.

"Most likely not. That was a small group, watching for smugglers and riffraff. Not permitted a radio."

"No radio," Hershel told the others. "Now, let's see if we can find Tehran."

It took them another two hours. They showed the old man the address they needed in Tehran and he nodded.

"I lived there once. I know the area. Can help for more rials?"

Hershel chuckled. Sharpies all over the world. "Another ten thousand," he said and the old man grinned.

He showed them the way to within a block of the address, then they put the weapons back in the canvas tote bags and stepped out of the car. It was an hour to daylight. Their work in this house had to be quick. They gave the old man the money and he turned around and drove away.

Hershel cased the house by walking past it slowly on the other side of the street. It was a middle-class area by Iranian standards. The houses were individual but with no lawns. They were built almost on the street, which was narrow and at places winding.

Hershel came back to where Ichi and Roger waited in the shadows of a stunted tree.

"Must be a back door. Narrow walk along one side. Ichi, you work the back door. Roger and I will go in the front. Make it a silent entry and keep it silent as long as possible. Now I wish we had brought suppressors along for the Ingrams. Let's go."

They gave Ichi time to vanish behind the house, then they went up two steps and tried the door. Locked. Roger went to work on it with a set of picks and in a minute had the lock open. Hershel pushed the door inward while staying against the front wall of the house. Nothing happened.

Hershel pushed past the doorjamb and inside the room. Black. No shades of gray. No night lights. No night vision goggles. He let his eyes adjust. A front room. Two doors off it. He moved silently to the first door and sensed Roger come in behind him. He turned the knob slowly and edged the door open. A faint light showed.

It came at him without warning, only a slight growl gave away the attack, then the gleaming white fangs in the dim light. A large black dog leaped at Hershel, who reacted from days of practice with a forward thrust kick that put all of his 145 pounds behind the blow. His hard-soled half boot caught the dog in the throat just under snapping jaws and broke its neck. The dog continued forward with its momentum. Hershel sidestepped it and checked the rest of the room.

He saw a bed on the far wall, a small table used for a desk, and a typewriter. On the bed lay a body that looked more dead than alive. The man lifted up on one elbow.

"What, Bruno, what?" he asked the large black dog in Farsi.

Hershel surged to the bed and saw both the old man's hands on the ends of skin-covered arms and wrist bones that looked as if they might break apart at any time.

"Bruno is dead," Hershel said in Farsi. "Are you Muhammad Al Kashan?"

The old man's eyes wavered. They stared from deep sockets that seemed strangely filled with the dark brown orbs. He looked around quickly.

"You are not my friend."

"No."

"You come to kill me?"

"No."

"We come to talk about the *Achille Lauro*. The ocean passenger liner you planned the hijacking on fifteen years ago."

A faint smile touched the weathered, skin-stretched face. The man's eyes turned back to Hershel.

"You have come to kill me. You must hurry, the great one with the honed sharp scythe has called at my door often in the past month, but each time I have driven him away. I am tired. I am no longer able to fight with the specter."

"You are one of the two leaders of the ship hijackers?"

"You say I am, you must know." His right hand worked slowly under the thin sheet that covered most of him. When it came out it held a .45 automatic. It was so heavy he had to slide it up his thigh. He couldn't lift it to aim. Hershel took it away from him.

For the briefest second the old face smiled. "You must have the list by now, and know what it means. But you are too late. The Big One has started. Work is under way on a strike against the Great Evil. Your treatment of the Arab nations and the powerful oil-producing countries will take an immediate about-face to one of submission and co-operation."

Hershel scowled. "This Big One, we have heard the term before. What does it mean?"

"What I said, American camel shit eater. A massive attack on the soil of the Great Evil. A catastrophic strike that will leave hundreds of thousands dead and dying. I can say no more."

"Who is the leader of this group working on the Big One?" Hershel asked. The old man didn't hear or pretended not to. Hershel repeated the question, louder, more insistent.

"The leader? He could be anyone who loves Allah and hates the Great Evil. Anyone. I can say no more."

Hershel started to ask him more about the leader when gunfire exploded from the rear of the house. It was the chatter of the Ingram. A moment later a man dove into the room with a submachine gun of his own. He was not Ichi. Roger fired three rounds at the man who came to his feet and sprayed the far wall with rounds. Roger fired twice more and the gunman kneeling on the floor flopped backward and never moved again.

"Clear rear rooms," Hershel's earpiece told him.

"Clear front," Roger said. He kicked the weapon away from the terr on the floor, then checked the man. He was dead.

Hershel had ducked to the left when the shooting started. Now he moved back to the bed and stared down at the old hijacker. He had figured the man was over eighty.

Muhammed cried out in terror. He clutched his chest. His face went gray and he shivered. He bellowed in pain again, then gasped for breath. "Heart," he whispered, then his hands fell and he stopped breathing.

"Muhammad is gone. Heart attack probably," Hershel said. "He's bought the farm. Check the desk."

Both Roger and Ichi worked over the desk with the aid of their pencil flashlights.

"Yeah, a list that looks like it could be similar to the one we found before," Ichi said.

"Look at this," Roger said. "Some kind of high-tech ignition detonation device like I've never seen before. This stuff is far too sophisticated to be used on a terrorist bomb. It's high-level stuff for missiles and nuclear bombs."

"What the hell these guys doing with it?" Ichi asked. "Maybe they're just dreaming of what could be."

"Take one of them along with us," Hershel said. "Put everything in those watertight plastic bags we brought. We'll let the big boys play with them."

They searched the house for an hour. When they checked outside it was daylight. No one had responded to the sound of gunfire.

"Why not stay right here until dark?" Roger asked. "Doubt if this old boy had much company. Just a keeper who isn't doing his job. I'll drag the body into the back porch and then check to see what we'll have for breakfast."

They stayed. Ichi found eggs, milk, rolls, and fruit in the small refrigerator. They ate the eggs, peeled the fruit, and drank bottled water. It was a long day. They left one man on guard while the other two slept on mats made of blankets on the floor. Ichi found a map and he tried to locate the next address of the second man. He couldn't.

It was slightly after 4:00 P.M. when someone knocked on the front door. Hershel went to the door and looked out through a narrow crack.

"Hello, it's me again. I've brought you some groceries."

Hershel frowned. Speaking was a pretty woman maybe twenty-five, dark hair, well dressed, and with a sack of something. He opened the door.

"Oh, where is Salman?" she asked.

"He had to leave."

"Didn't he tell you about me? I come every day with food to be sure poor Muhammad eats correctly. He's such a thin person."

Hershel let her in. "I'm sorry but Muhammad passed away during the night, a heart attack."

Tears formed in her eyes. She wiped them away. "I . . . I

knew it was coming. He was so frail. I didn't want to admit that he might die." She shook her head.

"Would you like to sit down a minute?"

She nodded. "Losing someone you know is always a shock. Life seems so fragile. A person is alive one minute, and the next he's snatched away forever and ever."

Hershel brought her a glass of water and she drank some.

"So, are you notifying the family, his friends?"

"Salman didn't cover this possibility. He said he had to go into town for two days. I filled in."

"I do know one of his relatives, a grandson I think. I'll tell him."

"I wasn't sure what to do," Hershel said. "Oh, I'm not familiar with the city, could you help me find an address?"

"Yes, of course."

"It isn't on my map. Here it is." He gave her the street and house number. She frowned.

"This is a fairly new area. It doesn't show on most maps yet. I can explain how to get there."

"Good, can I get you some tea or coffee?"

She hesitated. She seemed a little suspicious. At last she nodded. "Some caffeine-free tea would be good."

"I'm not sure where things are yet. Did Salman show you?"

She smiled. "Yes, I'll be glad to help."

In the kitchen she found the tea, heated the water, and set out two cups at the small table. If she saw the row of three bullet holes in one cupboard she said nothing.

A moment later Ichi stepped into the room with his Ingram.

"Tell her we need her to show us where the address is. She has a car. I saw her get out of it before she came in. We need her car."

The girl looked at Hershel. "What's going on? Who is this foreigner?"

"Did you know what Muhammad did for a living before he became ill?" Hershel asked.

"No."

"He was a professional terrorist."

"I don't believe you."

"Remember the Italian luxury liner that was hijacked about fifteen years ago and some people were killed? He was one of the ringleaders in the operation."

"I remember the story, but surely . . ."

"Yes, surely. Why else would an old man have a keeper who also carried around a submachine gun?"

"I never saw him with one."

"He had one. He fired at us. We returned fire and he was killed. We're a kind of international police who go hunting terrorists. You really didn't know about him, did you?"

She shook her head. "No, I didn't. He looked so pitiful, a sick old man with nobody to care for him." She hesitated, stifled a sob, then watched Hershel closely.

"I guess I should believe you." She twisted a strand of black hair that fell over her shoulder. "My name is Salimah." As if it were a sudden idea she brightened. "Oh, are you hungry? I have some good things in the sack."

They were.

"We have one more member of our little group. I'm Hershel, you've met Ichi, and our third man is Roger."

Roger came from the other room holding the Ingram but with a big grin on his face. She stared at him and then smiled.

"Sorry, I've never seen a black person close up this way. You're a handsome race. Yes, handsome is the word. Come now and eat."

By the time they ate the bakery goods and fruit she had brought, it was nearly dark outside.

"You do have a car?" Hershel asked.

"Yes."

"Would you help us find the next address?"

"Are you going to shoot people there?" she blurted out, then put both hands over her face. "I'm sorry. I'm not . . . I don't have . . . I've never seen anyone who was shot to death. Please forgive me." She took two long breaths, then looked at the three of them.

"Yes, I think it would be good for me to help you find this address. Is this where the other man lives who stole that big ship?"

"Yes. We want to take him back to England for trial."

"Then you're English."

"I am. Ichi is Japanese-American, and Roger is an African-American."

"America must be a marvelous place with so many different nationalities and people living in the same area."

"Yes, wonderful, but there are problems."

"Everyone has problems. Let's go find that address."

A half hour later they stopped down the street from the suspected house.

"This is a new area. People with lots of money live here. Some places have fences and armed guard patrols. Here they have only fences."

Ichi looked at the homes. "Fences over here mean security systems as well," he said. "We won't get in this one easily."

"Maybe the girl can help us get inside the gate," Roger said.

"No, she's helped us enough. We can't put her in any danger." Salimah must have sensed that they were talking about her.

She watched Hershel. "Maybe I can help. What's the man's name you're hunting?"

"Hymar Sharif."

"Oh, yes. I've heard Muhammad talk of him. He's much younger than Muhammad. The older man looked up to Hymar. He never told me why. They did this bad thing together?"

"Yes, with a lot of other men to help them."

"Let me go to the door. I can tell them that Muhammad is extremely ill and wishes to see him."

Hershel told the others what they had been talking about in Farsi.

"Good idea," Roger said. "Then we move her back out of any danger."

Ichi shook his head. "I don't know. I'll let you two decide. If she volunteers, that's another matter."

Hershel worked it over for twenty seconds. She could make the difference in them getting in easy or having to blast their way inside. She was on.

They planned it quickly, then the three men slid out of the car and into the shadows along the walls on the left side of the street. Salimah drove the car to the address and stopped right in front. Automatic lights came on, bathing the front of the house, the sidewalk to the street, and the street itself.

She left the car and walked up to the gate in the wall and pushed the bell button. A voice came over a speaker.

"Yes? What do you want? Identify yourself."

"I am Salimah, good friend to Muhammad Al Kashan. I want to talk to Hymar Sharif about Muhammad."

"He isn't here right now."

"It's urgent that I see him tonight. Muhammad is deathly ill."

There was a pause. Then a new voice came on.

"Where does Muhammad live?"

She told him.

"What is the name of the man who lives with him?"

"I don't know. We were never introduced. He left the room when I was there."

"Salimah, about twenty-five. Yes I remember you. I can give you ten minutes. Push open the gate when you hear the click."

By that time Hershel and his two men had run along the wall bent over to conceal themselves until they were at the gate. When it clicked, Hershel pushed the gate open and the three men charged up the sidewalk to the front door. No shots were fired. Hershel motioned Roger to go around to the right and Ichi to the left.

Hershel remembered thinking that in a house this size Sharif could have a half-dozen bodyguards. He knocked on the door and to his surprise, it opened.

A young man not out of his teens stood there frozen in place by surprise. Hershel grabbed him by the throat.

"Where is Sharif?" he demanded. He brought up the Ingram and put the muzzle against the youth's head. Then he eased his left hand off his throat.

The youth tried to talk, failed, and motioned toward a set of stairs that rose to a second floor at the sides of a large two-story room expensively furnished.

The young man moved up the stairs rapidly, went down a hall to the second room. He pointed to the door. Hershel thought of knocking, then snorted, lifted the Ingram in his right hand, and pushed open the door.

Inside it was like the killing house. He swept his glance across the twenty-foot room. Two men on the right looked at some papers. A man was seated at a desk in the center and another man reached for a weapon on the left.

Hershel swung the Ingram to the left and a three-round burst to the chest brought the weapons man to his knees. He fell facedown on the expensive carpet. The man at the desk scrambled to get something from a top drawer.

"No!" Hershel shouted in Farsi and moved the Ingram to cover the desk. The two men with papers stood without moving, as if they had seen this scenario played out before.

"Which of you is Sharif?" Hershel demanded.

"There is no one here by that name," one of the paper readers said.

Hershel snapped the Ingram to single shot and fired one round into the man's thigh. He whimpered and fell to his knees.

"Which one of you is Hymar Sharif?"

The man behind the desk waved one hand. "May I speak?" he said in Farsi.

Hershel nodded.

"My English must be better than your Farsi. Mr. Sharif is not here tonight. He was called away to a meeting."

"All right. If you won't tell me, I'll simply kill all of you and in the process, I get the man I want. You first, behind the desk." Hershel lifted the Ingram and walked three steps forward. He leveled the weapon at the Arab's chest and began to squeeze the trigger.

"Wait, wait," the man behind the desk said. "All right. Yes, he is here, but down the hall. He is . . . occupied."

"He's with two women," one of the paper readers said.

"Good, then he won't bother us. Search this place. We want anything that even looks important. Code books, invoices, shipments. Anything about explosives. Let's do it."

They pulled drawers, rifled the desk, took the papers the men were working on. Stuffed it all in a large backpack.

"Hey, look at this," Ichi said. "Complete schematics on the structure of the Empire State Building. And another one for the White House. What in the hell are they thinking?"

"The Big One?" Hershel asked.

"We're done here," Hershel said in Farsi. "Take us where the big man is with his two whores."

There were not two women with the man on the bed. There were three, and all three were naked and blondes.

"Oh, God, he's got a gun," one of the girls bellowed in English.

The man dove for the side of the bed. One of the girls was in his way and he pushed her to the floor, fell beside her and came up with an Uzi. Before he could fire it, Hershel pounded three rounds at him. One clipped the weapon, knocking it out of his hands. Another hit him high in the shoulder and spun him facedown on the floor. The third round buried itself in the mattress.

Hershel jumped over two naked women and kicked the Uzi out of reach. He looked at the three females. All under thirty, all three standing around the king-sized bed, still naked and unconcerned about it.

"He hasn't paid us yet," one snapped.

"Business before pleasure, haven't you ladies learned that yet? Now get dressed and get out of here." He looked back at the man on the floor who had pulled a pistol from under the bed but hadn't got it aimed yet. Three more rounds from the Ingram stitched up his right arm bringing a scream of pain.

"Now I think we have an understanding, Sharif. You

reach for a weapon, I shoot you. I shoot you enough times, I'm liable to make a mistake and kill you. Understood?"

He had automatically switched to Farsi.

The man on the floor nodded and pushed up with his good hand so he could sit and lean against the bed.

"Get dressed. We're going for a ride."

"You'll have to kill me first."

"That's a better idea." Hershel lifted the Ingram and forced the muzzle into Sharif's mouth. "Good-bye, Sharif. This first one is for the man you killed on the *Achille Lauro.*" He began to squeeze the trigger.

Sharif waved with both hands, and said something through the muzzle in his mouth. Hershel pulled the weapon free.

He heard something at the door and whirled. Roger came in with his weapon ready.

"Oh, yeah," he said, watching the three women dressing. "Too late again."

One of them still topless, walked toward him. "Not too late, big guy. I can use a little black stuff now and then. You have five hundred dollars?"

Roger pushed her aside with the barrel of the Ingram and went over by Hershel.

"Sharif, you were saying?"

"Money. I can make you and your men rich. Name the figure in the millions. Anything you want. I'm legitimate now. Real businesses. Really. Ask the girls."

"Get your clothes on before I stuff a thousand dollars down your throat and choke you on it," Hershel said.

The G-16 talked in Hershel's ear. "Hey, man, we got new company. Two cars pulled up at the gate, and each has three men. All of them look like they're armed. Coming inside about now. Salimah moved her car down a half block before they came. Can you get out with the package?"

"Negative right now." He looked at the dressed women. "Ladies, is there a back way down from here?"

"Sure. We don't want no trouble. You come this way."

Sharif had his pants and his shirt on by that time. Hershel

nudged him onto his feet and they walked to a side door that led down a flight of steps. The other two girls didn't come with them. Roger took rear guard.

They were halfway down two flights of steps when the bottom door burst open and two men came in with Uzi submachine guns, stocks folded out.

"Hold it right there," one of the men bellowed in Farsi. Then both Arabs lifted their weapons.

★ TEN ★

"Don't shoot, idiots!" Hymar Sharif barked. The men at the bottom of the stairs looked closer, saw their leader, and they lowered their weapons.

"Put them on the floor and lay on top of them," Hershel yelled in Farsi. The two men hesitated, then did as they were told. The Specialists and guests continued down the steps. Hershel and Roger each kicked the men on the floor and took the Uzis.

Roger looked outside the door. He used his radio. "Ichi, where the hell are you? We're at the side door. Any more of these shooters around?"

"Yeah, four more somewhere. I'm on your side of the house but haven't spotted any more men. Inside, I figure."

"We have the package, is the car still there?" Hershel asked.

"Was a minute ago. We could make a run for the front gate, but my money is on somebody watching it."

"We'll stay in the shadows of the house," Hershel said. "Move our way and cover our hindside. We're going, now."

Ten steps later, an automatic weapon opened up from the gate. The rounds went high. The men hit the dirt, but the woman only frowned and knelt down.

"Why are they shooting?" she asked.

Nobody answered. Hershel pushed Sharif ahead of him. "If any of our people takes a round, you get half a dozen, Sharif. You might want to remind your shooters of that."

When the rounds stopped coming, Sharif bellowed into the night, "Stop shooting at me, you filthy camel shit eaters. You trying to kill me? You know my voice. Now stop."

There was no shooting for a minute. Hershel prodded the terrorist to his feet and they ran across a slash of moonlight from the house to the gate. The weapon there remained silent, but two opened up from the second-story windows of the house. They hadn't heard the warning from their leader.

Hershel felt a hammer blow to his right leg and nearly stumbled. He had hold of Sharif's shirt and he pulled himself up as they both ran for the protection of the stone entranceway. The door had swung open.

They pushed past it and Hershel shoved the terrorist to the stone floor. "Stay there," he said in Farsi, then he turned his Ingram and pounded off a dozen rounds at the windows where the rounds had been fired. He heard glass break but no shouts of pain.

Roger came into the protection of the gate with the woman in his arms. "She got hit bad in the chest," Roger said. "No way she can make it."

"Put her down. She has a chance in here. Where's Ichi?"

Just then the slender Japanese from Seattle slid into the gate structure. "Hey, the gang's all here. I'll go get the car."

Hershel shook his head in the faint moonlight. "No, let's all go down there. We have the wall for protection. Leave the girl here. The rest of us move, now."

He pushed Sharif ahead of him as they both bent over to stay below the wall and jogged toward where Salimah's car sat on the street. Ichi worked as the rear guard. They were halfway there when Ichi pounded off four five-round bursts at someone behind them.

Then a weapon in the house across the street opened up and a dozen rounds slammed into the rock wall beside the men. Hershel turned and sent ten rounds at the muzzle flashes, then ran on toward the car.

He pushed Sharif into the backseat and dove in behind him. Ichi took the wheel and Roger piled into the backseat as well. Salimah sat in the passenger's seat. She had been crying. Now she wiped her eyes and watched Ichi start the car.

"Hurry," she said. "I see more men coming from the gate."

The firing from behind began at the same time and the men ducked in the car even as Ichi got it moving down the street. Hershel heard several rounds hit the car and one broke out a side window. Soon they were around a corner and out of range.

"Anyone hit?" Hershel asked.

A small mewing-like sound came from the front seat, and Salimah fell against the door. Ichi looked over the seat and saw the blood on her neck.

"She caught a round in the neck and will bleed to death in two or three minutes. Nothing we can do. Blood all over the place."

"Keep rolling," Hershel said. "They'll be driving after us. Kick it, Ichi."

Hershel did a quick search of Sharif and found a knife and a hideout revolver. He took both, jammed the terrorist in the bottom of the car, and put his feet on his back.

Then he shot out the rear window and watched for the pursuit. It came quickly. He used one of the Uzis for greater range and when he was sure the car behind them was shooting, he sent a full magazine into the oncoming rig, blasting out its headlights, shattering the windshield— one lucky round found the driver's forehead killing him instantly and sending the car into a metal-tearing crash against a stone building.

Ichi took another corner on squealing tires. The second car caught them moments later. This time Hershel used the Uzi on single shot and aimed for the windshield. He hit it twice, then three times, but the rig kept on coming. He pushed the lever to automatic and blasted out the remaining rounds in the magazine, shattering the windshield and bringing the rig to a halt after it crashed into a parked car.

"Where to?" Ichi asked.

Hershel took a deep breath, his first in several minutes. Combat always got his blood pumping too fast. He tried one more long breath and let it out slowly.

"We move north toward the Caspian Sea. Should be about sixty miles, if we're lucky."

"Hell, I feel lucky," Roger said. "I didn't get hit. You did. Let me look at that leg."

"Just a scratch."

"Oh, hell yes, let me look."

He tore open the pants leg and found the bullet hole.

"Damn, it went in but it didn't come out. We've got three days till somebody digs out the lead."

"Three days, easy," Hershel said. He winced when Roger bandaged it with some first-aid gear from his tote bag.

"Now, go to bed, get twelve hours sleep, and stay off it for at least two weeks," Roger said.

"Sure, doc."

"What about Salimah?" Ichi asked. "We can't just let her sit there in the front seat all the way to the wet."

"Find a back street somewhere and we'll take her out," Hershel said. "Her family will find her. It's all the time we can give her."

"But she helped us," Roger said.

"Yes, she helped. So did that blond hooker back there who also got herself shot to death. We have to move on."

They put Salimah in a small park beside a picnic bench, then all three left by different routes and got back in the car. Before they moved from the car, they had bound Sharif hand and foot with riot cuffs and put a gag around his mouth.

Hershel sat in the front seat and watched street signs. They were lost for an hour, then found their way through the metropolis of seven million souls, and hit a highway heading north. By that time it was nearly daylight.

"We travel during the day, or hole up somewhere?" Ichi asked.

They were nearly out of the city by then, when Ichi pulled to a stop beside a small store.

"Bakery, and it's open. Bakers work all night. I bet they have some good sweet rolls of some kind. Maybe some Danish."

Hershel seconded the idea and went in alone with only a slight limp on his right leg. No blood showed on his pants. He came back with three dozen pastries that looked like Danish but were better.

"One more store, Ichi, a green grocer, or a market, or whatever they call it where we can stock up on some fruit. We can live on these rolls and fruit for a week."

They found the fruit they wanted in a little farmer's market well out of the city. Hershel bought three big sacks of apples, bananas, some pears, and a dozen plums. Then they were on the road again working through sparsely populated areas and off the main highway but headed directly north toward the small village of Shahsavar. From the maps it looked to be right on the sea.

Ichi drove an hour into daylight, and then he found a good-looking lane that led into a grove of trees. Ichi wheeled into the trees only to find a curious pair of men staring at them and holding leashes on two large dogs. He turned the car around and went out, then continued. Five miles on north they found a better spot with no lane and a woods that would hide the car. No one lived in this bit of countryside.

Sharif had said no more than two or three words during the night. Hershel figured he'd been sleeping most of the time. Now he sat up and began to wail. Roger cuffed him alongside the head twice.

Hershel took the gag off. "What do you want, Sharif?" Hershel asked him in Farsi.

"Why am I still alive? You are a hit squad. I must be the target."

"You're going to England and stand trial for your part in the *Achille Lauro* hijacking."

"I had nothing to do with it."

"You're a poor liar, Sharif. We know you were the main man behind the takeover. You just weren't on the ship."

"You're not going to execute me?"

"Not unless we have to. We'll kill you if it looks like you're being rescued or escaping."

"What do you know about Abdel Salim?" Ichi asked.

"Nothing. Who is he or maybe what is it?"

Roger cuffed him again, jolting his head to one side.

"Hey, I'm a stupid man, what do I know of this name?"

"Because you work with him or sometimes for him, I would guess. You're a fellow terrorist, only now you're old and fat and not as good as you used to be."

Sharif laughed. "Old and fat am I, but I know things. Wait until you find out what we've planned for you . . ." He stopped. "See, I told you that I'm stupid."

"So you are planning something," Hershel said. "Tell us what it is and you live until we get to the coast."

"Live? I was a dead man when you put those plastic things around my legs. I'm a dead man already."

Ichi rolled the car well into the woods, checked from the rear to be certain it couldn't be seen from the road. When he came back, they unloaded and ate the fruit and pastries. They gave Sharif some to his surprise.

Hershel prodded him. "We hear that bin Laden is planning a huge operation. He's the number one wanted terrorist in the world, and we figured that he might ask you for some help."

"Why would he do that? I'm a nobody. Unemployed." He grinned, his eyes sharp, black holes. "Then you have heard about the Big One. It will be a great blow against your country."

"Just what is this Big One, Sharif?"

"I've said too much already. I can't tell you because I don't know for sure."

"But you do know who the leader of this project is. Is it Osama bin Laden?"

"I don't know. I wish I did. It will be glorious."

"Will hundreds of thousands die?"

"Oh, yes, perhaps more."

"Not much action since the ship hijacking?" Hershel asked. "We heard you lost your confidence after that one."

"Not at all. I retired for a time to enjoy my money. I was paid well for what I did."

"Most killers are paid well."

"I am not a killer. I'm a political activist. If some eggs get broken while making the omelet, it's not my fault."

"Like throwing an old man in a wheelchair off a ship at sea?"

"That's not what happened." He turned away and wouldn't talk about it.

Hershel gave up on that tack. He checked his watch. A little after eight in the morning.

"We'll stay here until near dusk, when we drive again. Maybe we can dodge any police and army guards that way." The others had no arguments or suggestions.

"Let's sack out," Hershel said. "I'll take the first four-hour watch. Get some sleep, we'll need it tonight." Hershel checked the cuffs on Sharif, then prowled the woods searching for a good lookout spot. He didn't want an army patrol or some policemen to sneak up on them. They had left several bodies behind them. The authorities would be furiously searching for them. With luck they had left no trail north. With luck.

Hershel found the spot he wanted just behind a fallen log in a flush of young trees and brush. He could see out easily, but anyone on the road couldn't see him or the car. He settled down to wait.

At times like these Hershel had time to think. As always, he thought about his young wife. Nathania had been living at their home near Haifa. She had been shopping at a small market when terrorists struck with a car bomb near a big store. Nathania had been close to the rig when it exploded and was shattered by the blast. He had been working with the Israeli secret service, the Mossad, and had been home on a short leave. They couldn't find enough of her to bury. For three days he walked the streets, not sure where he was, wanting revenge that he would take in the most hideous fashion he could think of.

Twice he crossed into the Lebanon occupied area and sought out known terrorists and blasted them with grenades and his automatic Uzi. He cut up six nests of terrorists before he burned out the hatred inside him and went back to the Mossad. They guessed where he had been, but they couldn't prove it and charge him with unauthorized attacks. He stayed with the Mossad for another three years.

Then the offer had come from Mr. Marshall so he could expand his work, strike at more terrorists on a full-time basis, and he had jumped at the opportunity.

Whenever he thought of his wife a sudden coldness gripped him; it swept through him and left him shivering with a still vital rage. Slowly the cold turned warm and then into the white-hot heat of iron in a fire. It seared into his brain and burned away the new hatred until he was limp and still furious, but with reason again that told him he must satisfy any more vengeance through the work of the Specialists.

He shook his head to clear it. Memory was sometimes too vivid, too demanding. Sweet Nathania had been only twenty-five, a student at the university in advanced mathematics and electronic engineering. She had been four months pregnant with their first child when they both died.

He blinked and took a deep breath and watched a car coming down the highway. It was a French Fiat, six or eight years old, and rolled along about fifty miles an hour. It went past and the man driving never wasted a glance at the woods. Good.

Hershel watched the rest of his time, ate an apple and another of the rolls. He had seen twenty or thirty vehicles, but none of the people in them even noticed the woods. He had tensed when a motorcycle went past, but it looked like a civilian, not military or police. He had one more bite of the apple and called Ichi to stand guard. Suddenly he was weary. He could use a good chunk of sleep. Ichi growled when he woke up and chattered in Japanese for a moment, then grinned.

"You can't know when I'm swearing at you that way," he said. He took his MP-5 and the borrowed Uzi and went up to the lookout spot that Hershel showed him.

Hershel slept until they woke him at 4:30. They ate fruit and rolls again, wished they had coffee, and made ready to move. The prisoner was more talkative now, but Hershel told the others he said nothing important. Mostly complaining.

An hour later it was nearly dark and they packed up, reloaded empty magazines, and were set.

"Might be a good time to use some juice on our talkative friend," Ichi said. He was the holder of the drugs. Hershel nodded and Ichi took out the kit, chose the one that would not knock out Sharif, but make him cooperative, drowsy, and keep him quiet in case of any close inspections by the police or army.

Sharif saw the needle coming and tried to react, but he was too late. The drug squirted into his arm. Five minutes later he was smiling and chuckling as they helped him into the backseat of Salimah's car.

"They could have a stolen car notice out on this license plate," Hershel said. "Let's keep a sharp eye out for cops and military."

They drove. There was little traffic. It picked up as they came toward the coast and the small town they were aiming for. They could see the glow of the town ahead.

They came around a sharp turn in the road, and Ichi put on the brakes.

"Look at that, must be a million animals ahead of us all over the road like a flood," Ichi said.

"Goats, a huge herd of brown and white and black goats crossing the road going somewhere," Hershel said.

Ichi brought the car to a stop twenty feet from the sluggish brown and black tide and waited.

"How long is this going to take?" Roger asked.

"Can't be more than a few hundred of them," Hershel

said. "Some of these people have their whole family wealth in goat herds."

They waited.

"Where are the guys minding the animals?" Roger asked.

"Usually in back prodding them along," Hershel said.

They waited. The stream slowed, then only a few stragglers came across. In the dim light they saw four men plodding along behind the goats. When they came closer, the Specialists saw the men were soldiers, all with weapons they were lifting.

The road was clear. Ichi hit the gas pedal and the old car plunged ahead. "Fire when ready," Ichi yelled and pushed his Ingram out the window and began firing at the soldiers.

✶ ELEVEN ✶

MOUNTAIN HOME, IDAHO

Thursday night Charlie made it to the bar after five pilots had gathered around their favorite table. He brought three pitchers of beer and the pilots cheered.

"Missed you this week, Charlie," Captain Clooney said, slapping him on the back. "Mostly we missed your free beer." They all laughed and Charlie sat down and poured a beer into his glass.

"Hey, I have to work sometime. My editor is getting on my tail about deadlines."

The talk went back to flying and Charlie settled in, enjoying the talk, pouring fresh beer for the men, and making himself generally helpful. He begged off after an hour, saying he had to get some work done today.

"Hey, my editor is going to expect to see an outline one of these months. With the advance she gave me, I expect I better send her one."

"Take time out tomorrow night for poker," Captain Clooney said. "Going to be at my place. You know where I live. We want you and your two hundred bucks to show up."

"Hear you got cleaned out last week," a pilot Charlie hadn't met said.

"Oh, yeah, cleaned and reamed out good. I'm looking

for some recoup. Damn right, I'll be there tomorrow night." He finished his beer and left the pilots to talk about afterburners, inside turns, lock-ons, and intercepts.

The next night he arrived at the Clooney home fifteen minutes before the game was to start. He was the first to show. He wanted to meet Mrs. Clooney and the girls. Depending on how persuasive he was, the women in the Clooney family could be a big part in the showdown, when it came.

"So you're the writer Marv has been telling me about," Beth Clooney said as soon as they had been introduced. "I always wanted to write, but then I became busy with two small ones, and they take up a lot of time."

Beth was short, slender, blond, and looked to be full of energy and ideas. She didn't bubble over, but the vitality of the woman was obvious. Charlie liked that.

"Mrs. Clooney, you can . . ."

She waved him silent. "Mrs. Clooney is Marv's mother. I'm Beth. Call me Beth."

"Good, I'm Charlie. Beth, you can always find time to write if you really want to. Just block out a period of time when the girls are at school or nothing else is going on, and do your writing then. Even two hours a day will get you moving good. What do you want to write?"

They were off on a half-hour talk about writing as the pilots assembled. Then Charlie had to hurry out of the kitchen to claim his chair and buy his two hundred dollars worth of chips.

The game started slow, with one- and two-dollar bets. There were six men playing that night and it built up larger pots. Charlie started as he had before jumping at tries on flushes and straights, losing every hand for the first six. Then he won the seventh to stay in the game. After that he won just enough to stay nearly even.

Whenever he dealt, he cheated. If he was behind, he cheated to win. If he was too far ahead he cheated giving another man a good hand without his knowing it.

After sandwiches and cheese and crackers and fruit juice at ten o'clock, Charlie began to lose in earnest. In three hands he was cleaned out of chips and going light on the last pot. Clooney had been winning, and the last time Charlie dealt, he had sent him four nines.

"Hey, partner, you need some cash?" Clooney asked. "No new money, but nothing says I can't give a friend a couple of bucks." He slid a hundred dollars in chips to Charlie who protested. Then everyone shrugged and said, "Why not?" He took the cash and played more conservatively. By the end of the night he had lost half of the hundred and gave Clooney back the other fifty.

"Hey, I'm good for it. Pay you back at the next game."

As they were breaking up, Beth came in and talked to Clooney for a minute, then came over to Charlie.

"Say, Charlie, would you come to dinner tomorrow night? I'd like to bribe you with some good roast beef, then ply you with questions about writing and about my writing. Maybe, if I'm bold enough, I'll ask you to read something I've written."

Charlie grinned. "Hey, I don't get a home-cooked meal very often. If it's okay with the captain, I'd love to come."

"Oh, I asked Marv first and he said sure to invite you. I'm glad. We'll eat about seven, because Marv has a late flight tomorrow afternoon. We'll see you then. And remember, I'm not a pro at this writing game."

"I'll be gentle," he said and Beth blushed and hurried out to the kitchen.

Charlie took Captain Clooney's hand at the door. "Hey, thanks for the loan, I'm gonna learn how to play this game eventually. Thought I was doing better tonight."

"You were. It's those wild shots at flushes and straights that can sink the best poker player. Have to work the odds. Better to be trying for three cards than just one out of the deck. You'll get the hang of it. See you tomorrow night."

Charlie laughed softly on the way to his rented car. Oh, indeed they would see him the next night. He figured one more poker party and he should be ready to move. Oh, yeah, one more week.

When he got back to his apartment, he worked the

E-mail and reported in that he had the hook in good now and was about ready to land the fish. He figured another week, two at the most. He headed to a tavern closer to his apartment and sat at the bar. Charlie had two drinks, then began looking for a likely lady for the evening. A half hour later he found her and they went to his apartment. He figured it was high time for a small celebration.

LONDON, ENGLAND

El Ali Katami spent most of his free time in London at a large flat he had rented and been there for almost three years now, working in and out of the country on a variety of passports. He was known in his neighborhood as a Saudi millionaire with oil income who was generous with his spending.

He had an English cook and a live-in butler who was one of his operatives. The maid came in during the day but slept out. The Scimitar lived in London because it suited him. It had all of the luxury and convenience he wanted. He had grown accustomed to the Western way of living, eating, even entertainment.

At some point he had been exposed to opera. He went to most of the big productions in London and sometimes Paris.

He had an "office" nearby in the warehouse district, a rather large building that formed a working area, where the five men he kept on permanent payroll operated. One was a mechanic, the second an expert on explosives and bomb making, a sharpshooter, one driver, and the last a procurement man who could buy, beg, borrow, or steal anything from the latest in blasting equipment to the best in intelligence-gathering material and equipment.

His small office in the back was furnished like a den, with carpet, a desk, a fine hi-fi music system, a large wall TV set, guest chairs, a refrigerator, and a microwave for emergencies. The den was cooled and heated precisely to seventy-two degrees inspite of the undependable London weather.

Now he sat down behind his desk and looked at the three items put there with red tags on them. All urgent.

One was an E-mail printout. He read it and smiled. The main project was moving ahead on schedule. In fact it was a week ahead of where he expected it to be.

The second red tag was from Egypt. A phone call that had been recorded and typed out. Project four was ready and coordinated. All incidents would take place the next day precisely at twelve noon.

The call had come from Hamal, his top explosive expert who he had sent to Egypt to coordinate the tasks. He was good at his work, not only providing the packages, but in making sure of the timing. In this project, timing was vital.

The third red flag was placed on a note from Imad, his manager of the London office and also one of his top expert snipers. There had been two inquiries by neighbors about what exactly they did in the warehouse. The neighbors said they saw few trucks coming and going and were naturally curious.

Imad said he had given them a story about technical research projects that were hard to describe and some of them were classified by the government, so they had to maintain a certain amount of security. He said the explanations had satisfied the neighbors. Imad suggested that their time left at that location could be less than two years and suggested that some plans should be made for checking out another site to have for backup.

The following day at 11:45 A.M., El Ali called his four men into the office, providing them with drinks and snacks, and invited them to watch the news reports. He had a satellite to pick up worldwide TV as well as CNN news.

Promptly at 12:15 the first report and video came in on CNN of a blasted building in downtown Egypt.

"It was a two-story building before the bomb went off," the TV spokesman said. "The device had been simply leaned up against the front of the structure in a backpack that students use. It exploded twelve seconds after twelve noon, destroyed the building and killed two workers inside having lunch and injured six more. The building was owned by Trans American Oil, with extensive holdings in the Near East.

"Egyptian authorities said that there was no clear reason for the bombing, yet they did find a copper plate at the edge of the blasted building that had engraved on it the picture of a scimitar. A scimitar is a saber made of a curved blade with the cutting edge on the convex or curved outward side. Historically it was an Arab and Turkish weapon.

"Pardon me, ladies and gentlemen," the announcer said. "We have another bulletin coming in. Now we have reports and pictures of three more bombings that took place at or near the noon hour in three more countries. All involved American business firms. The two- or three-story buildings were shattered and destroyed by the powerful bombs. The other attacks came in Saudi Arabia, Syria, and Lebanon. In each case there was a signature left by the bomber. It was the copper plate with the picture of a scimitar engraved on it. We return now to our regular programming."

The Scimitar turned off the set and watched his four men. Each responded in his own way, but all showed pleasure.

"In the months and years to come, the whole world will learn to shiver when the name of the Scimitar is brought up." He smiled at his four men, their eyes glowing with a fanatical fury that the Scimitar counted on.

✴ TWELVE ✴

Ichi and Hershel both began firing as the sedan surged ahead down the highway. When the vehicle jolted forward, the soldiers all dropped to the ground and let the hail of hot lead sail over their heads. Only two were wounded. When the car raced past them, the soldiers began firing at the rear of the sedan.

The Specialists were at a disadvantage then, since they had to lean out the windows and fire at the soldiers. The Iranian soldiers used fully automatic rifles, and sent dozens of rounds at the retreating car. One tire on the left side rear blew and the sedan swerved and slowed, then plowed ahead with tire rubber and cord flying into the roadway. The soldiers fired until the rig vanished into the night, then ran for their car parked a short distance away. They piled in and gave chase.

Ahead in the wounded sedan, Ichi came up from his crouch behind the front seat and kept the car on the road.

"Don't know how much longer we can stay with this crate," Ichi yelled. "Lost one tire, and they might have hit the gas tank. No gas gauge so I can't tell."

Hershel fired once more out the window, then gave up and looked ahead. The glow of the small town looked inviting, but he wasn't sure they could make it.

A grinding sound came from the rear of the car.

"We're running on the rim," Ichi said. "Good for maybe two more miles. Any casualties?"

Roger swore softly in the backseat. "Just one of us hit back here," Roger said. "Those rifle rounds pounded through the back of the car and the rear seat and nailed old Sharif good. Looks like he took at least three rounds right in his spine. He was dead before he hit the floor."

"Who has the camera?" Hershel asked.

"I do," Roger said. "I'll get three or four shots of him for positive ID. Damn, hate to lose a prisoner when we got him this far." He took four head shots making positive ID.

"Now all we have to worry about is getting out of fucking Iran," Hershel said. "How much longer can we stay in this gas guzzler?" Hershel asked. "If they get one of their cars running, they'll chase us down quick."

The motor coughed, sputtered, then stopped. They rolled to a halt within twenty feet.

"Everybody out," Hershel said. "Chances are those soldiers back there are halfway here."

Five minutes later they were two hundred yards off the road into the black countryside. They saw headlights coming up fast from the rear. The vehicle stopped at the dead sedan and they heard yells of glee.

"Double-time it," Hershel said. "We need some distance between them and us."

They had their G-16 personal radios on so they heard the whispered words, and they all took off heading for the village lights ahead.

"How far to the town?" Ichi asked.

"My guess, about ten miles yet," Roger said.

"Plenty of time for those grunts back there to radio ahead and get a good-sized search party out to block our way."

"So we fool them," Roger said. "We turn north, go back across the road and get the hell out of their way. When we have five miles off the road west, then we can turn back north and find the wet."

"Gets my vote," Hershel said.

"Amen, brother," Ichi agreed and they turned back toward the road. They waited in the brush near the highway as two cars went past, then a truck, before it was clear enough for them to race across the road. Once across, they settled down to a ground-eating jog that Roger said would move them six miles an hour. They were in good enough shape they could keep it up for two hours before they took a break.

"Damn," Hershel said. "Wish that we'd brought the rest of those sweet rolls."

"Wish no more," Roger said. "I've got half of them. Now let's keep moving."

After an hour they took a break. Roger automatically became the field leader when they were in a combat or firefight situation. He had spent three years as a Navy SEAL.

"I know one thing," Roger said when they had rested for five minutes. "When we get back to camp our troops are going to do more running and conditioning. You two are pathetic."

"Easy for you to say, you're not even winded," Ichi said. "You're right. We need more training runs."

Roger checked the skyline. The lights of the town had faded to the east. "We turn north now and strike for the water and find us a boat we can steal or buy. These damn kit bags should be strapped to our backs. We've got the cord. Tie on each other's, then we move. Next time we bring rubber hose to use to tie our spare weapons on our backs."

On the north route they passed three small farms with houses, two with lights. They kept moving. One place had a dog that set up a barking fit, but they ran quickly past.

Far ahead they saw lights, moving red and white lights in the sky.

"Choppers," Roger said. "They're looking for us or somebody else. Those stream-type lights turn the night into day for thirty-yard circles."

The choppers went the other way and the Specialists kept on hiking.

"Five more miles to the water," Roger said. "Don't ask me how I know. I can smell it."

A short walk later they came to a road that headed generally north and they took it, walking on the shoulder. It was easier than jumping farmer fences and working through brush and wood lots.

Two miles up the road they saw headlights coming. The three men edged into a ditch, then into a field and went flat on the ground as an old army rig rumbled past. They could see at least six soldiers in it, all with their rifles pointing skyward.

"Looking for us?" Hershel asked.

"Who else?" Roger asked.

He looked at his pocket compass.

"Off the road. I don't like that mounted patrol. We'll head due north."

The choppers came back. Almost without warning they lifted over some woods and six of them spread out in a line in front of the surprised Specialists. Their stream lights picked out landing sites and the birds set down. The moment they touched ground armed men leaped out of each one and formed up in a perimeter around the chopper.

Roger counted. "Ten men per bird. That means there are sixty automatic rifles out there and probably some machine guns."

When the last man off-loaded each bird, the choppers jolted upward and went back the way they had come.

"What the hell we do now?" Ichi asked.

"We wait and see which way they move," Roger said. "We see if they form up in a column of ducks or in a skirmish line. That tells us what they know about where we are."

As he said it they saw the shadows in the field five hundred yards ahead of them form into skirmish lines that joined the ten-man squads. There was a whistle and then the men began to work forward, straight at the three Specialists.

"Well, Roger?" Hershel whispered in the mike.

"I'm thinking. We're slightly left of center on their line.

They are spread five yards apart. That puts twenty of them to our left, about a hundred yards. We run to the left keeping so damn quiet our future mothers-in-law couldn't hear us going out their daughters' window. Move."

They ran.

They had five hundred yards to work with and in the end that proved to be barely enough room. They heard some shouted commands repeated down the line, then the Iranian troops began to jog forward in a basic frontal assault.

The three Specialists squeezed beyond the last man in the long line and went flat in the grass and weeds.

When the Iranians were fifty yards past them, Roger whispered that it was time to move.

"We keep heading north," he said. "No way we can miss a puddle the size of the Caspian Sea."

They hiked again. By this time they had distributed the rest of the sweet rolls and the last four apples and ate as they walked.

Twice they saw and heard the helicopters behind them. The troops worked away from them. This must have been a beating group, with the job of containing the quarry and scaring a prey toward the center where the masses of troops would cut them into small chunks.

Thirty minutes later, the Specialists came to a road that carried a lot of traffic. When they looked closer from a ravine twenty yards from the highway, they discovered that all of the traffic was military.

"Twenty trucks in that last convoy," Hershel said. "They on maneuvers or are all those jaspers hunting our hides?"

"Best bet they're looking for us," Roger said. "We wait for a spot of dark here and then we all go across at once. Hope none of those guys have night vision goggles."

It was another five minutes before Roger gave the order and the three men dashed across the road and vanished into a field of wheat. They had come through low mountains in the car on the way north, now they had the fertile, but narrow coastal plain to work through. It was good farmland in a country with very little such land.

A mile farther north and they all could smell the sea.

"Is that saltwater I smell?" Ichi asked.

"Is the Caspian Sea salty or fresh water?" Roger asked.

"It has no outlet, so it's probably salty," Hershel said. "I'll tell you for sure as soon as we start swimming out to meet our boat."

"Swim?" Ichi yelped. "Thought we were going to buy a boat."

They came to another road, not as well traveled, and crossed it quickly without spotting any cars.

Roger heard them first. The roaring, grinding, clanking sound was soon evident to all three.

"Tanks?" Ichi asked.

"Yep. More than one," Roger confirmed.

"What the hell are they doing out here?" Hershel asked.

"Let's hope it's an exercise, because that means they won't have any live ammunition," Roger said.

The tanks rumbled past a quarter of a mile east of them. The next smaller road had direction signs that Hershel read.

"Nothing about that little town we were looking for," he said. "But there is a village called Chalus two kilometers straight ahead."

"What are we waiting for?" Roger asked. He took three steps ahead in the soft moonlight and then saw what had stopped the other two. Directly in front of him twenty feet away stood three Iranian army troopers with rifles pointed right at them. Each one wore his steel helmet and they looked ready for a fight.

"Down!" Roger bellowed. He swung up his Uzi, thumbing it to full auto, and dove forward. As he dove, he triggered a six-round burst at the three soldiers. He hit the grass and weeds, rolled and came to his stomach, and fired ten more rounds at the two men still standing—they went down before they could get off any aimed shots.

Roger came to his feet and charged the three, the Uzi up and ready. One of the men screamed and lifted up with a knife in his hand. Roger pumped two more rounds into the Iranian's chest, slamming him backward. Roger touched carotid arteries on all three, then came back and asked Ichi to get a fresh magazine for the Uzi out of his kit bag.

"Let's move," Roger said. "We just announced to half the Iranian army that we're here, we're armed, and we don't mind using our weapons. I figure we have about ten minutes before this spot will be swarming with choppers."

They jogged toward the Caspian Sea. A half mile later they came over a small rise and saw the first signs of dawn. Directly ahead of them was a road, and the Caspian Sea lapping at a smooth coastline.

There was no sign of a town. There was no port, no inlet, no harbor.

"Where the hell we supposed to get a boat?" Ichi asked.

"We go north," Hershel said. "Should be some boats up that way. If not, we can walk all the way to Russia."

They hiked along the edge of the water. It was almost daylight. There was no sign of any harbor or any boats.

"Sitting ducks," Ichi said. "We're cannon fodder out here in the open. I can't even see a port."

Hershel stopped. "We better find a place to hide out until it gets dark."

They angled back inland and found a spot about half a mile away from the surf. They crawled into a copse of trees and brush that would keep them hidden unless a platoon of troops really searched the area.

Hershel woke up two hours later.

"Can't sleep anymore," he said. "Trying to figure out where the damn town is. Should be here somewhere."

"We must have cut north of it," Roger said. "Don't worry, there'll be some boats up here soon. People have been fishing this Caspian Sea for five thousand years."

By noon, Ichi was up and they decided to cut inland another mile, pick up some cover in the trees and brush, and watch for the first bunch of boats.

Two hours later, Ichi saw a stream that emptied into a good-sized river. They turned and followed it toward the coast without a word. A river could mean an inlet of some kind, and probably a small harbor.

"Got to be something here," Hershel said. They had crossed the coast highway, a sad little two-lane affair with more potholes than were reasonable, and then skirted a farmhouse and found the mouth of the river five minutes later.

The dock was so small it almost wasn't there. Two rowboats and a small fishing boat were tied up. The tiny boathouse at the land end of the pier looked no more than six feet square.

Ichi and Roger remained in some brush as Hershel went forward and spoke in Farsi. He took two steps onto the wooden dock when a woman came out of the shack with a large pistol in both hands.

"Who are you? What do you want?" she asked.

Hershel grinned and tried to keep from laughing. The revolver wasn't cocked and he doubted she could hold it up long enough to fire.

"Easy, miss, easy. Don't let that thing fall or it might break your foot. My name is Hamal and I come looking for a boat."

"There are no boats for sale here."

"No, I only want to rent one, to go fishing."

"We don't rent boats either."

She was small, slender, with dark pools for eyes and a mouth that had a touch of makeup.

"Maybe just this once, you might rent us the fishing boat. You can come along and pilot the craft back to shore."

"I don't understand."

"Put the gun down before it hurts someone. Please."

She sighed and let the weapon swing down and point at the ground.

"I must be careful. Sometimes people try to steal our boats. Then how could we make a living?"

"I understand. But I have money." He took out a roll of rials so she could see them. At three thousand to a dollar he could give her a bunch. He peeled off twenty of the thousand-rial notes and held them out. Not quite seven dollars.

She frowned. She wore a shawl over her head, a loose-fitting white blouse, and a long dark blue skirt to her ankles. Now she pulled the shawl up so it covered all of her face but her eyes.

"For ten times that amount I will consider it. How do I know you won't rob me and steal the boat?"

Hershel used his best smile and most convincing tone of voice. "Miss, you do not know what might happen. But I won't steal your boat. I won't need it. You'll have to trust me."

"You know I can't do that."

"I'll give you seventy thousand rials. Almost all I have."

She smiled. "Much better. When my father comes back, he will take you out to sea." She turned toward the boat shack, then gasped.

"Quickly, inside. The secret police are coming. They are always bad for us. Come now before they see you. They might drive right on by."

They ran ten steps to the shack and ducked inside. No one else was there. The girl looked out the small window on the land side.

"They are stopping. I must go talk to them." She looked at him. "I don't know why, but I trust you. And seventy thousand rials is more money than we have made in a month fishing. Stay quiet."

She pulled the veil closer and walked out of the shack. Hershel watched her through a crack in the wall. A civilian car stopped at the head of the small dock and two men in mufti got out. She waited for them at the pier. He couldn't hear what they said.

The tone was cordial, friendly. One of the men smiled and reached out to shake her hand. She pulled back and nodded at him. He laughed and walked away. She watched them until they drove down the road, then went back to the shack.

Her face was still flushed. She let down the veil and frowned at him.

"They were not nice. I told them my father was watching them. They told me there were some strangers in this area who were wanted by the police and the army. I should watch for them." She looked sternly at him. "You are a stranger."

"How many strangers are they looking for?"

"They weren't sure, one or two, maybe five or six."

"I am definitely not six. Now, the boat. I'd wait until dark to leave, so no one would be suspicious of you."

She smiled briefly, then returned to her small frown.

"And so you could hide in the dark, yes?"

"Yes."

"How many rials do you have?"

"Not sure. Maybe ninety thousand."

Her eyes went wide for a moment and he saw they were a deep brown and now darting from side to side.

"I am a modern Persian woman. I know many things the men don't realize. I was in London for six months. My name is Sadira."

"Good. You should have rights the way English women do."

"I don't know if I could live that way. It would take a lot of changes. Not in Iran, not in my lifetime."

He moved toward her and held out the roll of bills with the rubber band around them.

She put them in a drawer in a small desk, then smiled.

"Now, you have one friend or two? You all must stay hidden until dark. Then we will take our trip."

A moment later the car that had been there before returned and the two civilians ran toward the shack—both had out automatics.

The girl's eyes went wide and one hand flew to her mouth.

Hershel pulled the Ingram from under his loose-fitting Iranian clothes and stood beside the open door, waiting.

✶ THIRTEEN ✶

SOUTHERN LEBANON

Abdel Salim stood in a small room in a village in Lebanon only ten miles from Israel. He was five feet four inches tall, and sturdy at 170 pounds. He had two scars on his Iranian dark skin, one that flashed down from his left eye almost to his mouth. Shrapnel from one of his own bombs had caused that one. The other scar was along his chin from a knife wielded by a man who tried to be a lover to one of Salim's wives. Salim received the deep cut, the other man, a funeral.

Salim's brown eyes narrowed and his heavy brows over a full black beard drove needles of doubt toward the man who stood in front of him.

"Nothing? You have found out nothing more about the celebration? It's a national Jewish holiday. Check the World Wide Web, you camel shit eater. Get out and don't come back without the information."

The young man shivered and hurried away.

Salim sat at the small desk his host had provided and looked over the timetable again. They would go ashore at Haifa in a rubber boat, three of them would be enough. They would be disguised as tourists with backpacks and sleeping bags. The packs and bags would be filled with plastic explosives. They would go in after midnight, and work their way silently to the objective once they got past any patrol boats and guards on the Mediterranean coast.

After sinking the boat and motor, they would slip through a park area, then work quickly through the six blocks of businesses and residences to the new bleachers and go under the structure when no one was watching. He had checked bleacher construction on the WWW. There were only four basic types and Israel would use one of them. The team had memorized the main supports for each type. Once the team was safely away, all bombs would be set off by electronic detonators.

The backpacks and sleeping-bag bombs were ready. They were heavy, but he had chosen two large men to be with him. Salim had been able to pick from twelve volunteers for the mission.

This was the type of action he loved. Striking at the heart of the infidels, the non-Muslims, the Great Evil. He was a soldier of Allah. His people accepted donations only of enough money to do their work and maintain a simple lifestyle. No mansions for them. No stretch limousines, fancy foods, or luxurious accommodations.

Salim ate his noon meal of goat cheese and bread as he remembered a small problem. Achmed. The man was sincere, but he simply was not a soldier of Allah. He had no real skills, and the first small raid he went on, he made three vital mistakes and caused one of his men to be seriously wounded. He simply had to go.

Salim had called the man in. Achmed was thirty years old and a goat herder from the rural areas far to the south, who said he had a vision he should fight the hated Jews.

Achmed was a tall man with a skimpy beard and almost no mustache. His dark hair was thinning and he would be bald before he was forty. Deep-set dark eyes peered at Salim.

"You called for me, worthy leader?"

"Yes, Achmed. I have important work for you to do back in your region. You must tell of your strikes against Israel with us, and you must recruit more young men to come and take your place. You have done your duty to Allah as a soldier. Now you must be a recruiter and send money and young men to me."

"I still want to be a soldier."

"You will be, but on a different front. Soldiers do as they are ordered. Now I order you to report back to your home. To take up your old life and as a second duty to recruit new men and money for the holy cause. You can do that. Now, say good-bye to your friends here and leave before nightfall. You have a long trip."

Achmed had stood there a moment more, unbelieving. His face worked and he sniffed and then turned slowly. "Yes, sir, Abdel Salim, I will do as you order."

Salim hadn't watched him leave. Now, he checked the map of Haifa he had spread on the desk. The holiday was always the same. A parade down the main street ending at the old soccer stadium where new bleachers had been built for this celebration.

That evening, just at dusk, they set out from Lebanon in a fishing boat that held the eight-foot-long rubber craft. The weather was stormy, which would help them. Rain began the first hour they were on the water and by the time they had traveled the twenty miles down the coast to Haifa, the rain had increased to a downpour. Salim welcomed the rain. It would make the job of the Israeli patrol craft along the border that much harder.

Salim wiped rain from his face as he powered the small rubber boat through the choppy sea toward the coast. The fishing boat had left them four miles offshore. Even the good Israeli radar would not be able to spot the low profile of this tiny rubber craft in this rain and running sea. Good. One of his men threw up silently over the side. It was his first strike. His name was Sarihah, and he was from Tehran. Each carried a Glock 18 automatic pistol with an extended magazine holding thirty-two rounds of 9mm parabellum. They hung on cords around their necks and under their civilian shirts. Salim had a La France

M16K submachine gun on a sling around his neck and under his floppy civilian shirt. The weapon was only twenty-four inches long and had a magazine with thirty 5.56 rounds.

Salim had the boat close enough to shore now so the soft purr of the motor might be heard by the shore police. He hoped they were inside out of the rain. Salim's crew came closer, and he saw the lights he always used as guides. It was a small beach between some rocky outcroppings. On shore there was a band of trees and parks they could work into and use as concealment as they hiked the mile into the heart of the city and toward the old soccer stadium. The workmen must be finished with the construction by now. Salim checked his wristwatch. Just after midnight. Good, their timing was good. The rain continued but came now as a drizzle.

Salim touched the waterproof packet in his pocket that contained the small transmitter that would detonate the bombs—it was safe. He turned the small boat slightly more toward the light, then idled the engine down and listened. There was an incoming tide, that would help. With luck he could turn off the motor and catch a wave and run silently into the beach.

No, it wouldn't work. Drifting now, he found a strong current was pulling them left of the target beach. He moved up the throttle and powered the boat back on line. They were only fifty yards off the shore. All three put on their packs then, tying them firmly to their bodies. Now the rain came again in torrents almost blinding Salim.

A patrol boat surged out of the darkness and the rain, its engine growling loudly in the night, a searchlight scanning the area between the boat and the shore. Salim watched the beam come toward his boat, then it slowed, stopped, and reversed directions. The next time the beam swept his way, the patrol boat had passed their position and was devoured by the windy sea. The patrol boat continued on down the coast.

Salim powered forward, judging the waves, then pushing the throttle to full forward so they could catch the top of the next forming wave. They slammed forward with the rush of the powerful wave, careened near the front of the curling mass of water, then eased back as it crashed into white foam and the boat glided silently into the sand to a smooth stop. The three jumped out of the boat, slashed with sharp knives so it would sink in the heavy surf, and hurried up the sandy beach to a copse of trees and brush thirty yards away.

They dropped to the ground just inside the first concealment, the heavy packs testing their strength as they waited and watched for any shore guards. The rain continued. Salim held up his hand and then touched each man for total silence. An Israeli soldier in a poncho, carrying a submachine gun, slogged along through the soft beach sand, stopped a moment to stare out to sea, then continued to the far outcroppings and disappeared. The trio waited a moment longer, then came to their feet, adjusted the heavy packs, and walked through the parklike natural woods. No words were spoken. Salim used hand signals and the men continued forward, watching ahead and on all sides for any more signs of military guards. They moved cautiously inland past a playground, through more trees without underbrush, and at last to the edge of the deserted park. The time was almost 1:00 A.M. The trio moved through the deserted, dark park for half a mile before edging into a street and walking toward the old soccer field.

They saw several cars moving along the street. Once they spotted a police vehicle, but it crossed the street ahead of them with light bar on top flashing as it hurried to a call farther on.

Salim felt the familiar surge of energy, the high he could find no other way. Danger, destruction, fighting for Allah. It was all there and he gloried in the moment. Then he studied his surroundings. They were only two blocks from the celebration site. Already people would be coming to get in line for the best seats. If they were on this side of the stadium, he would have to move his men around them. Still, they did look like students or tourists. They wore ordinary clothes purchased from a Jewish store and were all relatively young. They would pass a walk-by inspection.

The rain had tapered off to a soft mist. Salim walked casually now, as if in no hurry in case anyone saw them. He could see the backs of the bleachers now, over three stories tall. They worked down the street, walking slowly toward the bleachers. Salim saw a line of people a block away under streetlights, sitting and standing on the sidewalk leading toward the main entrance. Some were sleeping, some talking. Two small fires blazed where people tried to stay warm.

The three Iranians faded to the left, away from the line, and found the rear of the bleachers. Salim and his men lay in shadows for ten minutes watching the area. They spotted no guards, no roving patrol, no protection. Salim huddled with his two men. "You have three minutes to place the bombs in the spots we picked out on the blueprints. Get them solidly in place, then push down the lever arming the electronic detonator. Go." They drifted singly next to the bleachers, then vanished under them, each taking his assigned section.

Salim placed his bombs quickly and walked away from the beams and supports to the back of the bleachers. He checked the street behind, but saw only one car going the other way. No guards or walking people. He sauntered across the street and half a block away to a tree where they would meet. The other two came a few minutes later.

Salim had picked out a vacant building a block from the bleachers where they would be able to see the whole area. It was up a slight hill. They wandered up there and slipped inside, then looked out the windows. Salim let the other two sleep and he stood watch. It would be almost noon before the stands filled with the hated Israelis. All they had to do was wait. That was the hardest part. At least the rain had stopped and the clouds blew away to show a sprinkling of stars overhead. It would be a bright sunny day for the celebration.

Salim didn't sleep. He watched the area slowly come awake and people began moving around. Guards soon showed at the back of the grandstand, soldiers with their submachine guns. They were too late. Salim smiled.

By 11:30 that morning Salim could see the stands filling up. Now even the top row was filled with people looking over the side, talking, shouting to each other.

The parade had started earlier, wound through the Haifa streets for three miles, and would end here just before noon. Salim touched the pouch in his pocket that held the electric signal box that would set off the bombs. Yes, it was still there and safe.

He roused the two sleepers. They came to the window to watch the scene.

"Are the stands full yet?" Sarihah asked. The strapping youth who had thrown up on the boat stared at the target with an eager look.

"Soon," Salim said.

"I could go check," Sarihah said. "Walk around to the front and take a look."

"What if a soldier stops you," Salim said. "You don't even speak Hebrew."

"I'll fake it, there are Arabs all over Haifa."

Salim nodded and the youth went to the door, eased out, stood around, then walked toward the bleachers. He was only halfway to the front of the bleachers when two Israeli soldiers stopped him. Sarihah pointed at the bleachers and stood there.

Salim took out the black box with the two switches on it. He might have to blow the stands if Sarihah gave it away. He pushed the first switch and his finger hovered over the second. If they searched his man it would be all over. Sarihah would sacrifice himself for the glory of Allah.

Then the soldiers waved and Sarihah turned away from the stands and walked down a side street. Salim relaxed, took his finger off the second switch, and pushed the first one back to off.

Five minutes later, Sarihah came into the front room of the building. He had slipped in a rear door.

"Their security is tight. They told me if I had no ticket, I couldn't go to the bleachers. They held up a ticket to show me. I shook my head and walked the other way. I could see that the stands were filled."

"Then now is the time," Salim said. They could hear a band playing as Salim picked up the black box again. "We are too close, we must move back another two blocks to be out of the blast area."

They went out the back door and up the street. On the hillside they could see the old soccer field and the new bleachers built on the open end.

Salim looked at his men. "*Al hamdo lillah,*" he said. All thanks and praise to the Almighty. His men both repeated the phrase, then Salim pushed the second button.

A tenth of a second later six blasts shook the whole area, coming almost at one time. A great shock wave of air blasted past the three men six hundred yards away. A shroud of smoke and dust billowed into the air, then the back of the bleachers blasted outward as the whole assembly fell into itself.

Bits and pieces of wood and metal shot into the sky from each of the six locations. The blast rumbled through the air like a dozen thunderclaps. The Iranians put their hands over their ears too late to shield them.

Sirens wailed. Even from that distance they could hear the shrieks and cries of the wounded and injured. A moment after the blast, the whole bleacher area, forty yards wide, had smashed downward into a roiling mass of timbers, metal braces, seats, and bodies of the dead and dying.

"Time to go," Salim said. He turned and with the two men headed not toward the park they had come through into town, but due north toward Lebanon. They had a little over twenty miles to hike and knew it would be dangerous. After strikes like this, the Israelis routinely put out screening patrols beyond Haifa covering all roads and trails leading north.

They walked for two hours, trying not to appear to be rushing. By then they were just out of the city itself moving into a few roads and fields. Far ahead they saw a roadblock, with cars lined up at a checkpoint. They moved into the field next to it and into some brush where they waited.

"It will be best to wait until darkness to work our way to the border," Salim said. "We will stay here out of sight. Go to sleep, I'll keep watch." Salim moved some plants and grass so he could see out past a small tree toward the roadblock. Any trouble would come from that way.

Salim nodded and came up with a start. It had been a long day. He had been up now for almost thirty hours. Perhaps he should wake up one of the men. No, he needed them sharp for the hike through the military lines at the border on both sides. He didn't want to get shot by friendly Lebanon forces.

A half hour later he nodded off again. This time he roused Sarihah.

"I'm sleeping at the switch here, Sarihah. You better take over. Wake me in three hours."

Salim saw the young man at the lookout, then drifted off to sleep at once.

Gunfire awoke him. Sarihah had his pistol out and fired to the south. Bullets zipped through the thin cover over their heads. Salim came up with the M16 shortened automatic rifle. Sarihah pointed to the south and Salim turned that way. Three Israeli soldiers were moving forward across a field with little cover. Two charged forward as the third covered them with a barrage of rounds. The two Iranians ducked. The third man woke up and grabbed his pistol, but the gunmen were out of range.

Salim waited for the next rush, then leveled in the M16K and pounded off two three-round bursts, cutting down one of the Israelis. The other two hesitated, then dove behind some boulders and out of sight.

"That should hold them for a while," Salim said. "We have to figure out how to get out of here."

Sarihah didn't answer. Salim looked over to where he had been ready to fire when the enemy came within range. Sarihah had turned over on his back. His shoulder and chest were one mass of blood. He tried to talk, but only a whisper came out.

"He's hit bad," Abarku said.

Salim rolled over and looked at the wounds. The shoulder had caused most of the blood. But the chest wound was the most dangerous. The round had penetrated a lung, missing his heart by inches. It could have cut a major artery.

"Hurt bad," Sarihah said. The words forced.

The "no prisoners" code blasted into Salim's head. He had a policy of never taking prisoners and never leaving any of his men to become prisoners. There was no chance that Sarihah could run or even walk away from that copse of trees.

"What are they doing out there?" Salim asked.

Abarku lifted his head around a small tree and then pulled it back at once. "The one man is still down in the open. He isn't moving. Can't see the other two. Oh, just saw a rifle barrel lift over the . . ."

Six shots blasted through the trees, nipping off small branches, one round coming dangerously close to Salim.

Salim cursed himself. He had not checked the terrain closely enough before he holed up here. Now he looked. There was a small ravine leading away from the trees. Could be a small stream in it. With some good crawling they could get to the ravine unseen, then move left and generally north past the riflemen and the roadblock. With luck. But not with Sarihah.

Salim unhooked his M16K and handed it to Abarku. "Take this, get to this side of the hole here, and fire six shots at those rocks the riflemen are behind when I tell you. Then as soon as you fire, crawl toward that ravine in the brush. Try not to make the brush move any. I'll be right behind you."

"Sarihah?"

"You know he can't be moved. We'll have to leave him here. Now move over and get ready. I'll fire the pistol at them, then we move."

Salim checked to see that there was a round in the chamber. His other man moved into position and Salim nodded. When Abarku fired toward the Israelis, Salim put one round through Sarihah's head, then fired twice at the rocks. Then they moved. Salim looked back at one of his best men. There was no other way. None of his agents had ever fallen into the hands of the enemy. None ever would.

They went around the riflemen before the Israelis knew they were gone, then around the roadblock. From there it was a hike north. The two Iranians slipped through the Israelis' front lines, then into Lebanon without any problem. It had been a good hit against the hated Israel, but it had cost him a good man. Salim shrugged. He could always get more men for his teams. One Iranian for five hundred Israelis. It was a good exchange.

★ FOURTEEN ★

NEAR CHALUS, IRAN

When the two secret Iranian police were twenty feet from
the door of the shack, Hershel stepped out and leveled the
Ingram at the pair.

"Drop your weapons," he barked in Farsi. Both men reacted with shocked surprise. One lowered his hand but
held the pistol. The other jerked his automatic up to shoot.
Hershel fired four rounds into the man's chest and swung
the Ingram toward the other man. He stared at the submachine gun for a moment, then dropped his weapon and
put up his hands.

"Inside," Hershel ordered, and the secret policeman
walked in, looking nervous and still in shock.

Hershel tied his hands and feet with riot cuffs and put a
gag in his mouth. He let the Ingram vanish under his shirt
where it hung on a cord around his neck.

He motioned the girl outside. Hershel went to the policeman and started to roll his body off the dock.

"No! He will be found here and we will be shot," the
girl said.

Hershel nodded and picked up the corpse and carried it
to the fishing boat and put it on board. Then he talked to
the girl.

"We must leave now. Somehow they know we're in this area. Is the boat ready to go?"

"My father will be furious."

"Not with ninety thousand rials. I'll call my friends. We must move as quickly as we can."

Hershel looked at Sadira and saw the indecision, then it faded and she smiled. "Yes. We can go. We have fuel. Bring your friends."

She went on board the boat and began getting it ready to sail. Hershel hurried to the road despite his limp, across it, and to the thicket where he had left the other two Specialists.

Hershel stumbled a little when he went into the brush and Ichi eyed him critically.

"How's that leg?"

"The slug is still there and I'm still walking and it hurts like hell if you really want to know. More important, we've got a boat and two secret police found us. We better get moving."

"Let me look at your leg," Ichi said.

"Do it on the boat. Let's choggie."

They walked quickly down the rise and across the road to the dock.

"You zapped both the cops?" Roger asked.

"One of them, left the other one tied up."

"A good way to get us all killed," Roger said. "We don't leave unfriendly witnesses."

The girl came out of the shack and looked at the newcomers.

"Sadira," she said and held out her hand. Ichi took it, told her his name, and Roger did the same. Her smile brightened when she looked at Roger.

"I've never seen a real Negro before," she said softly to Hershel.

"He won't bite," Hershel said. "Let's get on the boat."

Roger went into the shack and came out with the tied-up secret policeman. He didn't say a word, simply carried him to the fishing boat and dumped him on the small deck.

"Don't want him smelling up the neighborhood," Roger said.

Ichi cast off the lines and Sadira gunned the engine. The thirty-foot fishing boat slanted away from the dock and picked up speed. It smelled of fish. Hershel watched the countryside as they pulled away from Iran. He saw no troops, no choppers, nor did he see any Iranian patrol craft on the Caspian Sea.

When they were three miles off the shore, Roger dumped the corpse of the Iranian secret policeman into the sea and watched him sink. He and Hershel looked at the tied-up secret policeman.

"No loose ends," Hershel said. The ex-SEAL nodded.

"I agree." They waited until Sadira went into the little cabin. Then together they picked up the bound Iranian secret policeman and dropped him overboard. Hershel didn't even blink. It made no difference if the man drowned or was shot to death.

A half hour later, and five miles off the coast, Hershel told Sadira to stop the boat. From his carry bag he took out a small transceiver, extended an antenna two feet, and made a voice transmission in Farsi.

"Moonrider, calling Moonrider. This is Floater One. I repeat. Calling Moonrider. This is Floater One. Over."

They waited. The small speaker on the transceiver remained silent. Hershel made the call twice more with no results.

"This box will reach out nearly twenty miles. We had no definite time frame. Which means we keep repeating the call until we get an answer."

"Which means we have plenty of time to look at that leg," Ichi said. He had the small kit of medical supplies. Hershel nodded and pulled down his pants exposing the bloody bandage on his right thigh.

"You didn't say it was bleeding," Ichi said.

"You didn't ask."

It took Ichi ten minutes to take off the wrap and treat the entry wound with some powder and salve, then bandage it again.

"Now sit down somewhere and stay off it for a couple of hours. It might just start to get better. We still have to take out that slug, wherever the hell it stopped. We have two more days."

Sadira asked Hershel how long they would wait there.

"Not sure. Depends when we can make radio contact. Might be in ten minutes. It might take all day and all night."

She nodded and put out four fishing lines. Each had twenty hooks on it, baited with pieces of some small fish. Each line had a small bell attached. Sadira pointed at the lines and then at Roger.

"Watch them," she said in Farsi. Roger looked at Hershel.

"She said watch them. You're now our fisherman."

Hershel kept transmitting. He worked it every fifteen minutes, but there was no response.

Twenty minutes later, Sadira returned to the deck from the small cabin. She handed each of the men large sandwiches and cups of dark coffee.

"We'll have fish for supper," she said and Hershel translated.

A bell on one of the lines rang and Roger looked at the woman.

"Let it ring five or six times, then we pull it in," she said. Hershel told them what she had said.

"Five or six fish that way," Hershel said.

He kept trying on the radio. The far coast of Iran slid past gently as the fishing boat drifted slowly to the north.

"You sure there's somebody out here watching for us?" Ichi asked.

"Supposed to be," Hershel said. "Another boat, a larger one that's on duty along here most of the time. It might be out of range right now. If it is too far out, it's supposed to move in within ten miles of the coast at least once a day. So relax, enjoy the sun, work on your tan."

"We must fish," Sadira said. "We must catch sturgeon to prove where I have had the boat. It is watched and someone will come when I return."

She began pulling in the lines with hand winches. Roger jumped to her side and took over the winch, winding in the first line. There were eight fish on it, some ten pounds or more. Most of them were sturgeon, some abasks, and two whanfish. They rebaited the empty hooks and let the line out again.

The other three lines came in quickly with Roger winding. More than two dozen fish flopped in the fish boxes on deck by the time they were done.

"It is a good catch," Sadira said. "This is as much as we get sometimes when we fish all day. I will have a lot to show them when I return."

She had taken off her shawl as soon as they were at sea. Now she took off an outer garment and wore a brown blouse with short sleeves. She stood beside Roger and watched him. Sadira smiled and touched his bare arm.

"Do you like me?" she asked in Farsi. Hershel grinned and translated for her.

Roger began to sweat. He shuffled his feet and looked away, then back down at the small lady with the wonderful smile.

"Yes, I like you, Sadira, but we are on a dangerous trip here and I don't want you to be hurt."

She listened to Hershel translate Roger's words and then laughed softly.

"You would never hurt me. I know. I lived in England for six months. I've been kissed even. I am not innocent."

Roger nodded during the translation. "You are right. I would never hurt you." He frowned and looked up, then pointed. They could all see it then, the wake of a fast-moving boat coming toward them.

"Patrol boat?" Hershel asked the woman.

She nodded. "Usually they stay closer to shore. If they come we are doomed."

"How many men on the boats like this?"

"Usually, three. I have seen some with more, but usually it's three."

"Let them come near, even tie up with us," Roger said.

"Then we take them out. We can use their boat and send Sadira back to her fishing."

She looked at Hershel for translation. He told her. She frowned. "They will know my boat. Probably already have radioed in about me being too far from shore for best fishing."

"This is the only way," Hershel said. "Otherwise they will kill all of us including you. Act as naturally as you can."

The three Specialists hid where they could. Roger went into the small cabin with his Uzi cocked. Ichi found a spot just under the lip of the small hold where he could hide and pop up suddenly with his Uzi snarling. Hershel stood on the far side of the cabin where the approaching boatmen couldn't see him.

Sadira gave them a running commentary as the boat came closer. She pulled fish lines, found several more good catches, and baited the hooks again and let them down. She was on the last line when the patrol boat came within hailing distance.

"Why are you so far out of the fishing grounds?" a voice asked on a bullhorn.

"Catching fish. Bigger sturgeon. Look at this twenty-pounder."

"Is that all you have caught?"

"No, some smaller fish, too."

"We will come on board and look," the bullhorn voice said and the craft edged closer until a seaman could grab the rail and quickly tie the boats together.

A second man came from the patrol boat's cabin, then a third, and they stared at Sadira.

"You are not properly clothed," the tallest of the men at the rail said.

"I usually don't see strangers this far at sea," Sadira said. "Where is your other man?"

"Other man? We are only three and we can handle you." The speaker stepped on board the fishing boat.

Hershel came around the cabin and fired six rounds at

the man who had just boarded the fishing boat. Seconds later he heard the other weapons barking and the other two Iranian sailors went down with multiple bullet wounds. One of them tried to get up, but Roger finished him with four more rounds.

Sadira had dropped to the deck with the first gunfire, and now she lifted up and stared at the dead man on her boat. Roger hurried up and lifted the man and pushed him overboard. Ichi jumped onto the patrol craft and went inside the cabin. He looked out a moment later.

"Piece of cake. I can motor this thing. Come on board and we'll go for a ride."

Hershel and Roger dumped the two dead Iranians into the sea and unlashed the patrol boat from the fishing craft. Roger reached out and touched Sadira. She pushed up and kissed his cheek, then his lips, and just then the sea pushed the boats and the two people apart.

"Fish well, and pretend nothing has happened," Hershel called. "Hide the money where the police would not think to look. Fish your usual schedule and you should be all right. We wish you well."

Ichi nudged the throttle forward and the patrol boat surged ahead through the calm Caspian Sea. He made a long looping circle and came around the fishing craft again, then headed to sea more and to the north.

Hershel took out the radio transceiver and tried again.

"Moonrider, Moonrider. Calling Moonrider. This is Floater One. Over." He called in Farsi and they waited.

Nothing.

He made the same call again. This time the small speaker came on.

"Yes, Floater One. Read you. Do you have a global positioner device?"

"Afraid not, Moonrider. We're about six miles offshore, just above Chalus. Your approximate?"

"Floater One. We are ten miles out north of your position. If you transmit every five minutes, we can plot your location."

"Will do, Moonrider."

Roger scowled. "Hey, you told him where we were. Won't every patrol boat in the area come charging at us?"

"Nope. This little transceiver scrambles the transmission. Nothing fancy but enough to require a good crypto man to figure it out. By then, we'll be gone from here."

Hershel made another transmission.

Ichi came out of the cabin. "Any direction I need to aim?"

Hershel grinned. "Take us north at ten knots and just a smidge more away from the shore. We have company coming to meet us."

Two hours later, and just before sunset, a three-hundred-foot Russian freighter steamed up to them and gave a greeting. The captain was surprised to see an Iranian patrol craft, but at once had the Iranian markings painted out and put on a towline.

"I am claiming the ship as salvage at sea," the captain said. "I can sell it for enough to retire on. My lucky day."

A day and a half later, the *Baku Belle* docked at Baku in southern Azerbaijan. The Specialists had given their weapons to the Russian captain in exchange for him booking air passage for them on the first flights out of Baku heading for Istanbul, Turkey.

It took them two more change of planes, then they landed in London's Heathrow Airport where a car and driver met them for a fast trip to the Marshall headquarters.

LONDON, ENGLAND

An hour later Hershel lay in the hospital bed in the Marshall infirmary where the house physician had just removed the lead slug from his thigh.

"You'll stay right here for a week," the doctor told him. He meant it.

The next day the Specialists gathered around his bed and spread out the papers that he and the other two had brought back from Iran. They had been partly translated. Mr. Marshall pointed to one.

"Again we find the list of potential targets in the USA. This is nearly the same list as the ones we have seen before. You say that Kashan claimed that he had no connection with any other group, especially Osama bin Laden. How then did he get this list? Where did it come from?"

"It could be a wish list that Osama bin Laden circulated to all of his terrorist friends," Kat Killinger said. "Sounds like the sort of thing he would do. Like saying here is a list, if I can't get to all of these, maybe someone else can."

"Possible," Wade Thorne said. "I wish we had some way to give weight to the different targets. There's no number one through ten here for us to deal with."

"This list might not be that important," Mr. Marshall said. "What else did you bring back?"

"A lot of paper that needs evaluating and complete schematics of the White House and the Empire State Building," Hershel said. "We don't know what it all means. We'll compare it with other material. Then there were some printouts and other papers."

"The White House and the Empire State. Interesting. Expanding the list." Mr. Marshall frowned. "The FBI director told me that the list I faxed to him were the same targets as those the bureau had noted as potential terrorist objectives. However, he said there was a growing feeling, after the Oklahoma City disaster, that local and foreign might be moving away from the traditional targets, and more into the countryside, the Midwest, even the Southwest.

"The director said that they could give us numbers from one to thirty on their list. The Washington Monument was number four, sport stadiums in general were number twelve, Hoover Dam was number twenty-one, and Prudhoe Bay oil fields was the least likely."

"Anything ever develop on those four bombings in the Near East with the Scimitar's signature on them?" Kat asked.

"We haven't been able to get any direction or reasoning on those blasts," Mr. Marshall said. "Our people are still working on it."

"Anything said about the Big One?" Wade asked.

Roger nodded. "Yeah, we talked some about it with Al Kashan. He knew the term. He smiled when he talked about it. Said that hundreds of thousands would die when it happened. We asked him about the leader and he wouldn't say. Finally he said that the leader could be anyone who loved Allah and hated the Great Evil."

"Then when we were with Sharif he, too, knew about the Big One," Ichi said. "He grinned and worried us about it. But when we tried to pin him down about what the Big One was, he would say that only the core group knew what the project was and when it would happen."

Mr. Marshall frowned. "I haven't been able to get much more from my contacts all across the Arab world. The term is familiar, the terrorists seem to be looking forward to it like some celebration. But nobody knows what it is or when it is scheduled to happen. All I hear is that the Big One will strike on American soil and it will be devastating. So we still have three major suspects, bin Laden, Scimitar, and Salim."

"Sounds like something Osama bin Laden would cook up," Kat said. "Is there any way that we can find out if he's working on the big project? Do we have any spies in his camp?"

"Mighty hard to get anyone inside that group," Mr. Marshall said. "But we're trying. First we have to figure out exactly where he has his new headquarters."

"We're tilting at windmills," Hershel said. "We can't fight them or stop them until we know who we're looking for."

"I have twenty contacts working on it," Mr. Marshall said. "They tell me almost daily that they've never heard of such a project."

"So until we get some facts about it, what can we do?" Wade asked.

"We work over these lists and data we received from the two raids and see what we can come up with," Mr. Marshall said. "A friend of mine from British Intelligence will be around tomorrow to lend us a hand. Let's get to work."

★ FIFTEEN ★

SOMEWHERE IN AFGHANISTAN

Osama bin Laden watched critically from under bushy, dark brows as the four men talked about the project. It was not moving as quickly as he wished. Fazul as well listened to the two explosive experts go through the difficulty in either transporting or making enough explosives to do the job.

"Chemical fertilizer is the easiest, but now it is much harder to buy than it used to be," one of the men said.

"How many people will be there?" bin Laden asked.

The youngest man at the table, Ayman el Hage, looked up quickly. His beard was not as long as any of the others and he had worried about this. But now he was on familiar ground. "There will be a sellout, a total of eighty-six thousand people. The stadium will be filled and there will be a horde of national TV people in the area to give us immediate and top-notch worldwide coverage."

"There will be four trucks loaded with the explosives at the four main entrance/exit points," al Sura said. "All will be set off electronically, so they will fire simultaneously. The destruction will be massive. More infidels may be killed in the stampede trying to get out the blocked exits than in the actual explosions.

"We'll use four extended vans, they will hold enough

explosives with partitions put across just in back of the driver's seat. They will be purchased at used truck lots in nearby towns, then driven to the pickup points in the rural areas to get the fertilizer and other components."

Osama bin Laden held up one hand. "How do we know there will be that many people there?"

"It's a regional final game of World Cup football, or soccer as the Americans call it," el Hage said. "Sellouts have been automatic for this level of play."

"So we have a timetable, a deadline," bin Laden said. He frowned, took a long drink from a tall glass near him. "I do not like deadlines." He sighed. "In this case it must be so."

There were looks of relief on three of the men around the table.

"How many men do we have in the country now who we can rely on?"

"Six, with two more a week set to move in through Canada for the next four weeks."

"Fourteen men?" bin Laden asked. "I remember when we used to go out with just three of us. We carried everything we needed in packs on our backs."

"The projects are much larger now, and involve massive amounts of explosives," Fazul said. "This will be a bold strike that the Great Evil will remember for many years."

"Are we still secure in this house?" bin Laden asked.

"Yes," Fazul said. "No one in this end of the town knows who we are or what we do. The place is large enough that we do not attract attention. We have purchased as you suggested the three houses on each side of this one, and four across the street. Our people will live in these houses and create a solid secure area."

"Our welcome in this country is growing thin," bin Laden said. "The political winds blow one way and then the other. The Taliban even now is losing some of its control over parts of Afghanistan. We need to seek another nation where we can function without harassment. Fazul, look into that. Libya might be one to consider. I have always had the highest regard for al-Qaddafi, and he has been kind to us on several occasions. Another area might be Sudan."

Bin Laden looked at the others around the table and nodded, dismissing them. Only Fazul remained. Fazul was thirty-two years old and had been with bin Laden since he was eighteen. He had risen through the ranks and now was the leader's right hand.

"Have we received anything from our favorite Prince?" bin Laden asked.

"No, nothing in the post or by wire. I'm sure it will come. The Prince is probably busy this time of year. He has been a loyal supporter in the past and I'm sure he is still of the same mind."

Osama took a long drink from the tall glass. It was his favorite cold drink, pink lemonade. His dark bearded face slowly built a frown.

"It is immensely important that we keep pressure on the Americans and the Israelis. Both must be driven out of the Middle East. The Israelis are killing small children in Palestine and the Americans, innocent people in Iraq. The majority of the American people support their dissolute president, which means the American people are fighting us. Therefore we have a right to target the ordinary American civilian.

"I would love to have at my disposal any number of weapons of mass destruction. America has all sorts of them and the world thinks nothing of it. It is okay if the Jewish state has some of those same mass killing weapons. But if a Muslim state like Pakistan tries to defend itself against the Hindu hegemony in South Asia, the Western world says everything should be done to prevent them from getting these weapons.

"We don't consider it a crime for a Muslim country to try to get nuclear, chemical, or biological weapons. How can the Great Evil nations consider it anything but normal self-defense? Our Holy Land is occupied by Israeli and American forces. We have the right to defend ourselves and to liberate our Holy Land.

"We will do what we can do. Early in 1999 we held the first great meeting of the International Front of Islamic Movements. It is a good step. It is an umbrella over all organizations fighting the jihad against Jews and crusaders. The response from Muslim nations was greater than we hoped for. We have urged them all to start fighting, or at least to start preparing to fight against the enemies of Islam.

"Yes, two of our brothers started their jihad before they had sufficiently prepared. That does not mean fighting the way of jihad is wrong. We have urged all Muslims to study the case of each of their countries and to decide when they can start their jihad. If the time is not suitable, this does not mean they should just sit. It means they must work hard in preparation. You have to do many things before waging jihad, and every Muslim should prepare himself very well for this."

A buzzer sounded on the table. Bin Laden picked up a small handset. "Yes?" The leader listened for a moment, then put down the phone and smiled. "We have a visitor coming, someone who is a stranger to us, but who knows the way and the passwords. The sentry believes that the man comes from Saudi Arabia."

"Then it must be good news," Fazul said.

Ten minutes later the courier had turned over his packages to Osama bin Laden and left.

Fazul waited until the guard and the courier had departed, then he opened the carefully sealed packages.

"Yes," bin Laden said when the first package revealed a large amount of banded hundred-pound British notes. The second showed banded stacks of one-hundred-dollar bills, fresh and unused. Fazul counted the bundles and made some notes on a page.

"Yes, our Prince has provided for us again. We have here more than a million dollars in hard currency. We are in business again."

Osama bin Laden looked at the stacks of money and nodded. "Now if we can only make good progress on our dream target in the heart of the Great Evil."

✷ SIXTEEN ✷

MOUNTAIN HOME, IDAHO

Charlie arrived at the Clooney home exactly on time for supper. He had been surprised when Beth Clooney called it supper. No flirting with the "dinner" idea, just a good old-fashioned American supper. Beth met him at the door.

"Charlie, good to see you again. Marvin is in the shower. He'll be out shortly. Come in, come in."

They went into the kitchen where she was finishing the meal.

"Just a few more things to do here. Do you mind waiting out here?"

"Not at all, Beth. The marvelous smells are making me hungry already. I always like to watch a pretty lady at work."

She smiled. "Well, thank you. I'm hoping that after supper you'll have time to look over one of my short stories. I know you write articles, but I'd appreciate your reading it and telling me what you think. It's only ten pages."

"Beth, I'd be glad to. Hey, we writers have to help each other out." Beth gave him a big smile, then turned back to the chicken roasting in the oven.

Beth Clooney was a tall, corn-fed farm girl from Iowa. She was almost five-nine and slender with long blond hair she wouldn't cut yet, clinging to her high school cheerleader days. Her dark blue eyes were large, inquiring, over a thin nose and high cheekbones that gave her the look of a high fashion model.

Beth was deeply religious, found a new church wherever her family moved and attended church every Sunday with the girls, even though her husband never went. She didn't talk to him about it. He had told her once that religion wasn't something he believed in and they had left it at that.

For the most part Beth was happy and easygoing, however she was also the disciplinarian in the household. With her husband gone for weeks at a time flying with the Air Force, she had taken on many of the husband's usual functions of keeping the household going. She was a military wife, that was part of the job.

Beth had been writing since high school, nothing to publish but just for her own entertainment. Lately her interest had expanded. She wanted to write and be published and had talked with a lot of people who said the romance field was best for a woman right now. Romances were the easiest to get published.

Under her easygoing attitude was a stern, farm-tough will of steel that she didn't let show often, but that she could always rely on to help her in tough times. Right now it was the best of times for her. She had a great husband devoted to his job of flying, who never looked at another woman, who was a great father to their two girls, and who took special care of her. She watched this new man and smiled. Even Marvin's poker sessions were special. They had brought this writer to her house. Maybe he could help her with her novel.

Captain Marvin Clooney came in still drying his dark hair. "Hey, thought I heard a strange voice out here. Now if you'd said, 'Hey, beats me, I fold,' I'd have known right away who you were." He held out his hand. "Hi, Charlie, how goes the writing game?"

"Slow, but I'm getting some ideas. That's the important part. How goes the sky flying?"

"A bitch today. We had some low-level bombing runs

that always give me the jeebies. I mean one false move with the controls and you kiss the dirt down there at nine hundred miles an hour. It ain't no fun."

"Your fighter can do close support for ground forces?" Charlie asked.

"Not our prime, but in a pinch we can cover. Of course at even nine hundred miles an hour on a strafing run with the 20mm cannon, that means one round hits the ground every three hundred feet or so, depending on your angle of attack. We can scare the hell out of the other side, though."

Clooney rubbed his face with his right hand and threw the towel on a chair. Beth picked it up and gave him a long, serious stare.

"Okay, no more fly talk. This is supposed to be a literary affair. I promise to be quiet and sit and listen."

"Not a chance, Marvin," Beth said. "You'll get in your share of talking. Now, why don't you go bring the girls. We're ready to eat."

Charlie did a second take when the daughters came in. Both were blond, the image of their mother, and maybe four and six years old.

"Thank God, they look like their mother and not me," Clooney said as he seated them at the table. The two girls reminded Charlie of his nieces back in Iran, except for the blond part. The little ladies held most of his attention through dinner. Beth noticed and teased him a moment about them, then went back to talking about writing.

"This published novelist told a group of us who want to write that we should pick a genre, some specific kind of novel. I told him I wanted to write historical romances and he laughed at me."

Charlie shook his head. "The man might be published, but he's also an idiot. Women today buy over seventy percent of all books sold, and a great percentage of those are romances. They sell by the millions. I'd say go right ahead and work on romantic historicals. It's certainly easier to have a romance published than a mainstream novel."

Charlie saw Captain Clooney tune out as they talked about writing the rest of the meal. He simply wasn't interested and didn't feel the need to pretend that he was. Charlie tried to move the talk away from writing for a moment.

"Clarice, you must be in the first or second grade," Charlie said. "Which one?"

"First," she said and giggled.

Beth excused the girls and they rushed off to their room for some deep, dark secret girl games.

The talk went back to writing. They cleared the table as they went into plot and characters and the eventual problem that the heroine must solve, and of course win the love of the main male character.

Captain Clooney was there but didn't participate. He had his nose deep into a magazine about vintage military fighters.

"Hey, look at this. Here's a guy who is selling his P-51. Isn't that amazing? Damn, wish I had about fifty thousand I didn't need. I'd love to have a fifty-one. They are classics."

"I'll help you save up for it, Marvin," Beth said with a grin, then asked Charlie how many historical romances she should read before she tried to write one.

"Read at least twenty-five," Charlie said. "Write down the plot and the characters for each one."

An hour later Beth was running out of questions. Charlie brought the captain back into the conversation with a question about the F-15.

"Can the F-15 really do Mach two point five the way the military spec books say they can?"

"Oh, hell yes. Nothing classified about that. It's in all the books on modern American warplanes. Usually when you're going that fast you're at altitude. The higher the faster. Mach one is slower at a thousand feet than it is at thirty thousand feet. I used to know why, but I don't remember now. Yeah, what a boot to slam along at Mach two-five. That's about sixteen hundred and fifty miles an hour. One of our guys figured out that's almost twenty-eight miles a minute."

"Somebody says wait a minute, and you're twenty-eight miles farther across the globe," Charlie said. "Now that's amazing. I envy you guys. You know, I should get an assignment doing a story about your F-15, what is the name, the Eagle. Yeah, then I could get some clearances and take a ride. Any of them have trainers with two seats?"

Clooney grinned. "Fact is there is a two-seater, two or three different models in fact. We don't have one here at the base."

"Gives me something to think about."

They talked for a half hour more and then Charlie said he better be getting home.

"Poker Friday night," Clooney said.

"Oh, yeah, I've got to win back some of my money," Charlie said and then thanked Beth for the dinner and went out the door.

As he started his rental car he nodded. Oh, yes. Charlie grinned. He was on the right track. About two more weeks and he'd have that flyboy right where he wanted him.

That Friday night they played poker at Captain Johnny Ralston's condo. He was a bachelor and had a table filled with goodies for before, during, and after the game.

As usual, Charlie lost the first two hands. Then he started winning. When he dealt, he won again.

"What got into you?" Clooney asked. "Hey, last week you were a patsy. Now you actually won three hands in a row."

"My luck has either turned, or I'm learning how to play," Charlie said. He promptly lost the next hand.

When they broke at 9:30 for snacks, Charlie was a hundred dollars ahead for the night. Clooney was fifty down.

"Never seen this many kinds of cheeses except at the grocery store," Charlie said. It was all delicious. They had to yell at Charlie to get him back into the game.

He won the next hand. Clooney was down another fifty. When Charlie dealt the next hand, he gave Clooney three kings and a six and an eight. Clooney went for it drawing two. Charlie made sure one of them wasn't a king. Then he dealt himself the two cards he needed and let Clooney bid up the pot.

"You trying to get healthy on one pot?" Grabowski asked.

Clooney didn't react, just sat there with his poker face in place.

The others dropped out, but Charlie stayed in until at last Clooney called him. He showed his full house, sixes over threes and Clooney swore and threw down his cards. He was fifty dollars light in the pot.

An hour later, Clooney had lost again and owed Charlie two hundred he had borrowed. The game broke up and Charlie left with Clooney.

"Look, man, it was a bad night. I'll pay you next week, okay?"

Charlie shrugged. "Whatever. I made almost two hundred from the other guys. I'm almost back to being even for the games."

"Well, I'll pay you next week, or tomorrow if you need it. Just give me the word. To me it's not a gift. A gambling debt. I have to repay you." Clooney paused. "Yeah, principle of the thing. See you next week."

Charlie thought it through again. It was his idea to go with the gambling debt to get his hooks into Clooney. The gambling and going to Clooney's house served two purposes. It gave him a small hold on Clooney when he came up short and owed cash to Charlie. Then he could threaten to go to the pilot's commanding officer and cause all sorts of hell for Clooney. The captain could even get thrown out of the Air Force.

In the end, the gambling might not be enough. So Charlie would simply kidnap Beth and the two girls and hold them until Clooney did what he was told to do. He might confess to his CO his gambling and offer to retire, but before that happened Charlie would have to take the family hostage.

Charlie didn't think Captain Clooney would turn himself in for gambling. If he threatened to do that there was the kidnapping. One thing he had learned about Clooney—he was a conventional family man. Nothing was more important to him than his family. That's what would be his downfall, and what would win the game for Charlie.

Once Clooney got "lost" from his formation, he'd have no option but to continue the defection. He would know that his family was in mortal danger if he tried to turn back or turn in Charlie to his CO. He'd do it all the way. Yes, Clooney was on the hook. That was the kind of strong family man Captain Clooney was.

LONDON, ENGLAND

"So exactly where does this leave us?" Wade asked.

Kat looked at him, frowned, and stood and began pacing up and down the room. They all watched her. They knew she liked to think on her feet. Walking up and down in front of a jury had developed this habit.

"To evaluate, it seems to me that we still have three suspects who are capable of doing the Big One. We have Scimitar, Osama bin Laden, as well as Abdel Salim. We know that the first two are capable of doing such an act. Recent information about Salim and the Haifa terrorist bombing shows that he is still in the mix and willing to take chances to do his evil work.

"The new information from the last two raids on terrorists has given us more details about what they might be thinking. The White House seems a dream for them, not a reality. The Empire State Building is a potent possibility.

"Which brings us back to where we were. We have three potent terrorists we have to watch, monitor, spy on, do whatever we can to find out the target of this Big One.

"We know the most about the first two men. We must learn more about Salim. He may be the most dangerous because we know so little about him. We know that the Scimitar is a danger. We know he's done large jobs before.

We know that his current price is over five million dollars for a major terrorist act.

"What we don't know is much about him. No photos, no fingerprints, no voiceprint, no retina ID. We're blind. Wade had the closest thing to an encounter with him. It might help if Wade could give us a run-through on what he saw, did, found. Anything he learned about this ghostly figure that might help us."

Wade picked up the pictures, and then put them down. He glanced at the others.

"If it would help, I can give you my impressions. They aren't much. It was four years ago just outside of Cairo. In those days, Egypt was at odds with many of the nations in the Arab League. Some wanted Egypt thrown out for its close ties with the U.S. and with Israel.

"There was a government-staged rally in a soccer stadium with over fifty thousand people attending. It was billed as a way of assuring the government that the people of Egypt believed in the path of foreign affairs the leaders were taking. They said they wanted to stay in the Arab League with the chance of helping to persuade a more liberal line.

"At the height of the speeches and talks by officials, a truck laden with banners proclaiming Egypt as a leader in the Arab world drove in the gate. It was covered with all sorts of posters about Egyptian loyalty and signs of support for the leaders. The truck came to a stop at the edge of the huge crowd. It could get no closer to the speakers.

"The driver was an Arab man with a full beard, large sunglasses, and a dark burnoose that covered his head and down to the waist. He left the truck and began to walk away. Soon he started to run. His sudden movement caught my attention and I tried to track him as he moved. That's when I saw the beard and the sunglasses. He came straight toward me for a time, then turned where the crowd had thinned and began to sprint flat out.

"Ten seconds later I understood why. That's when the bomb went off. The whole truck had been loaded with explosives. At the final count a hundred and six were killed, and almost two hundred seriously wounded. With the explosion came a rain of propaganda leaflets, blaming Egypt for a dozen problems in the Arab world, and demanding that the state of Egypt be thrown out of the Arab League and boycotted economically by all Arab nations.

"This was the first time that most of us had seen the sign of the sword, the scimitar that was printed on each of the leaflets that rained down on the crowd after the explosion.

"Hundreds of people saw the driver, but by the time they realized what had happened, this man we believe to be the Scimitar was lost in the crowd and never caught."

Mr. Marshall motioned toward Kat. "Katherine has our dossier on this man. Can you brief us?"

Kat took up a file and glanced at it. "Briefly we think his real name is El Ali Khatami. He's about forty-six years old, stands six feet three inches, and is thin at 175 pounds. He has softer brown skin than most Arabs, heavy black hair, and often wears a full black mustache. His eyes are burnt umber brown, unless he has colored contacts on.

"We think he was born in Lebanon and went to some Western-style schools there. His English is excellent, colloquial, and he picks up accents remarkably fast. We believe he also speaks Farsi, Arabic, German, French, and Russian."

Ichi had been working through a stack of paper they had brought back from Iran and he waved them.

"Remember the sheets that had the picture of a scimitar on them? Here are several more. Not sure where these came from."

"Interesting, Mr. Yamagata," Mr. Marshall said. He handed the papers to Hershel. "What do the papers say?"

Hershel scanned them quickly. "They are in Farsi and a kind of manifesto of purpose and intent. A pep talk to the troops. They don't list any targets but the faithful are promised that the Scimitar will have projects for them now and then, and that they should not despair. He says:

" 'The way of the true revolutionary is rugged, tough, dangerous, and sometimes exceedingly boring. We all must wait and watch, and do what we can every day to bring down the Great Evil, to batter it and make it bleed everywhere and every time we have the chance. In the end we will win. We will throw Americans out of the Middle East and send them packing to their own land across the sea.' "

"So what do we do next?" Kat asked. "We have to do more than wait and watch."

"I can check with MI-6 and see if the Brits or Scotland Yard have any evidence of any terrorist threat in this country," Duncan said.

"We'll keep after my unofficial friends at the FBI for any kind of action against those targets listed in the U.S.," Mr. Marshall said.

Roger Johnson stood and paced to the window. "Then actually what we are doing is sitting and waiting for something to go boom before we can do anything about it. I don't like that."

Wade took a deep breath. "So we can do something. We'll do an in-depth check on the three or four top targets on the list in the U.S. and see what shows up. There might be something. Right now we'll grab at any straw that looks like it could be a small part of a terrorist threat."

Roger grinned. "Yeah, now I like that. We can have some action here at last."

Wade frowned. "Roger, you just got back from Iran. Wasn't that a little bit of action?"

"Yeah, sure, Chief. But, hey, that was two days ago."

★ SEVENTEEN ★

MOUNTAIN HOME, IDAHO

Charlie felt more at home now in his Western-style clothes. He had taken to blue jeans and T-shirts, with a cotton flannel for chilly evenings. Charlie liked them and bought three more pairs of jeans for his suitcase to take home.

He slept late most days, took a turn at the local library in case anyone watched him, and generally pretended that he was researching. The disguised Arab checked behind him twice that day. There was no one following him, he was certain. Charlie knew about doing that work. No one paid any attention to him. Strange, but comforting.

Charlie made a report to his contact, found a query on the E-mail, and answered it.

"Not sure of timetable yet for new project. Perhaps within a week. Making contact with buyer again tonight. Will report any progress. Need firm location of the new land parcel. Thanks." He signed it "Charlie" and sent it. His man in Seattle would have the message within minutes. What a great advancement in communications the Internet was.

Thursday night he checked in at the bar and bought the pilots a pitcher of beer. He confirmed the poker session the next night. They would be at Grabowski's place.

"Yeah, we recruited two new patsies," Clooney said.

"That means at least four hundred bucks of fresh money. I love that."

The next night the game went according to Charlie's plan. He lost the first two hands, then won one, and stayed even until two of the new guys dropped out. With four of them left he began to zero in on Clooney. Every time Clooney stayed in the game, so did Charlie and three times out of four, Charlie beat him on big pots.

By 11:30 the game was down to three and Clooney was on his last twenty dollars. He borrowed a hundred from Charlie and promptly lost that. On the last pot he went a hundred short on the pot and lost when Charlie dealt and arranged for himself four deuces to win the pot.

"Damn, I'm down four hundred for the night," Clooney said. "My own fault. I owe you another two hundred I'll pay."

"No rush," Charlie said as they parted at the driveway.

"Oh, Charlie, Beth wants to squeeze some more writing secrets from you. She's offering you a fresh salmon barbecue dinner tomorrow night if you can come. I told her it might not be enough notice. What shall I tell her?"

"Sure. I can get along without Burger in a Box for one night. What time?"

They set the time for six, then Captain Clooney shook his head.

"Hey, I'm into you for four hundred dollars. I don't know when I can pay you. I'm good for it, but not for a couple of weeks. Can you go along with that? A gambling debt. I always pay up."

Charlie laughed and smiled. "Hey, what are friends for. I was down for the first two or three games. You're just on a bad luck streak. Don't worry about it. I'm not broke. Fact is I came out over a hundred ahead in cash tonight."

"For sure you don't mind?"

"Hey, friends help out friends. Don't worry about it. See you tomorrow night for that salmon. You firing up the grill or is Beth?"

"Hey, the grill is man's work. I'm good at it. Don't be late. Salmon takes about five minutes and it won't wait."

"I'll be there."

Charlie grinned as he drove to his apartment. Yeah, he was halfway there. One more game and he should have Captain Clooney right where he wanted him.

Saturday night, Charlie watched Clooney work the salmon on the grill. He'd done it before and it was delicious. Beth provided her own mix of tartar sauce and the side dishes. The meal was great.

Beth was worried about plotting.

"Say I have this idea for a novel, but it isn't a whole novel-length idea. How do I plot something like that to flesh it out and make it long enough, say even for sixty thousand words?"

"Novels are tough. Somebody told me that a novel was no big problem to write, the really, really tough job was selling it. True. But plotting isn't all that tough. Remember the basics.

"Take an intriguing character and put her in a desperate situation that looks insurmountable. She tries all sorts of ways to solve the problem or beat the situation. Each time she does a new thrust, she gets farther into trouble or more evidence turns up against her to prove she is the killer, say. Then she tries again and again. Each time deeper into trouble. Then at last through her own efforts, her own skill and knowledge, she beats the problem, wins the day, marries the guy, and lives happily ever after."

Charlie looked at Beth who had been writing furiously in a notebook.

"And through her own efforts and skill she wins the day, marries the guy, and is happy ever after."

"That's it. Just don't paint yourself into a corner that nobody could get out of. A novel is a huge exercise in logic. If it ain't logical, it won't play as a novel. I've written three and haven't sold a one. But I had a good teacher. Maybe someday."

Beth looked up puzzled. "But you're a professional writer. You earn your living by writing."

"Yes, but not novels. Articles for magazines, one nonfiction book, and a lot of newspaper work."

"Oh." Beth frowned. "Then it's harder to write novels than it is newspaper stories and articles?"

"Different. It's another skill. Like the difference between roasting a turkey and baking a pie."

Dinner was over and they went into the living room. The two small girls, Kathy and Clarice, were both there. Charlie went to the entry hall and came back with a small package he had left there when he came in.

He unwrapped it and gave a book to each girl. Charlie had carefully selected the books to be right for the ages of six and four.

"A book!" Clarice yelped. "A book all of my own. Can I go look at the pictures?"

Kathy was less enthusiastic, but Clarice told her she would help her with it.

"Girls give Uncle Charlie here a big hug for the books," Beth said.

The girls rushed up, gave him a quick hug, then ran off to their room.

"That was thoughtful of you, Charlie," Beth said. "Clarice is just getting into books and reading."

They talked more about writing, then about the test program that Captain Clooney was on with his squadron.

"Going to finish in a week or so when we have a full-scale flying problem. Hope all of our guys can pass the mustard."

They talked for another hour, then Charlie excused himself and said he better be leaving. He thanked Beth for the dinner and Clooney for the salmon, then headed for his apartment.

Charlie smiled to himself. Oh, yes, he had the fish on the line, now all he had to do was yank the line hard and set the hook. Next week's poker game should be enough to do the job.

The following week went quickly for Charlie. He drank beer with the pilots after work twice. Thursday night he met a lady at the bar who was interested in seeing his apartment. She checked out the bed and decided it would be a good place to spend the night.

Saturday night the poker party was at Captain Johnny Ralston's where, as usual, he had a huge spread of expensive snack food, cheese, and wine.

The poker game was late getting started because they couldn't get the eight guys away from the food table.

With eight in a game the pots grew large quickly but also drained the table stakes. After the second hand, two men were broke and dropped out. After the fourth hand another man went busted.

Then the serious poker began. After two hours of playing, Clooney went broke again. He owed Charlie three hundred for that night.

Clooney pounded the table with his fist. "Hey, I know. I'm always lucky at this. I'll cut the deck with you for double or nothing on that three hundred I owe you."

"You don't want to do this, Clooney," Charlie told him. Ralston told him the same thing, but he waved it all aside.

"Hey, I'm the one deciding here. Just like on a missile strike. I'm the one calling the shots. Now, you want to chicken out on me, Charlie, or will you cut the deck double or nothing?"

"Not my kind of gambling, Clooney." He shrugged. "What the hell, I don't have anything to lose. It's all found money. Let's do it."

Now it was down to pure chance for Charlie. He couldn't control the deck. He hadn't shaved the cards. It was up to the luck of the cards.

Clooney went first. He turned up a ten of spades and grinned.

"Hey, I've got you on the odds. More cards under ten than there are over ten. Three to one, in fact. Oh, yeah, this is where I'm going to get healthy again. Go ahead, Charlie, cut yourself a loser."

Charlie rubbed his hands together, stretched his fingers, then reached for the deck. Only half of it was left on the table. He made a riffle of the cards but didn't stop. The second time he reached for the cards he picked up half of them but held the card facedown.

"Come on, come on," Clooney said.

"You still sure you want to go through with this?" Charlie asked. "We can both put down our cards right now and call it off."

"No way, not a chance, not with my three to one odds. Turn over the fucking card."

Charlie turned it over. A jack of diamonds.

Clooney threw down his cards and stormed out the front door. He forgot his jacket. Charlie grabbed it and hurried after the man.

Clooney stood at his car, pounding his palm against the flat top of the roof.

"Damn, another six hundred down the drain." He pounded his hand again. "Why the hell do I get into these messes?"

Charlie came up and handed him the jacket. Clooney stared at him.

"I owe you a fucking thousand dollars. I can't pay you right away. My credit is in a mess. Nothing in the bank."

Charlie had lost his smile, now he was stern and cold. "Clooney, I need the money. Something has come up and I'm a little short. I need that thousand now or by tomorrow night."

"I told you, I don't have it."

"Come on. You must have some savings, a CD at the bank. Something."

"Nothing I can touch. You'll have to wait. Told you my credit is shot."

"Wait how long, for two or three paydays? I don't have that kind of time, Captain."

"Be a friend here, Charlie. I need some time."

"I can always go to your commanding officer out at the base."

Clooney jumped back as if someone had hit him. His face built a scowl and he glared at Charlie. "You wouldn't do that. I could get kicked out of the service for this kind of gambling. I've seen it happen."

"Then get me the money tomorrow."

"I can't, I just can't. There must be some other way."

"What do you have worth a thousand? You could sell your car and give me a thousand."

"Not a chance. No jewelry, no motorcycle, nothing to sell."

"There might be one way."

Clooney looked up, a shred of hope on his face. "Another way, what?"

"The next time you fly and you're carrying a nuke, you could get lost and fly where I tell you to."

Clooney jumped back a step, his face showing pure fury. He trembled and he fisted his hands and scowled. "Hell no. Fucking goddamned no. I'm not going to turn traitor for a lousy thousand dollars."

"What else can you do?"

Clooney took a swing at Charlie who had been waiting for it. He slammed it aside with his left hand and crossed a right fist into Clooney's nose. The pilot staggered backward a step, then covered his bleeding nose with his hand.

"Sonofabitch," he shouted. He charged Charlie who danced out of the way and tripped him. The pilot sprawled on the ground.

"Stop it, Clooney. You're out of your league. You're a shitty poker player and you fight like a girl. Listen to the rest of the deal and stay on the ground.

"You fly where I tell you to, land, and we fake a crash at sea but you're saved. The plane and the nuke are gone. You get a bonus of a hundred thousand dollars from me, and a clean alibi for the Air Force. No blame. They hunt for the missing nuke bomb but can't find it. You tell them that your instruments went crazy and your displays were dead wrong. You can do it and come out clean. And be a hundred thousand richer. Think about it, flyboy. Think about it."

Clooney shook his head. "Not a chance. No way am I going to turn traitor and hand over my plane and a nuke weapon along with it for a lousy thousand-dollar debt."

"Then kiss your Air Force career good-bye. I'm going to your CO tomorrow on base and show him your IOU for five thousand dollars, a gambling debt. I'll ask the Air Force to attach your pay until it's settled."

"You can't do that. I didn't sign anything, let alone an IOU for five grand."

"Oh, but it will look like you did. Remember that autograph I got of yours the first night at the bar? I still have it and I'm good at copy work. What's it going to be, Clooney? Out of the Air Force, or fly that jet of yours where I tell you to?"

Clooney jumped up and rushed Charlie. He caught him and spun him around, but Charlie slammed a punch into Clooney's gut and he doubled over and leaned on his car.

"Bastard. This was all a setup from that first night in the bar. You ugly fucking bastard. But there is no way in the world that I'll do what you ask. I can live without the Air Force."

Charlie turned and walked away. There was one way that would force Clooney to do what Charlie wanted him to do. Now it had come down to that and Charlie knew that it would work.

GARMSAR, IRAN

Abdel Salim thought for a moment about the raid on Haifa. A hundred and forty-six killed and over two hundred injured. No, one more had died, his friend and comrade in arms, Sarihah. It had been a successful mission. Now he was thinking of larger projects.

He had been working from time to time on a huge strike against the Great Evil itself. He would hit the United States with such force that the people there would remember it in their history books.

Salim knew that Osama bin Laden had developed or obtained large amounts of biological elements that could be used in warfare. Salim called his plan "Water Strike." Twenty agents would infiltrate through Canada and Mexico into the U.S. as tourists. The loose border stations with both nations would allow each man to bring in various biological elements. They would be dumped into the water supply of the twenty largest cities in the nation at precisely the same hour of the same day. The cities would include New York City, Washington, D.C., Chicago, Los Angeles, Atlanta, and Dallas. Millions and millions of Americans would be dead before the authorities knew what had happened. The various biological elements would cause different problems in different parts of the country. It would be a strike more deadly than a nuclear explosion.

The ones who became sick first would each infect dozens of others with the contagious disease. Those dozens would infect hundreds and those hundreds would spread the disease to thousands who would soon infect millions, as the numbers of sick and dying would race into astronomical figures. The whole nation would collapse; the U.S. threat to the Arab world would be smashed for a hundred years.

Every other attack on the West would pale by comparison. He smiled, just dreaming about it. The name of Abdel Salim would be shouted from the rooftops of the whole Arab world.

He would put in a call to bin Laden, and send his top aide to Afghanistan to present the plan to the great man himself. He felt certain that bin Laden would either help him with the biological agents, or decide to participate fully and supply him with money and agents to complete the operation. Yes, it would be a great day.

✴ EIGHTEEN ✴

KETTERING, ENGLAND

The six Specialists wheezed and puffed as they came in after a six-mile run. They had to stay together, within ten yards of each other. The rule had a purpose. In a firefight a team stays together, but not on top of each other. The usual combat distance between men is five yards. In intense situations it's sometimes expanded to ten yards so one hand grenade or lucky mortar or artillery round won't wipe out more than one or two men.

Back at the castle they used their individual styles to catch their breath.

"Man, I hope we aren't going to increase the distance a mile a day much longer," Duncan Bancroft said. "Us older guys are about as tough as we're going to get."

Two of them laughed. The rest were still catching their breath. Kat bent over at the waist and let her hands trail on the ground. Wade stood with his hands on his hips panting. Ichi did two karate kicks and then sprawled on the ground.

Roger Johnson, their ex-Navy SEAL, led their workouts. He shook his head watching the others. He had only started to sweat on the last mile.

"Come on, you tenderfeet, we were plowing along at about seven minutes to the mile. Little old ladies in Barclay

Square can go that fast. Okay, okay, we'll hold it to six miles for the next three days."

The rest of them groaned.

J. August Marshall watched his team from his third-floor study window. He would give them the ten minutes agreed on, then the training would continue.

Exactly on time, Mr. Marshall and one of his men brought two boxes to where the Specialists rested. He placed them on a table near a thirty-yard firing range not far from the castle.

The team gathered around. Mr. Marshall greeted them and then pointed to the box on the table. "We have something here for you to familiarize yourself with. There's a chance we may never need this weapon, but you should know about it. I want all of you to fire this rifle until you're comfortable with it. The weapon will be available if you like it and want one. Mr. Johnson will continue."

Roger went to the boxes and took out two rifles that looked more like short two by fours.

"I used one of these in the SEALs. It's not new, but it is a little unusual. It looks funny, but it can slap out six hundred rounds of 4.73mm a minute. It's classified as an automatic rifle, and called the G-11. Heckler and Koch make it. The unusual part of it is that it fires rounds without metal casings. No brass to clean up. Nobody knows you've been there. Since there is no brass, no one can match extractor marks to a specific weapon."

He held up an oblong of rounds. "Each round is encased in a sleeve of solid propellant with a special thin plastic coating around it for separation. When fired, the propellant counters the low cook-off threshold caused by the lack of brass, heating up as much as it would with a brass casing. This chunk of firepower holds fifty rounds.

"The weapon fires on full auto, three-round bursts, or single shot."

He pushed in the wad of rounds, chambered one, then turned and fired it in three-round bursts at the targets thirty yards away. He tore one paper target in half.

He pointed to Ichi and tossed him the weapon. Ichi

caught it and studied it a minute. Then he went to the firing line, and rattled off four single shots, then two three-round bursts, and then six shots on full auto. It climbed on him.

"Yes, did you see that?" Roger asked. "On full auto it is going to climb on you. It helps if you can hold it sideways and get a natural spread of your rounds across a large target. Kat, give it a try."

When they all had fired the weapon Ichi said he wanted one and Roger elected to keep one as well.

"Mr. Marshall said we should move on to the Wild West range. After we work through it, he wants to see us back in the main hall."

The Wild West range was an acre and a half of winding trails, pop-up targets controlled by pressure plates in the trails. The targets were chosen in a variable unrepeatable sequence by computer and there was no way to know what would come up next to challenge the shooter.

Ichi went first and five yards down the trail he triggered three rounds at bad guys with submachine guns. He blasted them with his MP-5 sub gun and moved on. Ten feet farther along two terrs lifted up holding a blindfolded woman between them. He moved the MP-5 to single shot and cut down both terrs without hitting the woman.

When Ichi was three targets into the range, Duncan moved in behind him on the same course but with different targets.

A half hour later all six had been through the course, and read printouts from the computer in the small wooden shack at the far side. Each shooter was scored, rated for hits, number of rounds spent, and the time from target pop-up to hits. From the three inputs an overall score was recorded. The six-mile run had worn them down. Roger used his position as conditioning guru to look at all the scores.

"That does it," he said. "We've got to keep the troops in better condition. If that had been a real shootout with real terrs, probably half of us would be dead. We have to be faster and more accurate."

He grinned. "But, hell, it wasn't all that bad. I was the only one who killed a hostage." They all laughed and headed for the castle and the great hall.

The great hall was just that, over eighty feet long, with a three-story ceiling, wall hangings, and with battle armor and medieval fighting tools on every side.

When it was first built back in 1130 it must have hosted a room full of knights and ladies, earls and counts, and maybe a king or two. Now it looked huge and empty, except for a table and seven chairs at the far end. Mr. Marshall waited for them. When they were seated in front of the table, he spread out some folders and papers, then looked up.

"Kat and gentlemen, you have a new assignment. Ordinarily we would let this one pass. But I've been advised that it may have some bearing on the terrorist target lists we have recovered recently and that this man might have some input for us.

"In this case we have an old Arab man who was at one time in the thick of the terrorist activity. In thirty years of bombing and terror, even the best of men get old. For several years he was a close associate of the Scimitar, and we are told, one of his teachers. The man's name is Jamal Hussein. He lives in Iraq and we have an address, which is probably not current. All of these men move at irregular and frequent intervals.

"I've talked this raid over with Wade, and we agree the men to go on this one are Ichi, Duncan, and Wade. We hope that Hussein might give us some idea what big jobs the terrorists are working on, or at least shed some light on the list or the Big One target. Any questions?"

"We have an inside man in Iraq to help us?" Ichi asked.

"Not on this one. We had a man there who really worked for the CIA but he hasn't been heard from for over three months and we and the CIA assume he's dead."

"How do we get into Iraq?" Duncan asked.

"The easy way. You'll drive to the border of Kuwait and Iraq and slip across at some unguarded point."

"And walk the rest of the way," Ichi cracked.

"We'll have detailed instructions and equipment selection this afternoon, and all return to London tonight," Mr. Marshall said. "The small jet will take off from Heathrow tomorrow at six A.M. with the strike team."

KUWAIT BORDER

The chopper from Kuwait City set the Specialists down at a U.S. Army Advanced Recon Base a mile from the Iraqi border. It was a closed, highly sensitive base, but Mr. Marshall had talked with the commanding general of the area and told him their mission. The general gave orders that the three civilians would be brought there and outfitted with whatever they needed.

Wade, Ichi, and Duncan were hustled into a camouflaged prefab building that looked like a Hollywood wardrobe trailer. It was half filled with Iraqi military uniforms and civilian clothing. They were quickly outfitted in shirts and pants that would let them blend in with the rest of the population.

They were given headdresses to help conceal their Western look. Their faces and hands were swabbed down with a stain to turn their complexions into a more Arab shade. Large, dark sunglasses completed their makeup.

Each had a loose-fitting outer garment that would allow them to conceal weapons under it. For this mission, Ichi chose his MP-5 submachine gun, Wade took an Ingram sub gun, and Bancroft picked out the G-11 caseless automatic rifle to give them one weapon with a little more range. They all carried Glock model 18 pistols with thirty-three-round extended magazines. The auto 18 was specifically designed to give completely automatic fire by holding the trigger back. Ichi had his knives in his leg holders.

Each man had a money belt with two million dinars in it. At the exchange rate of about 1500 dinars to a dollar, that meant the Specialists each had about $1,350 worth of Iraqi money.

"Let's get out of here," Ichi said. "What are we waiting for?"

Wade had been talking with an army major who had been unhappy when they arrived but he had his orders.

"We're waiting for word from the border," Wade said. "A car from Iraq will come close to the border and be left. We pick it up and drive north. We have Iraqi identification papers so keep them in an outside pocket where you can get to them quickly. If we're stopped we fake it. I know the language so we should get by."

"How far up country do we have to go?" Duncan asked.

"Not far. This guy used to live in Basra, only thirty miles north of the border. Then he moved on north and west to a small town, but we hear he is now in another small town called Rumaylah near a large lake. With any luck, we'll find him there. That place is about forty air miles from the border, so is probably about fifty-five or so by road. Not too far."

"Unless they have roadblocks every ten miles," Duncan said.

"At least the car is legal, not stolen," Ichi said. "It could be a walk in the park."

"Except it's an Arab park and those guys get damn trigger happy," Duncan said. "I had one assignment in Baghdad a few years ago. It was no fun at all. Hope we can get in and out in a rush."

The army major came into the room and nodded.

"Let's go," Wade said and they followed the officer out the door to a waiting Humvee. They climbed in and rode north.

The actual border marker along there was a double strand of barbed wire on steel posts. The driver waved at the fence.

"Word is that the border here hasn't been surveyed for fifty years. It could be half a mile either way. But we use this one. We don't know when you're coming back, so you'll have to drive or hoof it into the base. Good luck."

He let them out two hundred yards west along the wire

where they saw a car. It was an old French Citroen, but looked in good condition. The keys were on the seat.

Wade drove since he spoke Arabic. Ichi took the front seat and Duncan sprawled in back.

"Nap time," he said and folded his legs and half lay on the seat.

"They said there was a dirt road north of here about five miles," Wade said. "Then we turn east until we find the main north road. Somebody said we couldn't miss it."

They did.

It was an hour after dark when they took over the French car. By the time they found the north road it was nearly 10:30 and they had fifty-two miles to go to find the village where Jamal Hussein was supposed to be staying.

They had driven about ten miles north when lights glared suddenly at them from the rear and a siren wailed. "Cops out here?" Wade asked. He saw the car move up beside him, and he turned the Citroen gently off the narrow road onto a wide shoulder and stopped. The patrol rig angled in front of them preventing them from moving forward. Both doors on the car ahead popped open and two men in uniform came into the headlights.

"Stay cool. Duncan, keep sleeping. Ichi, sack out too. I'll handle the talking."

A soldier came up to Wade's window and held out his hand. "Your papers please."

Wade reached for them and for a moment forgot his name on the documents, then he remembered.

The officer read them, frowned, and handed the papers back. "What are you doing out here so close to the border?"

"From the Interior Department checking the border. There's a big dispute about just where it is. We're looking for a good spot to survey to prove our claim. It's a little complicated."

The talk was all in Arabic.

The soldier lifted his brows.

"That's out of my jurisdiction. Usually they tell me when

government officials are coming. They certainly didn't provide you with much of a vehicle. The other two?"

"Sleeping. Been a long day. A shame to awaken them."

The soldier shrugged. He looked bored with the whole operation.

"Very well, on your way. Next time tell your superiors to notify the border guards. We like to know when you're coming."

Wade said he would do that. The vehicle pulled out of the way and Wade drove back onto the highway.

For two hours they drove north. Wade saw signs pointing to towns, but none of them was the one he wanted. He went ahead to a village where the only light was in a small store. He stopped and realized it was only a little after 1:00 A.M. He bought some rolls and asked the way to Rumaylah.

The old man behind the small counter had no teeth, and he squinted from watery eyes.

"Rumaylah? Nobody goes there anymore. Why you going there? Oh, well, it's on up the road and then to the left about ten more miles. Used to have relatives in Rumaylah."

Wade paid for the rolls and left.

"We might be able to find this place after all," Wade told Ichi, who grabbed one of the rolls.

Ten miles later they found it. The village huddled against the shores of a large lake that was one of a string of lakes and rivers that worked halfway up the country. The shopping area was buttoned up tight. They saw lights on in only two houses. He figured there might be three hundred people in the whole town.

Wade used his pencil flash in the car and read off the name of the street. It was 721 Al-Rahwa. Every other street had lost its sign. Three blocks down they found the right one. Now they realized that the houses did not have numbers. The dirt streets had no curbs or sidewalks.

"How can we find this house if they don't have numbers?" Ichi asked.

Wade brought the car to a stop and went out the door.

Two men came down the street. One weaved a little; the other was supporting him. It was almost 2:00 A.M.

Wade approached them and both stopped. Before Wade said a word the smaller man spoke.

"Yes, I know. I know. He found the strong drink somewhere. Not at my house I assure you. He just found it. Now I must take him home before he gets in trouble."

"You both are already in trouble. I'll deal with you later. Right now I must find house 721 on this street. Where is it?"

The Arab laughed. "See, we have no numbers on our humble houses. That's for the rich people in Baghdad."

"Would you know the name?"

"Yes. I live on this street. What's he called?"

"Jamal Hussein."

The small man smiled in the darkness. "No, you won't find him here. He left two weeks ago. Sneaked out in the middle of the night. Took everything with him. I can show you his house."

"Yes, do that, and I won't report you and your drunken friend here. It would go hard with him."

The smaller man frowned. "I keep telling him. He won't listen."

"The house?"

"Yes, it is three doors down. The one with the fence around it. A new fence. The man was afraid of everyone."

"Good, now on your way. I'll forget that I saw you. Go."

The two walked away, the bigger man leaning heavily on the shorter one.

Duncan and Ichi came out of the car on Wade's motion. They walked down the street to the fenced house. The gate was unlocked. They went in quickly and to the shadows at the side of the house.

Wade motioned to the back. The rear door was unlocked. Strange. Wade checked for booby traps, but found nothing that would indicate one. He used his pencil flash and moved through the door into the back room, then into the kitchen.

The three began a systematic search of the vacant and stripped bare house. Hussein had lived there. It was their only chance of following him.

After an hour of searching, the three sat on the floor in the unfurnished house.

"Has to be something here somewhere," Wade said.

"Fine-tooth-combed it already," Ichi said.

"We do it again," Duncan said. "It's that or go home with nothing."

They searched the place again for two more hours. Duncan went to the back door and looked at the small rear fenced yard. It was almost daylight. He found some pieces of paper and grabbed them. One was a scrap of paper from a lined sheet. Nothing written on it. Another showed a receipt for some purchase. The other small papers had no writing. He kept looking.

At the rear side of the lot he found a thistle. Clinging to some of the thorns was a shard of paper. He pulled it off and wounded one finger with a stab. He used his flash to examine the paper. The writing was Arabic. He ran into the house and showed it to Wade.

"Something? Let's see." He shone his light on it and read it. "Tuesday, two A.M."

"Yes," Ichi said. "they must have moved out at two A.M. But where did they go?"

Now it was fully light. There could be curious neighbors. They heard an alarm clock ring next door through the morning quiet. A moment later a man came out the back door of the house, stretched, and then walked toward the house where the Specialists sat. There was no way to hide from him.

He came in the back door humming softly. When he saw the three men with weapons, he stopped. The man scowled.

"What are you doing in my house?"

"We're looking for the man who used to live here," Wade said in Arabic.

The man shook his head. "You are strangers here. Your

accent is bad. Why do you look for the man who lived here?"

"He owes us money. We can't find where he went. Do you know?"

The man nodded. "He owes me money, too. Left without paying his rent. He was not a good man. I paid a man to follow him if he and his friends left at night. They did. My tracker went behind them all the way to Jalibah, but lost them there."

"Where is Jalibah?"

"Small place at the edge of the dry lands. Sixty kilometers to the west."

"Did you collect your money?"

"No. They caught my friend following them, and beat him up. He still is not well."

"Thank you. I want to give you some money for your help." Wade handed the man 150,000 dinars, about one hundred dollars. The man looked at the money and delight formed in his eyes.

"You are good, I thank you. May Allah watch over your safety."

"We'll be leaving in a few minutes. Thanks for your help."

The old man nodded, counting the money again. He smiled at them and hurried out of the house and across the lot to his other house, larger and better kept than this one.

Ichi looked up and frowned. "Oh, yeah, a big help. I can't find the name of that town on our map. It just ain't here."

★ NINETEEN ★

FORT JOHNSON, COLORADO

George Sampson parked the four-year-old pickup in the lot outside of the Tri County Farmers' Cooperative and stretched. George was his American name. He was tall and thin with dangling arms and a sharp-featured face with a nose too long. Brown eyes hovered over the nose and now danced with the emotion and danger of the next step. This was the crucial part and it made him nervous. Good to be nervous, Sampson told himself. He looked over at his partner, John, and grinned.

"It will be all right. We're legitimate farmers, and in this country we can buy whatever we want. They'll be glad to sell it to us. Now get tough and keep your mouth shut." John was dark as well, with black hair under a straw hat, an oversize body at six feet four inches and 260 pounds. He was strong as a camel and twice as skittish. John touched the 9mm pistol in his belt under his loose shirt, lifted his thick brows, and nodded. This was his first time being undercover on an assignment. Usually his work was simple: infiltrate, place the bomb, walk away, set it off, and work his way back home. Now America. If anyone asked he would tell them he had been frightened half to death the minute he and George had driven over the border from Canada. He had almost thrown up when the inspectors at the U.S. border asked him where he was born. He said Buffalo and the man only nodded and passed them into the United States. Here he was in the heart of the Great Evil.

It hadn't looked so evil so far. For six days they had been in Colorado, now for the vital part.

"Come on, we walk in like we know what we're doing," George said. "We don't haggle over the price. It's set." George pushed in the door and was amazed at the variety of goods that were there for the purchasing. They looked at some tools, then went up to the counter.

"Yes, sir, may I help you?" the man near the cash register asked.

"Right, we need six hundred pounds of Xcello-Grow. It still come in the fifty-pound sacks?"

"We have it that way, or in bulk," the store man said.

"No, the sacks are easier for us to handle."

"Sure, twelve bags, I'll write the order and the lot man will load you up. Pull your rig around to the side to the big double doors with the loading dock."

George waved at John and he went out the front door to the truck. John was the regular driver. George saw another man in the place, maybe he was a customer. He walked over and looked at George with a small frown.

"What the hell you buying fertilizer for this time of year?" the man asked. He wore jeans, a blue shirt, and a much used and crumpled cowboy hat.

George grinned at him. "Hell, I'm stocking up."

The man behind the counter nodded. "It is a little unusual to buy this much fertilizer this time of year," the clerk said. He was Lyle Broderson, owner of the co-op and curious about all things agricultural. "Most of the row crops around here are past the fertilization stage. Could I ask what you're growing?"

George grinned. "Nothing, actually. We just rented the old Handshoe place east of town. I know that fertilizer is cheaper this time of year than in the spring, so we're getting stocked up. Figure to save some cash that way."

The customer snorted. He was a large man, well over

six feet and solid. His face looked like he'd been kicked by a horse. His nose had been broken and didn't set correctly. A large bruise showed on his right cheek and up into the hairline. A small bandage perched over his left eye.

"Sure, save some money, but you also tie up all that cash when it could be in the stock market. I made a buy yesterday you wouldn't believe. It was an IPO and I swear I got in on the base price of seventeen-seventy five. Before the close of trading it had more than tripled to sixty-two fifty. I made myself over twenty thousand dollars in one day."

"Not all of us play the stock market," the counter man said. He looked back at the customer. "You're right about the lower price. Save maybe twenty percent." He held out his hand. "My name is Lyle, this is my store. You must be new in the area."

"Yeah, we are. Me and my cousin just rented the place. Probably be in here for a lot for equipment and advice. Haven't done any farming around here before, so we'll need some help."

"I can give you all sorts of free advice," Lyle said. "Some of it is even worth the price. Don't mind my rich brother over there. He's so nuts about the stock market that sometimes he forgets to do his farm chores."

The brother in the crumpled cowboy hat chuckled. "Hey, bro, at least I don't have to buy eggs and bacon at the grocery store like some damn city slicker."

Lyle tore off a sales slip and held it out. "How do you want to pay for this, cash, check, or plastic?"

"Oh, cash. For as long as it lasts." George looked at the total on the slip and counted out the money. He was good with money. The hundred pennies to a dollar made it simple. George had the bills on a small roll he took from his pocket. He didn't want to flash around too much cash.

"Right, and I owe you eighty-seven cents in change," Lyle said. "Coming right up. Lot man should have your sacks loaded. Hope your springs are in good shape."

Two minutes later, George walked out where the co-op

man loaded the last two sacks of fertilizer on board the pickup. He jumped down and checked the springs.

"Almost flat on the iron. Should be okay if you take it easy and don't hit any bumps." The lot man was in his twenties, George decided. He waved at them as they stepped into the pickup and drove away.

"*Al hamdo lillah,*" George said. "All thanks and praise to the Almighty," he went on. "See, I told you it would be easy. These Americans are absolute fools. They'll sell anything to make a few dollars. We have one more load to go. Then we can get busy mixing and wait for the call."

John drove the pickup carefully with the heavy load. He had been scowling ever since they left. "Did you see that man in the cowboy hat inside? I didn't like the way he looked at us."

"John, you dropped into Arabic just now. Never do that again. We speak only English, then nobody can get suspicious. The brother in the hat. Yes, I saw him, talked with him. Big man on the stock market. He's all talk, nothing to be afraid of. Now, we have half of the fertilizer we need. We drive away about fifty miles to get the other half. We'll do that tomorrow."

"Still don't like the way that guy in the hat looked at us. He was suspicious. I know he was."

"Forget it, John. We've got work to do."

In the farmers' co-op, Larry Broderson still wasn't happy. "Hell, brother of mine, those guys looked pure and simple like A-Rabs. Dark, heavy five o'clock shadow on the beards, black hair, brown eyes. Hell, they're A-Rabs sure as hell."

"Larry, there are thousands of Arabs in this country. Lots came over from Kuwait and other countries after Desert Storm. All perfectly legitimate, honest citizens trying to make their mark in a new and strange culture. It's hard. I read a story about some in Denver."

"An A-Rab is an A-Rab. Don't trust them. Especially those two. Still wonder about the fertilizer. You know any farmer around here who buys fertilizer after the growing season is over? Name me one."

Lyle frowned. "No, I guess I can't. But that don't mean some of them don't build up a supply to be ready."

"Fertilizer bombs," Larry said. "Hell, can't remember what else it takes, but this damn chemical fertilizer is about half of the story. Then they mix it with some activating chemical and then light the fuse and baloooooooooey. There goes the Oklahoma City fed building."

"Brother, you've been reading too many of those novels about terrorists. Just relax and read the *Wall Street Journal*, or check your stocks for today. Bet your IPO dropped at least fifty percent today."

"Bet you a six-pack of beer that it's up," Larry said. "I'll call Denver right now and check with my main man." Larry made a strange face, then sucked in a quick breath and exploded with a sneeze. Before that one had ended he sneezed again, and then a third time louder than the first one. He shook his head. "Damn allergy is back and I don't even know what causes it."

He took out a cell phone and dialed. "Yeah, Axel, my man. How is our Digital Output doing today?" He listened, then grinned. "Yeah. You, too, buddy. Keep up the good bidding." Larry folded the tiny phone and put it in his pocket.

"Make it a six-pack of Bud Light, brother Lyle. Digital Output went up over six points. It's at sixty-eight and fifty. You lose."

"Get one out of the cooler. You have anything else you want to wager on?"

Larry took off his crumpled hat and tried to redefine the crease through the top. He turned it around in his hands, then looked at Lyle and nodded. "Yeah, a bottle of Jack Daniel's that those two assholes who just left here are going to make a fertilizer bomb."

Lyle chuckled. "Hey, I get healthy here in a rush. So how do you prove it, go out and ask them?"

"Be one way. But since I think they're terrorists already, I'll slip up on them and take a look."

"My brother the CIA spy."

"Hey, I was in the National Guard for four years. Learned a lot about patrolling and cover and concealment. I was lead scout in our platoon."

"Little brother, don't do anything stupid. I don't want to have to go into the county seat and bail you out."

"Those two A-Rabs? Hell, I can take them with one arm tied."

"Even that big one?"

"He's got a soft gut. About three in there and he folds like the morning newspaper. Damn, soon as it gets dark, I'm going to take a look at the old Handshoe place. Don't worry, I'll take along my little .38 with me, the one I filed a notch in the grip for that rat I shot in my backyard."

Just after ten o'clock that night, Larry drove the last half mile toward the Handshoe farm without lights. He parked in a field entrance a quarter mile from the farm buildings and moved up on foot. It felt strange without his rifle and pack, but it was easier this way. Halfway to the buildings he stopped and sucked in air and sneezed. It exploded like a small thunderclap. Then he sneezed again. "Damn allergy. I've got to go see Doc Smarley about that."

Larry went to the back edge of the farm yard and studied the layout. Lights on in two windows. Pickup in front of the house. An extended van near the barn. There was a granary, a machinery shed, two more small buildings, and a large Quonset hut, the big kind for storing corn or grain that stretched for seventy-five feet down toward the barn.

He didn't move for five minutes. Good technique. There was no dog. Good. He hadn't seen anyone else around the farm yard. Larry could hear the TV rumbling along inside the house. The doors were open.

He checked the barn first, coming up behind it and through a small door. His penlight showed nothing unusual. Just an unused barn with four stalls and a pile of grass hay and a pitchfork.

Next he looked over the machinery shed. It had an open front and the only rig in it was a backhoe that looked in

good condition. That left the Quonset hut. It was closer to
the house. He shrugged. Had to be done.

The back door away from the house was not locked.
The Quonset was set up to be used to dry grain as well as
store it with blowers and heaters along the walls. Inside it
was mostly empty. Toward the roll-up front door he found
the stacks of fertilizer. Beside them sat another stack of another brand. That would make twelve hundred pounds of
fertilizer. What in hell for?

Then he saw the barrel, a regular fifty-five-gallon steel
barrel. He tried to read the label on the top, but it had
been smudged. Some chemical.

A fertilizer bomb—it was the only conclusion. He heard
the front door start to roll up and he scrambled toward the
side where he saw some old boxes and lumber. He crawled
behind them just as the top lights came on. Bright as day.

The two men came in the door chattering in some foreign language.

"No, English. We have to talk English." It was the one
who had done the talking at the co-op. "We need one
more barrel and one more load of fertilizer, then we will be
ready."

Larry shivered. He hardly believed what he had just
heard. The bastards were getting ready to make a bomb.
He had to tell somebody. He had to get out of there and
tell the sheriff. Before he could stop it another sneeze
came. It brayed into the empty Quonset, and was followed
by a second and then a third.

"Shit," Larry whispered. The two men at the fertilizer
jumped up and ran toward him when they heard the first
sneeze. Larry saw that both had out handguns. His .38
wouldn't do much good. He pulled it out and shot at one
even though they were still fifty feet away. They split and
came at him from two directions.

He had four rounds left. He never carried extra rounds.
What the hell? Maybe he could get one of the pricks before they got him.

Three rounds slammed into the boards near him. Automatics, they had automatics. He waited. They came closer.

They had no cover, but he couldn't risk using up his rounds until they got closer. Pretend to be hit? Hell no. He had qualified with the .45 on the range. Now he had to do some good with his .38.

They were thirty feet away now and moving up. He chanced one shot and caught one of them in the leg. The man shouted something in a foreign language. Then both of them charged him firing as they came. He ducked down, pushed up the gun, and snapped off the last three rounds. A bullet slammed into his shoulder and he dropped the gun. He pushed it under some boards and waited as they stormed over him. He was on his stomach and didn't see the kick coming. It slanted off his head and he saw the lights dimming, then they went black as he passed out.

✶ TWENTY ✶

JALIBAH, IRAQ

Back in the car, Wade asked what ideas the others had to find the town. There were none. Duncan checked the map, but he couldn't find the small place.

"So how in hell do we locate this rattrap little town?" Duncan asked.

"What men always do when they are lost," Wade said with a grin, "we ask for directions."

They drove down two more streets before they found a house with a man outside. Wade left the car and walked up to the man, who looked at him cautiously.

"Yes?"

"Sorry to bother you, but I'm from Baghdad and I'm lost. I'm going to Jalibah. Can you help me?" Wade used his best Arabic.

There was a long pause.

"We have nothing of value in our house."

"No, I'm not a robber. I'm simply lost. Just tell me how to drive from here to Jalibah. Is it close?"

"Not far. Why are you going there? It is a hideous town."

"I have a relative there who is ill."

"Oh."

There was another long pause. "All right. It's about forty miles to the west in the dry lands."

"Is there a highway that goes there?"

"Yes. It is not well marked, but there is only one road in that direction. Go to the end of this street, north two blocks and then turn west."

"Thank you. Thank you very much."

"Go with Allah."

"Yes, go with Allah."

When Wade walked back toward the sedan, he saw another car parked near it and a man staring at Ichi who sat in the front seat. Wade hurried up. He called out when he was close.

"Hello, can I help you?" he asked in Arabic.

The man turned and looked at Wade.

"This person won't talk to me. He is suspicious."

"The man is mute. He can't talk and he's terribly shy. Seldom does he come out in public this way. We keep him at our home."

"You are not from this area?"

"No, from Baghdad."

"Then you'll have to come to the police station and register. All visitors in our town must register. It will only take a few minutes."

Wade walked toward the man until he was next to him. Before the policeman knew what happened, Wade slammed the side of his hand into the man's neck, then punched him hard in the jaw. The cop went down moaning and reaching for his gun. Wade kicked the hand away and clamped his fingers over the policeman's mouth.

Ichi was beside him a moment later. They bound the cop's hands and feet with plastic strips, put a safe gag around his mouth, and eased him into the backseat.

Duncan found the cop's car keys in his pocket. "I'll drive his rig to the end of town. Stay behind me."

"Go west," Wade said. "That's the direction we need to go to find our man."

Ten minutes later the police car was a half mile out in the dry country and the policeman himself was safe in Wade's sedan. They found the road west and worried about the cop.

"How far from town before we let him out?" Duncan asked.

"Ten miles," Wade said. "Be a good conditioning hike for him. And give us time to get to that town before he reports us."

Later when they untied the man and took off his gag, he sputtered and swore at them.

Wade turned his head toward him and scowled. "We could have killed you—easier than doing this. You have a ten-mile hike back to town, so you better get started."

The policeman shouted threats at them as they drove away.

Wade checked the time. Just past 7:00 A.M. Now all they had to do was find Jalibah.

Two hours later, after driving over bad roads, they came to the desert settlement of Jalibah. The old man at the door had been right. There was no way they could miss it. This was the end of the road.

Now all they had to do was find someone who knew where the man lived, which would be dangerous, but there was no other way.

Wade stopped the car at the far end of the village. This town could have no more than 150 people. He saw no reason why there was a settlement there in the first place. It was the very edge of the real desert. He had seen no telephone or electric lines coming here. Cell phones would help the communications problem, but where would they get electricity?

He shut off the engine.

"We wait until we find somebody who looks friendly and can tell us where to find our target," Wade said. "If he's really here. Duncan, you take the first watch. I can use some sleep."

Duncan watched everything. He'd wake up Ichi in two hours if no likely looking person came along. There wasn't much of a town to look at here. They were at the end of it with only the desert staring back at Duncan. At slack times like this, Duncan wondered what they were doing at his old stomping grounds, the British Secret Service, MI-6. He had been with the agency for six years and his career there seemed to be stalled. When Mr. Marshall offered him this job, he grabbed it fast.

The diversified types of projects they would work were what had intrigued him. His background meant that he was a good team player. He knew that his contacts in almost every major capital city in the world would help the Specialists. Those contacts were invaluable at times in aiding them to obtain weapons in foreign nations. He wasn't an expert on the Arab world, but the rest of it was his playpen.

He eased out of the car and walked down the dirt street. There were two houses about a hundred yards along. No dogs. He had learned a healthy respect for dogs early on. It had been on a simple stakeout on a foreign diplomat they knew was importing cocaine in his diplomatic pouches. They couldn't stop him from doing that, but they could clamp down on how he sold it.

The man's visit to a suburban house had been routine, and they were about to close in and arrest the buyer when a silent attack dog came out of the side of the yard and knocked Duncan down, making him drop his weapon. The animal dove in for Duncan's throat and only his wrist in the wide-open canine jaws saved him from having his throat torn open. He recovered and caught the animal around the neck and throttled it before it could do any more damage.

The whole attack had been viciously silent. The only noise was a weak growl as the eighty-pound German shepherd died. They continued the work, caught the pair in the drug sale, and sent the buyer to prison, and the next day the drug dealer was booted out of England.

Duncan almost wound up as a professor. He enjoyed school. His parents sent him to Cambridge and he took his diploma in English literature there. But then the government service called and he joined. His one regret about this job was that it left him precious little time for sailing. He sailed his boat only twice last year.

He tried not to think of his two young daughters living in Scotland with his ex-wife. That part of his life had been filled with mistakes, overseas assignments, and long stretches of not getting home. Few agents in the field were married. Even fewer stayed married for long. His fault, his mistakes, his regrets.

A car moved slowly through the street a quarter of a mile down the way almost at the other end of the village. Duncan watched it. It turned a corner and faded away. Nothing.

He walked back and leaned against the car. This would be an ideal time for a cigarette if he smoked. He didn't. Not since college. Too dangerous in the field.

He heard another car, closer this time. Curious. Little else stirring in this small place.

A car suddenly raced around the closest corner to the Specialists' sedan aiming directly for it.

"Company," Duncan shouted. "Everybody awake and on the triggers, I don't know what the hell we have coming here. Look alive. Wade, get ready to talk to whoever this is."

The car came within twenty feet of them, head-on, and stopped. Duncan saw two men get out of the official car and walk forward. Both held long guns.

"How do we play it, Wade?" Duncan asked. "Two of them with rifles. Terrible-looking uniforms but they must be cops."

"We talk," Wade said from the backseat. "I'm getting out. Cover me."

Wade opened the rear door and stepped out. He shielded his eyes with his hand against the glare of the desert sun.

"Hey, can you help me, I'm lost," he said in Arabic.

The two men came on forward until they were almost at the rear of the car.

"Who are you?" one of the men asked.

"I'm from Baghdad, Hashim Jamar. What place is this anyway? I ran out of road."

"You are in Jalibah. Almost no one drives here."

"I'm lost. This is the desert?"

"Close enough. You have just driven here from Rumay-lah."

"I've been lost all night. How do I get back toward Basra?"

"You are really not lost. We heard you were coming."

"Heard? I didn't even know I was coming."

"Lift both hands high. We can spot an assassin a kilometer away. Lift your hands."

Wade did. There was nothing else he could do. The Arab walked toward him and now Wade could see the full beard, the burnoose, mixed with military pants and boots.

"Now," Wade said in English.

A three-round burst from an Ingram stitched holes up the Arab's chest, slamming him backward. At the same time, Wade dove behind the car as the other man brought up his weapon. Another three-round burst from the back-seat of the sedan blasting just beside the other Arab changed his mind and he ran.

Ichi bailed out of the car on the far side.

"Stay with him, Ichi," Wade said and he lifted up, join-ing Duncan from the car as all three ran after the second attacker.

"They knew someone was coming," Wade said as they ran. "Damn cell phones, probably. Which means that old man we asked directions from worked both ends on this deal."

Ichi shouted from ahead. They heard gunshots, a burst of six rounds from a heavy weapon, and they changed di-rections, went down the next street, and caught up with Ichi who had hidden behind a small truck on the unpaved street.

"He went into the yard of the third house up there. Didn't go in the door. He must be hiding there. That probably isn't where he's heading."

"Ichi, you take the far side of the house, we'll go down this way. Watch yourself."

Wade and Duncan ran to a stone wall twenty feet from the target house. Ichi blasted across to the far side without drawing any fire. Then on a hand signal, they all moved from cover to cover along the walls of the house.

Nothing.

The Specialists met at the far side where there was another trail of a dirt street. Across the way in a small house, the front door closed.

"Could be it," Wade said. "I'll pay them a visit. What time is it?"

"Just past noon," Ichi said.

"Too damn early for a social visit. I'll make it a police call."

They drifted across the road. Ichi and Duncan took up covering positions near the front of the house as Wade walked up to the door and knocked, standing to one side. His three raps on the door were followed by three hot lead rounds of rifle bullets splintering through the light door.

"Right house," Wade said. He saw a window four feet to his side of the door and fished a flash-bang grenade out of his vest pocket. He smashed the glass with the muzzle of his Ingram, waited a moment for the answering six rounds of hot lead, then pulled the pin on the nonlethal weapon and threw it inside.

He pushed back to the door. Four seconds later the grenade went off with a shrilling, ear-smashing six blasts, followed at once by six strobes of light so intense that they jolted through hands held over the eyes.

With the last bolt of raw white light, Duncan kicked open the door with one blast from his boot and splintered it, ramming the pieces inside the room.

Just like at the kill house, Duncan took the right side, diving that direction. Wade dove in on the left-hand side. They rolled and dodged behind furniture and listened. Something stirred in the left side of the room. Wade lifted up from behind a sofa, then jolted downward. A handgun blasted, but too late.

Duncan had crawled silently toward the sound, and as

soon as the gun went off he bolted forward, and dove at a figure crouched against the wall. Duncan slammed into him with his shoulder, jolted the handgun away from his fist, and powered him backward to the floor. He quickly bound the man's hands and feet.

"Got him," Duncan said.

Wade came to his feet and prowled the rest of the room silently as a cat and found no one else.

"Clear front room," Wade said. Ichi came through the front door and ran to the door that showed on the back wall. He peered around the frame, then dove into the room. There was no reaction.

"Clear back room," he said.

Wade darted through the room to another door. This one was closed. He tried the knob. Unlocked. He twisted and then pushed the door open hard. A thin shaft of light came out. Wade dropped to the floor and looked around the door frame from the floorboards.

A bedroom. The window curtains were closed. A lamp beside a cot bled soft light into the room. On the small bed lay an old man. Sitting across from him was an even older-looking woman.

Wade stood and walked into the room. "Jamal Hussein?"

The woman stood as well as she could. A rounded back showed stooped shoulders. She lifted her head and glared at him.

"I don't allow firearms in this house," she said with conviction.

"Is your husband Jamal Hussein?" Wade asked in Arabic.

"Is your mother the whelp of a camel whore?"

Wade smiled. He stepped to the bed and looked at the man lying there. He had to be well over eighty. His head was bald, his eyes dark pools, deep-sunken into his skull. Skin flaky and the color of soft brown chalk. Wrinkles so deep his expression became lost in them. The eyes shifted from the woman to Wade.

"Yes, I am Hussein. Go ahead, kill me."

"Why should I kill you?"

"You've been after me for fifteen years. So kill me now and take back proof and the rest of my family can live in peace."

"How many people have you killed with your bombs?"

"How many lice on the head of a bastard child starving in the streets of Baghdad?"

"You know the Scimitar?"

"Everyone who hates America and the Western Great Evil knows the talented Scimitar."

"But you know him personally."

"It was a great honor."

"You taught him from the early days. You were his mentor."

"I knew him."

"You taught him how to kill hundreds of people at a time."

"For the love of Allah."

"But now your great Scimitar is a common criminal killing hundreds, thousands for money. His last job he was paid ten million dollars. More dinar than would fill this room."

"You lie. The Scimitar fights for Allah."

"And for the Scimitar. Mostly for the Scimitar."

"Again you lie." The old man coughed, then again, for sixty seconds he couldn't quit coughing. His ancient wife hovered over him yelling at Wade to leave.

When the coughing stopped. Wade looked at Hussein with surprise. He had curled in on himself. His eyes were glassy. He shivered.

"We have come to take you back to England to stand trial as a multiple murderer for the Hill Street Bombing eight years ago."

The old man laughed. His eyes came clear again and he laughed once more, shallow, without humor. "You want to put a dead man on trial so you can execute him? You English are absurd, stupid, camel dung eaters. You have an ambulance, a doctor, and a nurse to keep me alive? How would you get me across the border? You are stupid, young man."

"What is the Scimitar planning now?"

"He doesn't tell me."

Wade stared hard at the old man. The harsh looks splattered on the weathered face and bounced off like soft rain.

"You do not know we Arabs well, do you, young man? We have long memories of misdeeds and being cheated by the Western Great Evil. We plan and we plan. You may have heard of the Big One, the grand plan to hurt the United States in a way no nation or people or individual has ever hurt you before. We are patient. In Allah's good time we will strike at your vitals. We will punish you for your evil deeds and your thefts of our lifeblood. Soon you will be at our doors, begging us to help you."

"What is this Big One?" Wade asked.

The old man tried to laugh but coughed instead. It sounded like his lungs would come out of his mouth. When he quieted, he wiped his nose and his eyes, then looked at Wade with a deep anger.

"You will never know until it happens. Then it will be far too late."

"Is Osama bin Laden behind this Big One?"

The old man on the bed snorted and looked away.

"Is this Scimitar we hear about part of the Big One?"

"That is for you to find out. I have nothing more to say."

"I bet the Scimitar knows. You were his teacher. He idolized you. He has a long list of targets, right?"

"We all have a long list of targets in the Great Evil, the United States."

"You helped him make the list?"

"Yes, years ago."

"So which one is at the top of his list now? Is that the Big One?"

"I don't know. He told me but I forgot. I'm an old man getting ready to die. Leave me in peace."

"Like the way you left a thousand families grieving for the relatives that you killed?"

"Long ago. Long ago. I . . ." He stopped and looked away. Then he chanted something in Arabic. He said the words over and over. When he looked back, the old man's eyes had rolled up showing only whites. His body trembled and shook. His wife screamed at them.

"You have killed him. You have killed him."

Ichi stepped in and took three Polaroid pictures and put them in his pocket.

The old man lifted up, then fell back. His eyes seemed clearer. He said four words. Words that Wade didn't understand. The words came over and over again in a chant. His breath wheezed in and out with barely enough to keep him alive. Then he stopped breathing. With a gasp, he began breathing after ten seconds. His arms went limp but he was alive. The old lady lifted a broom and took careful steps around the bed and swung it at Wade.

"Get out of my house. Let this great hero of Islam die in peace." She rushed at them. Wade waved the Specialists outside.

"What did the old man say, his last words?" Ichi asked.

"Strange. Rantings I guess. He said over and over. 'My home in the mountains.' Over and over he said it. Maybe he was born in some mountains and wanted to go back."

Wade shrugged. "We didn't get much. We know that Jamal Hussein won't be causing the world any more pain and suffering from his ingenious bombings. We don't have to kill him because he'll be dead in two or three days. Let's get back to the car and try to get out of this damn country."

They walked toward their car. A small truck eased along the street a block over. They came around a corner and could see the sedan they came in. Duncan held up his hand. They stopped.

A second car had parked beside their sedan and the other car. A man in a uniform checked inside their car. He leaned out of it and looked around, then he turned toward them.

"Oh, yeah," Ichi said. "Going to be simple as spooning goose grease into a sieve to get back across the border."

FORT JOHNSON, COLORADO
THE OLD HANDSHOE PLACE

George and John stood looking down at the unconscious Colorado farmer. John bent down and stared at the man's face.

"It's that guy from the co-op store."

George agreed. "Yeah, now what we have to figure out is what to do with him."

"Nothing to figure out. We snuff him and dig him a deep hole somewhere. We can't let him go."

"Right. I wonder if he told anyone he was coming out here to snoop around?"

"Maybe his brother the co-op man?"

"Probably. We better set a guard at night."

"You want me to kick this guy in the head again about four times?"

George shook his head, took out his automatic, and shot Larry three times in the heart. Larry gave one last roll of his head and a long sigh, then he died.

They used the backhoe twenty yards behind the barn. John had worked for the Power Supply Organization in Saudi Arabia and knew how to operate one. He went down ten feet, they rolled the body in not touching his wallet or personal items, and covered him up quickly, pushing in the dirt with the side of the backhoe. Then they packed it down, running over the spot with the treads until the ground was solid and looked like somebody had been practicing driving the backhoe. John moved the rig over fifty feet and dug a shallow hole and partially covered it. Then he put the backhoe in the machine shed.

"Now we find his car or truck," George said. "He didn't walk out here." They found the truck quickly. George jumped the wires under the dash to start it, then they sat there deciding what to do.

At last George had a plan. They took both trucks and drove east until they found the waterway George had remembered.

"The Beebe Seep Canal," George said. "We park his truck as close to it as we can drive, then we make some shoe tracks up to the water and take off our shoes and get out of here."

"Yeah, could work. They might think he drowned himself and he's downstream somewhere."

It was after 3:00 A.M. before they got back to the farm. Nobody was there.

"We'll start our guard duty tomorrow night," George said. "That guy won't be missed tonight."

Just after 5:00 A.M. Lyle Broderson had a phone call at home.

"Lyle, Jenny. Larry didn't come home last night. He left all mysterious about eleven. Said he had an errand to run but he wouldn't say where he was going. I saw him take along that revolver he owns. You know anywhere he might have been going? Ain't like Larry not to come home."

"Jenny. He did say he wanted to check out a couple of guys. He did have a wild look in his eye when these two guys bought some fertilizer."

"They farmers?"

"Going to be. Rented the old Handshoe place."

"So why would that upset him?"

"You know, fertilizer bomb. These two guys were dark, could have been Arabs. But we have several Arab families living in the county now."

"I called Sheriff Wilson. He says he's talked to all of his patrol units to watch for the pickup. I gave him the license plate number. He says not much else he can do."

"You want me to ask him to check out the Handshoe place?"

"Yes. Anything that might help."

Lyle called and left a message for the sheriff with the night deputy. Told him Larry was missing and he said something about going out to the old Handshoe place. Might be a spot to look.

It was just after seven when Lyle opened the store. There were two farmers waiting for him. He knew farmers liked to get an early start on their work day. He handled their needs, then checked with Sheriff Wilson.

"Willy drove out there a half hour ago. He said the two men were up and having breakfast. Things looked normal around there for a place that's been empty for a year. The men said they had been in the area only five days and didn't know anyone. Yes they said they had met you at the co-op but that was about it, so far. Their English wasn't good but they said they had recently come from Poland."

"Nothing suspicious?" Lyle asked.

"Not a whisper. We'll keep looking for Larry. Oh, something just came in. Just a minute."

The line went silent for a moment, then Sheriff Wilson came back on.

"Might be something. One of our cars just spotted Larry's pickup on the banks of the canal up near the reservoir. I'm heading up that way. You want to come along?"

A half hour later they stopped on the banks of the Beebe Seep Canal.

"It's Larry's rig," Lyle said. The driver's door stood open. The deputies searched it carefully.

"No bloodstains or any sign of violence," Sheriff Wilson said. "But then there's no suicide note, either." He looked quickly at Lyle. "Now no cause for alarm, we always have to consider suicide when a car is parked at a river or canal. Normal procedure. We'll check the canal downstream. If somebody went in here, the current would take him down five or ten miles quickly."

"Larry wouldn't commit suicide. He had too much to live for. His stock market involvement alone was more than enough."

"Right. I'll drive you back to town. The men will do a sweep along the canal."

The rest of the day, Lyle worked the store, handled customers' needs and even one complaint, but he was always thinking about Larry. About four, Sheriff Wilson called.

"We swept the canal and didn't find a thing. So we've ruled out suicide. Not much else we can do. We tried for fingerprints on Larry's pickup, but came up with a lot of smudges and the rest were Larry's. We have him on file from when he was a deputy. We'll keep watching and waiting for some development. Maybe he'll just walk into somebody's farm with a whale of a hangover. Been known to happen."

"Thanks, Sheriff Wilson." Lyle worried the rest of the afternoon. Why would Larry take his gun? He must have been going to the Handshoe place and he figured it would be dangerous. It had to be the Handshoe farm. But then how would his pickup be fifteen miles away?

Still it all fit. Larry was suspicious of the Arab-looking pair yesterday afternoon. He figured they were spies or terrorists getting ready to make a fertilizer bomb. He said he was going to check them out. So he tried it after midnight. What if he was caught? Yes his little brother must have been caught. The big question was what did the pair do with his brother?

For the last two hours of business, Lyle could think of little else. He would go to the farm and find out. He'd had six years in the National Guard. He knew how to use a rifle. He had an AR-15 he had bought the kit for and adapted it so it would fire full automatic like a machine gun. It was illegal, but so was kidnapping his brother. Yes, they must have caught him and kidnapped him. They'd hold him until time to set off their bomb. He had no ideas about what their target might be. Denver maybe. Nothing up here worth blowing up.

That night Lyle waited until ten o'clock before he went to the Handshoe place. It was only four miles outside of town. He had decided to drive in with his lights on, get them both outside, and then fire over their heads and put them on the ground. Then he could question them safely.

When his pickup's headlights swept across the kitchen door of the house, he saw it open and two men came out.

Lyle turned back to keep the lights in their eyes and stopped. He left the lights on but turned the engine off.

Lyle stepped out of the pickup with the AR-15 in hand. He had already jacked a round into the chamber and pushed off the safety. Staring into the headlights meant they couldn't see Lyle.

"Just a friendly visit," Lyle called. "Heard somebody rented the old Handshoe place."

"Yes, we did. What do you want?"

Lyle fired a three-round burst six feet to the left of the two men. They started to run.

"Hold it! Stop or the next rounds go into you. Stop and get on your knees on the ground, now!" Lyle's booming parade-ground voice stopped both men and they turned to face him and went to their knees.

"Where is my brother? You met him yesterday in my co-op store. What did you do with him?"

"Don't know what. . . ."

Another three-round burst cut up dirt four feet to the talker's left.

"Try again, asshole. Where's my brother?"

Lyle had been concentrating on the speaker. He didn't see the other man take a pistol from his belt under his shirt. The first notice came with a pair of quickly spaced shots. They missed.

Lyle turned the AR and sprayed a dozen rounds into the man with the pistol before he could fire again.

The talker screamed at Lyle and surged over to where the shot man lay on the ground at the edge of the light beam.

"He asked for it, dumb bastard. You, the live one. Leave him alone and talk to me. Where is my brother?"

"I don't understand. Why did you shoot my friend?"

"He tried to shoot me. Old tradition out West. We call it self-defense. Now where the hell are you holding my brother?"

"We don't have your brother. Can I see if my friend is alive or dead?"

"He's dead, just like you will be in about ten seconds if you don't tell me where Larry is."

Lyle moved up, keeping to the side of the headlights so he could see the man without being seen. He came within ten feet of where the man stood.

"I'm calling the police. You just murdered my friend."

"You take one step and I'll blow your legs off. Understood?"

The man started to move, then stopped. "Look, we can work this out. I haven't seen your brother, but I can forget about John there and forget you came out here. I can give you twenty thousand dollars right now to forget about all of this."

"I bet you can. One more time. Where is my brother?" Lyle pushed the AR back to single shot and aimed at the man's legs.

"I don't know what—"

Lyle fired. The single 5.56mm slug drilled into the knee-cap on George's right leg and he screamed and went into the dirt. He kept screaming, but there was no one within three miles of the farm to hear him.

Lyle moved up to the wounded man. He kicked him in the side, rolled him on his stomach, then grabbed his hands and fastened them behind him with the plastic cinch bands like the ones they had used in the National Guard. He didn't bother with the man's ankles.

"Think I'll have a look around." Lyle went back to the truck, took out his flashlight, and turned off the headlamps. Then he checked the barn, the machine shed, and stopped at the large Quonset hut. It was locked. Lyle lifted the AR and put four rounds into the padlock blowing it open and off the walk-in door. Inside he used the flashlight and found the fertilizer and the two barrels of some chemical. Bomb. Larry had been right.

He found the light switch and turned on the overheads. Lyle searched the open area. There was no place to hide a person. At the far side he saw some splintered boards and when he looked closer he saw that the boards showed several bullet holes. Could be they were firing at Larry? That brought more questions and he searched the area carefully where the rounds had hit and six feet on either side.

He found it under some boards, a .38 revolver with all five rounds fired. He checked the grip. A half-inch-long notch had been filed into the plastic.

This was Larry's .38.

Lyle ran outside to where he had left the wounded man. Almost too late he remembered he hadn't found the pistol the dead man had used. He ducked to the left and saw the muzzle flash as the terrorist fired three times. The rounds missed. Lyle lifted the AR and emptied the thirty-round clip in and around the flash of the pistol. He heard a scream. It came loud, then softer and softer until it faded into silence.

Lyle pushed a fresh magazine of thirty rounds into the AR and moved up quietly to the spot he had seen the muzzle flashes. There was no reason to be quiet. The second man lay half over the first one. The flashlight showed four rounds in his chest and two in his neck.

Lyle sat down suddenly. He had never killed a man before. Deer in season. Yes, but never a human being. Justified. Yes, damn right, but still, two men lay dead. He felt an overwhelming surge of pain and anger at the same time. He had killed.

He stood silent for a minute, then thought back to his army training. The army trained men to kill. He had killed for a good reason and when he was being shot at. Self-defense.

Ten minutes later he unloaded the AR-15.

He sat there wondering what to do now. Call the sheriff from the phone inside?

No.

Leave the dead men here for someone to find?

No.

Bury them?

How?

He remembered spotting the backhoe in the machine shed. If it would run . . .

An hour later he had carried the two men in the back-hoe's bucket a quarter of a mile into a field and dug a fifteen-foot-deep hole. He rolled the two terrorists into the hole along with the pistol. Lyle stared into the hole for a long time, then threw in the AR-15 and the three magazines. He would never need them again.

It took another ten minutes with the backhoe to fill in the hole, and drive back and forth over the spot with the tracks to pack it down. After the first good rain no one would be able to tell the backhoe had ever been up here. Lyle drove the rig back to the machine shed and parked it where it had been. He found a hose and washed the blood down on the ground where the men had died. He washed it through grass and weeds and dirt until it was little more than a slight pink misty color. After a good rain . . .

Lyle sat in his pickup a moment before he started it. He left the lights on in the house and drove away.

The next day he used a pay phone next to a bar and disguised his voice and called 911.

"Hey, something crazy is going on out at the old Handshoe place. You best send somebody out there and figure it out."

"Sir, your name please," the operator said just as he hung up and moved slowly away from the phone so no one would notice him.

The next day the sheriff announced that he had found at the old Handshoe place a stash of fertilizer and chemicals needed to make a fertilizer bomb. Two vehicles were also seized along with a number of weapons and ammunition in the house and over twenty thousand dollars in cash. The two men who had rented the farm were not at the farm and were missing and wanted. A statewide man-hunt was under way.

Lyle stared at the same spot on the wall he had picked out five minutes before. The backhoe had been so convenient, so easy. Then it hit him. Now he had no doubt that the two terrorists had used the hoe the same way he had. His brother lay somewhere out there on the old Handshoe place. Now he prayed that it wouldn't rain. That afternoon when the cops were gone, he was going to start a foot by foot search of the land. He'd dig into every spot where the earth had been disrupted. It might take him a week, but in the end he was sure he would be able to find his brother's body.

✴ TWENTY-ONE ✴

MOUNTAIN HOME, IDAHO

Charlie settled down behind his notebook computer and punched up his E-mail. Two messages. He read the first, then grinned. So, his man was ready up north. Now all he had to do was turn the screws on the pilot Captain Clooney. Yes, it was coming together.

He sat back and thought about it a moment before he read the second message. The greatest terrorist in the whole goddamned world had no idea what was going on right under his nose. Not a single flicker of an idea.

Charlie leaned back in the chair, put his hands behind his head, and laughed softly. Yes, it was going to work. Oh, he wouldn't bad-mouth the big man too much. In three years working with him, Charlie realized just how much he had learned. That combined with his own natural deviousness and looking out for himself would now prove to be an unbeatable combination.

He punched up the next message and read it critically:

"Friend in the Greater Good. Have facilities ready here in California. Understand we will have sufficient budget to set up permanent facilities. Will be ready for you when current project is finished. Immediate move in on your orders. Keep me informed."

Charlie sent a quick note in reply:

"All on schedule, keep fluid on arrangements. Will advise you in advance of my arrival." He signed it "Friend" and hit the send button.

He turned off the set and looked at the phone. It was time. He dug out a number from his billfold and dialed it. The connection went through at once and surprised him. He thought he might have trouble calling Deadhorse, Alaska.

"Yes, this is Frank," the man on the other end of the line said.

"Frank, Charlie, your friend."

"Good, I was hoping you would call. They're here. Have rented a chopper and took a flight today. Not sure where they went but it was over a two-hour flight."

"Good. They're hunting a facility. Stay on them. You have the needed tools?"

"Yes. One long and six short ones. Should be enough."

"You received my shipment?"

"Yes. Much appreciated."

"You'll have to account for every dollar. You know the six men you hire must be three from each shift so we can be covered no matter what time of day."

"Done, and the men are ready. They like the extra money."

"The deadline is coming closer. I'd say within a week. Maybe a little more depending on the air flight schedule. I'll let you know at least twenty-four hours in advance. You have an answering machine on this line?"

"Yes, as instructed."

"You're a good man, Frank. You'll get your ten shares as promised."

"Oh, yeah, my retirement."

"Just be ready when it's time to move."

They said good-bye and Charlie hung up.

He smiled. Loser was he? That's what they called him in Lebanon. He had an American father and a Lebanese mother and none of the people in Lebanon accepted him. The kids in the American school there called him a loser.

He grinned. Yeah, what a loser. He figured this little operation should bring into his coffers at least twenty million dollars. There were several customers and it would be up for bid. He smiled as he thought of it.

Yes, there were arrangements to make. A chopper, crating, then renting a transport plane. In Seattle he would re-crate it with farm machinery signs and trademarks, and get it on a good-sized boat. That would be the tricky part.

He smiled, daydreaming about the auction itself. What a boot! He couldn't think of a bigger rush than watching representatives bid for his treasure. Oh, yes, it would be great. Loser? Ha.

One step at a time. First the grab, and then an evening up with the great man if it came to that. He remembered the humiliation the big terrorist had heaped on him. It had been almost ten years ago now, when they both had been learning this new trade. They had been assigned as a team to take out two guards on a gate before the car bomb was driven into the U.S. compound of a huge oil company.

They had crawled up on the guards in the darkness. Then the big man had knifed his guard to death quickly. Charlie had misjudged the second man, his knife missed, and then he panicked and shouted for help. The guard had his weapon up and ready to fire when Charlie's partner drove his knife into the man's spine, paralyzing him instantly and killing him a few seconds later.

They gave the signal with a small flashlight and the car came driving through. The explosion went off on schedule and was termed a great success.

But for months, the other man bragged about how he had saved Charlie when he missed his assignment and tried to run away. They had fought with fists about it, and Charlie had been beaten badly. It was over then. Charlie had realized if he ever wanted to stay in the organization he'd have to forget his embarrassment about the incident and move on. He did and soon became a lieutenant working under the same man.

But the old hatred was still there. This time. This was

his chance to make a fortune and get even with his former partner at the same time. Yes. Two benefits from one major effort. He liked it.

RUMAYLAH, IRAQ

The three Specialists looked around the corner of the closest house toward their sedan and studied the scene. A car had parked twenty feet from their rig. They saw one policeman in uniform looking over their car. He undoubtedly had seen the dead body.

"He won't be friendly," Duncan said.

"No room for diplomacy," Ichi said.

Wade scowled. "We move up as far as we can without being seen. Then I'll go out and talk to him. If he draws his gun, take him out. Then we get back in the rig and drive. How is our fuel supply?"

Ichi shook his head. "Not sure. I wasn't watching it coming in. We haven't done more than a hundred miles. Should be good for another hundred."

"We hope. Let's move up silently."

When they were as close as they could get unseen, Wade called, then stepped away from the house where the cop could see him. "Officer, what's the trouble? I just left my car for a minute."

The cop turned, hand on his hip where his pistol hung.

"This is your car?"

"Actually I borrowed it from a friend in Basra."

"Did you kill the man beside the car?"

"Kill? Of course not. There wasn't anyone there when I left the car an hour ago."

"Put your hands up. You're under arrest." The cop pulled out his pistol. At the same time two shots punctured the stillness of the desert. The policeman jolted a step backward, screamed, and tried to shoot his pistol. His legs buckled and he bellowed in anger and frustration as he collapsed to his knees, then pitched forward on his face and didn't move.

Duncan ran up and checked the policeman's neck for a pulse. He shook his head.

"We better roll," Wade said. They dumped the body from the car, then piled in and Ichi drove down the road they used to come into the small town.

They saw only a few vehicles in the village before they cleared it and drove down the uneven asphalt toward Rumaylah.

"Go back the same way we came?" Ichi asked.

"If you remember the route," Wade said.

They rolled along for five miles before they met another car. They were almost to the next small settlement when they saw a rig with flashing lights coming toward them.

"It's moving fast," Ichi said. "Any ideas?"

"Play it straight," Wade said from the front seat. "It might not be a police car."

The rig came closer, then it was near them and racing past.

"Ambulance," Ichi said.

"Could be for our buddy Hussein," Duncan said. "He was about ready to go."

Over the rough and potholed road, it took them over two hours to drive to Rumaylah. As they approached it, they found more traffic. By that time it was almost 2:00 P.M. Ichi remembered the number of the highway south at the outskirts of Rumaylah and he turned into it.

A mile later they came to a police car stopping all vehicles leaving the town. The cop was on the driver's side. As they waited in line, Ichi and Wade traded places in the front seat.

When they came to the front of the line, Wade stopped the car.

"Yes, officer, how can I help you?"

The policeman looked into the car and waved them forward. "We're looking for an older car with one man in it. You may move on. Quickly now."

Wade drove on.

"Glad it wasn't us they're hunting," Wade said. "Doubt

if anyone over here knows anything about what happened in Jalibah this soon. At least let's hope not."

They drove south, watching for any trouble. Wade repeated over and over the words of the dying terrorist.

"He said them a dozen times: 'My home in the mountains.' I still can't figure out if he was raving, or if he was hoping to get to where he was born in some hill country."

"Could the phrase have anything to do with the terrorist hit list?" Duncan asked.

"Don't see how it could tie in," Ichi said. "As I remember, none of the targets were really in the mountains."

"Must have been raving," Duncan said. "He was really wigged out there at the last. Probably didn't know what he was saying."

They let it cook for another ten miles. The road here was no better than the other one, and sometimes they could make only twenty miles an hour.

"Better than walking," Wade said. They had traded off and Ichi was driving again. It wasn't quite 3:00 P.M. when Ichi saw a car coming up fast behind him. He watched it. The rig was older than their sedan. It went past him, then pulled back into the lane on the two-lane road. A moment later another car came up. It stayed side by side with the sedan and Ichi frowned.

The car in the lane ahead slowed and Ichi had to slow. The car beside him slowed as well and then edged in toward him.

"We're being hijacked," Ichi said. He pushed the muzzle of the Ingram out the open side window and sent six rounds through the backseat side window. Both rear windows shattered. There was a pause, then the car next to the Specialists' car hit the brakes and swerved in behind the sedan and stopped.

Ichi charged forward and banged his bumper on the car ahead of him. He was ready to hit it a second time but the car turned off onto the shoulder of the road and let them pass.

"My guess is it'll be a couple of months before they try a

hijacking like that again," Ichi said. "That one driver is going to remember the hail of bullets taking out both his rear door windows. Right now he's probably wishing he had a pair of clean shorts to replace the ones he's wearing."

Later Wade saw a village to the left. He drove down a narrow road to it and looked for a road that led south. He didn't find one. He stopped at a small store and asked. When he came back he was grinning.

"Lady said there was a rough road that went all the way to the border. Not much used anymore but it's passable. We'll try it. Might save us from another shootout."

The road was rough and only a track in some places, but it had two small bridges to go over ravines and it looked as if it had been used lately.

"The woman said they were eight miles from the border," Wade said later. "By now we should be within three miles. We could make it after all."

A mile later the odds changed.

"Two vehicles coming straight at us," Wade said. "They can see our dust trail. We can see theirs. My guess is they're some Jeep ripoffs. We'll wait and see how many bodies they carry." When the rigs were a half mile apart, Wade made the decision.

"Okay, they have three men per Jeep. Six to our three. They all have long guns; we have one, the G-11, and two sub guns. Any suggestions?"

"Yeah," Duncan said. "We split up and go three directions. Two to one is better than six to three. We can let two men get up close enough for our short guns."

"I'm for it," Wade said. "We work generally south. Let's move. Now."

The three left the sedan and two ran to the right and one to the left. When the drivers of the Jeeps saw the move, they turned their rigs one each way. The rig on the left chasing Duncan and his automatic rifle was soon stopped by a wadi it couldn't cross. Duncan found a small ravine and looked over the top. The three men were coming toward him, all had rifles. He let them get within a hundred yards, then zeroed in with the G-11 on the first one to stand and move forward.

He fired single shots, getting off two rounds before the man slammed backward. Hit, maybe out of action.

The other two moved slower. One crawling behind what he must have figured was concealment.

It wasn't. Duncan put two G-11 rounds into the soldier, then one more to stop him as he tried to crawl away.

Then Duncan waited. It was five minutes before he saw the third man running back for the Jeep. Duncan ran forward and found a good firing position. From two hundred yards he put six rounds into the Jeep engine. When the Iraq soldier tried to start the vehicle, he couldn't. It ground and ground. That was when the soldier threw the keys into the desert and jogged to the south and to the right where the other Jeep roamed the area hunting for its prey.

Duncan heard the submachine guns chatter, then the heavier sound of what could be AK-74s, the updated version of the old AK-47. He saw the man he had chased join the other three. Four to two. Duncan shifted his position, then tried to figure a way where he could get behind the Iranian troops and put them in a crossfire. It was time he moved before those long guns made dead men out of Ichi and Wade.

It took Duncan ten minutes to run, walk, and crawl to where he wanted to be. It was a small hump in the desert that gave him good sight lines on the four Iraqi troops looking for Ichi and Wade. He watched as one man about two hundred yards away lifted up and ran to the left. He must be trying to get behind the Specialists.

Duncan sighted in on the man, led him, and fired a three-round burst. Two of the 4.7mm rounds ripped into the soldier and he sprawled in the dust.

Duncan saw one of the trio left lift up and look behind, then drop down quickly. They had left the Jeep a hundred yards in back of them. Duncan grinned and put four rounds into the engine, then tried for the gas tank and found it on the second shot. The Jeep exploded in a large ball of gasoline fire.

Two of the soldiers ahead drifted to the left, then when they thought they were out of range, lifted up and ran. Duncan followed them with a dozen rounds on single shot. He missed them but rushed their movement. When they were out of range, Wade and Ichi lifted up from behind a small rise and jogged forward to where Duncan sat.

"Glad to see you and your long gun, buddy," Ichi said. "Wade nailed one of them."

"I owe you a beer," Wade said and they all laughed.

It took them two hours to hike the rest of the way to the border. This section was unmanned by both sides. They walked past a three-strand wire fence and then to a well-traveled road on the Kuwait side. A half hour later a Humvee patrol unit rolled up and gave them a lift.

On the ride back to the Advanced Recon Base a mile from the border, Wade kept trying to figure out what the old terrorist had meant by his last words. They haunted him: "My home in the mountains," he had said. He worried about it all the way back to London.

✳ TWENTY-TWO ✳

MOUNTAIN HOME, IDAHO

Charlie knew the timing had to be right. Captain Clooney wasn't flying this morning. He would be tied up on base all morning in some ground school tactical problems. Charlie grinned thinking of all the money he was going to have. Twenty million. Now that was real money.

He drove toward the Clooney home and stopped a block down in front of a vacant house. He locked the rental car and walked toward the Clooney place. Nothing unusual, just a man moving down a suburban street in the middle of the day. It was almost noon and the girls and their mother should be home.

Charlie knocked on the door as anyone in the area would do and waited for it to open.

"Charlie, what a nice surprise," Beth Clooney said. Her bright smile genuine, her blond good looks impressive even without her company makeup on.

"Beth, could I talk to you a minute? It's about Marvin."

Her smile faded. "Oh, about the gambling trouble. Yes, of course come in."

He stepped inside and she closed the door. Her pretty face turned into a frown and she shook her head once. "I didn't even know he was getting in so deeply. Can't we work out something?"

"Let's sit down, Beth. I really didn't think it would go so far. Marvin really isn't much of a gambler."

They went to the living room and sat on the sofa three feet apart. He watched her closely. She was nervous, jumpy. This gambling debt must have hit her hard.

"I have some money," Beth said. "It's in stocks and I can sell them. I don't mind. It's my husband I'm talking about here. His career. I won't let his one big mistake ruin it. It would kill him. I'd do almost anything to help him."

"Are the girls here?"

She looked up, her soft frown curious. "Yes, in their room. Kathy is having a nap." She cleared her throat, moved on the couch, and rubbed her hands together.

"This is hard for me, Charlie. To find out that Marvin had gambled so much. That's why I'll get the money. A thousand. I can have it for you in two hours. No big problem."

Charlie shook his head. "Too late, Beth. Far, far too late. The wheels are turning. For a minute there I thought you were going to offer to go to bed with me."

"Charlie, I've never been so . . ."

He held up his hand. "It's far too late for your little games, Beth. Oh, I was tempted. But that wasn't in the plans." He stood up and Beth stood, too. Before she could move he caught both of her hands and bound her wrists together with one of those plastic cinch cuffs that police use.

"Charlie, what in the world?"

"You haven't figured it out yet? Your devoted husband was going to dump his career just to prevent me getting what I want. Isn't that a killer? He was going to go to his CO and tell him the whole thing, and they would come after me. He'd be thrown out of the Air Force for gambling and endangering the service and his plane and the whole security system.

"I couldn't let him do that, Beth. That would spoil all of my plans that I've worked on for so long. So, you and I and the girls are going for a little ride."

He turned her around, then slipped a folded scarf over

her head and bound it tightly around her mouth tying it in back of her head. Her eyes went wild. She tried to talk.

"Just relax, and everything will be fine. We're going for a ride. Your van is in the garage, right?"

Beth nodded, her eyes moving from side to side.

"Good. Let's go out there now. No trouble and nobody gets hurt."

He led her into the hall, then to the kitchen and into the garage. He opened the van's sliding side door and put her inside and fastened her seat belt. Then he cinched a plastic cuff around her ankles so she couldn't walk. She moaned and groaned at him but no words came through the gag. Her eyes burned into him with fury but he looked away.

"I'll be back in a minute."

He went into the house and found the girls' room.

"Clarice, your mom wants you out in the garage. She said right away. Why don't you take your game with you?"

They went to the garage where Charlie promptly placed the cuffs on her wrists and ankles and put her in the seat beside her mother. Lastly he tied a gag around her mouth. She closed her eyes and wouldn't look at him.

A few minutes later the four-year-old, Kathy, sat in the big backseat by the others bundled up the same way. He fastened the girls' seat belts.

"Now for a short drive," he said. He had found the car keys and garage opener in the kitchen. He opened the garage door, drove out, and closed the door behind them.

It was a twenty-minute drive to the house he had rented the week before. The place was almost out of town and the only one around for two blocks. It had probably been a farmhouse when the town was much smaller.

No garage. He drove close to the back door and checked the situation. Nobody could see the side door of the van. He opened it, cut off the plastic around Beth's ankles, and led her to the back door and into the house. He put her on an old couch in the living room of the minimally furnished house and put a new plastic tie on her ankles.

"Now, Beth, don't get ideas about running away. I have

your two girls. Remember that. I'll go bring them in. Then I'll tell you what this is all about."

She tried to reply but the gag stopped her.

He led in Clarice and carried Kathy and put them in a bedroom with a sagging mattress. He applied new plastic cuffs around Clarice's ankles, then went back to Beth.

Charlie sat beside her and stared at her. He grinned and took the gag off her mouth. She sputtered and swallowed, then could talk.

"I don't know what this is about, but my offer still stands. I'll pay you two thousand dollars instead of one. Just don't hurt the girls."

"Darlin' Beth, I wish it were that simple. The gambling money isn't important."

Beth frowned. "Then it's because Marvin's a pilot." She watched him but he didn't react. "Oh! You're trying to steal his plane. Make him fly it . . . You bastard."

Charlie chuckled. "Oh, yes, I've been called that before. This is the real world out here, Beth. The strong take from the weak. Marvin is one of the weak ones. You better listen to this phone call. It's almost one o'clock. Marvin will be in the pilots' lounge. He has a flight at two-thirty today. Just listen."

Charlie took out a cell phone and dialed. It took them three minutes to find Captain Clooney, then he came on the line.

"Yeah, Clooney here."

"Captain, this is Charlie. Remember what we talked about the other night? Today is the day. You have a flight at two-thirty. You will follow my directions exactly, or you'll never see your wife and girls again."

"Bastard. You wouldn't do that. Beth wouldn't let you."

"Right now I have Beth and the girls in a secret place. Talk to Beth a minute."

He held out the phone and Beth grabbed it.

"Honey, don't do anything he asks. We're fine. He has us in a strange house, but he hasn't hurt us."

Charlie grabbed the phone. "So, Captain, convinced?

You do exactly what I tell you to do this afternoon or your family will die in especially painful ways, all three of them. Then when I find you, you'll join them in hell. Understand?"

The voice that came over the phone was husky with anger. "Yes, understood. You leave them alone, unharmed, and I'll do anything you say. You bastard."

"Listen. You'll have one nuclear device on board when you take off. At the first chance, you get lost from your flight. Turn off your radio and then fly as I tell you."

Charlie gave the pilot detailed instructions. "I'll be listening to the radio news. A missing Eagle will be big news around here. Just don't disappoint me. You do your part and you'll get a bonus of a hundred thousand dollars and a family that's healthy and safe.

"You don't do what I tell you and you're a dead man along with your family. In that case I'll use your wife up before I do her. You really understand?"

"Yes, you fucking bastard. Nothing else I can do. Damnit."

"Now you're getting with the program. Oh, as a bonus I'll cancel that gambling debt of a thousand dollars. See, I'm not such a bad guy after all. Now get out there and fly that Eagle. You'll be worse than dead if you don't." He put down the phone.

Beth's eyes were large with shock when he looked at her.

"Don't worry, old Marve is going to do just as he was told."

She gasped. "You're not just stealing his plane, you're stealing a nuclear bomb."

He ignored her tirade. "I need to get to your van's radio and check the progress of my little plan. Don't worry. I'll come back when old Marve gets to where he's going."

"You . . ." She screeched in frustration. "I wish Marve had never met you. How I wish he'd never gambled with you. You slimy, shit-faced, murderous terrorist."

"Hey, Beth, maybe you're not so dumb after all. Think of how much I can get from the highest bidder for that nuke. It should go from twenty to thirty million dollars. Now, I've got to get out of here. I'll let you know when he lands."

He walked out while Beth yelled at him.

LONDON, ENGLAND

The six Specialists, Mr. Marshall, and two experts on the Arabic language who had been brought in for this session sat around the conference table on the second floor of the London office. Wade had reported to the group what the terrorist said about the Big One.

"He told us that the strike would be devastating, and that we would come to the Arab countries begging them to supply us with goods and services. I have no idea what he meant by that."

"So it's still up for grabs," Roger said. "This Big One could come from bin Laden or from Abdel Salim or the Scimitar or half a dozen other big-shot Arab terrorists."

"Do we have anything more on bin Laden and his current activities?" Kat asked.

Mr. Marshall shook his head. "Not a thing. Some of our earlier sources have dried up. We're wondering."

"If we knew what the Big One was, we might have a better idea who could do it," Ichi said.

Wade told them the phrase that the Jamal Hussein had repeated over and over in his delirium.

"My home in the mountains," Wade said again. "It may mean nothing, just the demented ramblings of an old man about to die."

John Bursing, the Arabic expert from the British Foreign Office, shook his head. "Not likely, not likely. The man was an international terrorist for years. He fought with every ounce of his mind and body for what he believed in. We called him a criminal, a murderer, a mass killer, but he was always true to his beliefs and his calling.

"I can't believe, even in his last days or hours of his life, that he would not take the chance to ridicule and throw something in the face of those hated Westerners who came to hunt him down."

"What if we use different words that mean the same thing for the two nouns in the phrase," Kat said. "Like, my bungalow in the hills. Or my casa in the Cascades." She shook her head. "No, that makes no sense at all."

All nine of them talked and brainstormed for another hour, then Mr. Marshall called a halt. "All of us will go off by ourselves somewhere and let this percolate. Something might come to the surface. See you all back here in an hour."

Kat went to her office and sat facing the wall, closed her eyes, crossed her arms, and tried not to think about it.

Hershel went for a walk in the soft afternoon rain. He got wet and foot sore and came back without an idea in the world about the phrase.

Duncan sat in his office flipping playing cards at his rain hat. When he got one in, he thought about the problem. Nothing that made any sense developed.

Roger threw darts in his office. Ichi practiced karate moves. Wade sat in his office working on a crossword puzzle. He had most of it done in the first half hour, then couldn't get the last key word. Just before the hour was up he had it. Habitat. He went back to the meeting with an idea.

They assembled with fresh cups of coffee, cola, and three cups of tea.

"So," Mr. Marshall said. "What do we have?"

They all shook their heads except Wade.

"Had a thought. Maybe we're making it too hard. If we work just with the two nouns we have what? Home and mountain. What about mountain home? Could it be the name of a place?"

"There's a Mountain Home town in North Carolina," Roger said. "Not much around there to blow up by terrorists."

"Yeah, I drove through a Mountain Home in Alabama once," Ichi said. "I had two flat tires at the same time right in town. I still think some kids let the air out while we were having lunch. Not a big terrorist target there either."

"What about Mountain Home, Idaho?" Wade said. "There's an Air Force base there. Now that could be a target."

Kat pulled out a map of the States and zeroed in on the Idaho town. "The town is in the southwest part of the state about thirty-five miles southeast of Boise."

"The air base could be a target," Mr. Marshall said. "Why else would the terrorists be interested in it?"

Wade and Hershel both spoke up at once.

"The nukes they have there," Hershel said.

"Right, the Air Force has tactical nuclear weapons they fly on board some of the aircraft there," Wade said. "If they carry them, they go on practice missions with them, the live ones."

Kat held up her hands. "Now wait a minute. We're jumping hoops of logic too fast here. Slow down. We have two words from an old dying terrorist, and we're pinning our hopes on him, and that he was talking about the Mountain Home Air Force Base? Isn't that a little out of left field?

"I mean we have three suspects here. We don't know what any of them have planned. We have rumors and talk about the Big One, a huge hit at the U.S. But we don't know what it is or who might be doing it. We have one terrorist who said that hundred of thousands would die. So, okay, that could be a nuclear explosion for that high a body count. But it might be something else."

"What?" Wade asked.

"I don't know. Granted the nuke does seem like a good possibility that it could be big enough for hundreds of thousands. But are we jumping to conclusions here that this is the Big One?"

She looked around. For a moment Kat thought she was in front of a jury she had to convince. No, she was just injecting some logic in here, putting on a slow down before this train ran off the tracks.

Mr. Marshall looked up. "Quite right, Katherine, to

slow us down a bit here. We're working in a vacuum, we have few facts, we have three potent and active suspects. True, we have no absolute pointer or clue that gives us a method or a target. Still, this idea that the terrorist knew the words Mountain Home has to mean something. The question is, how much can we stake on the point that this is indeed the Big One?"

Duncan sipped at coffee and then looked up. "We can't be sure. But this is the one good lead we have. In this business we can't afford to overlook anything. How much time would it take to check out this air base and see what happens there? If it's a wild goose, we just chase it a while and look around for a better goose."

Hershel nodded. "I've been in this spook business for long enough to get a feel for things. A hunch I guess you'd call it. This Mountain Home idea seems to me to have something potent about it that we haven't found before. True, we still don't know which of the three might be working the flimflam here, but I'd vote that we give the place a good looking over."

"I've never heard of this Air Force base," Roger said. "Is it a big one?"

"Nothing strategic about the place," Ichi said. "I've heard of it. It's a relatively small base. Is there a chance the terrorists might think that security there might not be as tight as at some of the larger bases?"

"It would be tight," Duncan said. "Any military installation with nuclear weapons has horrendously tight security, no matter where it is."

Ichi spoke up. "What you're saying is that Mountain Home Air Force Base might not be the target, but it could be the place where the terrorists could try to steal a nuclear weapon for later use."

"Certainly one scenario," Mr. Marshall said. "Maybe it's a matter of logistics. The terrorists want to steal a weapon close to the target they intend to bomb. Are any of the U.S. targets on our list anywhere near Mountain Home, Idaho?"

Kat checked her map book.

"Hoover Dam is about five hundred miles due south at the bottom of Nevada. Going the other way, it's fifteen hundred miles north to Prudhoe Bay, Alaska, the thirty-year-old oil field."

"Then there's the Denver stadium packed with sixty thousand people, and the stadium in San Francisco all within easy jet flight range," Ichi said.

"Let's say somebody wanted to steal a nuclear bomb from an Air Force base," Mr. Marshall said. "How could they do it?"

Duncan looked up. "Heard about it being done once. A chopper moved ten men over the fence at the end of a runway. They shot out the tires on a jet bomber about to take off, removed the nuke, put it in a sling, and were gone before base security arrived. Took them something like four minutes for the whole job."

Hershel waved at Duncan. "Sure, but today every base that has nukes does defensive training against a chopper steal. They can respond in two minutes, or less time with fifty-caliber long-range rifles."

"Someone could put a ringer pilot on base for a regular guy and steal a jet on a practice mission," Kat said. "But on most bases I've seen that would be almost impossible."

"So what is our next step?" Mr. Marshall asked.

Wade looked up. "You might suggest to your friend at the FBI that Mountain Home Air Force Base be put on a special alert about a possible plot to steal a nuclear weapon."

"I will certainly make that suggestion. What else?"

Kat spoke up. "It might be a good idea to send one of us to each of the four potential targets: Hoover Dam, Prudhoe Bay, Denver stadium, and San Francisco's stadium."

Wade and Mr. Marshall looked at his team. The other five Specialists nodded in agreement.

Mr. Marshall smiled. "Yes, good plan. Wade will make the assignments. One person each place. You'll take the large jet from Heathrow as soon as you pack a bag and get out there. I'll alert the crew. First I'll call the FBI."

Wade looked around the table. "Any volunteers?"

Kat waved. "I'd like to do Prudhoe Bay, I've never been to Alaska."

"You're elected." Nobody else spoke up. "I'll take Hoover Dam," Wade said. "I've done some work in that area."

"Put me down for San Francisco," Ichi said.

"I'll do Denver," Roger said. "Maybe I'll see a Bronco practice."

"You'll all go by our jet right to Las Vegas," Mr. Marshall said. "Then it'll take Kat on to Seattle. The rest get connecting flights. Kat, better go commercial on to Fairbanks and up to Prudhoe so not to attract attention. The rest of you work out your route with our travel specialist. That's it. Good luck."

SOMEWHERE IN AFGHANISTAN

Osama bin Laden polished his personal AK-74 rifle with the curved thirty-round magazine as he listened to his top aide. Fazul Abdullah shook his head in anger and disappointment

"It is the second one that we have had destroyed. We don't know where the two men are we had placed north of Denver. The news wires were alive with reports about an abortive fertilizer bomb-making action. The goods were seized along with money and guns, but our two men were not found.

"Neither have they checked in on the Internet as they were supposed to in case of an emergency. We must assume that they have been lost."

Bin Laden ate from a bowl of fruit staining his long black beard. He used a finger bowl of water and a cloth to clean his beard, then turned his angry eyes on his aide.

"The other two teams are in place with their bombs?"

"Yes, sir. They have reported in and are awaiting the final execution order on the given day."

"The target date, a soccer/football game, is still scheduled for the same day?"

"It is."

"But it is far too short a time for us to send in new teams. We can't do the project with half the bombs we need." He put the AK-74 on the polished desk surface and pulled it to him, lifting it and aiming at a picture on the wall.

"No, it's not too late. Order the two teams that have their bombs ready to go at once to the areas not covered. Go to small towns and get the package put together. They must hurry, but there is still time. Send them twice the money as usual so they can bribe anyone they need to. It must be done fast. There is still time. They must move on it today."

Fazul smiled. "Yes, you are right. There will still be enough time. I'll E-mail and telephone them at once." He turned and hurried out of the room. Osama bin Laden nodded slowly, then a soft smile replaced the frown he had been courting. He swung the rifle around at several targets in the room.

Yes, this was the important one, he must give it every chance to succeed. With fast work there should still be time to have everything in place and ready. If it was Allah's will.

⋆ TWENTY-THREE ⋆

DEADHORSE, ALASKA

Phil Lawrence stood in his room at the Prudhoe Bay Hotel, the only one in Deadhorse, and looked out the window. The hotel was Spartan, to be kind. A bed, a chest of three drawers, a chair, a small closet, and a bathroom down the hall. The entire structure was made from a series of portable trailer homes pasted together. Weird.

The small imitation of a town outside was just as strange. This was a company town, owned and run by the huge American oil corporations that built it and the Alaskan pipeline and now work the rich deposits of oil in Prudhoe Bay. Most of the area was taken up by the "camps" where the oil field and pipeline workers lived. The camps, too, were made up of a series of trailer homes, some put together to form larger units. The men lived, ate, and slept in the camps.

The men did now. He scowled. But not for long.

The gravel street outside was built on the permafrost, as was every trailer home in town and every part of the oil operation buildings. The trailers all sat on a foundation of crushed rock hauled in. When the oil was gone, the government required the company to dig out the crushed rock and put it back where it came from and leave the permafrost pristine again.

He heard that there were only twenty-four legal residents in the town of Deadhorse. The two thousand men who worked in the oil fields were not residents. They were classified as transient workers and lived in company barracks and facilities in the company town's exclusive camp.

The few stores and the Prudhoe Bay Hotel were the exceptions in the town. There was only one place where he could rent a helicopter. He had made certain of that before he arrived. The price it cost him was amazing, but when you had a fifteen-million-dollar budget, you went right ahead and paid what was required.

Lawrence turned to the other man in the room, Fred Smith, and grinned. "So, this is the famous Prudhoe Bay oil field. We will learn a lot about it in the next few days."

The other man nodded, not yet used to the feel of the Western-style clothes they had purchased in Fairbanks two days ago. They had spent three days in that central Alaskan town, trying to get used to the nearly twenty-four hours of sunlight.

"Damned pants don't fit right," Smith said. "I don't know how these Americans stand them."

"Get used to them, Mr. Smith," Lawrence said and chuckled. "Your light brown hair looks good, and that beard of yours is gone along with your mustache. With the green contact lenses you look almost American. Now try to get used to the clothes and to be called Smith. It's a common American name."

"Is this really necessary? Why do we have to look like Americans? We say we are from Italy. They're dark."

Lawrence's smile vanished. His face turned hard and his eyes became cold steel balls. "Enough of this whining. You will do precisely as instructed with no more complaining. We have much work to do to get ready. We're not even sure of our time schedule; we don't control that. So we must be ready as soon as possible.

"Tomorrow we will rent the helicopter I arranged for. We will establish our cover as scientists here to test the ozone layer. We will be friendly, gregarious, good neighbors, and devoted to our task. For the next two or three weeks you are Fred Smith. After this job is over you can take your well-earned hundred thousand dollars and have a long vacation. Now it's work. Understood?"

"Yes, Scimitar, understood."

"No!" the word came out with cutting edges. "Never use that name again while we are on American soil. Never. I am Phil Lawrence, from Milan, Italy. I am a scientist." He sighed. "Yes, we had to change our appearance. Americans can become highly suspect and suspicious."

"Yes . . . Phil, I understand. We will be ready. We rent the chopper tomorrow and scout our location." He hesitated. "I can't get used to you without a mustache, and that hair is light brown. Your eyes are green like mine, not brown. Amazing what they can do these days in a hair-styling place."

"They can do whatever we ask them to do. Now, let's see what kind of food they have here at the hotel. I understand it's the only place in town to eat. There are a hundred and eighty rooms here, so there will be a crush at the restaurant. We will become well acquainted with the food and the people. Remember, we treat everyone, especially the serving people, with friendship and respect. Let's go eat."

The next morning they went to the small firm that rented and repaired helicopters. Most of their trade was when the oil companies needed an extra, or one of theirs broke down. They had three they could rent to anyone with the cash.

Hal Fitzgerald, of Fitzgerald Helicopters, stared at the Italian pilot's license with helicopter rating and nodded.

"Hail, I guess it's okay. Long as you sign for the insurance and the daily rate. How long you need this bird?"

"Possibly for as long as two weeks," Lawrence said in perfect and unaccented English. He even had an Alaskan twang to his words. "We're not sure of the climate conditions, which can close down our research in a rush."

"Understand. I need to check with your bank in England, not that I don't believe your credit card. Usually takes about an hour. Why don't you come back then and we'll be all set to get you airborne."

"Fine, we'll be back."

Fitzgerald watched the pair as they left. He frowned. Something ticked in the back of his mind, but it never turned into anything solid. The taller guy seemed American all right, but something seemed askew. Maybe it was the three hours of sleep he had last night. He snorted and picked up the phone to check on the bank. At three thousand a day he didn't want to come up with an expired credit card, especially one from England. Did that seem strange? The man explained an English credit card was easier to use than one from Italy. That was true. Fitzgerald nodded again. He didn't speak any Italian at all. The phone rang twice, then someone in London picked it up.

Outside in the soft sunshine of early morning, the two men walked the short distance to the hotel and had coffee.

"He was suspicious," Fred said. "Right now he's checking our passports and our ID."

"Not a chance, Fred. He wants the business. He just doesn't want to get cheated. He'll contact our bank in England that issued our card, come up with a high six-figure balance, and be thrilled to have us as customers."

An hour later they checked out the chopper with the owner, did a quick test flight for him, and then took over the bird.

"Be good to bring her back here each day when you're finished with your work," Fitzgerald said. "Then we can service her, juice up the fuel tank, and have her ready for you the next day."

They took off and angled inland, following up the highway toward Fairbanks for five miles, then swung to the east for another five before turning north. They checked out what had been reported as an ice field that held solid during the sometimes warm weather of summer.

They crossed miles of slushy snow and melting ice, then lifted farther inland where the landscape slanted upward. They found what they wanted about ten miles from the coast of the bay. It was near two frozen lakes and had an ice and snowfield more than a mile long that looked flat and available.

"We'll set down and take a closer look," Lawrence said. He angled the bird down to the middle of the ice field and they both stepped out. The ice was solid under an inch of soft snow.

"Didn't think it snows much up here," Fred said.

"True, but when it does in the winter it hangs right in there until summer before it melts." Lawrence jumped up and down on the ice. It held.

"Yes, I think we have our site. Let's set up that fake instrument panel and make it look like we're working just in case anyone flys over."

They unloaded two cardboard boxes from the cargo section of the chopper and from them took out a tripod with a small telescope on it. There were several other instruments that looked scientific, but really had little to do with the ozone layer or anything else. They had bought the outlay in Seattle and figured it was enough to con most people.

They nailed down to the ice fluorescent red signal banners three feet wide and twenty feet long on two sides of the experiment. It would make the spot easier to find the next time, and might help establish their cover story and camouflage their true purpose in the Prudhoe Bay area.

"Let's get back to the hotel and set up the laptop," Lawrence said. "It's about time to contact Charlie in Mountain Home and see how he's progressing."

"I don't trust those E-mail messages," Fred said. "You know how the American government monitors everything. I hear they monitor all E-mail inside the country and going out and coming in. They have a giant system called Echelon. You know about it?"

"In detail," Lawrence said. "It's a computer-based keyword recognition system that routinely scans the satellites, fiber-optics and cable transmissions, faxes and E-mail for certain key words. Several nations including England and Australia are monitoring U.S. transmissions since the U.S.

can't legally do it themselves. They get the input of any key words used and shoot them to the U.S."

"So we're okay if we don't use any key words," Fred said.

"Most people who talk about this Echelon system say it looks for words such as bomb, explosive, terrorism, kill, sniper, hit man, C-4, dynamite, fertilizer bomb, assassination, those sort of words, plus a long list of other words that NSA considers sensitive."

"Yeah, but there must be billions of phone calls and E-mail and faxes every day," Fred said. "How can they monitor all of that?"

"Anytime a message hits the atmosphere by microwave or to a satellite, it's fair game and can be picked up by anyone with the right equipment. They call it their Super Cray computers that listen to all this talk, then grab any conversation with the sensitive words and send an audio recorded message to the right authorities. Most of what they get is harmless, but they have a record of it if they need to check back."

"So we don't use the key words and they never even know that we're here," Fred said.

"Now you've got it."

They flew back to the chopper rental firm and parked the bird, then went to the hotel.

In Lawrence's room they set up the computer, plugged it into the phone jack. It had a built-in 56K modem and Lawrence checked into his network server and put in Charlie's E-mail address: Itype@OLC.com. He typed in this message:

"Landed at expansion site today. Scouting possible locations. New one about ten miles south of the big lake, near two smaller ones. Over a mile of good terrain. What's your schedule? Reply soonest."

He checked it again, then sent it and a small window popped up telling him that his mail had been sent.

It would carry his usual E-mail address: UK@Gtrade27.com. and in parentheses (John Brookhurst) as the sender.

"Done," Lawrence said. "We should have a reply tonight or in the morning, depending on when Charlie reads his E-mail."

"Still don't trust it."

"Better than a phone call, and much harder to trace. They keep phone records forever and the police have easy access to them."

"We're having two more men come in?" Fred asked.

"Tomorrow. Don't want to overload the hotel, here. We'll need all four of us for the end game."

"When will it happen?"

"Depends on Charlie. Within a week I hope. Get this one over and back to more pleasant and simpler jobs."

It was midafternoon by then. Fred looked out the window at the rows of barracklike buildings where the oil field workers stayed.

"What do two thousand men do on their off hours around a bleak, strange frozen hellhole like this?" Fred asked.

"I read that there are good recreation facilities for the men, theaters, sports fields, probably a basketball court, all sorts of activities. Not like they have a lot of time. They work twelve-hour shifts seven days a week, and then have a break every so often. Most of them rotate to Seattle or Anchorage for their time off. Tough job but the pay must be double what it is in the other states down south."

"Still seems strange, two thousand men here and no town. Unreal. You mean the oil companies feed those two thousand guys three times a day? Where do they get the groceries?"

Three truck tractors with forty-foot trailers hooked on behind blasted past the hotel and through the gate of the oil company compound.

"Yeah, I guess I see where the supplies come from. Can fly in stuff they really need fast. Supplies and drill goods and such. Have their own planes. Hey, what about schools? I didn't see a schoolhouse anywhere."

Lawrence laughed. "Don't need any schools for two thousand men or for twenty-four adults who live in the town. Medical problems? They are flown by air evac to Barrow, about two hundred miles to the northwest. Really serious cases would go to Fairbanks, I'd guess. Let's check on the net and see if we have any response from our little friend down there in Mountain Home."

There was no response from Charlie.

Fred sat on the bed and lit a cigarette.

"No smoking in here. You know how I hate that smell."

"Sorry. Forgot myself. So, what are we going to do until morning?"

"I have two books that I need to read. One is *The Mastery of Power: How to Get It and Hold It*."

"Sounds boring." Fred fell back on the bed. He was short and sturdy, a good man with a gun who could use his hands as weapons in a street fight. He had a scar on his right cheek from a knife fight years ago. "Can't get used to it being broad daylight here at nine o'clock at night. Damn sun doesn't set at all up here in the summer, right? I thought it would still be freezing."

"Gets up to ninety degrees on some good summer days," Lawrence said. "Now get out of here, I want to get some reading done."

"You enjoy reading that kind of stuff?"

"You want your hundred thousand pay for this job?"

"Oh, yeah."

"Then get out of here and let me read. Tomorrow we'll go out again with the chopper and take along a sling big enough to do our job. Remember, whatever we do has to look natural and routine. Just another research job we're doing this time up here in the north country. That way we won't attract any attention, even though we're the only strangers here."

⋆ TWENTY-FOUR ⋆

MOUNTAIN HOME, IDAHO

Charlie rolled out of his bed in the rented house, dressed quickly, and at once went to check on his prisoners. He'd taken the cuffs off the wrists of all three, figuring that they wouldn't be able to get the ankle cuffs off.

Yes, all three were still sleeping in the one big bed in the locked second bedroom. Then he looked outside and swore. The fog was so thick he couldn't see to the corner. By the time he walked to the kitchen, the rain began.

"Damnit. How in hell can they take their flight in the goddamned rain?" He knew the answer. The flights would be scrubbed for the day. He went to his notebook computer and punched up the Internet and sent his E-mail to the Scimitar.

"Rain and fog here today, Thursday. No chance that the game can be played today. Hoping for tomorrow. All else is ready."

He had checked and found no incoming E-mail. He hadn't counted on feeding his guests for more than a meal or two. Now it looked like he had to give them something to eat at least for today. He'd wait until they were up, then go to the store.

Charlie had stocked the kitchen with a few essentials and some staples. He turned on a small radio and listened to the local news as he broke two eggs into a skillet and pushed down the toast. Just as the toast popped up, he sensed someone behind him. He spun around to find Beth standing there, bare-footed, the cuffs still on her ankles and wearing a long shirt she evidently had used as a nightgown. Her hair was rumpled but she had a curious little smile.

"The girls are still sleeping. I just wondered . . ." She looked up at him and her smile was full and open.

"It's just that I had this dream . . ." She sighed and turned away. "Whenever I have a sexy dream Marvin always helps me get over it. I thought that maybe . . ." Beth closed her eyes and shook her head. She stood tall, her full breasts showing under the T-shirt.

Charlie dropped the toast on the counter and turned toward her. "Look, it was just a dream. This isn't like you, Beth. Forget it. I have big plans and they don't include messing around."

"What's the matter, don't you like what you see?"

"Oh, damn yes. You've got a body a man dreams about and it's all right there in front of me."

"So?"

"The kids might come in."

"Lock the door."

"You do this often? Cheat on your husband?"

"Never have before." She shuffled toward him, the cuffs making it a slow, hard move. She kept her arms at her side and didn't stop until her breasts touched his chest.

"Woman!" He stared down at her. Slowly his arms came around her and hugged her to him. "Oh, damn, you sure know how to get a man going. Hell, where?"

"Right here on the floor. Get out of your clothes. I hate to make love to a man with his clothes on. Reminds me of high school."

He let go of her and pulled at his belt. He stepped back, then suddenly self-conscious, he turned when he pulled down his pants. Just as he reached for his shorts, Beth grabbed a four-inch paring knife off the counter and swung the blade at Charlie's side.

"Hey," he bellowed. He tried to jump away, but the blade caught his side and slashed a two-inch-long gash a quarter of an inch deep. Charlie brayed in pain and surprise. His right fist came down like a hammer and slammed into Beth's wrist jolting the knife from her hand. He caught her right wrist and twisted her arm behind her and pushed her away from the ledge where two more knives lay.

"You fucking bitch! You tried to kill me." He spun her around and slapped her face hard, knocking her head sideways.

"Almost," she said. "Hit me again you sonofabitch. I almost had you. Another two or three inches and you'd be down on the floor with me clubbing you with a frying pan."

He grabbed one of her breasts and twisted it until she screamed. Charlie snorted.

"I almost had you, Charlie, you lying sonofabitch."

Charlie pushed her away, grabbed a kitchen towel, and pressed it over his cut side. "Woman, get back with your kids before I change my mind and kill you right here. I don't need you or the kids anymore. Remember that. I don't need you. Move." He shouted the last word and she shuffled her feet forward a few inches at a time until she was out of the room.

Charlie looked down at his side. Blood oozed from the wound around the towel. He moved the towel and looked again. It wasn't as deep as he feared. No more than a quarter of an inch slice. He could fix that. Charlie took a small towel and cut it into a square and folded it four times. The Arab used clear tape and fastened the pad in place over the cut, then tied strips of the towel around his waist as a bandage. It would have to do until he got to a doctor. At least it would stop the bleeding. Maybe he'd get some bandages and disinfectant at a drugstore later.

Charlie looked at his eggs on the stove. Burned. He threw them out, cleaned the skillet, then broke three eggs in the pan and fried them sunny side up. That bitch wasn't going to stop him from making his breakfast.

He checked on the prisoners. They had tried to open a window, but he had nailed shut the one in their bedroom. Now he locked the door and put a straight-backed chair under the handle so it wouldn't open even unlocked.

At eight that morning, Charlie called the Clooney home number on his cell phone. It rang only once.

"Yeah, Clooney."

"Yeah, this is Charlie. You won't be flying today, right?"

"Charlie, you bastard. I'm gonna find you and kill you."

"Not a chance, Marvin. It's a big town. No flying today, right?"

"Right, they canceled, said to take the morning off. I want to talk to Beth."

"Not a chance. She tried to knife me this morning."

"Good for her. Hope she cut you good."

"Just a scratch. You get on that bird tomorrow and do your thing and your family will be safe and well and you'll be a hundred thousand dollars richer. Remember that."

"Not doing this for the fucking money. I want my family safe. You've got to guarantee me that, or I get sick and can't fly. I can do that and you can't stop me."

"I can. I will. If you play sick and don't go with the first flight, you lose one member of your family. Simple, deadly. Your choice."

The line went silent for a long pause. Charlie heard some quick breathing and sniffing. Then Clooney cleared his throat. "No, don't do that. I'll be on the first flight we take with the weapons. Just keep my family safe. You feeding them?"

"More than they deserve. Now shut up and pray for good weather tomorrow."

Charlie hung up without saying good-bye.

He sat at the kitchen table going over his priorities. He had his men and a crew ready. They had rented a chopper large enough to move the bomb. He had arranged for a storage trailer where they could crate the bomb and mark it as well-drilling machinery. Then they would get it ready for a transport back to Seattle. There in the bustle of a larger port, they could find ways to move it on a ship or fly it to one of three possible countries where he would be welcome to hold his auction.

As soon as the Eagle was designated as missing and out of formation by the Air Force, Charlie would roll out his rented Gulfstream business jet.

The pilot on standby said it would be a 2,300-mile trip. Well within the range of the Gulfstream II. At 580 miles an hour the flight would take a little over four hours. He figured it out on a piece of paper. The Eagle jet would be flying on the deck most of the way which would cut its speed to about 900 miles an hour. At that speed and taking a few detours, it still should make the flight in just under three hours. So Clooney would have landed well before Charlie could arrive.

He would phone his team the time of departure so they could be near the landing area in their chopper before the Scimitar arrived. Yes, it should work. He would communicate with his team by cell phone. They would come and pick him up if possible.

Charlie leaned back and grinned. Twenty million dollars. Oh, yeah. He hadn't decided where he would settle down. England maybe, or the south of France. He could pick up French easily. Australia was a thought, or even the USA. He could take his time deciding once he had the cash in the bank.

Oh, yes, this was an exciting time. He heard someone pounding on a door. Beth, probably wanted some food for her kids. He had Cheerios and milk. That would have to do.

LONDON, ENGLAND

The Marshall Gulfstream II business jet lifted off from Heathrow International Airport at 10:00 A.M., gained five hours on the time changes flying nonstop to New York, and arrived there after a six-and-a-half-hour flight at 11:34. Two Marshall people helped them get through customs quickly and back into the air.

Their refueled jet headed out for a 2,580-mile jaunt to Las Vegas, and made the trip in five hours but also gained three hours on the clock and landed at a little after 2:00 P.M. They dropped off Wade Thorne and the others. The jet took on more fuel, then headed for Seattle where Kat would land to change to a commercial flight. She would land a little after 4:30 P.M. and grab an already booked flight with Alaska Airlines heading for Deadhorse.

In Vegas, Wade picked up a reserved rental car, a Mercury Grand Marquis, and a cell phone. He headed for the dam and phoned first to let them know he was on schedule. The manager there had been briefed by the FBI as to why he was coming.

He arrived in time to join the last tour of the day. There were twenty people in the group along with one of the Hoover Dam officials in charge of publicity. After taking the tour, Wade found half a dozen places where security seemed weak or relaxed. But a nuclear bomb overhead wouldn't worry about weak spots. He talked with the tour leader and the PR man after the tour.

"Have you noticed any suspicious people here lately?" Wade asked.

"Yeah, had one old coot who claimed the dam was ruining the fishing in the whole western United States. He was a nut case pure and simple. No threat."

"Anything else?"

The tour leader and the PR man looked at each other. "No," the PR man said. "We had the vice president here a month ago, and we did a total electronics area sweep before he came. Found nothing."

"Have you ever had an alert here about any type of sabotage?"

The PR man laughed. "What are they going to do, drop a bomb over the side? Our engineers estimated that a two-thousand-pound bomb would only make a small dent in the dam."

"Actually I was thinking of something more powerful than that," Wade said.

The manager frowned. "What's larger than that?" Recognition washed over his face. "Hey, that would probably do it. We have worst-case scenarios covering a nuclear blast. But not a hell of a lot we could do. You're just talking worst case here, right?"

"It's always good to have the worst-case situation plotted out. It's never going to happen, but we need to make these checks from time to time."

"Might be interesting. Anything else, Mr. Thorne?"

"How about a tour of the guts of the place, where the public doesn't get to go?"

"Sure. Our instructions from Washington were for total cooperation."

There wasn't much else. Some tunnels, some access areas for service, a computer room where continual scanning of the dry face of the dam was done to register and keep track of small cracks.

"The small cracks serve as pressure releases in certain parts of the dam," the PR man said. "That way we know which ones to repair and which ones can wait."

Back on the top an hour later, Wade asked the last question. "Have you had any more thoughts about any threats to the dam or the people who run it?"

The PR man and the supervising engineer who Wade had talked with before shook their heads.

"Doubt if we're high up on any of the terrorists' hit list," the engineer said.

"Strange, that's what the FBI man in charge of the Oklahoma City office said six months before the bombing there." Wade walked out to his car. It hadn't been much of a research job, but there wasn't much to investigate. If this was the target, there would be no prep work the terrorists had to do. No inside contacts, just fly over and drop the bomb and get out of the way.

He drove back to Las Vegas and checked in at his hotel. There wasn't much more he could do. He sent an E-mail to Mr. Marshall reporting what he hadn't found, and suggested that he go on to Mountain Home, Idaho, the next day.

He had an immediate response. "Go to Mountain Home. The rest of us may join you there."

In the Las Vegas hotel, Wade thought about his career. He had been set in the CIA until his wife was murdered by a foreign agent aiming for him. It hit him so hard he simply quit and went fishing and back to his horse ranch in Idaho for a year. His savings ran out about the time Mr. Marshall contacted him. The first time he had said he wasn't interested. He'd had an offer to work on a Formula One auto-racing team as a substitute driver. It took him two months to get back in the groove of racing but he'd been in three races and managed not to crash any of the cars.

Then the lead driver had a wreck, a bad one, and wound up in a wheelchair for the rest of his life. The same week Wade quit and went fly fishing on the River of No Return in the primitive section of Idaho.

But how long can you fish? Three months later, he accepted a new offer by Mr. Marshall and flew to London to begin putting the team together. He stored his snowboard and buckled down to the Specialists. That left plenty of time to work on his Italian cooking and three trips to Egypt where he did some research on a little known pharaoh.

Now they had the team formed and everyone had been bloodied over a two-year period and they were moving into more important missions. One element here he enjoyed was that they never had to stop and think about what ramifications their work might have on the United States position in the world or its foreign policies. The CIA thinking was far in the background. They worked for the good of all people, everywhere.

SAN FRANCISCO, CALIFORNIA

While Wade worked the dam, Ichi checked out 3Com Park, formerly called Candlestick Park. They couldn't be sure yet that the target would be for a nuke. The terrorist list had been made years ago, and had concentrated on places where there were large numbers of people at one time. Sports stadiums were often listed.

Ichi contacted the general manager at the park and found that Mr. Marshall had talked to him that morning. The story was that they were checking out the safety ramifications of various places that had large concentrations of people. The idea of an atomic or even a terrorist attack wasn't mentioned. Ichi had the run of the park. A guide showed him around. His name was Arthur and he'd been at the park since it opened.

"This is behind the scene at the scoreboard," Arthur said, unlocking a door and showing Ichi inside. "Nobody gets to come back here. Takes one electronics wizard repairman full time to keep this monster in full operation."

Ichi had the entire tour, and noted several spots where large explosives could be planted to bring total panic to the crowd and achieve a big body count just from the stampede. He filed it for future reference and wound up his tour and contacted Mr. Marshall who told him to fly to the air base in Mountain Home, Idaho.

DENVER, COLORADO

Roger had limited cooperation when he went to Mile High Stadium. The general manager had taken a call from the FBI, but said the idea was crazy and he didn't have time for it. He turned Roger over to a PR assistant who took him on a limited tour of the stadium. During the whole time they talked football, and the Broncos and their chances for the coming season.

Roger found that the entrances and exits to the stadium were poor to say the least, and would be ideal for small explosions to block them before the terrorists set off the main blast. The explosions and panic would be devastating.

He talked his guide into a walk on the playing field. Roger stood, looked up at the stands, and could almost feel the presence of seventy-six thousand cheering fans. He couldn't help it, he did a few moves and made a run down the field.

The guide waited for him.

"Happened before?" Roger asked.

The guide shrugged. "Yeah, but it seems to make a lot of guys happy. What's to hurt?"

Two hours later, Roger phoned in his report to London, and on his way out of the stadium, grabbed a copy of the *Denver Post*. The headline screamed out at him: FERTILIZER BOMB PLOT FOILED.

He read the story. "Early today, Sheriff Wilson of Weld County, just north of Denver, captured two tons of fertilizer and chemicals needed to construct a fertilizer bomb at a farm near Fort Lupton. Sheriff Wilson said all the ingredients were there for making a bomb but they had not been put together yet.

"A local merchant said he sold the men who had rented the farm six hundred pounds of the fertilizer just two days ago. He had no reason to suspect they weren't farmers as they said they were."

Roger gripped the paper hard, ran to the street, hailed a cab, and went to the nearest car rental firm. He rented a car and drove as fast as he could to Fort Lupton about thirty miles north of Denver. He left Denver on freeway U.S. 76 and then turned off on U.S. 85, which led directly to Fort Lupton. He found the town, and then the farm cooperative where the newspaper said the fertilizer was purchased. Inside, he talked with the owner.

"Yeah, I own this place," said Lyle Broderson. "You're not from the newspapers are you?"

"No. I'm an investigator. You said in the story that the two men looked dark, like they may have been Arabs?"

"They were dark. I'm sure they were Arabs. They killed

my brother. Just glad that the sheriff found the bomb. I didn't know that's what they would do with it. I sell tons of fertilizer every year."

"Has the FBI been here?"

"Sure, they talked to me early. Told them all I know."

Roger thanked the merchant and found a phone booth. A minute later Mr. Marshall came on the line. Roger told him about the bomb plot that was busted near Denver.

"If we're thinking Mile High Stadium in Denver, it would take more than one bomb to hit the place," Roger said. "Three or four bombs probably."

"Stay around there and see what else you can find out. I'll call my contact with the FBI and see if he can get some kind of clearance and cooperation with the FBI for you there."

"In the meantime, I'll do some snooping at other co-ops that sell fertilizer. Usually just one in each small town. If bin Laden has one bomb going, there might be four or five more. I'll see what I can dig up."

"I'm sure the FBI will put out a news bulletin to all Law Enforcement Agencies warning them of the situation and maybe putting a freeze on any more fertilizer sales in large quantities."

"I'll keep you posted," Roger said.

"Should I come out with some more team members?"

"Might be a good idea. Come here not Mountain Home. Denver might just be our target for the Big One. This does smell like bin Laden more than the other two terrorists. Just a hunch. I'm staying at the Rocky Mountain Plaza in Denver. Let me know if you're coming in."

Roger wondered if he should talk to Sheriff Wilson. He didn't think he could learn anything that the store owner didn't know. He seemed to be personally involved. Instead, Roger picked out a town about twenty miles away, still in the farming area, and drove there.

He stopped at Brighton, seven miles south along the highway to Denver, which boasted 14,764 residents. He saw the Farmers Feed & Supply Cooperative just off the main street and drove in. He found the owner/manager and introduced himself.

"Good to meet you, Roger, I'm Halley Milner. What can I do for you?"

"You heard about the fertilizer bomb scare up at Fort Upton. I wondered if any strangers have bought or tried to buy fertilizer from you?"

"Not a big time of the year to sell fertilizer. Only sold two loads and both to long-time resident farmers I know. No Arabs got any fertilizer from me to make a bomb. We make the buyers sign for it now, and even if I know them, they have to show two picture IDs. Don't know what other dealers do, but that's our policy."

"Sounds like a good idea. Any idea what dealer might not be so particular who he sold to in this area?"

"Don't like to rat on anybody, but old Brill Hemphill over in Lafayette ain't too particular. We got an association and all, and he's a member. Almost got thrown out two years ago."

"You any special hate for this guy?"

"Nope. He's an idiot, that's all. Might go over and see him. Almost due west of here past the interstate. Maybe fifteen miles all told."

"Thanks, I might check him out."

On the way to Lafayette, Roger spotted three more feed sales places that also sold fertilizer. He checked them all. No luck with a prospect.

He arrived at Lafayette at about five o'clock and hit the Hemphill Farmers' Co-op. Brill himself wasn't there. George asked his by-rote question.

The salesman, who said he was Jake, looked around to see if anyone was nearby. He moved closer to Roger.

"Cain't say for sure, but there was two guys in here about two weeks ago who sure looked like Arabs to me. They bought a ton of Xcello fertilizer in hundreds and we loaded up two pickups. Said they was farming over by Dacono. They had some IDs but Brill never even looked at them. Don't usually sell a ton of Xcello this time of year."

Roger took the name of the buyer and the salesman

knew the farm. It had recently been sold. A mile the other side of Dacono right on Highway 52. Two big red barns and a low rambling farm house. Well kept up place.

Roger thanked Jake and found a telephone booth. He wanted to tell Mr. Marshall he might have a lead. The industrialist had already left for New York. Roger didn't bother calling him on the plane. Instead, he slid into his rented car and headed for Dacono. If they were Arab, he didn't have the slightest idea what he would do. He didn't even have a handgun with him, a weapon was always too much hassle on the airlines. He'd figure out what to do when he got there.

☆ TWENTY-FIVE ☆

DEADHORSE, ALASKA

After a stop in Fairbanks, the Alaska Airlines jet landed on the new gravel-surfaced runway at the airport at Deadhorse. Kat had been setting her watch with every time change but she was still surprised to see that it was 11:30 P.M. and the sun was up. It was summertime in Alaska, perpetual summertime, when the sun would make a feeble attempt at setting before it soared into the sky again for another long, long sunlit day.

She had slept most of the way from Seattle, and knew she had to get on local time. She had gained eight hours since leaving London at ten that morning. So far it had been a twenty-three-hour day for her. The only hotel in town was just across the gravel street from the airport. She walked there with her travel bag. Kat had learned to travel light working with the Specialists.

She had looked up everything she could find on Deadhorse before she left London. The town itself had from twenty to forty full-time residents. The huge work force was considered a transient group and not residents. The men drilled for oil and moved it down the pipeline to Valdez, Alaska.

An advance reservation had been made at the Prudhoe Bay Hotel for her and she slumped on the soft bed in her room. It was not what she had expected. The place had 180 rooms and some of the management people from the oil fields stayed there. The whole hotel was made from combinations of trailers, the house size that usually sit up on blocks in trailer parks. A few were even set two high for a second floor. It was just after one in the morning when she lay down to sleep. It had been a long and wild day.

The next morning Kat woke up and tried to remember what day it was. Her watch told her it was Friday, the second day from London. She dressed and went downstairs. The restaurant at the hotel served breakfast all day. She had two large glasses of orange juice and pancakes. The whole place only had three customers and one waitress.

One of the two men stood out. He was striking with light brown hair, and a complexion that looked suntanned. She figured he was in his mid-forties. She worked on her hotcakes and looked up when someone stopped by her booth. She glanced into green eyes and a smile.

"Hi, looks like we're in the middle of the breakfast trade. Not hard to spot a newcomer in a town this size." He held out his hand. "Phil Lawrence, here on a research project."

She blinked, then nodded. He was the striking man she had noticed before. She put down her fork and took his hand. It was soft. Kat smiled. "Katherine Jones, a writer here on an assignment. Not much of a town, is it?"

"Not much." He hesitated. "Well, I'm on my way. Have to get some work done while the sun shines."

They both laughed. "I'll probably see you again in this crush of people," he said.

He waved and walked out the door. It was automatic with her. She pegged him at six feet three inches tall, and a lean 175 pounds. She frowned and went back to her hotcakes and sausage. There were three or four small businesses in this minuscule town. Kat decided to walk the street and see what they were. She would fake her cover by writing now and then in her notebook computer. Kat took it out of her shoulder bag, turned it on, and put down her thoughts on the man she had just met. Phil Lawrence, his age, appearance, and the color of his hair and eyes.

She finished breakfast and did her tour. No sidewalks, just one street. Everything here was built on permafrost. Kat knew little about that feature of most far northern areas. It had to do with the ground temperature and zero degrees and the amount of water in the soil and how far down the ground froze and stayed that way. She knew that in some places the permafrost went four thousand feet deep, and in other areas there was little or none. However much it presented definite problems in construction with the frost heaving upward in the winter and then in warm summer months losing its weight-bearing ability—even large buildings could sag and fall apart.

She walked the one block-long business section. The four businesses were all slanted toward the oil drilling and pumping work that made up the only industry in the area. Well, almost. She heard there was one commercial fisherman who lived there.

So far that morning she had seen few women. One at the desk of the hotel, the others were waitresses at the restaurant. Kat had dressed as she figured an experienced traveling writer would. She had on a good pair of brown slacks, a brown button-up shirt, and a light brown jacket. Her shoes were serviceable, soft-soled tennies. She was glad for the shoes after two minutes walking the gravel street.

She talked to men in two of the small firms. Both were busy and gently worked around her. It felt like she was in the Old West where there was one woman in town for every two hundred men. She saw a welding shop, a machine shop with dozens of metal working machines, a helicopter rental firm, and one store that had only oil-drilling supplies.

"Sure, the big companies have their own stocks, twenty times as big as mine," a talkative man at the supply store told her. "When they burn up a certain part, they come charging in here to get one to use until their plane flies in a new supply from Detroit or Pittsburgh or wherever the parts are made. Yeah, they need me. Put that in your story, lady."

Kat thanked him and typed in some notes about the firm in her notebook computer, then she went back outside. It was warmer than she expected. She had read that sometimes in midsummer the temperature rose to ninety degrees. She wondered what that would do to the permafrost.

Kat went back to Fitzgerald Helicopters, and talked to the man behind a small counter. The building was a trailer like the rest in town, not high enough for a hangar. She wondered how they covered the birds in bad weather.

"Hey, I told you I'm writing an article on this area. Would you have a chopper and a pilot available for me to take a guided tour of the oil fields, the start of the pipeline, and the company town?"

He was in his thirties, blond, and had a grin that lit up his face.

"Hey, you bet." He held out his hand. "I'm Hal Fitzgerald, your pilot. When do you want to go?"

She took his hand in a firm grip. "Hi, I'm Katherine Jones. Good to meet you. Go? Probably tomorrow after I get my feet on the ground. I'm in from London. That was a wild series of airplane rides. I'm still on London time, which would be just after dinner."

"London? You're a long way from home. Not a lot of tourists up here. I used to fly at Niagara Falls. I could get a charter just about anytime, anyday, I wanted to. Got boring the same old route."

"A lot of other business up here?"

"Not much. Mostly when one of the oil companies loses a bird or it's down for repair and they need a replacement."

"You rent out choppers to people not in the business?"

"Now and then. Have one out now to some guy who says he's doing a scientific study on the ozone layer. I don't know much about that. Out in space somewhere."

"I bet that was Phil Lawrence."

"Could be." He looked in a book on the counter. "Yep, right on. How did you know?"

"Met him at breakfast. Not a lot of strangers in town. He's a scientist?"

"Said so. Has an Italian pilot's license and a ticket like mine to fly choppers."

"Why would someone studying the ozone layer need a chopper?"

"He said something about triangulation for his instruments or something like that."

"Well, I'm off on the rest of my walking tour. I understand I can't see much of the oil companies area if I'm not with a tour group."

"That's what they say. If you're a customer of mine I can take you on a pickup tour of the company village. Over two thousand men in there now working twelve-hour shifts seven days a week."

"They don't get time off?"

"Yeah, they rotate them out of here to Seattle or Fairbanks every so often, but I don't know the timetable. It's mostly just hard work around here."

"Thanks, Hal. I'll talk to you later about that chopper. Maybe I can whittle down your price."

"Maybe, but probably not."

"Hey, you don't get that many customers." She put on her best smile, turned, and walked out the front door into the warm weather of the Prudhoe Bay summer.

MOUNTAIN HOME, IDAHO

That same Friday morning, Beth Clooney woke up crying. Her ankles were still bound together with those tough plastic strips. Charlie had taken them off the kids, knowing she wouldn't let them run away without her. She tried the door: still locked.

Beth hobbled back to the girls and checked on them. Both sleeping soundly. She couldn't let them know what was happening. Already they were frightened enough. Beth slipped on her skirt and blouse. She had to think of something. If there ever was a time, this was it. Beth set her jaw. She might be able to get to him yet. She would simply do anything, anything at all, to protect her girls and to save her husband.

Beth went back to the door and knocked on it five times. A moment later she heard footsteps, then the door unlocked and he pushed it open.

"Up already?"

"Yes, the bathroom."

"That could be a problem. There's a window, a big one."

"So stay with me, I'm not proud or bashful."

"Girls sleeping?"

"Yes, and if you touch them, I'll kill you with my bare hands."

Charlie looked at her a moment, the near smile faded rapidly and he nodded. "Hell, I'm no pervert. Come on to the bathroom."

"Take the cuffs off my ankles?"

"Not a chance. I should have killed you yesterday when you stabbed me. You're damn lucky I didn't."

In the bathroom she didn't even wait for him to turn around. She pulled up her skirt and started to pull down her panties. She was still covered by her long blouse. He turned at last, then opened the door and stepped outside. Score one point for her. He had some feelings after all.

"What are you getting out of all this?"

He answered from around the door. "Getting? I'll be rich. I should clear well over nineteen million dollars. You know how much money that is?"

He came around the corner and watched her pull down her skirt.

"Relax. It will be over soon. Cloudy outside but no rain. Weather report on the radio said rain moving in rapidly.

"They'll fly," he said. "I checked with flight ops and they said to suit up and be ready. Good chance they would fly."

He took her back to the room. Out the window they

could see rain begin to pound against the windows and thunder rolled.

"Shit," Charlie said. "Another lost day. Does it always rain in this hellhole of a country?"

"Only on nights, Sundays, and flight days. You lose again, Charlie."

He kicked the wall, then went out and slammed the door. She heard him lock it. Beth looked around. She needed something sharp to cut the plastic cuffs off her ankles. There was nothing in the room that would work.

Before she finished her inventory the girls woke up and wanted to go to the bathroom. She called to Charlie. He told them to go ahead and waited for them to come back to the room.

"Have Cheerios ready for you in a minute. Then I have to go get something to feed all four of us. We're stuck here for another day. Damn flight has to go tomorrow."

"You check with Flight Ops?"

"Don't need to. I know the procedures out there. They won't fly this flight in this weather." He rubbed his eyes, then the top of his head.

"Fucking headache." He scowled and massaged his head as the girls came back.

Ten minutes later she saw him through the bedroom window as he drove away. Now, she had about an hour to get free. How? She searched the room again. Nothing in her skirt pocket, not even a nail file. She looked at the window. She couldn't get out of it with her ankles bound. A mirror on the dresser caught her attention and she grinned. She used one of her shoes with the hard leather heel to smash the mirror.

It broke into a dozen long pieces and two fell out. One was sharp and big enough to hold. She picked it up carefully and sat on the bed, then began sawing at the tough plastic ankle cuffs with her homemade knife. Beth ripped up the sheet and wrapped a piece of the cloth around the bottom of the jagged chunk of glass for a handle. Then she sawed again at the plastic. The strip was less than a quarter of an inch wide and half that thick. But it was tough.

After half an hour of sawing at it, Beth was halfway through. Another ten minutes and she felt the plastic snap in half. She pulled the wraps off her ankles and was free. Beth tried the door. Locked, the window nailed shut. But now she could break out the glass.

Beth used her shoe again, broke out the glass from the two-foot-wide window, and made sure all of the shards were gone at the bottom. She had just let the oldest girl out the window and dropped her two feet to the ground when Charlie's car came through the now drizzling rain with the horn blasting. He ran up to the window, picked up Clarice, and pushed her back through the window, then jumped up and crawled through it himself.

Charlie had screamed something at her but she didn't understand until he was inside. Then he slapped her so hard it staggered her. Beth set her feet and held up her fists. She'd taken a self-defense course years ago. All she had to do was kick Charlie hard in the crotch. He didn't give her a chance.

He ripped the blouse off her back, tore off her bra, and unlocked the door. Charlie pushed Beth and the kids into another room. This one had no bed, no dresser, and the window here had been nailed tightly shut as well.

"Enjoy your new home. You don't eat again until it gets dark." He went out and locked the door. Beth slumped to the floor and leaned against the wall. Tears spilled out of her eyes and she couldn't keep from crying. Both girls hurried to her and sat beside her.

"Don't cry, Mommy. It's going to be all right. Daddy will come and hit the bad man and knock him down and take us all home."

Beth held both her girls. She couldn't think of anything to say. She knew that Marvin wouldn't come. He had no idea where they were. The cellular phone Charlie had used couldn't be traced in a town like this. If they were going to get out of this alive, she had to use her head, or her body. She realized she was bare to the waist, but the girls didn't say anything. She held them to her so tightly they winced.

Beth stopped crying. No time for that. She had to figure out something to do to get them out of this.

DACONO, COLORADO

It was dark when Roger turned off U.S. 25 north into the small town of Dacono. He continued through the two-stoplight town, and two miles beyond saw a pair of large red barns near the road and a new rambling split-stone farmhouse. This should be the place. He drove on past a half mile and parked in a field just off the highway.

On the drive, he had done his planning. First a recon. He'd see what he could find. If the barns were locked, that would be a good indication of a problem. What farmer locked up his barn?

When Roger used his SEAL techniques of silent approach, he found lights on in the house, but the two barns and three smaller buildings were dark. He slid through the cool mountain night silently toward the first barn. It had a haymow door on the peak, a large drive-in door for machinery at ground level. To one side was a man-sized opening with a large white-painted Z on the cross boards. The moon hid behind high clouds drifting over. He waited for a sizable cloud to shade the area, then he ran to the small door and tried the pull handle. It opened.

Inside, Roger found inky darkness. He let his eyes adjust to the even more intense dark, but it didn't help. He took out the pencil flash he always carried and checked around.

A barn. Smell of cows and manure, strong odor of urine. Cows had been here, but none now. The large area in front of the stalls was empty, but had been covered with hay.

Five minutes later, he was sure there was no bomb or sacks of fertilizer in this barn. He slipped out the back door, skirted a large pile of cow manure mixed with straw. He edged to the side of the barn and peered around.

The moment he touched the far side of the barn, two

yard lights snapped on, flooding the whole area around the barns with daylight. He heard a screen door slam and looked up to see three men running out of the house, all armed with automatic rifles.

"Which position?" one of the voices asked.

"Fourteen and fifteen. Could be one or two of them. That's on the off-side barn."

Roger turned and sprinted into the darkness behind the off barn. When he was out of the glow of the lights, he slid to the ground and turned so he could see behind him. The three men charged around the barn like well-trained infantry. They checked the area, kicked out hiding spots near the barn, and then came back together at the edge of the light.

"Where is the bastard?" one man asked.

The reply came in a foreign tongue that Roger didn't know.

The three stood talking a minute more, then one ran back toward the house. The other two went to the barn closer to the house. In the bright lights, Roger could see them checking a back and side door on the building. Looking at the locks? He couldn't tell. Then they, too, went back to the house.

Roger was curious about the second barn. It must hold something they didn't want found. But what? It could be a prize herd of dairy cows—or a fertilizer bomb. He checked the ground around him. It hadn't been plowed recently. He found what he was looking for, two fist-sized rocks. He walked gently toward the second barn. A moment later the yard lights snapped off. Roger ran then, until he was within thirty feet of the big building. He threw both rocks as hard as he could at the near side of the barn. At once, the lights came on again and a small siren wailed. Vibration sensors, Roger decided. Now he was sure there was something in that barn that the men there didn't want anyone to know about. There was no way he could get in there tonight.

The first automatic rifle fire caught him by surprise and he dove to the ground. They were random, none coming near him, but they were a warning to anyone trying to get into the barn.

Roger jogged back toward his car. After about twenty shots, the firing stopped. Roger drove away without lights until he came to the first crossroad that would take him back to the small town. It wouldn't have a hotel, but maybe a motel along the highway.

His recon was over. Now he needed a battle plan and for that he would need some troops. The sheriff's men, the FBI, or maybe just the local fire department. The more he thought of it, the more he liked the plan. He would need a good bow, some arrows. Roger grinned as he drove back to find a bed for the night. One thing he remembered was a field of corn that grew almost up to the barns. Ah yes, a good old cornfield. Roger laughed. This was almost like being back in the SEALs.

★ TWENTY-SIX ★

DEADHORSE, ALASKA

Kat finished her tour well before noon, retreated to her room to write up some notes on her computer as if she were doing research for a story. She put down everything she could remember about the different men she had talked with. She said she had no idea what Phil Lawrence was doing, but there was little chance he was performing any legitimate research on the ozone layer.

She had dug into the ozone problem a year ago and this time came out of it more confused than before. Kat went to lunch at 12:30 more from habit than hunger. She stared at the menu for several minutes and at last ordered a fruit salad and orange juice.

The waitress had a tag that said she was Martha. She grinned.

"Yeah, I didn't figure you to be a meat and potatoes lady three times a day. Fruit salad and OJ coming up. You know for a long time I couldn't call it OJ, but now it doesn't bother me. You think he did it? I do. He did it. Yeah, he might have blanked it out, you know psychologically, doesn't remember it so doesn't think he could have done it." She giggled. "Sorry, some of the guys call me the running mouth. I'll have that salad for you in a shake."

Kat grinned as the young girl left. Nineteen, maybe

twenty, and probably the daughter of the owner and waiting her first chance to get out of here and down to Anchorage or maybe Seattle. She wondered how long Martha had lived in Deadwood. She'd ask her when she brought the order.

Someone knocked on the table as she thought about Martha. Kat looked up quickly.

"Oh, Mr. Lawrence."

He stood there in the same clothes he'd had on that morning and smiled. "I was wondering if this seat is taken? The place is so jam-packed. Would you mind sharing the table with me?"

She looked around and laughed. There were only six people in the whole restaurant. "Hey, the place is packed. I hadn't noticed. Yes, by all means, sit and relax and order whatever you want as long as you pay for it."

"Figures you wouldn't be a cheap date." He slid into the booth, his green eyes sparkling.

"You have a good morning researching the ozone layer?"

He frowned. "Now how would you know about that?"

"I'm a journalist. I ask a lot of people a lot of questions. I'm curious. How do you go about testing the ozone layer from down here? Would you use a spectroscope?"

He laughed and she liked the sound of it. Phil certainly was attractive. Good manners, and he had a job.

"I make it a policy never to talk about my work with people who aren't really interested. But, to answer your question, no, I wouldn't use a spectroscope. For that you need an in-hand specimen to examine, and I certainly can't reach up thirty miles and pull down a sample."

He signaled to Martha who came over with a large smile and the body language to go with it that practically said "anytime you're ready." Phil gave his order, a hamburger with everything and a pot of coffee.

"I live on coffee," he said. Martha wrote down the order.

"Yes, Mr. Lawrence. I'll have the cook do you up a

great burger fast and get it right back here. Anything else I can do for you?"

The trite phrase became more than it sounded like and when he shook his head, she left reluctantly.

"You know Martha has a huge crush on you."

He shifted in the seat and nodded. "Yes, but I try to discourage her. She doesn't have much contact with men unless she goes out to the airport."

The food came and they ate in silence. Then they both hurried off to other tasks.

Kat fired off an E-mail:

"Mr. Marshall: Established here in Deadhorse. No evidence of any conspiracy. People are friendly. Only twenty residents in the town, so a stranger stands out. One man here says he's doing research into the ozone layer, which seems far-fetched. Should I stay another day here? Kat."

Late that afternoon after another tour of the town, Kat phoned the restaurant and had them send up a hamburger and a strawberry milkshake for her dinner. That way she wouldn't run into Phil Lawrence again.

That Friday afternoon Phil Lawrence rocked back in the hotel chair and contemplated Kat Jones. Jones, a common name. She was not a common woman. She was sleek and slender and well proportioned and got his blood heating up every time he looked at her. She turned down his invitation for a drink, but maybe tonight after dinner she would be more receptive. A woman couldn't work all the time.

That afternoon he found her and followed her unnoticed. She did what he thought she would do, went back to all of the businesses and talked with them. Then she looked at the oil company compound and he imagined she was trying to find out how to get a tour of how and where the two thousand men lived during their off hours.

Phil talked to the man at the helicopter place and rented a sling that could be used to haul a heavy object.

There were only three empty business storage trailers in town that were available for rent. He had signed for one the first day he was there. They landed the chopper just in back of it and left the sling there. The trailer was modified so it had a large opening door along one side.

His right-hand man, Smith, was staying in the storage trailer during the day. He had reminded Phil that their two new men were coming in from Fairbanks that afternoon. Phil was on hand to meet the Alaska Airlines 737 jet passenger liner that landed on the gravel airstrip. They stood by as 128 men came off the plane, fresh back from their break in Fairbanks or on south in the other states.

The last two men off the plane stood looking around as if they didn't know where they were or where they were supposed to go. Smith walked over to them and talked a minute, then they went to the baggage area and picked up heavy suitcases. Smith brought them back and nodded to his boss. Phil waved them after him and led the way to the storage trailer.

Their names were Eldridge and Nelson. He spoke briefly to them once they were in the trailer.

"You'll stay at the hotel, eat at the café, and work here," he told them. "Not a lot to do for a day or two, but when it happens it will go down fast. What did you bring us from Fairbanks?"

The men pointed to the suitcases.

"You gentlemen do good work."

"Good. Now get over to the hotel, and tell them you're working with me on the ozone layer project, get rooms and rest up. I want both of you here tomorrow morning at eight A.M."

He left the suitcases with Smith. The men took flight bags with some clothes and personal goods and left for the hotel.

Now, all he could do was wait, and Phil Lawrence was not used to waiting.

That evening at dinner, he didn't see Kat. He asked Martha the waitress about it.

"Oh, Mr. Lawrence, she wasn't feeling too good so she had some supper sent up to her room." Martha paused. The top button on her blouse was open exposing generous cleavage. "Anything else I can do for you?" She bent over the table and her blouse swung out a little exposing more breast.

"Yes, Martha, there certainly is something you could do for me, but I can't mention it. Thanks anyway, Martha, for the preview."

She grinned and stood up. "Can't blame a girl for trying."

After his dinner, Lawrence went to the room he had seen Kat leave that morning. He knocked on the door. He heard her fix the chain, then the door edged open an inch.

"Yes, who is it?" Kat asked.

"Hey, Phil Lawrence. That offer of a drink still stands. I can bring them here to your room."

"I don't think so, Mr. Lawrence. Thanks anyway." She tried to shut the door but his shoe stopped it.

"Come on, just one drink to celebrate another day's end where the days never end. Starting to get on my nerves."

"I understand, but I really am not in the mood for a drink. I was about ready to get in bed with a good book."

He stepped back and kicked the door next to the knob. The screwed-in fitting in the door chain ripped out of the wall and the door slammed open. Kat had jumped back just before the kick.

Lawrence stepped into the room and closed the door. Kat moved back and stared hard at him. She was fully dressed.

"I don't know how you behave in Italy, Mr. Lawrence, but in this country you don't kick down a lady's door."

"Now, Miss Kat Jones, relax. I'm not going to hurt you. You and I are going to come to some kind of an understanding. If you won't have a drink with me, the least you can do is get undressed and go to bed with me. I assure you I will be as gentle or as rough as you wish. Strictly up to you. Don't try to scream or use any force. I'm good at the physical end of it. On the other hand, sometimes a little fight heightens the lovemaking. Don't you agree?"

DACONO, COLORADO

Roger stayed overnight in the motel room just outside of town. He was up at eight buying the material he needed. The bow was hardest. He found a used one in a small sporting goods section of a hardware store and bought six long arrows. He also took a gallon of paint thinner. He asked the clerk for some thin black wire and the clerk found it. At a fabric store, he bought two yards of cotton flannel and a pair of scissors. He was ready.

Back in his car, he called the hotel in Denver on his cell phone and checked for messages. There were three. The clerk read them:

" 'Roger. Hershel, Duncan, and I will be arriving in Denver at ten A.M. Friday. Meet us at your hotel. Marshall.' "

"Second message was: 'Anything more on your suspect? Heard about one fertilizer bomb takeover there. Same people?' The third message was: 'Roger and Mr. Marshall. Ichi here, nothing happening in San Francisco that I can find. Shall I meet you in Denver?' "

"Yes, thanks for the messages. If anyone else asks for me, tell them that I'm hung up in Dacono until about noon. I'll contact them after that at the hotel."

Roger drove east to the suspect farm, went past the two big barns and down the road three miles, then came back and parked a mile away in a driveway where heavy farm machinery went into a field. He took his gear, the bow and arrows, the paint thinner, scissors, the wire, and cloth with him to a small clump of trees half a mile from the suspect farm. There he strung the bow and practiced with the six arrows he had, careful not to break any. He could shoot with some accuracy at thirty yards. All he had to do was hit the barn. He used the scissors and cut the cotton flannel in foot-wide strips, folded them, and wrapped them around three of the arrows with the flannel almost at the arrowhead.

He practiced with two of them, shooting them into an already harvested field. It took a lot of power to get the clumsily wrapped arrows thirty yards. He might have to go closer. He wrapped the three other arrows and fastened the cloth tightly on all of them with the black wire. Then he was ready.

Now he moved with extreme caution as he went across a fence toward the farm. He doubted if they would have the vibration sensors out this far. He went another fifty yards and came to the corn. It was field corn, seven feet tall and not yet ready for picking. The sea of wide green leaves covered him completely as he walked through it heading for the barn. When he was fifty yards from the back of the locked-up barn, he paused and watched the whole area. He worked his way closer but remained hidden. He could see the house between the barns. There were two pickup trucks in the yard, but he saw no activity. Good. He brought up his gear to the thirty-yard point. He was still covered by the tall corn, and could move up another ten yards if he had to.

Roger took out his cell phone and dialed 911.

"This is Weld County Emergency."

"Yes, driving by two big barns east of Dacono. One of the barns is on fire. Better bring the sheriff, too. Somebody told me they had a fertilizer bomb in the barn."

"Is that about two miles east of Dacono?"

"Yes."

"Who is calling, please?"

Roger hung up the phone. He opened the paint thinner can and saturated the six cloth bands on the arrows with paint thinner. Each band was about three inches thick. He lifted the bow, nocked an arrow, and lit the cloth on fire. Roger pulled the arrow back to the limit and aimed it at the roof of the barn. It was a shingle roof and looked as dry as a desert in summertime. He fired the arrow. It sailed out, hit the side of the barn ten feet from the roof, and fell to the ground. The next arrow sailed higher, hit the very edge of the roof, and stuck. He moved up ten yards and fired two more arrows. One hit the roof and the arrowhead stuck in the shingles. A small fire had started on the roof from the second arrow. He fired the last two and both hit the roof, but one rolled off to the ground. Now three arrows were starting to burn the roof. In the half hour that it would take the local volunteer fire department from Dacono or Fort Upton to arrive, the whole roof should be on fire. He took all of his gear and walked back through the cornfield. He stashed the bow, paint thinner, and scissors in a small dry irrigation canal.

He dialed 911 again.

"Weld County Emergency. Fire or police?"

"Fire. A big barn is burning about seven miles west of Fort Upton. It's really roaring."

"Thank you, we already have that fire. Units have been dispatched."

Roger hung up and walked back to his car. Before he got there he heard sirens coming from the west, that would be Dacono's volunteers. He hoped they were good. Roger looked over at the barn. The back of the roof was burning, but it didn't look like the rest of it had caught. They should be able to save it, but they'd have to go inside. He drove toward the fire and saw a dozen other cars there. In some places a barn fire became a social occasion.

Two red pumper fire trucks swung into the fire and almost at once they had hoses working on the barn. Roger was close enough that he saw one man standing in front of the truck-sized large door on the barn arguing with a fireman. The door must still be locked. A minute later a fireman came up with three-foot bolt cutters and sliced off the padlock. They pushed the big doors open and firemen vanished inside.

A moment later two sheriff's cars whined into the yard. Roger moved out of his car and walked up closer. A man began shouting at one of the deputies.

"This is private property, you have no right to come on our land, let alone go inside this building."

"Tell it to the judge," the deputy said and three of them ran inside the barn. Roger walked closer where a group of ten spectators watched. No fire had shown on the front of the barn. The smoke had changed from black to white.

Five minutes later, the deputies and two firemen pushed

an extended Ford van out of the barn and well into the yard. The doors were all open. The deputies found the three men who lived there and handcuffed them.

"Look at that," one of the spectators said. "Deputy told me that van is all rigged as a rolling fertilizer bomb. Like the one they used in Oklahoma City. Be damned. Right here in our little county."

The deputies came around then and told everyone that they would have to move back at least a half mile.

"Is it really a fertilizer bomb?" Roger asked.

The deputy nodded. "Sure as hell is. If it got set off it would flatten all these buildings around here for a quarter of a mile. Huge damned thing. Somebody called in a tip."

By that time, the fire was almost out. The three men from the farm were stuffed in a patrol car and driven away. Two more sheriff cars arrived with two officers in each.

Roger walked back to his car. He'd love to be in on the questioning of the two bombers. No chance out here. At the car, he took out the cell phone and called the hotel. He asked for Mr. Marshall's room. The desk patched him through.

"Hello, Marshall here."

"Mr. Marshall, Roger. I'm on my way back to Denver. Looks like another of the fertilizer bombs has been found, and two bombers captured by the county sheriff. I'm sure the FBI are on their way here from Fort Lupton."

"I would guess you had some part in the affair."

"True, I'll explain it all later. I wonder if this will knock out bin Laden's plan to blow up Denver? If these bombers are indeed part of bin Laden's operation."

"Working on that. The FBI tells me that they defused another fertilizer bomb about fifty miles below Denver last week. That would make three strikes for somebody. If there's a fourth bomb, it might not be used."

"Good. See you at the hotel in about an hour."

•   •   •

At the Rocky Mountain Plaza Hotel, Roger went to his room and changed clothes, then called Mr. Marshall. Everyone had gathered in his room, 1204. Roger knocked on the door and went inside.

"How the hell did you do that one all by yourself?" Duncan asked.

He told them.

"My contacts in the FBI tell me that there may be another bomb. When they questioned some of the captured men, they hinted that there are four bombs. The football stadium was the target."

"So the FBI is working at finding the other one?" Roger asked.

"Tell me they have fifty agents flooding the small towns around Denver. They have contacted every fertilizer seller in the state and asked about suspicious sales. Right now, they're following up on ten of them."

"So, was this the Big One?" Hershel asked.

"Could have been," Mr. Marshall said. "Four huge bombs at the four exits at that stadium could have killed twenty, maybe thirty thousand."

"Wade find anything at the big dam?"

"Nothing. Nor did Ichi in San Francisco. Kat may have something up in Deadhorse. A strange character who she says doesn't seem to be what he says he is."

"What about Mountain Home Air Force Base?" Roger asked. "That has to be connected to this whole scheme somehow."

They all looked at Mr. Marshall. He stared out the window at the snowcapped Rocky Mountains on the horizon. "Yes, I think the old terrorist's words did mean the Mountain Home air base. And the other terrorists who said that hundreds of thousands would die. That can only mean a nuclear explosion. Which brings us back to the air base at Mountain Home and its supply of nuclear weapons."

"But hundreds of thousands wouldn't die if the terrorists used the weapon on Prudhoe Bay," Duncan said. "Maybe two or three thousand."

"Yes, that's right," Mr. Marshall said. "But the old men

might not have known what the target was. They could have assumed that it would be a large city."

"So, what's next?" Roger asked.

Mr. Marshall walked over to the window and looked out at the mountains again. At last he turned. "All right. Nothing more we can do here. Roger has done the work nicely. He gets the Robin Hood Award of the week. Now it looks like we need to at least go up to Mountain Home and check on their facilities and their securities. The big jet will leave the new airport here tomorrow at eight A.M. See you all in the lobby at seven."

✳ TWENTY-SEVEN ✳

MOUNTAIN HOME, IDAHO

Mr. Marshall, Hershel, Ichi, Roger, and Duncan all flew into Mountain Home, Idaho, Saturday. Mr. Marshall had already been in contact with the base commander at Mountain Home Air Force Base. He had worked with him before when he was CIA director.

Hershel came along but was on official light duty. His right thigh where they dug out the bullet still gave him trouble, although it was healing. He figured it would be another week before he'd be ready to play at full speed.

The Specialists stayed at the Mountain Motel in town and Mr. Marshall went for a courtesy call to Brigadier General Hugh Petroff. They had talked on the phone about the chance that some agents were going to try to steal an atomic weapon.

Now the general leaned back in his swivel chair behind his big desk at the Air Force base and grinned.

"Marshall, we've got the best damn security force in the States right here. Ten times they sent in security busters, those experts who think they can break into any base and do what they want to do. It's their job and we pay them to try to beat us. So far we've knocked them out ten times out of ten. Only base in the world to have a ten on ten with those devils. And they're good."

"Hugh, we're not sure it's going to happen, but it might. These three outfits we're tracking are the best in the world right now at terrorism, for-hire killing, and large-scale bombings. We don't know what they're up to, but we have a couple of targets they've put on a list."

"Targets for terrorism?" the general asked. "Was this base one of them?"

"No, but Mountain Home is between two targets that were mentioned in a terrorist dream hit list. One of them is Hoover Dam, and the other one Prudhoe Bay, Alaska, where we get twenty percent of our oil."

The flying general sobered. "Well now, that does make more sense. A strike at either one would be a total disaster. But how are we involved here?"

"We think the terrorists might have pegged your base as the best place where they could steal a nuclear weapon. That's the only kind of attack that would wipe out Hoover, and it would kill off oil production in Prudhoe Bay for five hundred years."

General Petroff stood and walked around the office. He stared out the window, lit a cigar and put it out, then went back to his desk and sat down. "Marshall, you know about security. There's not one damn thing more I can do here to tighten the screws. We're drum solid and no way anyone can steal an active nuclear bomb from my base."

"Good, Hugh, then I won't have to worry about it. If you get even a whiff of any attempt, you let me know. We're staying at the Mountain Motel."

"I'll do that, Marshall. But no chance these terrorists can even find out where we store the weapons, let alone get their filthy Arab mitts on one of them."

"I'll take your guarantee on that, Hugh. Now I better get back to the motel and see what the E-mail has for me."

Wade flew in from Las Vegas and met the rest of them at the motel in time for a late dinner. He had nothing new to report to Mr. Marshall. Ichi came in later that night.

"All we can do now is wait and see what Kat turns up, then wait again and see what happens out at the base,"

Wade said. The rest agreed with him. None of them liked waiting.

PRUDHOE BAY, ALASKA

Kat stood halfway across the room from Phil Lawrence. He smiled, closed the door, and jiggled it into the right position, then snapped on the night lock.

"Now, sassy lady, we can do this any way you want to. It can be soft and gentle, or you can fight like a tiger. I'm kind of in the mood for a fight myself." He took a step toward her.

Kat's mind whirled. Just how much of her special abilities could she show and not give herself away? She decided on a minimum that would do the job.

He grinned when he saw that she hadn't retreated. He took three quick steps and reached for her hand. Kat grabbed his arm and using his forward momentum did a hip throw and slammed him onto the floor. She followed that with a hard kick into his right elbow that brought a wail of sudden pain. The throw hadn't hurt her left arm at all where the bullet had gone through. It must be healing quickly. She stared hard at the man on the floor.

Lawrence swore in some foreign tongue, then tried to stand up, pushing off with his right hand. He bellowed in pain as his right elbow gave way and he fell flat on the floor. Kat walked to the door, unlocked it, and pulled it open.

"I do believe that you were about to say good night, Mr. Lawrence. It hasn't been at all pleasant. I really hope that you understand now that I don't want to talk to you again, or even see you. Good night, Mr. Lawrence."

He struggled to his feet, and held his right elbow with his left hand. Phil Lawrence walked to the door and looked back.

"We'll settle this later, you bitch."

He left and Kat closed and locked the door, knowing that he could break in again anytime he wanted to. When he was gone she picked the lock on the room across the hall, then moved her belongings and clothes into the empty room there.

She plugged into the phone jack and sent an E-mail to Mr. Marshall, telling him about what she had learned— that Phil Lawrence wasn't at all what he claimed to be. But she didn't know if this would have any bearing on a possible targeting of Prudhoe Bay.

That done, she pulled the shades to shut out as much of the sunshine as she could, then checked her .32 caliber hideout. It had a full magazine. She slid it under her pillow, then crawled into bed and hoped that she could get some sleep.

MOUNTAIN HOME, IDAHO

In the house just outside of town that Charlie had rented, he put new riot cuffs on Beth's ankles, then nailed several boards across the inside of the window in Beth's room, so there was no chance they could break out.

He set out some milk and cereal and left them a loaf of bread and cheese.

"You guys are eating better than I am," he said. "I'll bring back some hamburgers for lunch. I've got to take a trip. Just stay here and don't cause any more trouble."

It was Saturday morning, the third day of rain. The morning had begun cold and with a hint of sprinkles. Then the rain came again and he swore all the way into town and to the apartment he had rented. There he used his computer and sent an E-mail to his man in Deadhorse:

"Take today off. Report sick. See if you can hire a helicopter to be ready to follow Scimitar when he makes his move. It isn't going down today. Raining here. You don't need to follow the other bird until I tell you that the jet fighter is on its way up there. Be sure to line up those six men. You better get one of them to work with you tomorrow. This is close to wrapping up. Remember the big payday when it's all over."

He checked it over, pushed the send button, and relaxed when the window popped up showing him that the mail had been sent.

Now, back to the house. Those two little girls were gems. He wouldn't be able to follow orders about them, he was sure. What the hell, he wasn't following the other orders from the Scimitar.

He stopped on the way and bought more groceries and six burgers at a local drive-through. At least he could stay on the good side of the kids.

When he walked into the house at the end of the deserted block, it seemed strangely quiet. When he unlocked the bedroom door where the three were held, he sensed danger but too late. The door opened inward and now came jolting forward, slamming into his arms that held the sacks of burgers. They flew to the floor and Beth tried to hobble past him.

"Stop," he yelled. She took another pair of sliding steps and he grabbed her from behind. One hand caught a breast in front and he saw that she was still naked to the waist. He walked her back into the bedroom now with both his hands holding her breasts and she winced at the pressure.

"Bastard," she said softly so he could hear. "You fucking asshole bastard."

Charlie chuckled. "At least you're talking dirty, maybe I have a chance of getting your panties off after all."

He spun her around into the room, picked up the sack of hamburgers, and motioned to the two girls.

"Eat all you want. It's going to be a long day. They can't possibly fly now even if it clears up. Maybe tomorrow. Now, no more trouble."

He closed and locked the door and shook his head. Charlie knew he was being stupid. He owned her, could do her any way he wanted to with or without her help. Charlie went into the kitchen and turned on a small radio and listened to the news. Weather would be breaking this afternoon. The weatherman predicted a clear, bright day tomorrow. Great! He did a little jig in delight.

After he ate a hamburger and drank a strawberry milk-shake, he went to the bedroom door and opened it carefully. The two girls were napping on the floor. Beth sat by herself leaning against the wall. She was still topless. He grinned. She stood and walked toward him, hips and breasts swaying.

"Charlie, you really want me, don't you? I can see it in your eyes. I told you I'll trade. Me, as many times as you can get it up, only don't make Marve go on that wild rogue flight tomorrow. Deal?"

She was close to him then. He reached down and fondled both her breasts and she began to breathe faster, her face flushed down her neck to her breasts.

"So, how about it. Me in exchange?"

He grabbed her and pulled her hard against his body Beth waited for the right moment, then she rammed her knee upward as hard as she could into his crotch. It was a glancing blow but it brought a wail of pain from Charlie. He pushed her away and bent over, holding his crotch with both hands.

For two minutes he couldn't speak. Then he flew at her. In his rage he slapped her half a dozen times. Each time she laughed at him. He controlled himself at last and panted out the rest of the pain.

Then he caught her by one breast and pulled her out the door. He locked it and pushed her forward.

"That hurts," she said.

"Good. Serves you right. You're a teasing bitch."

He took her to the basement door and pushed her through. "You get solitary confinement. This way you'll wonder what I'm doing to your two little girls. Now get down the steps and be quiet. If you're lucky you'll still be alive by tomorrow." He pushed her to the first step and waited while she hopped down. When she was halfway down he turned off the light plunging the cellar into absolute blackness. No windows down there.

Her voice came up from the darkness just before Charlie closed the door.

"Charlie, you even touch my girls, I'll kill you so slowly

you won't remember your name. Do you entirely understand what I'm saying."

He slammed the basement door and she heard a lock click in place.

The first thing she did was go back up the steps. It was one of the most difficult physical things she had ever done. She had to reach up and grab the wooden banister, then hop up with both feet. The first two times she didn't make it and her feet came back to the same step. Then she got the hang of it. There were eighteen steps. Once at the top, she found the light switch and turned it on.

Her trip back down the steps was slow, so she wouldn't make any noise. At the bottom of the stairs she saw that she could easily turn out the lightbulb. She would if he tried to come down. She looked around. There was an old bed and a dresser in one corner. It looked like someone had slept down there at one time. She looked for a weapon. What could she use? Under some old boards, she found a three-quarter size ax with a five-inch-wide blade. Yes.

What else would work as a weapon? She saw nothing else. There was some wire, a length of rope, a hammer, and some nails. It looked like someone had left in a rush without cleaning out the basement. The stairs were steps put on slanted runners, with the back of them open. That gave her an idea. She'd seen in the movies how a man coming down open steps like this could be tripped. Now how did they do it?

It took her over an hour to figure out a trap that would really work. She fashioned a noose that would pull up tight around Charlie's leg. Then she ran the end of the rope back through the open step to an old car axle and differential. She tugged it to a standing position beside the wall and pulled the rope taut and tied the end round the top of the axle. Now, when Charlie stepped into the noose, she would jerk the noose tight around his ankle and tip over the axle, that would ram Charlie's leg hard against the steps and hold it there so he couldn't get away.

Maybe he'd lose his balance and fall down the steps.

Yes, either way. Then she'd swing the ax at him. She frowned for a moment. Could she do that, injure him severely, maybe kill him? She set her jaw and scowled. For what he was doing to Marve she most certainly could. He was not a man, he was a monster. That was enough. Yes, she could damn well swing that ax at Charlie if she had the chance.

Beth found an old chair, put a blanket on it from the bed, and sat down near the rope to wait. Then she got up and unscrewed the bulb turning the basement into a black hole. She crept back to the chair and settled in. Wait. She had no idea how long it would be, but she would be ready the second that Charlie stepped in that noose. Yes, she would be more than ready.

☆ TWENTY-EIGHT ☆

MOUNTAIN HOME, IDAHO

The day was still Saturday, although it seemed as if it had been at least three days to Beth since she was jailed in the basement. She was still ready for him. Maybe it had been four hours. Beth had slept some but now she was totally awake. She listened critically to noises from up the stairs. The steps came from the kitchen. He might be in there fixing dinner? Not a chance.

The basement door rattled. She heard a lock being opened. Then a door squeaked and a shaft of yellow light stabbed into the darkness. Beth saw a man's shadow swallow up part of the light, then Beth heard the light switch at the head of the steps go on and off.

"Damn switch is broken," Charlie said. "Don't move, bitch, I'm going to go get a flashlight, courtesy of your van." She waited. Now her hand on the rope felt like a rock. She tensed the muscles, then relaxed them and put the arm at her side.

When he came back, she heard the footsteps above, then a piercing shaft of whiter light came evidently from the flash. It probed down the steps, then into the darkness. She prayed that he didn't see the loop of rope on the sixth step down.

"Look, I'm coming down so we can talk. Maybe we

can get on a friendlier basis. I don't want to hurt you or the kids. This is strictly business."

She didn't reply, didn't want him to know she was back from the steps and behind them. Beth took a deep breath and waited.

"Hey, I've got the light. You can't hide and there's no way out. I'm coming down now so don't think you can stop me."

He moved down slowly one step at a time, the flash probing into the corners of the basement but not hitting the area behind the steps.

Charlie stopped on the fifth step and did a complete search with the flashlight of the area he could see.

"So you are hiding. Maybe we can't talk after all."

Beth cupped her hands around her mouth and pointed her face away from the stairs. "Yes, let's talk," she said loudly, hoping he would think the voice came from the other side of the basement.

He frowned, then went down one more tread with his right foot.

Yes.

Beth jerked the rope.

The rope cinched up around Charlie's right ankle. She at once drew it tight, then pushed over the old axle. The tug on the rope turned into a two-hundred-pound pull as the axle hung in the air with one end on the ground, the other suspended by the rope that jolted the back of Charlie's leg against the step and pinned it there.

"What the hell?" Charlie bellowed. "Let go of me. Beth, stop this foolishness."

She didn't say a word. Instead she walked around the steps and moved up two treads before he saw her. He still had the flash. Beth lifted the ax and he shrilled in alarm.

"What you doing with that ax, Beth? Now put it down and let me go. I said I wouldn't hurt you or the girls."

Beth went up another step and swung the ax. She had never even tried to use an ax that big before. It hit the stair tread below the one Charlie stood on.

"Stop that," Charlie said, his voice betraying a sudden fear. "Beth, come on. I won't hurt you."

"You already have hurt me and the girls and Marve." She swung again, this time hitting the right step but drove the sharp ax blade into the wood half an inch, but an inch from his shoe.

"Third time," she muttered.

Charlie kicked out with his left leg, barely missing her arm. Beth lifted the ax again, almost over her head the way she had seen the loggers in the woods do. Before she could swing the blade, the axle gave off a screech and scraping sound as it pivoted around where it rested on the floor. It swung toward the steps, then rolled forward another three feet loosening the rope.

Suddenly Charlie no longer had his right leg pinned to the step. But it happened before he was ready and now he pitched headfirst down the steps toward Beth. She yelled and jumped out of the way off the steps and to the floor two feet below. Beth wailed as she sprained her ankle and wound up sitting on the concrete floor.

Charlie put out both hands to catch himself, did a good job of it, and sat on the steps, quickly pulling the noose off his right leg.

He had dropped the flashlight but saw it beaming along the floor six feet away and retrieved it. Charlie centered the light on Beth.

"Well now, good try, but I have no broken bones and only a slightly sore elbow. You don't look in such good shape."

Beth started to stand but he pushed her back down. "I've changed my mind, Beth, I do want to hurt you, in the worst way possible. I'm gonna fuck you right here until I can't stand up anymore. Twelve is my record, but that was with a compliant rag mop of a woman. She was nothing like you."

Beth tried to scoot backward but ran into the side of the stairs.

"Hey, don't give in on my account. I like a little fighting. The caveman syndrome."

Her skirt had skidded upward and bunched around her thighs. He stepped between her legs and spread them even more. He knelt down between her legs and caught her hands. The plastic cuffs went around fast and then he looped three together and had her hands tied to the stairway in back of her head.

A half hour later, Beth lay on the concrete naked, shivering with anger and raw terror. She was furious, but had no way to fight back. He had protected his crotch perfectly this time. He stood and dressed. She turned her head away so she didn't have to watch him.

"I suppose you feel like a big man now that you've raped me."

He chuckled. "What else to do on a rainy afternoon? The weatherman said tomorrow would dawn bright and clear. That means your husband's flight will be in the air. So, the game begins."

"It won't work. Marvin will never sell out his country just to save his family."

"Oh, but he will. I know the man better than you do. He'll do exactly as I told him. He knows where to fly, how high and how fast and where to land. Simple. With any luck he can claim that his instruments went out and that he had to ditch the plane in that big sea up there, whatever they call it. He'll be safe but his plane and the nuclear bomb will be forever in the deep waters of the sea. Then he comes home to you, maybe gets pitched out of the Air Force but he'll have that hundred thousand dollars in cash to help him smooth over any anguish. See, I'm not such a bad guy after all."

He checked his watch, then went over and twisted the bulb so it lit. "So that's how you did it. I should have thought of that before." He came back and stared at her naked form. "Yes, yes, what a body. You should have done better than a captain. You're a general's pussy material."

Charlie tied his shoes and took three steps up the stairs.

"Enjoy yourself down here. I have to go get us some sup-per so you patriots don't starve. Who knows, you and I might do an encore tonight after supper upstairs on the one good bed."

He laughed and hurried up the steps, closed the door above, and she heard the lock click shut.

Late that same Saturday afternoon at the Mountain Home Air Force Base, Mr. Marshall had brought along Wade, Duncan, and Hershel to talk with the general and his three top aides.

"We know that your people have done exceptionally well with your security, General Petroff," Mr. Marshall said. "But sometimes that is the exact second that you should be concerned with becoming too complacent, over-confident."

"I hope that we haven't," a bird colonel said.

"You've worked against the chopper hopping over a far boundary fence and grabbing a nuke from a fighter air-craft?" Hershel asked. Heads nodded. "What about a six-by simply driving out the front gate with a weapon?"

"We tried that ourselves with an imported driver not familiar with our people," General Petroff said. "He was stopped flat and almost ripped apart before our people ar-rived to explain that it was a test."

"I see by your flight schedule that you have twelve dif-ferent planes up tomorrow," Mr. Marshall said. "Are those routine?"

"Not at all," Colonel Calendar said. "These are re-quired mission flights with full armament, just like we were going into combat. The weather has put us behind on our mandatories."

"Would those planes be carrying nuclear weapons?" Duncan asked.

Colonel Calendar looked at his CO. "Sir, that would depend. Some might, others might not. It would all depend right now on your need to know. I can't see how there's any way that I can tell you that information."

Duncan grinned. "Colonel, I was an MI-6 agent in the British Secret Service for six years. You just told me that they will be packing nukes. There is more than one way to steal a nuclear bomb."

"But these fighters are all armed. If one plane was attacked, there would be three of his fellow pilots on the scene at once with full firepower ready to defend that target plane whether it was still in the air or had been forced down. That makes these chicks so secure that these flights don't even come under our security specifications."

"General Petroff," Mr. Marshall said. "Here is one risk that you don't have total control of. Since we know there may be a move to steal a weapon from your base, why can't you postpone these flights with the nuclear bombs on board, or simply send them up with all arms except the nuke or a dummy nuke with the same weight?"

"We could. But Will tells me that would put us another twenty-four sorties behind sked on our mission requirements. He tells me it just isn't practical to do it right now."

"The rain set you back?" Hershel asked.

The training commander nodded.

Mr. Marshall stood, and Duncan and Hershel did as well.

"Gentlemen, it would seem that we have given you our message and that we have nothing more to say. The weather is clearing and you should be flying tomorrow, probably at dawn. We wish you the best of luck, and of course, safe flights and return trips."

When they arrived back at the motel, Roger brought out an E-mail message from Kat in Prudhoe Bay. Mr. Marshall read it, then passed it to the other men.

"Mr. Marshall. Have yet to discover anything here that is suspicious. There are few strangers here, but would you need somebody on ground zero when you're going to blast the place off the face of the universe?

"One suspicious man calls himself Phil Lawrence. He looks on the Arabic side in spite of his brown hair and green eyes. He claims he's from Italy, and he does have an

Italian chopper pilot's license. He rented a bird from a local guy here to help with his ozone layer studies. I don't
believe he's really a scientist, and if he is, this is not the
right spot to try to discover the hole in the ozone layer.
Isn't that done with huge telescopes?

"At any rate he became a little too familiar tonight,
broke down my door, and waltzed right into my room. I
did a hip throw on him and kicked him in the elbow. He
wasn't pleased. With any luck I won't see him again. (That
might not be possible since we both stay in the town's only
hotel and eat at the only restaurant.)

"There is a helicopter rental firm here where birds can
be rented if we need one. Shall I put one on order? This
town really does have only twenty people in it. The two
thousand workers are in their own private compound with
living facilities and quite extensive recreational areas. I
never see any of the men.

"Let me know of any more work for me to do here.
Should I return there after another day of monitoring this
place? Let me hear. Thanks, Kat."

After Wade finished reading the E-mail he rubbed his
chin, then looked at Hershel. "Why would a man be in
Prudhoe Bay pretending to be a scientist when he wasn't?
In a town of twenty-four civilians, he'd stand out like a
circus clown. Brown hair and green eyes can be changed
with contacts and a hair job. Is it possible the man could
be one of our three terrorists, or a man in their employ?
Damned curious."

Hershel was making some notes on a pad. "Did we get
a description of him? Is he over six feet and on the slender
side? He could be putting on an act. One of our terrorists
was a bit of an actor someone said."

Duncan had been nodding as the others spoke. "Yes, yes.
It sounds right. Undercover, and on one of our target sites
from the list. Let's get a more detailed description of him."

Mr. Marshall's faint frown deepened. "Yes, I agree. I'll
get an E-mail off to her at once, asking for a detailed description and telling her to be extremely careful around the
man."

He went to his motel room and sent the message. Five minutes later he had a return E-mail. The others were there and read it with Mr. Marshall.

"Subject is about six-three, a hundred and eighty pounds or so, dark complexioned that could be Italian, and perhaps Arab. Hair is definitely brown, but the roots may be dark black. Contacts could change brown eyes to green. He's smooth. Could be an agent for one of the terrorists. Have we decided yet which one of the three we think is working the Big One?"

Wade read the message again, then grinned. "Gentlemen, I think we have found our terrorist. Without any better look at the man than Kat's description, I'd bet a box full of hot dogs that he is the Scimitar. Height is right. He could have put on a few pounds since I saw him. Sneaking around, working undercover, he has to be there for the Big One. Which could involve a nuke stolen from Mountain Home Air Force Base."

Hershel shook his head. "You're jumping to a whole batch of conclusions. Sure, the description fits your take on the Scimitar. But what else do we have to point him in that direction? Nothing. We have no connection between him and the air base here. Yes, he could be up there to set up the bomb once it gets there, but right now all nukes at the base here are accounted for, locked down and guarded around the clock by hardcases with real bullets in their submachine guns. How does he get the bomb?"

"Not sure, but it sure looks like Prudhoe Bay is the target," Wade said. "A nuke over the bay would make that a dead zone for a thousand years."

"And force the U.S. to buy more oil from the Arab states who could jack the price up double if they wanted to," Mr. Marshall said.

"We can't do anything tonight except maybe tell Kat who we think that stranger up there might be," Ichi said. "Heard the weather report. The clouds are clearing tonight. Tomorrow is set to dawn bright and clear, which means the fighter pilots will be out flying their missions again. From what Duncan said, they'll have the nukes on them."

"I'll send Kat a warning," Mr. Marshall said. "We'll be up early and out to the base. We might send Kat some backup early tomorrow. I'd say that without any new leads from other sources that the Scimitar is our target and that he's in Deadhorse, Alaska. Now, it's late. Let's get some sleep and be ready to travel again at six A.M. We'll check the flights of the F-15s tomorrow, and decide if we need to send Kat that backup."

The men talked a little, then scattered to their rooms.

Roger Johnson hadn't brought any books. He could find one in the rack in the lobby, but he watched some TV, then turned it off and tried to sleep.

It didn't happen. He found an international basketball game on cable TV and watched it for a while. Damn, he could have played in that league. He wasn't sure they had it when he graduated. He had a better jump shot than anyone did on the floor.

Yeah, hoop dreams. It would have been great to get picked up by the NBA, but it didn't happen. He had grown up in the projects of New York City. The big bad ones. His mother kept him out of trouble by keeping him playing basketball in grade and high school. Then he tried some of the semi-pro teams but they all wanted players with four years of college experience.

That was out of the question with his GPA, and the cost was the other factor. He was good, but not good enough to get a scholarship from any but one college in Iowa, and they would pay only half of his tuition and none of the dorm expenses. Impossible.

So it was the Navy instead, and three years later he wound up in the SEALs, the first response team of the Navy that goes anywhere and does anything always on a covert basis. He became fascinated with African languages and became good enough to get by in Akan, Chichewa, and Swahili. He handled a lot of explosives in the SEALs and it was on one of his demonstrations that caught the attention of Mr. Marshall, who helped him get an honorable discharge from the Navy so he could join the Specialists.

Each of the team was an expert in underwater work, but because of his SEAL training, Roger was the man for any diving job.

He flipped the dial again, found an international soccer game with commentary in French. He turned off the sound and tried to figure out what was going on. He'd never understood the game, but since it was the world's most popular sport, he should learn. He gave up after twenty minutes and turned off the lights. So far this mission had turned out to be a chase after a wild snipe. Tomorrow was another day, as Scarlett O'Hara would say. Maybe they would get some action tomorrow.

✵ TWENTY-NINE ✵

MOUNTAIN HOME, IDAHO

Three hours after he had sex with Beth, Charlie went back to the basement. She was dressed in skirt and shoes. He'd taken the ankle cuffs off before. She stared hard at him, then looked past him.

"Go away," she said.

"You can come upstairs now. The girls are asking for you."

The mention of her girls brought a change in Beth. It was as if she had shucked her private grief and thought of her children's welfare. She stood from the chair and hurried up the steps.

The girls were locked in the same room as before, but now she saw that they had eaten an evening meal, a TV dinner. Better for them than hamburgers. She hugged both of them and found her bra and blouse and put them on.

Charlie didn't say a word. He watched them a moment, then left, closed, and locked the door.

He took out his cell phone and dialed. On the first ring the phone on the other end was picked up.

"Yes, hello."

"Clooney?"

"Charlie, you bastard."

"I figure you know by now that the weather has

cleared. You'll be flying bright and early in the morning. You been notified?"

"Yes, our flight gets off at 1030."

"You remember exactly what you are to do, and how to do it?"

"How are Beth and the girls?"

"They're fine."

"I want to talk to Beth, right now. You owe me this much."

Charlie hesitated, then shrugged. "Sure, why not?"

He went into the bedroom and handed Beth the phone. "Marve?"

"Yeah. Are you okay? Has he hurt you or the girls?"

"We're fine. I'm worried about you. I know you don't want to do this. You don't have to. He won't hurt us." She had walked away from the girls and kept her voice low.

"No. No. You and the girls are worth a dozen bombs. I'm going to do what he says."

Charlie pulled the phone from her hand.

"Enough. Tell me what you're going to do, exactly." He listened. When Clooney had given him back the instructions he had memorized several days before, Charlie grinned. "Yeah, you've got it. Now, tomorrow morning you do it."

Charlie hung up without a good-bye. He left the room and locked the door. He hadn't put ankle cuffs back on the woman, but he didn't think she could get out of the room.

He dialed another number. "Yes, this is Charlie. I put a Gulfstream on standby. I'll want it for sure tomorrow morning. Have her ready to go sometime around eleven A.M. Yes, a one-way trip. I'll pay you before we leave."

Charlie smiled as he closed the phone. Now all he had to do was carry out the rest of the plan. A cold chill made him shudder.

The Scimitar. He was a problem. A difficult opponent. A quick shot to the back of his head would solve that problem. Charlie left the house and took a walk. It would burn off some of the nervous energy he felt. Everything was so close. By tomorrow night he should have in his control a live nuclear bomb.

He walked faster, went around the unfinished block where streets and sidewalks and houses would soon go in. He came back to his rental and sat a moment outside in the soft Idaho night. Yes, tomorrow. Charlie was sure that he wouldn't get an hour's sleep.

Sunday morning dawned with a washed blue sky. The Air Force base buzzed with unusual Sunday activity. The flight line was humming as four flights of F-15 Eagles were readied by their ground crews.

The first four Eagles gunned down the runway and took off two at a time precisely at 1031.

Mr. Marshall and Wade were in the Flight Control Center at the invitation of the young bird colonel, Calendar, who ran the operation. He was the same one they had talked with in the general's office the day before.

"First flight is up with no problems," Colonel Calendar said. "They are Red Four, scheduled for a two-hour mission run north and west, vectoring somewhere over central Washington and a turnaround near Wenatchee. On these birds we have our top four men, Johnson, Anderson, Chu, and Clooney.

"We'll be sending out a new flight every half hour aiming them four different directions. It's routine—when the weather cooperates."

"So far, so good," Mr. Marshall said. "Did you say there was coffee somewhere around here?" Mr. Marshall and Wade had decided not to send the corporate jet to Deadhorse, not yet. They would wait to see if anything happened to the flights that went up that morning.

Captain Marvin Clooney sat on the end of the runway with his wingman waiting for the final approval for takeoff. He had a vague idea how he might get away from his flight, but nothing planned in detail. There had to be some clouds somewhere that he could hide in for a few minutes. He'd watch for them.

"Red Four, cleared for takeoff," the small speaker in his helmet said. He signaled across at his wingman, got a thumbs-up, and both men pushed throttles forward. They rolled, then raced down the runway side by side until they took off in perfect formation, blasting into the sky, making a five-mile-wide circle as they waited for the next two planes from their flight.

Soon they were in formation heading on their pre-planned flight. Ten minutes out they ran into clouds and their plane-to-plane radio chattered.

"Let's go over them," their flight leader called. "About now."

Three of the planes angled upward at their cruising speed of a little under 1,650 miles an hour. Before the other three knew what happened, Clooney dipped his right wing and dove into the streak of benign clouds at thirty thousand feet. He was into the clouds in less than five seconds. A moment later the radio chattered.

"Clooney, where the hell are you? What happened?"

"I checked him when we started up," his wingman said. "Then when I looked over seconds later, he was gone."

"I saw him just a few seconds before he seemed to dive to the right and into the clouds. I couldn't tell if he was in trouble or not."

The three TAC One radio transmissions came in loud and clear at Flight Ops at Mountain Home.

"Red Four Leader, what's going on up there?"

"Damned if I know, Colonel. Clooney just vanished into some clouds. No transmissions from him. Don't know what happened. Request permission to break off the mission and try and find him. He might show up on our close-range radar."

"Granted, Red Four Leader. What's your approximate location?"

"We're twelve minutes from base on the assigned course, somewhere over central Oregon. Breaking off mission and starting search. Two of us will check out the ground under the cloud formation that's about twenty thousand. I'll work the clouds top and bottom watching for Clooney. How could he just vanish that way?"

"Sounds like some equipment failure," Colonel Calendar said. "Keep on it hard. We'll put up two search and rescue birds. Keep us informed."

Captain Clooney welcomed the clouds and when the others climbed he dove into them and vanished in a few seconds. He had plotted his position and now stayed with the clouds and turned north and then east until he ran out of the cover. He dropped down from twenty thousand until he was no more than a thousand feet off the ground. Down here, the close-range radar couldn't find him.

He knew his air speed had cut back from 1,650 at altitude to about 900 mph on the deck. He saw the open plateau of western Oregon/Washington. One or the other. Then he could see the mountains coming up. They would be the Bitterroot Range and the primitive section of Idaho where the river of no return ran through.

He heard the radio talk as the other pilots hunted him. Already he was far out of their search pattern. They were looking over the ground for a crash site.

"Sorry, guys," he said. A little later he turned off his radio. He had some tough flying ahead. His instructions were to stay below radar, hug the ground, then the mountains. He would have to take every valley he found and wind around the mountain peaks. The clutter on the radar screens around the mountains was heavy, and his occasional sightings on the screen would be hard to pin down.

He came on the first mountains almost before he realized it and turned north again heading up through the gut of Idaho the way he had been told. There were few residents in this primitive area, so there would be almost no one to report a low-flying fighter.

Clooney was surprised at how easy it had been so far. The other pilots had been concentrating on their own planes and he simply dropped out of sight. Now he had to stay low enough to confuse the radar.

Charlie had a friend in the Flight Ops section and as soon as Clooney dropped off their radars and was reported missing, the airman called Charlie on his cell phone.

"We have a missing dog. One dog has vanished. No one knows what's going on here."

"Thanks, buddy, a check will be in the mail."

Charlie called the airport to warm up the Gulfstream jet for immediate takeoff. He sent an E-mail to El Scimitar telling him the timetable. Then he phoned the Deadhorse hotel and left a message at his man's room that the Eagle would arrive that morning. That done, he pushed the rest of the food into the room with Beth and the girls, locked it securely, then drove to the airport. He used the cell phone again and called the Mountain Home police reporting strange doings at the house he had rented. They said they would check it out. He said his name was Hollister and he lived nearby. This was the first time he had disobeyed orders from the Scimitar. The family was supposed to be shot dead before he left the area. Tough, he just couldn't do it. The little girls really got to him. He shrugged.

The business jet was ready at the commercial gate when Charlie arrived and he stepped on board. He checked with the pilot.

"Yes, sir. Flight time to Deadhorse is four hours ten minutes, if we don't hit any headwinds. Flight plan is filed, we're ready to take off. Grab a seat, sit back, and enjoy."

Charlie did. He had arranged for a flight attendant and snacks. He figured it as they flew. The Eagle should get to Prudhoe Bay in about three hours at the slower on-the-deck altitude. That meant Clooney would get there at about 1:30 P.M. Now all he had to do was wait.

At the Mountain Home Air Force Base, Colonel Calendar stared at Mr. Marshall. "How could you know something like this might happen? There is no chance that his aircraft went down. We would have had the emergency signal. He seems to be heading north. There's not a lot of places up there we can watch for him."

"You have good evidence that he's heading north?"

"We have some spotty radar, but he's into a mountainous area up there in the nine- and ten-thousand-foot level. That always messes up radar. So much clutter you can't figure out what's real and what's a ghost."

Mr. Marshall nodded. "Thank you, Colonel Calendar. Give my regards to the general. We have to fly north. We'll be in touch if we find anything."

Fifteen minutes later, the Marshall Gulfstream business jet had been warmed up and was ready to fly. The Specialists ran up to it and jumped on board and it took off.

The pilot confirmed the flight time. "Yes, sir. A little over four hours from here to Deadhorse, Alaska, providing we don't hit any bad weather or high head winds."

A half hour out, Mr. Marshall used his new digital phone and called the Air Force base. It took him five minutes to get through to Colonel Calendar.

"Colonel, what's the status on the Eagle?"

"No firm sightings, no firm radar on his track. We think it's generally north, but we can't be sure. We've alerted Eielson Air Force Base near Fairbanks, Alaska, to watch for him. They'll have all their facilities looking. We've alerted the Canadian National Radar System to see if they can pick up a single jet headed their way, but we don't have much hope that their radar can do any better than ours.

"Somebody suggested we send up an AWACS to find him," the colonel said. "Trouble with that is we have a fifteen-hundred-mile-long target area that could be a thousand miles wide and no firm area to search. The AWACS can cover a two-hundred-mile radius. At even a thousand miles an hour, the Eagle would be out of a search area before we could get a new two-hundred-mile pattern established. It just won't work.

"So far Canada reports they have nothing to tell us

about our missing Eagle. We've pulled our three planes back from the spot of the disengagement. We're almost certain that the plane didn't go down or we would have heard from someone on the ground, or the three pilots and our S&R people would have found a crash site. So, we wait and hope."

Mr. Marshall thanked him and hung up. Later he called the Prudhoe Bay Hotel where Kat was and left a message since she wasn't in. He told her to rent a helicopter and have it ready to roll when they arrived. He checked his watch.

"Tell her that we should be on the ground there in Deadhorse at four P.M. today. Miss, if you can find her and deliver this message within the hour, I'll see that you get a hundred-dollar tip. My name is J. August Marshall. I would appreciate you finding her. Thank you."

★ THIRTY ★

OVER CENTRAL IDAHO

Captain Marvin Clooney turned on his radio and heard the chatter of pilots still searching for him. Two S&R helicopters were working over eastern Oregon and western Idaho. He tried to remember what he'd heard about radar in Canada. Did they have any kind of intrusion radar? He wasn't sure. If so, he should be able to stay under it by hugging the ground and swinging around the mountain peaks.

Once past the border there would be little to fear. There was the Air Force base just out of Fairbanks. He'd flown in there once on a training run. Eielson AFB, that was the name. He'd do a detour around it if he saw he was coming close.

He prayed that Beth and the girls were all right. Sometimes Beth could get a little headstrong. He hoped that she didn't fight back so much that she got herself injured or shot. His Beth had a temper. This was all to remind himself that he was becoming a traitor to his country to save his family.

A cold shiver slanted through him. Would Charlie leave any witnesses? He kidnapped the family. Would he simply shoot them dead before he left? Clooney slammed the idea out of his mind and concentrated on flying lower to the carpet of the fir and hemlock. That was his job now, stay low and slow.

He did have a way out of this mess if they followed through. Charlie said he would land on an ice field. They would take the nuclear bomb off the pylons under the fuselage, then the plane would be hauled to the sea and dumped in. He could claim that he had to eject when the rest of his instruments went out. His parachute dropped him on an ice field. Yes, he'd tell them the nuclear bomb was still on board and he could show the investigators about the spot where the plane went into the water.

Captain Clooney quit thinking about it and flew. He hit his first target almost on the nose. A town called Porthill, in Idaho and almost on the British Columbia border. From there he slanted west toward Prince Rupert on the British Columbia coast just below Alaska.

Clooney checked his watch. Halfway. Another hour and a half and he would land, dump the plane, and he would be "rescued" by the Air Force from Fairbanks. Most important, his family would be safe. That was the important factor here. Do the job he had been forced into, and save his family.

On board the Marshall Corporation business jet, Mr. Marshall had a long telephone conversation with Gene Vincent, the current head of the FBI. The two had been college classmates at Harvard many years ago.

"Gene, I wouldn't ask if it wasn't vital. Your people and the Air Force have been dragging your feet on this one. We're sure now that a terrorist is trying to hijack a nuclear bomb and plans to explode it over Prudhoe Bay and kill our oil production there for five hundred years.

"We've been on him most of the way, but now we need one small help from you. We need satellite tracking on Prudhoe Bay as soon as possible."

"It isn't quick or easy to shift a satellite track, August, you know that."

"Gene, we're backed into a corner now. There is absolutely no other way to get the information. We need that satellite moved so it can take pictures of the Prudhoe Bay area. It's an hourly orbit and that way the pictures of the area every hour should show us where the Eagle has gone down."

"We heard about the missing Eagle and its bomb load." There was some silence on the air. "You say it's absolutely vital to the security of our country, August?"

"Absolutely. There's thousands of square miles up there that the Eagle could crash-land on. We need to know exactly where it comes down and be there as fast as possible. Pictures of any unusual objects on the ice fields could save the day—and the oil fields. Did you know we get twenty percent of our current petroleum supply from Prudhoe Bay?"

"I didn't know that. All right, August. It looks like we don't have any other option. Why didn't my people get on this quicker?"

"Have to ask them. I've been feeding information to them."

"Yeah, I heard. So let me get on the other phone and change that orbit as fast as we can."

"Thanks, Gene. It could pay off big."

"I'll use your plane's fax number for any pictures we get."

Mr. Marshall gave the FBI director the plane's phone fax number and settled into lunch served by his steward.

Some of the Specialists slept. All of them ate. Hershel with his shot-up leg was appointed to be master of the plane's fax machine. He would stay on board in Deadhorse and phone Mr. Marshall when anything came in concerning the bay area.

They agreed that the target must be Prudhoe and the oil fields. Now they had to find out where the Eagle would land, and how the Scimitar planned to move the bomb from the landing area to the bay. That was one trip they had to stop before it started. If they could.

. . .

Captain Clooney passed Prince Rupert and headed across the long string of islands and a little bit of land that made up the stretch of Alaska that hangs down along the coast of Canada. He flew higher here since many of the areas were populated. At Juneau he took a compass bearing and headed straight for Prudhoe Bay. That meant he had to fly across a section of the nearly uninhabited Canadian Yukon Province. He was well west of Whitehorse, the largest town in the area. Most of the flight took him over a national park with few people in it. Here he dropped down again skimming the land below him sometimes less than fifty feet over the treetops.

His target now was the Alaska Arctic National Wildlife Refuge on the edge of the Beaufort Sea and east of Deadhorse. He would swing around Mt. Chamberlain, over nine thousand feet tall, and zero in on an ice field about five miles east of Deadhorse. That was the plan. The landing area was supposed to be designated with bright ground panels. With any luck he would see them on the first pass.

The last leg of the trip was one long snow scene. Lots of snow and ice. Now in the summer he did see an occasional small stream heading north. He spotted one tiny native village with three dead pickups near it.

Then he saw a road and figured he was too far to the west and eased back east a little. Five miles? How could he estimate five miles? Before he knew it he had flashed off the land mass of North America and was over water. This had to be the Beaufort Sea. He did a sweeping turn to the east to stay away from what must be Deadhorse to the west and came back around. He spotted a smudge on the snow now a short distance from the water.

The color panels. He slowed and dropped lower to check them out. Yes, two red and two green panels the way he had been told. One marker gave him a north landing direction. He made one more sweep over the area. It must be an ice field. It was flat and had some snow on it. He wondered how much. It looked smooth enough and long enough for a wheels-up landing. If he tried to come in with the gear down, the wheels would dig in and send the plane into an immediate flip and maybe explode or catch on fire. Gear up. An hour before he had fired off the three Aim-9 Sidewinder missiles and the three Aim-7 Sparrow missiles on the wings. That left the nuke hanging on its pylons midship under the fuselage. He had fired the wing-mounted missiles into some remote sections he passed over. Now hanging on the tips of the wings were the two large fuel pods carried for added range. The pods would take up a lot of the shock of the landing and would hang on until the plane stopped skidding on the icy snow. They were slightly lower than the nuclear weapon amidships and should protect it from any damage.

That was the plan. He came around again, slowed almost to stalling speed. He didn't look but figured his airspeed at about 145 knots, enough to keep him airborne. Then right at the end of the ice-covered runway he cut power and let the bird settle slightly nose first toward the snow. The belly of the Eagle touched the softness of the Alaskan snow, then the ice a foot below it. He heard the swoosh of the snow, then a grinding noise as the eagle's fuel pods took a beating as they cut through the snow and skidded on the ice. Now and then he heard some sharper sounds that must be loose chunks of ice. He was in the center of a quarter-mile-wide icy runway.

He stared directly ahead and saw where the ice field was not smooth. Ice had reared up three feet out of the ice pack. The upthrusts were directly in his path and he could do nothing to avoid them. At his last look they seemed to be twenty or thirty feet wide and right in front of his landing lane.

The smooth slide turned into a crashing, scraping metal-tearing sound as the right fuel pod hit hard ice upthrust and ripped off. That caused the wing on the other side to drop and the pod caught more ice there but blasted through it. He heard the terrible noises, then the heavier left wing with the fuel pod dipped again and tore off part of the wing tip. The Eagle was through the ice thrusts and back on the level ice, but now the bird went into a skidding 360-degree spin. It went around twice, then once more before the craft came to a stop less than fifty feet from a drop-off.

Clooney sat there a moment. He was down, alive, and would soon be "rescued" as promised. Clooney hit a button disengaging the electric locks on the hardware holding the nuclear weapon against the belly of the plane. He heard the familiar sounds as the nuclear weapon came free of the Eagle, and dropped a foot into the snow and ice below.

Slowly Clooney unhooked the flight harness, then popped the canopy and turned off all switches. His baby was down, but it was severely damaged. He had forgotten she would never fly again.

As he stepped out of the cockpit, he saw a medium-sized snow tractor heading toward him over the ice and snow. He saw four men on it. They came directly to the plane. One of the men ran out and examined the belly of the aircraft, nodded, and waved over the tractor. The tallest of the three strode to where Charley still sat on the edge of the cockpit. There was no convenient crewman with a ladder to help him get down. He at last jumped and hit the snow, nearly careened forward but caught himself and stood. He took off his flight helmet and put it under his left arm as was his habit.

The man who came up to him was three inches over six feet and dark-complexioned probably from the sun. Clooney wasn't sure what to expect. He held out his hand when the man stopped four feet in front of him.

"Captain Clooney delivering one Eagle and one intact nuclear weapon as directed," he said.

"You sure the bomb is not damaged?" the Scimitar said. "You didn't hook on a missile instead of a nuke just to get even with Charlie, did you?"

"No, sir. A deal is a deal. I deliver the bomb, and Charlie gets me off the hook with the Air Force and keeps my family safe."

"Good. Just so we understand each other."

The Scimitar didn't smile, he simply pulled out a pistol and shot Captain Marvin Clooney four times in the chest. Clooney staggered back against his aircraft, his eyes showing surprise and terror, then he stopped breathing.

The Scimitar didn't give Clooney another look. He turned to the three men on the tractor. "Let's move it, men. Get those white plastic sheets over this plane in a rush. You never know when somebody might fly over. Hurry now, hurry."

The Scimitar was in such a rush that he helped. They unrolled twelve-foot-wide sheets of white plastic and nailed them into the ice with long spikes. The sheets covered the plane from one side to the other. Extending thirty feet beyond the wings to make a gradual incline. They unrolled more of the plastic and stapled it together at the twelve-foot seams. In forty-five minutes they had most of the aircraft hidden except for the twin rudders that slanted into the air. They drove the tractor up close to have something to stand on, then draped the rudders the best they could with the white plastic and stepped back. Yes, from fifty yards it would be hard to know the plane was there.

As soon as the bird was camouflaged, the men on the tractor ducked under the plastic and hooked up a pair of ropes to the nuclear weapon. Then they tied the ropes to the tractor and skidded the bomb out from the plastic. It slid along like an awkward sled. When it was thirty yards from the plane, they paused.

"I'll bring up the chopper and we'll get this prize out of here," the Scimitar said. "Unhook the ropes and give me a ride."

A moment later the tractor headed back the way it had come, using the same tracks in the snow. Before he left, the Scimitar pointed to the other two men. "You're my guards. This is a valuable piece of property." He looked at the men. "You have automatic rifles and you can use them. Shoot anybody who shows up around here. Get that? Anybody, civilian, oil exec, cop, or military. Got that?"

The two men nodded and they dropped to the snow beside the bomb, one on each side.

.   .   .

A half mile to the east, behind a hump of snow-covered ice, a helicopter sat out of sight of the downed plane. Two men in white parkas and pants lay in the snow watching the men around the Eagle through field glasses. They saw when one of them shot the pilot as soon as he got out of the downed Eagle. They watched as the plane was hidden, then the bomb dragged out from under the injured bird.

"Two of them are leaving," one man said.

"Why? Four of them came, only two left. Two still out there as guards. We let the other two come back, or we go in now and take them down two on two, instead of two on four?" the second man asked.

"No contest, two on two." The men moved out, white blobs against the white snow. They spread forty yards apart and moved slowly forward. When they were fifty yards from the plane, they could see the two guards beside what they figured was a bomb.

They used hand signals and moved forward another twenty yards, then went flat in the snow. The stocks of their hunting rifles had been painted white for better concealment. Now they stretched out and each man zeroed in on a different guard.

The sound of the hunting rifles rang sharply. Neither guard heard the sound. Both took the 30.06 rounds in their backs and slammed deeper into the snow. Both were dead by the time the hunters ran up to the spot. They dragged the guards away from the bomb and piled snow over them. Now they checked over the automatic rifles the former guards had carried.

"Nice little piece," one said. The other snorted.

"Ain't no piece. It's a damn fine automatic rifle. Hold the trigger down and kick out a whole magazine full of rounds. Might come in handy when those jaspers come back. S'pose they went for their chopper?"

A moment later the answer came as a helicopter lifted off the snowscape four hundred yards away and came toward them.

"What the hell we do now?" the shorter man asked.

The other man laughed. "Hell, we wait for them to come. They won't even see us. When they land we blow both of them away, go get our chopper, and carry off the bomb just the way we planned."

A digital phone beeped and the tall man dug into his white parka and answered it.

"Yeah, Les here."

"Les, I'm about an hour out from Deadhorse. What's the situation?"

"Hey, we have the bomb. The plane landed, somebody shot the pilot dead, then they hauled out the bomb and went to get their chopper. It's coming now. We gunned the two guards on the bomb. Now we're about to take out the guy flying the chopper and his partner."

"Yes, good work. You boys earned a bonus. When you get rid of the other two men, fly that bomb to the trailer you told me about. Move the bomb inside and get rid of the chopper at the rental. Got that."

"Yes, sir. Their bird is here. Better talk later." He closed the cover and put the digital phone back in his parka pocket.

In the chopper, the Scimitar frowned as he looked down at the bomb. "Where are those two men we left there?" he asked.

Smith shook his head. "Damned if I know. Don't see them anywhere." He stopped. "Something moved near the bomb. Could be somebody in a white outfit. Yeah. Two of them. Want me to blast them with my rifle?"

"And maybe hit the bomb and ruin it. Don't be an idiot." The Scimitar pulled the chopper around in a turn and scuttered away from the prize. He was too late. The men on the ground both lifted up and fired ten-round bursts at the helicopter. The men felt the rounds hit the chopper and at once the Scimitar swore in Arabic.

"They hit something in the engine. Oil pressure is dropping like crazy; we've got to sit down in a rush before we crash."

He swore all the way to the ground. Just as they landed

the engine gave one final burst of power, then stopped suddenly.

"What the hell now?" Smith asked.

"We get back there and try to cut down those guys who are stealing our weapon. We go now. You have the long gun. My submachine gun won't reach more than eighty maybe a hundred yards. Let's move."

The Scimitar figured they were about a half mile from the prize. They had come down behind a clump of snow that may have hosted some ice upthrusts. The two men tried to jog through the snow, but couldn't, so settled for walking. The Scimitar thought it was the right direction, but when they came around another upthrust, they had to change course. The target was still four hundred yards away.

By the time they were at three hundred yards, they heard the sound of a helicopter ahead of them.

"Damnit, no!" the Scimitar bellowed. "Who are these guys? Nobody knew about this landing site except the pilot and"—he stopped—"and Charlie. If he's behind this hijacking I'll cut his balls off and make him eat them as I kill him so slowly he'll beg me to end it." They found some humps of ice and flattened out in the snow behind them.

"Your party, Smith. First chop down that helicopter. I want twenty rounds into the engine compartment. Just one lucky hit is all we need. Then work over the two men. They don't have a damn thing to hide behind."

"How about cutting down the men first. Then we can use their chopper. It's got a sling already rigged."

"Yeah, go. Do it. As soon as they land pick them off. Try to get the pilot first. Then they can't fly." The first two rifle shots went through the pilot's compartment of the chopper, clipping air and grazing a side window. The pilot dropped to the snow on the far side of the bird and waited.

The Scimitar looked at his man and scowled. "What the hell is the holdup. Shoot the bastards."

"Jammed, this piece of junk jammed. I can't get another round chambered."

By that time both rifles from the chopper by the bomb began shooting back, chipping ice off their meager cover. The Scimitar reached around the ice and fired a six-round burst from the sub gun, and saw the lead kick up snow in front of the target.

When the men at the helicopter saw there was no more dangerous firing, they moved the sling and put it around the heavy bomb by rolling it over, then the sling was ready and they both stepped into the chopper and eased it into the air. The sling tightened, held, and slowly the nuclear weapon lifted off the Alaskan ice and into the sky. Ten seconds later they gained altitude and headed toward Dead-horse and the last available storage trailer.

✴ THIRTY-ONE ✴

DEADHORSE, ALASKA

By the time Charlie's business jet landed on the long gravel runway at the Deadhorse airport, his two men had brought the nuclear bomb to a trailer used as a storage area in back of the welding shop. They off-loaded the nuclear bomb, wheeled it into the warehouse on a forklift, and began making a wooden box that would be marked "drilling machinery" so they could air freight it to Seattle.

As soon as he left the plane, Charlie called his man Warner on his digital phone.

"Yeah, Warner here."

"This is Charlie. What happened?"

Warner gave him a quick rundown of the shootout, the escape, and the shooting down of the other chopper.

"That had to be the Scimitar," Charlie said. "Too bad he wasn't one of the men you killed. I'll be there as soon as I can find you."

He received directions to the welding store and they hung up. Charlie couldn't keep down the ear-to-ear grin he sported. He jogged across the gravel street toward the cluster of what looked to be portable trailers just across from the small airport terminal. Yes, the prize was his. Now all he had to do was concentrate on keeping it. The Scimitar would be livid with rage and he would scream and bellow in total fury. Oh, yes, but that would be a sweet time to see the look on the Scimitar's face.

"Outstanding, men, just outstanding." He had the advance money from the Scimitar in a money belt around his waist. He had dipped into the thirty thousand to pay for the jet rental, now he took a roll of hundreds from his pocket and peeled off ten of the bills for each man.

"That's a bonus for work well done. You'll get your paycheck just as soon as we get this beauty boxed up and shipped to Seattle."

"That's good, boss, because that Scimitar guy is gonna be gunning for us in about a half hour. He must be coming back to town on his little snow tractor. And as you can see, there just ain't many places to hide in Deadhorse."

"Yeah, I noticed." Charlie picked up a hammer and helped the men work on building the box.

Forty-five minutes after Charlie's business jet landed on the long gravel runway at the Deadhorse airport, the Marshall Gulfstream jet arrived with the Specialists and Mr. Marshall. They had phoned ahead and Kat was there to meet them.

"Nothing, I have absolutely nothing," she said. "All I know is that a second non-oil company person rented a helicopter from my chopper friend here in town."

Wade looked up quickly at Kat as they walked toward the buildings of the little settlement. "Three chopper rentals in a week, and the man said this was unusual?"

"Yes, said it had happened only once before when a flock of reporters flooded the place."

"This is interesting," Mr. Marshall said, holding up a set of faxes he'd received on the plane's machine just before they left it. "Look at this one, a satellite shot of this area. There's a smudge of some sort in the lower left-hand corner. Then a shot of the same area by the satellite an hour later, and the smudge is gone. Why?"

"It flew away or somebody covered it," Kat said.

"You have our chopper on standby?" Wade asked.

"Right, ready to go with you listed as the pilot."

Ten minutes later, four of them were in the chopper heading east of the small town.

"The guy who sent the faxes said the smudge should be about five miles east of Deadhorse, and maybe a mile to the north."

They flew in that direction and a few minutes later Kat pointed ahead. "Looks like a chopper on the ground."

It was and as they circled they saw that no one was there. There were tire tracks of some sort of snow rig on the snow around the bird, and two more sets that angled on east.

"Let's follow the tracks," Wade said.

A quarter of a mile later, they saw something on the ground that they feared they would.

"Has to be a jet fighter," Wade said. They could soon see where the wind had whipped half of the white plastic sheets off the remains of the aircraft.

"Twin rudders," Ichi said. "She could be an Eagle. Let's land and I'll take a quick look."

"We better check out two bodies down there as well," Wade said. "They're just behind the jet."

They landed and all went to look.

"One more body," Ichi said. "Must be the pilot. He's still in his flight suit and his flight helmet is beside him. On the patch on his flight suit it says 'Clooney.' Looks like he took two or three rounds to his heart at close range."

"There's no nuke under the wing or belly," Wade said. "Looks like there was one on the center pylons, but it was dropped off and dragged through the snow to a sling."

Kat came back from a short walk to the side. "A helicopter landed over there and took off. It could have picked up the sling and moved our bomb right out of here."

"The pilot is dead and the bomb is missing. Where is it? How do we find it?" Marshall said.

"If the Scimitar has it, we're too late," Wade said. "He would attach his detonator timer device, plant it in a snowbank somewhere or slide it into the bay, and be off on the next Alaska Airlines flight heading away from ground zero."

"Two choppers rented," Ichi said. "One chopper dead in the snow. Maybe the outfit is fighting internally."

"Let's mount up," Wade said. "We'll notify whoever polices this area about the bodies later. That way the Air Force won't come charging in here and take over. First we find where the bomb is. Any warehouses around here they might have rented or used?"

He looked at Kat.

"No warehouses, only open trailers and some tents. Policing is done here by one cop who works for the North Slope Borough. That's something like a county. A few trailers for storage are in back of the business buildings."

"Let's go check them out," Mr. Marshall said.

The Scimitar and his one remaining man, Smith, raced the little snow tractor back toward the cluster of trailers that made up the town of Deadhorse. He knew it had to be Charlie who had the bomb. He probably thought he could sell it.

The traitor would die slowly. The Scimitar knew there was no place to hide in the small settlement. Four or five stores, the general store, and the hotel and its 180 rooms.

"We look for the chopper they used?" Smith asked.

"Right. The one with the yellow bands around the body. Should be only one like it up here. We can still make this work. First we get the bomb back, then we use some kind of a sled and we haul the bomb to the edge of the water. You will have the timer and the detonator all set. We dump it in the sea and drive back to the airport and get on the first flight out, or we rent a plane and fly out ourselves."

"You want me to set the timer for six or eight hours?"

"Better make it eight. That airline might have weather delays. We'll be on the four-thirty plane."

They trundled the snow tractor up to the back of the place they rented it from and left it, then began walking along the backs of the five stores searching for the chopper. They found it two trailers down. A double-sized trailer sat open on one side where a large door had been installed. The helicopter sat there and looked shut down.

Scimitar and Smith still had their weapons. They slipped up quietly and looked in the door. There was nothing there but one man who was picking up some cut-off ends of boards, a small forklift, and a long wooden box.

"Where's the bomb?" Smith asked.

"It's in the box they just built for it."

"You sure, Chief?"

"Absolutely. But where is Charlie? I want that bastard."

They waited a few minutes, then Charlie came out of an adjoining trailer. He was grinning. He talked with the man with the hammer, but they couldn't make out the words.

"You take the short one," the Scimitar said. "I want Charlie, the one with no hat."

Both men lined up their weapons and after a glance at each other, both fired. Charlie took a silenced slug in the shoulder and jolted backward grabbing for his pistol in a hip holster.

The other man caught a round in the chest and he went down pawing at the sawdust on the floor as he died. Both shooters ran forward quickly and the Scimitar kicked away Charlie's 9mm Glock. Charlie managed to keep standing but held his shoulder.

"Not this time, Charlie," the Scimitar said. "You almost made it, but you're just too stupid to think things through."

"Now, Scimitar, this isn't what it seems. We didn't know who it was out there coming for our weapon. We figured it was somebody else. You never identified yourself to us."

The Scimitar shot Charlie in the left knee with his silenced pistol. Charlie screamed in pain and then choked off the scream and sobbed at the drilling agony of the blasted-apart knee joint.

"At least we can use your helicopter, since you shot ours down. Seems fair. Anything more to say, Charlie?"

"Damn that hurts." Tears streamed down his face. "Look, I talked Captain Clooney into flying the bomb up here. Give me some credit. What's hurt? We still have the bomb to use."

The Scimitar shot Charlie in the left shoulder joint, smashing two bones and leaving his left arm hanging useless by his side.

"You fucked up, Charlie. You took on the master and you failed."

"How failed? You have the bomb. You're still on schedule. You drop it in the bay, boom, and you pick up the rest of the fifteen million. What's lost?"

"My trust in you, Charlie. You were my best man. You had real potential."

The Scimitar shot Charlie's right hand, the silenced shot making only a hissing sound. The slug blasted through the back of his hand tearing apart a dozen small bones. Charlie whimpered and fell to the floor on his back.

"Nobody steals from the Scimitar."

He shot Charlie in the other knee. A high keening sound spilled from Charlie's lips, then he turned his head and fainted.

"Bring him around," the Scimitar said, nodding at Smith. The man slapped Charlie gently, then with more force until he groaned, mumbled, and his eyes snapped open. At once he screamed. Smith slapped his hand over the scream before it could come again.

"Nobody cheats me, nobody deserts me, and sure as hell nobody double-crosses me on one of my projects."

The Scimitar shot Charlie once high in the right chest to hit the top of his lung, then once more in the gut to spout deadly digestive fluids and biles into his body cavity.

. "Sorry, Charlie, I should stretch this out for at least four hours, but we don't have the time." The last shot hit Charlie in the center of his forehead and shredded a dozen brain centers before it exploded out the back of his skull.

The Scimitar put a new magazine in his weapon and

scowled. "Smith, check to be sure the bomb is in that box. Then bring your toys over from the hotel room and get busy attaching the detonator and timer. We really should be dumping this beauty in the bay within the next three or four hours. I'll hide these bodies under something in case anyone gets curious."

The Scimitar watched him go. He felt a twitch on the right side of his face. That worried him. Something could go wrong in a rush here. He scowled, then went to the forklift, turned it on, picked up the bomb in its new box, and moved it gently back to the cargo net that was still attached to the chopper. He lowered it, backed away, then went to check.

He had to reposition the box once, then lifted both sides and the end of the cargo net. Yes, it would pick up the box safely. If anything happened suddenly, he could jump in the bird, start it, and fly away with the prize dangling below.

Wade Thorne set the chopper down in the area behind the store where they rented it. They had discussed on the way back how they would search for the bomb. It shouldn't be hard to find.

Kat had told them she had seen only two trailers behind firms that looked like they were used for storage. The Scimitar might have rented one of them.

"He has to jury-rig a detonator that will set off the nuclear device," Mr. Marshall said. "Then he'll put on a timer that will give them a few hours to get out of the area before the blast comes. The timer is off the shelf, and simple to install. The method of setting off the bomb without the right arming signals and the hardware that should be on it will be the challenge."

"How much time are we talking about?" Ichi asked.

"Two, maybe three hours, if the guy is good," Wade said. "I saw a demonstration put on by the AEC once. The work was on a dummy bomb, but it took the man almost four hours to fix it so it would detonate. That was before the preprogrammed timers they have these days."

The Specialists left Mr. Marshall in the hotel and moved down the back side of the hotel and the five business firms that made up the rest of Deadhorse, Alaska. They came to the first trailer set close to the back of the drill works store. The outside door held a thick hasp and a sturdy padlock. They moved on to the next store, went past it, and then ahead again. Kat was in the lead. She came around the corner of the back of the chopper store and paused.

Ahead she saw a helicopter not in the lot behind the rental office. At the very corner of the empty trailer she saw a man standing with his back to her looking the other way. He turned and glanced toward where she was only partly concealed.

Kat gasped. "That's the man I was uncertain of," she told Wade who was right behind her. "He must be working for the Scimitar."

"Where?" Wade asked.

Kat pointed out the spot where he was. "He's gone. That's a rental chopper. The bomb could be just inside." That's when they heard the chopper motor start and rev. It was still warm. Wade darted forward only to be met by a chattering of submachine gun fire that whipped past his thighs and nicked his pants leg. He dove to the left behind the wall of another trailer to get out of the line of fire.

The machine-gun fire slowed, then stopped. It began again as the chopper's blades started to turn as the turbines powered up. Wade took another look around the building and saw the bird lifting off, a cargo net below her with a long wooden box inside it. A man in the chopper door kept firing at them with the submachine gun until the helicopter slanted away to the east and went out of sight.

Wade felt the pain then; a round had nicked him in the leg. He'd look at it later.

"He's gone," Kat said. "What can we do now?"

✶ THIRTY-TWO ✶

DEADHORSE, ALASKA

"What do we do now?" Wade asked, repeating Kat's question. "We get in our chopper and chase them. They may not be ready to dump the bomb yet. We interrupted their work."

Wade took off in a sprint, past two buildings to the back lot where they had left the chopper. They still had the keys. Wade, Kat, Ichi, and Roger piled into the bird and Wade lifted off as soon as he had it warmed up and the turbines up to power.

"They went to the east," Kat said. "Low level and not too fast. Must be the bomb in that sling."

Wade turned the bird to the east and climbed so they could have longer sight lines. Roger picked it up first.

"There it is, at about eleven o'clock low, busting over the ice and snow."

"Got it," Wade said. "We can catch him easily, but what can we do then? We don't want to shoot him down."

"Why is the bomb in that wooden box?" Ichi asked. "Looks like it was ready for shipment. Have we misread this guy?"

"Maybe he didn't build the box," Kat said. "Remember that third party who might be in the mix here. Maybe they put it in a box to ship it, but good old Scimitar got it back from them."

"So maybe he hasn't had time to work on the detonator and get a timer set up," Wade said. "He needs some more time, so where can he do the work?"

"No place to hide around here," Kat said.

"All he can do is get rid of us," Ichi said. "Lure us way out here on the ice, then shoot us down and go back to his shop and finish the work. Before we could walk back he'd be done and have the bomb planted."

"Or we could do the same to him," Kat said. "Get him way out on the ice and drop him. What weapons do we have?"

The longest was a Colt M-4A1. Ichi frowned at it. "Five, maybe six hundred yards. Should be more range than they have with the sub gun I heard."

"So we let the fish run with the bait before he turns around and confronts us?" Wade asked. The other three concurred. Ichi put a fresh magazine in the Colt and was ready. It had thirty rounds of 5.56mm slammers.

"Should do the job," Ichi said. "If he gives us a chance."

"It's a gamble for him, but it's all he has left," Wade said. "He can't fix the bomb on the run. He has to put us down first, then fix the bomb and drop it in the bay. Do more damage to the oil rigs that way."

"Surprise," Wade said. "The Scimitar is coming back to us."

"Look out, he's heading straight at us," Roger said.

"Range?" Ichi asked.

"Hell, two thousand yards and closing," Wade said. "Lean out and get ready."

Ichi pushed open the door and locked it as Wade brought the chopper around and then hovered at about three hundred feet. The other bird was below him and climbing. Ichi put two more full magazines beside him on the seat, then aimed out the door with the muzzle lofted a little. He sent three rounds out to check. He couldn't see where the rounds went.

"Wish these things had tracers," Ichi said.

The other chopper came closer. "About eight hundred yards," Wade said. "You might reach him from here."

Ichi lofted the muzzle, fired a burst of five rounds, and watched. Then fired five more. The chopper kept coming forward. Ichi waited for thirty seconds, then shot again. This time he saw some of the rounds hit the other bird. He moved his sights and concentrated on the engine.

Another test of five, then he emptied the magazine into the engine compartment from what he guessed was three hundred yards. All at once, Wade dropped the chopper toward the ground and wheeled around at right angles to the other chopper, then turned again.

"Saw them firing back," Wade said. "Hope you got in some good licks."

Ichi watched the chopper with the yellow stripes turn and follow, then a thin stream of smoke came out of the back of the helicopter. A few seconds later the stream turned into a swath of black smoke and the chopper began to lose altitude.

Wade turned back to watch. There was no more firing from the yellow bird. It descended slowly, partly under control, then dropped the last twenty feet hard and smashed into the snow and ice. The sling had been moving back and forth from side to side from the motion of the helicopter. When the bird gave up and dropped, the sling had been to one side and the craft missed it when it hit the snow.

"One bird down," Wade said. "Good shooting, Ichi."

"How far are we from Deadhorse?" Kat asked. Wade looked back at the tiny company town.

"Three, maybe four miles. And about that far from the bay."

"So they could blow it up right here and do enough damage to set back the pipeline and the whole oil field by two hundred years," Kat said. "If this is ground zero, everything within ten miles each way is vaporized."

"So, we have to get the bomb before they set it off," Roger said. "We land, take our weapons, and move up on two sides of them and see what they can do."

"I bet you flunked risk management at the SEAL training academy," Ichi said.

"He's right," Kat said. "We have to go in and take out those two men and get the bomb. Just how we do the job is the problem."

"Our fifty caliber would go nicely now," Ichi said. "Or even a thousand-yard AK-74."

"Range to the target?" Wade asked.

Roger took another look. "Four hundred yards."

"About my estimate," Wade said. "Going down."

They landed gently and the four came out of the bird. "We'll do a forty-five on them," Wade said. "Roger with me. I didn't think we'd be in a war on this one. Two MP-5 sub guns and two Colt carbines. Let's go."

Behind the protection of the yellow-striped helicopter, the Scimitar watched the enemy deploy. He grunted. These guys were not amateurs. His only hope in turning toward the enemy bird had been to get within range of his shorter weapons. He hadn't. Smith had the top off the box and was working on the detonator mechanism. Good, but he needed more time.

Four guns to his two, and his were both submachine guns. He scowled as the four men worked closer to him with good infantry tactics of move and cover. They were still four hundred yards away. He was surprised they weren't firing again. Their longest weapon must have at least that range. He had a feeling these four weren't on the Charlie team. Then who were they?

He wanted to fire at them, but beat down the impulse. No use letting them know he had only short guns. He should have brought more men. His two Americans were dead, which left only Smith and himself.

The Scimitar saw the four men coming toward him separate so they could attack from different sides. Smart. He could hide behind the box and the chopper until the others came close enough so he and Smith could use their submachine guns.

The first shots came, drilling into the snow and ice near him. The Scimitar dodged behind the heavy wooden box that held the bomb. The rifle rounds wouldn't hurt the nuke inside the box. But soon the other two shooters would have his side of the box in their sights as well.

He'd been in tight spots before. His options: He could run for his life, abandoning his prize. He could fight it out, hoping he lived long enough to outlast the rounds they had for their long guns. He could attack, surprise them, and get into range for his sub guns. He could capture one of the two-man teams, and demand the chopper in exchange, then use that bird to take the bomb where Smith could finish his preparations on it.

The best option was the last one. He had to judge which of the teams was the weakest, then attack that one while defending against both pairs. Yes, it could work. He watched the teams working toward him. They stopped at two hundred yards.

Even at that range he had determined that one of the figures was a woman. She didn't move with the calculated ease the others did. She had little combat experience. He'd attack that team.

"How much more time do you need, Smith?" the Scimitar asked.

Smith looked up from the box. "Got hit twice by rounds. Nothing penetrated. I'll need at least another hour. Have I got it?"

"Maybe, first we need to discourage our friends out there shooting at us." The idea came slowly, then he pounced on it. The one policeman in the area, yes. He took his digital phone from an inside pocket and dialed 911.

Someone picked up.

"Yes, this is the North Shore Borough. You have an emergency?"

"Yes, someone is shooting at us. We're down in our helicopter about four miles east of Deadhorse."

"Someone shooting at you. Why?"

"We think they want to rob us. We have some valuable cargo in a sling but our chopper went down."

"Are you with one of the companies?"

"No."

"We have one patrolman there in Deadhorse. I'll contact him and see how he can help you."

"Get him here quickly or we'll both be dead."

"We'll do our best. What was your name?"

He hit the disconnect button and closed the phone.

The rounds from the others came faster now. They had moved again up to 180 yards. He listened carefully and figured out only two long guns were firing, one from each side. He pushed farther below the top of the wooden box. Three more slugs jolted into the box and two into the dead helicopter.

"Damnit, we can't just sit here and be slaughtered," the Scimitar said. "Leave the damn bomb for now. We need some leverage. On my signal, Smith, we charge out for that pair of gunmen on the right. It's the weakest pair. We do a lot of zigzagging and dodging and hope one of us gets there. Then we kill one and hold the other for ransom."

"Yeah, if we get that far," Smith said.

"You didn't think you'd earn this kind of money without a few risks, did you? Now is risk time. Let's go."

They both lifted up and dashed toward the right-hand shooters. The two terrs were ten yards apart, sprinting through the six inches of snow over the ice. They were halfway there when Ichi lifted up in front of Kat and blasted six rounds at the pair from the Colt carbine. All rounds missed the hard running pair. Wade was firing the Colt at the two terrs as well, but it all happened so quickly that he had no time to aim. Four of his shots missed the darting figures.

Before Ichi could drop down to the snow, a submachine gun chattered from one of the men in front of him.

Two slugs caught Ichi. One slammed through his right shoulder and the other one hit him high in the chest just below his clavicle spinning him around and driving him backward a step before he slumped to the snow. He dropped the carbine and pushed his left hand against his bleeding shoulder.

Kat turned and saw Ichi go down, bellowed in rage,

and turned her MP-5 submachine gun toward the two men rushing at her. Her first shots were short. She lifted the barrel without sighting and started to pull the trigger on a three-round burst. She heard the Colt firing from across the snow but didn't see any hits on the two men.

She aimed more carefully but before she could fire, a slug slammed into the weapon knocking it out of her hands and stinging her fingers. Then the terrorists swarmed over the two Specialists.

Smith grabbed Ichi and pulled him in front of him facing the other two shooters fifty yards away across the snow. The Scimitar grabbed Kat and jerked her away from her fallen weapon. He pushed her to the snow and dropped on top of her and only then did he see her face.

"Well, well, look at the writer. I had been worried that you weren't what you claimed. You some kind of a cop?"

"No. You ready to give up? You're finished up here."

The Scimitar laughed. "You make bad jokes, Katherine. You see, I have the perfect tickets to success. Who do I call to over there in the snow?"

"Talk to the wind, Scimitar. Not even that will help." There was no reaction to use of his name, but no denial either.

"Oh, but it will help." He lifted Kat to her feet and stood directly behind her.

"You over there with the guns. I have some property of yours. Two of them. If you don't do exactly like I say, they're both dead. Do you understand me?"

"Understood."

"First, lay down your weapons and begin walking toward your helicopter. I will be right behind you well armed. Move out now."

He lowered his voice. "Smith, keep them both here. Let the woman treat his wounds if she can. If they try to get away, kill them."

The Scimitar pushed Kat into the snow and walked toward the Specialists' chopper. Kat watched, then looked at the man the other had called Smith. Could she take him? Maybe. If she tried and failed, he would kill her. If she didn't, the Scimitar would get away with the bomb and leave them stranded. She moved slightly and Smith barked at her.

"No, lady. Don't move an inch or I shoot this one in the head. You want that?"

"Let me treat his wounds."

Smith nodded and backed off ten feet and kept them both in front of his submachine gun muzzle.

The Scimitar soon closed the gap until he was ten yards behind the two Specialists.

Wade turned and looked back at the man trailing them.

"So, you're the Scimitar," Wade said.

"Keep walking. When we get to the bird, I want the keys to it, then you walk off fifty yards toward Dead-horse."

"If we don't?"

"I kill you both."

At the bird, Wade started to hand the ignition keys to the terrorist, then held back. The Scimitar lifted the muzzle of his submachine gun and pressed it into Roger's throat.

"The keys or this one is dead."

Wade tossed him the keys.

"Now walk."

Wade motioned to Roger and they both headed away from the helicopter.

"He's going to shoot us both in the back," Roger said.

Wade nodded. "Probably, but not yet. He has to be sure that's the right key to the chopper. We've got ten or fifteen seconds to figure out what to do."

⋆ THIRTY-THREE ⋆

DEADHORSE, ALASKA

Wade and Roger kept walking away from their rented helicopter, waiting for the bullets to riddle their backs. When they were ten strides away, Wade whispered to Roger.

"When he looks away from us at the chopper, we run. Zigzag in different directions and sprint flat-out. He can't afford to let us live. We've seen too much of him."

Wade looked over his shoulder. The Scimitar reached into the chopper holding the keys. "Now," Wade said and both men ran through the six inches of dry snow, angling away from each other, zigzagging to make tough targets.

"Hey," the Scimitar shouted. Then came the stutter of the submachine gun. Bullets flew around the men from the quickly aimed weapon.

Wade felt a whack and a burning in his left leg, but it didn't knock him down. He jolted the opposite way and kept churning his legs to get as far from the spewing, deadly bullets as possible.

Wade looked back again. The Scimitar lifted the weapon and jammed in a new magazine. By then Wade figured he was fifty yards away and sprinting as hard as he ever had in his life. He saw an upthrust of ice twenty feet ahead and charged that direction. He dove the last six feet and skidded behind it. The ice was three feet high and he was out of the line of fire.

He lifted up and took a quick look over the top, then jolted down. The Scimitar was firing at Roger. He saw the big man stumble and go down, then crawl behind a small hump in the snow and disappear.

The submachine gun stopped firing. Wade took another look over the ice upthrust. The terrorist had climbed in their helicopter and started the engine. A moment later he saw the other terrorist run for the bird, jump in, and it took off. The chopper angled directly at the other helicopter and the nuclear bomb.

Wade stood and bellowed out Roger's name. The big ex-SEAL stood and waved. "I'm okay, Wade, did you get hit?"

Wade started to walk toward the other man, and only then did he feel the pain in his left leg. He stopped and looked down. There was a small tear in the pants leg and the back of it was pasted against his leg with dark red blood.

Roger ran up and put Wade down in the snow and checked the leg. "Oh, yeah, a damn scratch. Slug went in and out but it's close to the bone. Might have chipped it. We better keep out of sight until that chopper is gone."

"He heading for the nuke?" Wade asked.

"Sure is. Wonder how Kat and Ichi are?"

They both were worried the other Specialists might not have been able to get away.

"Thought I saw Ichi get hit just before they captured them," Roger said. He cut the pants leg and bandaged Wade's leg wound. "That should stop the bleeding. We'll get it done properly soon."

They sat in the snow and watched the chopper turn and land near the dead helicopter.

"They'll pick up the nuke in the sling and bust out of here," Roger said. "They won't worry about us. It's four or five miles back to town. In the time it will take us to walk back, they'll have the nuke primed, fused, and set the timer."

They watched the terrorists transfer the sling from the dead chopper to the working one. Then the bird lifted off with the bomb dangling in the sling below it.

Wade stood. "Let's find Kat and Ichi and see how the rest of the crew looks. I can walk." He took three steps and stumbled. Wade scowled. "Hell, I can walk but I'll need a little help."

It took them ten minutes to get to the spot where Kat sat in the snow. She looked up, relief evident on her face. "Good, I didn't know what to think when I heard all that machine-gun firing." She saw the blood. "Ichi's hit too. He's not feeling too good."

Roger knelt beside Ichi. "Hey, buddy, hear you picked up some stray lead."

Ichi opened his eyes where he lay on the snow and grinned. "Oh, yeah, a couple. They get away?"

"Again," Kat said. "We couldn't . . ."

Wade dropped in beside them and watched Ichi. "Hang in there, guy, we'll have you out of here in no time."

"How?" Ichi asked. "Walk?"

Wade rubbed one hand over his face. "Roger, look at this chopper and see how badly we damaged it. Might be something simple we can fix."

Kat and Wade stood and walked over by the helicopter. "You think Roger might make it run?" Kat asked.

Wade shook his head and frowned. "Probably not, but it's a shot we need to take. Otherwise it's a four- or five-mile hike. I doubt that Ichi can walk that far."

"We carry him."

Wade nodded. "You say this guy is the same one you met at the hotel? You think he's the Scimitar?"

"Has to be. He was there to make arrangements. I'd guess he's wearing colored contacts and that he bleached his hair, then colored it light brown as a disguise."

"Doesn't look Arabic."

Roger came out from the chopper and shook his head. "Not a chance, cap. Ichi blasted the oil line in two or three places and some ignition and a whole pot full of things are messed up in there."

"Figured."

"The Scimitar is still flying south, away from the bay," Kat said. "Why is he doing that?"

"Not sure, but we'll have to try to find him, once we get back to Deadhorse. Let's get moving."

When they came to Ichi he was sitting up in the snow. "So, we walk. I can walk. Lousy four miles, maybe."

"Emergency supplies," Kat said and ran back to the chopper. She looked behind the seats, in a panel in the side of the little cabin, and came back with only a flare pistol and three rounds.

"All there was. No sled, no first aid."

"You tied me up good," Ichi said. "Not even bleeding anymore."

"Keep the pistol," Wade said. "If we see any aircraft, we'll try it out."

Ichi stood with difficulty and wouldn't let them help him. "Nobody shot up my legs," he barked. But the pain showed plainly on his face.

They walked. Wade limped badly, but kept going. His left leg hurt with every step.

Ichi kept up for almost a mile, then he sank to his knees, arms crossed over his chest, pain etched on his features as he blinked back tears.

"Sorry," he said.

Roger knelt beside him. "You take it easy, man. Only three miles to the dead horses up there. Hell, I can run that in twenty minutes. Somebody hold this carbine and I'm gone. Be back with a Sno-Cat or something with wheels and room for four." Only then did Roger look to Wade for approval. A slight nod came, and Roger dropped his weapon in the snow and charged out at a steady six minutes to the mile pace toward the top of the tower on the airport they could barely see in the distance.

They all sat in the snow waiting. Wade worried about Ichi. A chest shot could be fatal. But the one Ichi took was high up, so the slug missed his lung. No big arteries up there so no chance he would bleed out on them. As long as they kept the bleeding stopped on the outside and kept him warm, he should make it another three or four hours. He'd seen a dozen upper chest shots like this one. Wade took off his jacket and wrapped it around Ichi.

"Not enough snow to build a snow cave," Kat said. "I always wanted to do that. The natives say it doesn't snow much up here. Seems strange this far north. Most of the storms start up here and head south taking their moisture with them."

They stared at each other.

"What now?" Ichi asked.

Wade took a deep breath and rubbed his face with his left hand. "Doesn't take a genius to figure out what the Scimitar is doing. He has the bomb, so he'll go somewhere that he can arm and fuse it. He must have a specialist with him. My guess is he'll keep going south away from everything where he can get the detonator on the bomb working and then attach an interrupt with a timer, maybe even a waterproof timer. Once he's got the bomb ready, he can fly back, drop it in the bay, return the chopper, and take a flight out from the airport."

"So how do we stop him?" Kat asked.

"Not sure that we can," Wade said. "He has a big jump on us. Say it takes him an hour to fix up the bomb so it will work. It could be that long before Roger gets a Sno-Cat or a chopper out here to rescue us."

"Then all he has to do is pick his spot and dump the bomb in the bay," Ichi said.

They stared at each other and to the west trying to will their rescue quicker.

Ichi heard it first.

Then Kat lifted up on her knees and looked west. "That's a chopper coming."

"Get that signal pistol ready," Wade said. Kat pulled it from a pocket, checked to see that it was loaded with a flare, then pushed the safety off and held the pistol pointing into the air.

They saw the bird a few moments later. It was high, maybe a thousand feet, Wade figured. When it was a quarter mile off, Kat fired the flare and reloaded with a second one. The red flare burst high in the sky and floated down on a small parachute.

At once the chopper changed course and headed toward the flare, then dropped in altitude until it was a hundred feet over the snow. All three waved at the craft as it eased over them, did a turn, and landed twenty yards away.

After the storm of snow settled, a man in uniform stepped from the chopper and walked toward them.

"Our one Borough policeman," Kat said. "What about these illegal weapons?"

"We'll have to bluff him," Wade said.

The policeman strode up and frowned. "You the party who called nine-one-one about a downed helicopter?"

"Yes, sir, officer," Wade said. "There's a little more to it than that." Wade explained the situation and the fact that a live nuclear weapon was somewhere to the south where it was being readied by an international terrorist to explode in Prudhoe Bay.

"Find most of this hard to believe," the cop said. "You have any proof?"

"Give us a ride south until we find the Scimitar, and we'll have proof for you. Otherwise this whole end of Alaska may be vaporized within ten to twelve hours."

"I'll have to call my boss," the cop said.

"That gives this terrorist more time to get the work done on the bomb."

"Sorry, have to follow procedures." The cop started to turn away.

"Not this time," Wade said. He lifted the MP-5 and fired three rounds into the snow beside the officer's boots. The cop turned slowly.

"Put the gun down. You're in big enough trouble now."

"Not as big as getting this area turned into ashes and steam from a nuke. Now, ease your weapon out of leather and put it on the ground. Then you're staying here with my wounded man, and Kat and I are going to dig out the Scimitar."

"Wouldn't advise it," the cop said. "Lots of big weather

coming in. Swinging in from the west on us. Weather guys say it will be here in an hour. Lots of rain and fog so thick you won't be able to see a foot in front of you. No chopper can fly in that goo."

"We've got to try. You use your radio or telephone and get a Sno-Cat out here to take the rest of you back to town. Let's rumble, Kat."

The cop stared. "You some kind of government agent?"

"I used to be CIA. Ichi here was CIA and Kat was with the FBI. Call Deadhorse."

Kat and Wade ran for the chopper taking both long guns with them and a sub gun. Wade looked over the controls. It was a four-place bird. He figured it out quickly, started the turbine, then eased in the rotor and they were off.

They flew two miles south but saw nothing. Another two miles, and they could see the storm coming at them. They paced it another half mile, then with the first drops of rain they turned and headed for where they had left the others sitting on the snow.

The cop and Ichi were about as Wade had left them. No transport was in sight. He set the bird down and waved them over.

"Make it snappy," Wade said. "We're about ten minutes in front of the storm. It's a dandy." They eased Ichi into the bird, then the cop crowded in and Wade took off.

"What now?" Ichi asked.

"First we transport you, sir, to the Alaska Native Hospital in Barrow," the cop said. "You'll go up by Air Medical and be there before the storm hits."

"Can't hurt," Ichi said. He looked at Wade. "Hey, you didn't introduce yourself back there. This is Officer Clyde Victor, of the North Slope Borough Police. He's not too happy with all of these illegal weapons."

"We'll explain later, Officer. Right now we're trying to save your hide and the rest of the twenty-one hundred people around here. How long will the storm last?"

The policeman shook his head. "No way of knowing. Our weatherman with the satellite pictures says it's fast-moving and should be out of the area in two hours. But that's just his guess."

Wade brought the chopper in to land near the heliport on the edge of the airport. He looked at them all. "We have to assume that the Scimitar had his work done on the bomb before the weather hit. If he's smart, he'll sit on the ground and ride out the storm. So here's what we have to do just as soon as we get Ichi on that ambulance."

⋆ THIRTY-FOUR ⋆

DEADHORSE, ALASKA

The policeman got out and ran into the airport and less than a minute later two attendants lifted Ichi onto a stretcher and wheeled him away. The first part of the storm came in with a light sprinkle.

"He'll be on the special medical airlift plane heading for Barrow in five minutes," Officer Victor said. The Air Medical plane took off just before the main storm hit with wind, rain, and fog.

They left the police chopper at the airport and scurried through the rain to meet Mr. Marshall in the hotel's small lobby. Wade briefed Mr. Marshall on the situation, then he sat down with the policeman for a talk. Five minutes later, Officer Victor agreed to work with them.

Kat found some first-aid supplies in the restaurant and put antiseptic on Wade's shot leg, and bandaged it securely so it wouldn't bleed anymore.

Wade suggested that they form a two-bird picket line along the south side of the bay and try to spot the Scimitar if he came in with the bomb.

"He must have it ready now and the timer set," Roger said. "He has to wait out the storm, then all he has to do is drop the nuke in the bay and leave. We have to shoot him down before he gets to the water."

Officer Victor shook his head. "I still can't believe somebody stole an Air Force fighter with a nuclear bomb on it and it's here about ready to explode."

"Believe it," Wade said. "After we get the bomb and neutralize it, we'll fly you out to the wreck of the F-15 Eagle."

The storm continued to pound the small town. Then the rain stopped but the fog was thicker. Wade groped his way to the helicopter store and told Fitzgerald the whole story.

"This Phil Lawrence really is a terrorist?" Hal Fitzgerald asked. "I'd never have figured it out. One of my choppers is shot up on the ice five miles out and another one is out there sitting out the storm?"

"About the size of it. We need to rent your personal chopper to set up our picket line."

"I can do that, but there will be charges to repair the other bird."

"We will take care of that. As soon as the fog blows away, I'll be here for that bird."

Back in the hotel, Wade put on dry clothes, then settled in the restaurant with the rest of the Specialists for coffee and food. He'd lost track of the time. With daylight almost twenty-four hours a day, it was hard to keep the time straight. Was it three o'clock A.M. or P.M.?

The fog and the last of the rain lasted for two and half hours, then Officer Victor told them it was time to fly. He took Hershel and Roger with him. Roger had run into town on his rescue mission, but heard that the policeman had flown out looking for a downed helicopter, so he waited.

Duncan and Kat went with Wade in the last rental chopper that Hal Fitzgerald had. They had one long gun and one sub gun in each chopper and doors that would open that they could fire from.

The last of the fog blew past as they lifted off. They stayed close together until they were about a mile east along the coast, then they parted. This time the Specialists had on their G-16 personal radios and kept in touch.

"We'll swing on east and watch that area," Wade said into his throat mike. "Victor, you take it west back over town and work along a quarter of a mile from the bay."

"Roger that," Hershel said.

Wade lifted up to a thousand feet so he'd have a longer view of anyone incoming. All three sets of eyes kept watching below and to the east, then straight south. The Scimitar could swing far south and then come north directly to the bay.

Wade flew out to six miles, then eight, then turned and came back along the bay of the Beaufort Sea. None of them saw an aircraft of any type. Wade turned and made the run again.

"Nothing to report from the west section," Hershel said on the radio. It came through weakly, but Wade understood.

"Roger that, Hershel, keep at it."

They patrolled both sectors for an hour. Hershel called in. "Hey, Chief, maybe we should take another run more to the south and see what we can find. Might have taken them longer to get the bomb ready to go swimming."

"Good idea, but let's maintain the picket fence along the bay here for a while, at least for another hour. Keep watching."

Wade boosted the little craft up to two thousand feet for a broader look at the whole area. He didn't have sunglasses and his eyes were getting tired of squinting against the whiteness of the snow and ice magnified by the bright sun.

He made one more round trip.

At the west end of his run near the town, the radio came on again.

"Hey, Chief, we've got something here. Definitely a chopper coming in from due south. Can't tell for sure if it has a sling on it, but we should know in five. We're heading to meet him at full speed. Come on down this way, south of you and to the west."

"How far is he over land?"

"Four or five miles. We should meet him out two miles. We still shoot the bastard down, right?"

"Yes, if it's the right chopper and still has the box, or a sleek silver nuke in the sling."

"Roger that. We're moving. The officer says we can't shoot at him."

"Tell him you shoot at the right chopper or at the officer, whichever he prefers. Knock that bird down over land if you can."

Wade pushed on full power and slammed at top speed to the southwest.

In the other chopper, Hershel had out the Colt M-4A1 and checked the magazine.

Officer Victor had relented. "If the sod is really carrying a nuclear weapon, figure we should stop him any way we can, short of crashing into him. Take your shots."

"One other thing," Hershel said. "This guy has a long gun, too, so we'll take return fire. Be ready to do some jigging and jogging."

The cop grunted. "So what's new? I flew one of these things in 'Nam a long time ago."

"Range?" Hershel asked.

"Half mile at least. He must see us, but he's coming straight on. If he stays on course we'll meet him three miles from the bay."

"That bomb is never going to get wet," Hershel said.

Hershel sighted in on the other bird, but it was much too far away. He waited. "Won't this thing go any faster?"

"We're at the max cruising speed now. He's coming up."

"Before we crash, I'll break to the right. I hope he does too."

"Range?"

"Six hundred yards. Fire away."

Hershel put the carbine to his shoulder and slammed out three rounds. He adjusted and fired a burst of five. He could see muzzle flashes from the other bird. He couldn't think about that. He took a spraying swipe at the other chopper holding down the trigger for fifteen rounds. Now they were so close he could see some of his rounds hitting the helicopter.

"Down, dive it, get away from here," Hershel yelled. At that same moment three rounds jolted into the cabin just in back of where the men sat.

The chopper wheeled right and down, then came up for a new sighting. Hershel moved to the other side of the chopper and fired again, this time at the side of the bird. He saw the Scimitar's helicopter take four more hits in the engine area. He waited. Nothing happened. They were within fifty yards of each other now.

The other gunman had changed sides as well. This time Hershel fired at the open door of the chopper and saw the gunman jolt backward. Hershel finished the thirty-round clip and jammed in a new one. They were within twenty-five yards of the other craft when Hershel fired again. He pounded a dozen rounds into the chopper's engine area and this time he saw smoke and the helicopter did a crazy turn and began to go down. It was soon within fifty feet of the ground slowly swinging left and right.

Suddenly it straightened, gained power, and then lifted up twenty feet as the sling fell away from the ship and the long slender box plunged fifty feet to the snow and ice below.

"Down, down," Hershel bellowed. "Land this thing. No we don't chase him. We have what we want. Land right on top of it if you can.

"Wade, we shot him up some and he tripped the cargo net. We have net and box on the ice. Hope the bomb is inside. We have our nuke expert to defuse this baby?"

"Mr. Marshall said he came in last night and has his tools and is ready and waiting. Mr. Marshall should be monitoring our transmissions. Right, Mr. Marshall?"

"I have you, Wade. The box is down. Is the bomb in the box?"

"Checking now. Hershel, you on the ground yet."

"Just landing. I'll tell you in a minute." The wheels and

skids hit the ice and Hershel limped to the ground. Roger leaped out the door ahead of him and ran twenty yards to the box entwined in the cargo net. One end of the box had broken open. There lay the shiny body of the weapon.

Roger touched his throat mike. "We have one weapon on the ice. Best send out that expert, Mr. Marshall."

"Right, Roger, we'll do that. Your location?"

"We're west of town, maybe five miles. About three miles from the water."

"Wade, bring your chopper into town to pick up the nuke expert. We'll be waiting at Fitzgerald's place."

"Roger that, Mr. Marshall," Wade said. "My ETA your place is about five minutes."

At the nuke, Roger tore the net aside and kicked some of the broken boards away from the box of the nuke. "There's a pair of additions on the top. Is one of them a timer?"

Hershel looked, then shook his head. "No handy digital readout to show us time remaining," he said.

"Wade and the expert should be here in about twenty," Hershel said. He looked at Roger. "You stay here and guard the bomb. Officer Victor and I will try to track down the Scimitar." The cop looked up and nodded.

They landed seven minutes later at the Deadhorse heliport. Hershel pointed at the chopper they had rented that the Scimitar stole from them. Hershel and the cop checked it.

"Oh, damn," the officer said. "There's a dead body in there."

Hershel looked. "Isn't the Scimitar. Now we're hunting for one man instead of two."

"Let's try the airline," Victor said.

They left their long guns in the chopper and ran to the terminal and its one ticket counter for Alaska Airlines.

"When is your next flight to Anchorage or Fairbanks?" Hershel asked the clerk.

"You just missed the flight to Fairbanks. It lands there in about an hour. Next flight out is to Anchorage in about two hours."

Hershel thanked the clerk and looked at the policeman.

"Officer Victor, can you phone Fairbanks and have the police there check the incoming flight for the Scimitar?"

"Yeah, from the office."

They walked to half of a trailer unit that was set up as the police station, and the cop made the call. Hershel gave him the best description they had of the Scimitar, but warned them that the man might have changed his appearance.

"That's right, Will. He's wanted here for at least two killings, robbery, assault, kidnapping, to name a few. He's armed, extremely dangerous, and violent. Watch yourself."

Officer Victor listened a minute, then said good-bye and hung up. "Usually only ten or fifteen people on that flight. They should know in an hour and he'll call me. He said he'd talk to every person on the plane."

Ten minutes after leaving Deadhorse, Wade, Kat, Duncan, and the nuke expert landed in the chopper near the nuclear bomb. The nuke troubleshooter took his kit of tools and looked at the now fully exposed bomb.

Wade had not been impressed by the man's appearance. His name was Nolan Olson, and he was five inches over five feet tall, nearly bald, and about forty years old. He wore thick glasses and his face had a soft pink glow. A dark mustache bristled on his upper lip.

"Oh, yes, a standard nuke with some additions. I recognize one device they used, but the others are new. This could take some time."

"How much time?" Wade asked.

"Hard to tell. No handy readout dial. You guessed they'd set it for eight hours. Means we should have more than seven left. I better get to it."

The small man stood on the boards beside the bomb and began checking wires and circuits. He used tools and removed a small unit from one side, then shook his head.

"They put on a break to make a trap. If I take out that next box, the whole thing goes up in one instant fireball.

This is not an easy one. Never seen anything like it before."

He stood and shook his head. "My best suggestion is that we lift this bomb and take it forty miles into the outback and let me work on it there. Then if anything happens, it won't knock out the pipeline."

Wade told Mr. Marshall the situation on his radio.

"Good plan," Mr. Marshall said. "He's the expert and he knows the chances. Move it quickly."

They hooked up the sling on the chopper Wade came in. Wade flew the bird with only the expert as a passenger watching the bomb in the net as they lifted it slowly, then powered due south into the frozen Alaska countryside. They set down at what Wade figured was forty miles due south of Deadhorse and twenty miles east of the pipeline. The landing site was a flat glaze of ice covered by snow. Wade unhooked the sling and Olson took out his tools and went back to work. He studied the two devices still mounted on top of the bomb.

"Damn. Three ways I can go here, and I'm not sure if any of them will work. Somebody put in some tricky secondary circuits and confusing double trigger mechanisms. It's going to take some time testing them to find out which ones are active and which are the dummies. I'd say three hours at least."

After a half hour, Olson shook his head. "Wade, get in that chopper and fly out of here. No reason you have to risk being here. I have a cell phone Mr. Marshall gave me. When I get this nuke defanged, I'll give him a call and you can come back and get me." He looked up and Wade saw his expression of anger, fear, and a lot of frustration.

"I'm sure I'll be back, Mr. Olson," Wade said.

"Hey, the risk is why he pays me the ridiculous big bucks. Beat it."

A half hour later back at the hotel, Wade told Mr. Marshall what Olson had said.

"He's the top man in this field," Mr. Marshall said. "We used him several times when I was with the CIA. I've seen him working on dummy bombs on all sorts of triggering mechanisms that terrorists might rig. He beat them every time but once."

Wade frowned. "Let's hope this isn't the day he can't figure out our bomb."

They waited.

Wade had no idea if it was day or night. He couldn't remember when he slept last. Three hours it would take him, Olson said. It already seemed like three days. He checked his watch. Wade had been back for an hour. Officer Victor was in his office making out a report. He had dead bodies all over town.

Mr. Marshall came up to Wade who had taken refuge in the restaurant and worked at keeping a cup of coffee warm with both hands.

"I phoned the Air Force at Fairbanks. They knew about the missing F-15. They said they would fly a team up here and notify Mountain Home. They also asked about the nuke."

"You told them?"

"Not exactly. They're assembling a team that should be here in three hours. A general is flying up in a fighter and will be here in a few minutes. I'll talk with him."

Ten minutes later they heard an Air Force fighter land at the airport and a car drove two officers to the hotel. Mr. Marshall met them and shook hands.

"I'm General Hans Running," the taller of the two said. "This is Major Lindsley. You must be Marshall. I remember you from when you were the CIA chief. You found our Eagle?"

"We did, General Running, and we need to talk." They went into the hotel lobby and sat down.

"General, the Eagle crash-landed on an ice field. The pilot is dead. He was shot by terrorists who tried to steal the nuke."

"Terrorists? First I've heard about that."

"We recovered the bomb from them, but only after they had jury-rigged it with a timer to explode. They wanted to set it off here and wipe out the whole Prudhoe Bay oil field."

"They put a triggering device on it?" Major Lindsley asked.

"Yes, but we have the best man in the world working on it right now forty miles out in the back country."

"Why didn't you call our experts on nuclear triggering?" General Running asked.

"Your men work on standard triggers and detonators. These are strange, unusual devices the terrorists put on, ones your people would never have seen. They are complicated and tricky with blind avenues and double retards and breaks to make circuits. My man knows about these. It's what he works with every day."

"I hope he can do the job," General Running said.

"Olson is forty-five years old and has been doing this type of work for the past twenty."

"We're bringing our people along anyway," the general said.

"You should. That's no problem. Now about the pilot. I heard from his CO that he was a top man in his squadron at Mountain Home, perfect record, good family man. We don't know what happened or why he flew up here, but my hope is that we treat him kindly. His wife might have some input about it. I can't tell the Air Force how to handle this, but my team pulled your feet out of the fire on this broken arrow, and we'd appreciate a little payback. Couldn't this be handled as a medical and an equipment problem?

"You could find that Captain Clooney's instruments went out on him. An autopsy could show that the captain suffered from a brain tumor that left him incapacitated at times. The captain brought his plane to a landing at the first available spot after he recovered. He died in the crash. No mention should be made of terrorists."

General Running frowned, then rubbed his face. He looked out the windows at the perpetual sunshine and at last gave a long sigh.

"Mr. Marshall. The Air Force appreciates your finding

the missing plane, and we hope deactivating that nuke. I have every sympathy with your suggestions. A spin on this might keep the Air Force out of trouble and benefit Captain Clooney's family.

"Just before I left to fly up here, I had word from Mountain Home that someone had kidnapped Captain Clooney's family and threatened to kill them if he didn't fly his plane up here. We're still checking that out. A spin on this might be good all the way around. I'll do what I can. Now, I'd like to go out and look at the Eagle crash site."

They flew the general and his aide out in a chopper.

An hour later Mr. Marshall had a call from Olson.

"All done, Mr. Marshall. The triggering device is neutralized and the timer has been stopped. The nuke is a virgin again. I'm getting hungry, can you send Wade out after me?"

"Good work, Mr. Olson. Wade will fly out there within a half hour. Keep the cargo net rigged and you can bring the nuke back to the crash site. We have a visiting Air Force general on the scene."

Wade made the flight, dropped off the nuke at the F-15 crash site, and brought Olson back to the hotel.

An hour later, twenty Air Force men swarmed the crash site taking pictures, recovering the broken-off parts, and getting it and the nuke ready for transport.

Captain Clooney's body was taken by chopper to the airport where it was flown at once in an Air Force plane to Fairbanks. Office Victor moved the two civilian bodies into town to a temporary morgue.

The Specialists tried to relax. Officer Victor talked to them twice about bodies around town and at the crash site. The third time he came back and shook his head.

"Fairbanks police say they checked two incoming flights from here and found no one who in any way matched the description we gave them. One officer talked with each passenger. He said he checked out the larger men and women, but all were legitimate."

"So, somehow the Scimitar slipped through," Mr.

Marshall said. "He must have changed his appearance radically."

Wade shook his head. "I'm not so sure that he's left town yet. He'd figure we'd be watching every flight out today. What about tomorrow? Mr. Marshall, I suggest we hang around and check out the first few flights that go out of here tomorrow morning."

★ THIRTY-FIVE ★

DEADHORSE, ALASKA

The Specialists looked at Wade.

"How could he still be here?" Roger asked. "Where could he hide out?"

"Right here in the hotel. It has over a hundred rooms," Wade said. "I'm not saying for sure that he's still here, but I'd think it would be a good idea to check out the flights that take off tomorrow morning just to be on the safe side. Next flight leaves here for Fairbanks at six-thirty A.M. I suggest that we have two people watching every flight, standing at the boarding gate, and giving everyone a body search if we have to. I think he's still hiding out around here waiting to get on a flight.

"Kat, you know him best. You and I will take it from six A.M. to noon. Can we check out those flights?"

Mr. Marshall rubbed his chin with one hand for a moment, then he nodded. "Yes, let's do it. Then if we don't catch him, we'll leave about noon."

"A question," Kat said. "Right now is it six-thirty in the evening or the morning?"

"The evening and I missed my supper," Roger said. "I'm hitting the restaurant right now."

The next morning when Wade and Kat walked into the

airport lobby, Officer Victor came in right behind them. The policeman took out his ticket book.

"Mr. Thorne. In view of everything that's happened here in the last two days, I'm going to have to give you a ticket for the dangerous operation of a helicopter over federal territory. The cost is forty-five dollars." He grinned. "Just kidding."

Wade told him why they were there. He went with them to the only boarding gate.

"I investigated the three deaths at the F-15 crash site and released the captain's body to the military. All three were killed by gunfire, but the perpetrators are unknown.

"We found two more corpses in a storage trailer, and the one at the airport in the rented chopper. What do I put in my report to headquarters? How do I explain six dead bodies?"

"You know the whole story. We figure that one of the men tried to double-cross the Scimitar and he struck back the only way he knows. So the perpetrator of the six murders may have flown out of town."

"Oh, I had a report from Fairbanks," Victor said. "The airport police there said they questioned three men off another flight yesterday. All three checked out. Two were workers here at the bay and the other one was an Alaska Airlines mechanic. No sign of the Scimitar."

Wade pondered it a minute. "He could have changed clothes in one of the hotel rooms and slipped through. Or he could have crossed us up and have let the first flights go, and taken the last one out yesterday to Anchorage."

"Either way, he may be away free and clear," Victor said.

"Maybe. At least we stopped him from blasting your town to cinders."

"Yeah, thanks for that, so I won't give you a ticket."

"Another good thing, the Scimitar won't collect the rest of his fee from whoever hired him to nuke the bay."

"Who do you suppose paid him?" Kat asked.

Wade snorted. "No doubt there. The Arab League or the oil cartel. Probably the cartel. By blowing off twenty percent of the U.S. production, the on-call market would need a twenty percent increase in sales, most of it from the cartel members, so the price would soar."

The loudspeaker called the first boarding for a flight to Fairbanks. Fifteen people, mostly men lined up with carry-ons. Kat and Wade looked over each person carefully as he or she came up to the ticket taker. Too short, too fat, not old enough. The first ten went through without a flicker from the two Specialists. The woman was Marsha from the café. The rest of the men simply could not be the Scimitar even in a disguise. They waited until the door closed and the plane taxied away from the gate.

"Next flight in an hour and a half," the cop said. "How about coffee?"

Wade and Kat agreed and they went into the small coffee shop. They had almost finished their coffee when five men in Air Force blue marched into the café.

General Running looked around a moment, then motioned with his hand at his men and walked alone back to where Wade and the others sat. He paused just a moment and when Wade looked up he spoke.

"May I sit down, gentlemen?"

"Please," Wade said.

He moved into the booth beside the cop.

"So, it looks like we came out clean on this one. Your expert did a good job on the ordnance. He knows more about our weapons than we like, but I'm thankful he did." The general stared at the policeman for a moment.

"We understand there are more fatalities on this mission. I know that will give you trouble, but for the Air Force's part, we're clear. We'll have transport up here within four hours to move the Eagle. Soon an official Air Force investigation will begin. Captain Clooney is already at our base and being prepped for a hero's return to Mountain Home. A medal ceremony has been planned. His wife and daughters are safe and back home.

"The ordinance involved is already back at Mountain Home where it is being evaluated."

"I hope your investigation goes smoothly," Wade said.

The general nodded and moved on. "I had a long talk with your Mr. Marshall. A good man. Looks like you people saved our asses here. That twenty percent would have caused a worldwide surge in oil prices. Right now we're in the process of moving out. Just wanted to thank you, and to have you pass the word to the rest of your people. Have you had any report on your wounded man?"

"He's in good condition at Barrow," Wade said. "Last I heard he'll be ready to travel in about a week."

"Good, good." The general stood. "Well then, good luck on all of your operations."

"You too, General," Wade said. The Air Force general turned and marched away. His men seated at a table near the door immediately came to attention and left with him.

Officer Victor watched the Air Force men go. He grinned. "I've always developed hives around anybody over the rank of major," he said. "Things never change." He itched a spot on his arm and shook his head. "Oh, those things I said about your illegal weapons. Now I can't even remember seeing, let alone hearing, any of that sort of weapon firing. You're clear with any authority I have. Now all I have to do is be ready with a lot of convincing answers when my lieutenant shows up in about half an hour from Barrow."

"You'll do fine," Wade said. Then he shook the officer's hand and they moved back to the loading gate. Another flight had been called.

People formed a ragged line before the gate opened. Kat, Wade, and Officer Victor watched each one. Again, almost all men. The tenth and fourteenth in line were women. Wade studied both closely. One was far too short to be the Scimitar. The second one walked with a debilitating arthritic limp and she was halfway bent over, perhaps with a curved spine. She shuffled more than walked, carried only a large purse and a small bag. She looked at Wade briefly from blue eyes, but didn't smile or frown. Only stared through him as he figured many people must do to her.

Kat also watched the woman, saw the shuffle, and

looked at Wade and shook her head a fraction of an inch.
There were two more women.

"Some of these women work in the kitchen and laundry
at the workers' compound," the cop told them. "They get
their time off just as the men do."

As they watched the last of the travelers enter the plane
Wade shook his head. "I was sure that we would catch
him trying to get on board," Wade said.

"No more flights until four this afternoon," the officer
said. "You guys waiting around?"

"Afraid not. Mr. Marshall said he wanted to take off at
noon. That about wraps up the detail for us here. We'll fly
back to New York and spend two days there, then be on
our way back to London. Oh, Officer Victor. If anyone
asks about us, you don't know us and you've never heard
of us. All right?"

"What? What? I can't understand what you're saying,"
the policeman said. "Who are you folks, anyway?"

On board the jet passenger liner waiting to take off from
Prudhoe Bay airport, the hunchbacked woman with the
shuffling steps had the help of two attendants as she pain-
fully slid into an aisle seat. The attendants assured her they
would not put anyone in the other two seats beside her.

When the two helpers left to greet other passengers, the
hunchbacked figure eased into a slightly more comfortable
position, moved the seat back, and stretched out long legs.
A moment later the blue contact lenses came off brown
eyes and a slow frown touched the much powdered and
made-up face. The Scimitar was still furious that his project had failed. At least he had escaped. He would meet the
Specialists another day, and they would pay for what they
had done to him. Until then, he would wait, and pray to
Allah for a just revenge.

About the Author

CHET CUNNINGHAM, an army veteran of the Korean War, experienced combat firsthand as an 81-mm mortar gunner and squad leader. He has been a store clerk, farm-worker, photographer, audiovisual writer, and newspaper reporter. A former freelance writer, he has published 283 books—mostly action, historical, and western novels. He was born in Nebraska, grew up in Oregon, worked in Michigan, went to college in New York City, and now lives with his wife in San Diego.

If you enjoyed NUKE DOWN,
be sure to look for the next
in The Specialists series

coming soon from Bantam Books

Here's a sneak peek . . .

DUBAYY, UNITED ARAB EMIRATES

Kat sat in a VIP waiting room at the airport at Dubayy. It had been a long flight in the Marshall Gulfstream II business jet. They had jolted away from London, grabbed the maximum cruising speed of 581 mph and headed for Cairo where they took on fuel and food, and flew on to Dubayy, something over 5,000 miles total.

They had been on the move for over nine hours and their workday was about to begin. It was dark and they had lost three hours, as she remembered, to the time zone monster. The Navy CH-46 was fueled and ready, the IBS and motor were on board and Roger had checked them out. The Specialists would take off in five minutes.

She had not worn her combat vest or harness during the long flight, but now Kat put them on to get used to them. She wasn't looking forward to the drop out of the chopper into the cold Persian Gulf.

"Time to move," Roger said at the door. He had made one last check on the boat and motor, and zipped up his radio in a watertight bag on his harness. The set could contact the chopper if they had any trouble.

"The pilot will give me a compass reading just as he drops us, so we know how to find that big ship," Roger said as they walked toward the helicopter. "This should be a piece of cake. We'll ask whoever we see first if the bad guys are wearing any kind of uniform so we can ID them. First we take over the torpedo boat.

"Oh, the locals just had word that one tanker was torpedoed this noon trying to run the blockade. She's limping into port here for repairs. After that all the tankers slowed and paid the ransom to get past."

"Do tankers move through there at night?" Duncan asked.

"Couldn't tell you. It's a rather wide area. I don't see why they couldn't. We'll find out."

"What if the torpedo boat is out collecting fees when we get there," Wade asked.

"We wait for it or I go up the side," Roger said. "I've done it before. I have rope, grappling hook, and magnetic plates. Either way we get on board. Hell, I can help Ichi go up if he can't climb the rope."

They filed onboard the big chopper and settled on the floor. Roger shouted so they could hear. "Flight time about forty minutes. We'll get a red light ten minutes before we drop."

Kat wasn't worried about jumping into the water. She was at home in the wet. The chopper would hover about eight to ten feet off the water and they would push the IBS out, then follow. They had float bags holding their weapons and ammo with buoyancy devices. Water wings.

Wade had decided at the last minute to take Ichi along. The doctor had said he would be all right if he didn't have to swim more than a few yards. He wouldn't be good on a rope climb. Wade would stay right beside Ichi until they both were on the luxury liner's deck.

"You guys grab me if I go under more than twice," he had told them at Dubayy.

"Piece of cake," Roger said. "I've done this water drop one thousand, two hundred and forty-eight times, and never lost a jumper. You'll be fine."

Wade wasn't concerned. He wished there had been a chance for a practice run, but this would have to do. There just wasn't time for the best possible training. They would go on gut instinct and experience.

The big rotors and motors made a continual blast of noise that killed most conversation. Roger looked up and saw the red light.

"Ten minutes," he shouted and all understood. They got to their feet and checked each other, including the float bags that were tied securely to their right wrists.

They moved to the rear of the helicopter where they would jump. Wade tied a thin nylon line on Ichi's harness and the other end of the ten-foot line on his own wrist. They would jump together and Wade would make sure Ichi got on board the IBS.

A moment later the green light came on and the rear hatch swung upward. Roger pushed the inflated IBS out the hatch, then stepped off the edge of the chopper into mid air. Kat was next in line. She took a deep breath and jumped. Almost at once she hit the water and went under. The cord on her right wrist attached to the float bag helped her pop up quickly. She could barely make out a dark shape directly ahead of her.

The blast of the chopper rotors had pushed the boat ahead of her twenty feet. She swam to it and saw Roger already on board. He grabbed her arms and dragged her and her float bag over the rubber side of the craft. Wade and Ichi swam up to the small boat, and they pulled Ichi in the same way Roger had her. Wade powered on board by himself.

A minute later Duncan and Hershel crawled in and pulled in their float bags. The chopper had left the moment the last man had dropped out of it. Now it receded into the night and a few minutes later they couldn't even hear it.

"Everyone all right?" Roger asked. He got a chorus of grunts and ayes, and moved to the motor. He made some adjustments, removed some waterproof elements and pulled the cord. The 35-hp engine started on the second try. The muffled sound seemed louder than it really was.

Roger grinned. "Hey, it works. Good. Hell of a long way to row. Now we take a reading with my handy-dandy wrist compass and we're off to Disneyland."

"Damn cold," Hershel said trying to squeeze some of the salt water out of his cammies.

"It'll dry in our first fire fight," Wade said grinning.

Roger took over. "First we take down the bridge. That's the key. Then we capture engineering where the bridge commands get processed. These ships are mostly run by computers. Now it's on hold just sitting there, but all of the other systems must work, air-conditioning, electricity, cooking, everything. If we can, we grab a steward or two who know the ship and can lead us where we need to go. Should be no trouble getting their cooperation."

Ahead they saw trouble.

"Heavy fog," Roger said. "That should stop all traffic through the Strait even if they wanted to go at night. Which means our little torpedo boat should be safely tucked up to mother ship at that open hatch. We hope.

"I figure about a thirty-minute ride in this IBS. We'll slow down when we can see the lights of the ship. These turkeys have thousands of lights on them for advertising. No trouble finding her even in pea soup like this."

Kat's teeth chattered. "I've never been so cold in my life," she said. "Not even in the channel swim I tried once."

They rode in silence.

"I have another four minutes. We should see the lady of the seas pretty soon."

They took the MP-5s and pistols out, checked them, and loaded in magazines.

"Put everything you want to take with you on your harness," Wade said. "We drop the float bags just inside the lower hatch. Roger, you guaranteeing that it's open?"

"Hell yes. If it ain't, sue me."

Ichi saw the glow ahead first. He pointed it out and Roger grinned. He'd never missed a ship yet on one of these drops. He cut the throttle by half and they crawled forward.

"Which side?" Roger asked.

"Try whichever one we come up on," Hershel said.

Four minutes later they were a hundred yards from the bow of the huge luxury liner. The fog had lifted slightly.

Ichi shook his head. "No boat, no hatch on this side."

Roger moved the IBS forward and around the bow of the big ship. They all saw it about the same time. Less than fifty yards ahead of them, a small boat with all running lights and a work light on the deck, gunned it's motor and angled in toward the side of the liner.

"Bingo," Roger said. "We're a little early for the ball.

We'll let them tie up and get lost, then we go in and take over."

They edged closer. "It's a Boghammar," Roger said. "Some country in Europe made too many of them for its patrol craft navy and sold them cheap."

"Do we cut it loose or keep it tied up there?" Wade asked.

"No chance we cut it loose," Roger said. "We might need it to make a fast getaway. We secure it and take out anyone in the door hatch."

It was almost ten minutes before the last terrorist left the Boghammar and stepped inside the big ship. Two lines came out the partly closed hatch door tying the patrol craft on tightly. The hatch door dropped again, but was still two feet off the deck.

"We move in now," Roger said. "Wade and I go on board and into the ship first and clear any sentries. Then we give you the word to follow."

Kat still shivered. Partly it was nerves. She'd never been on a seagoing operation like this. She felt the rubber boat bump the stern of the Boghammar and watched Roger jump on board, then Wade. Duncan held the rubber boat to the larger one, then used some line and tied it fast.

All was silent on board the luxury liner. Kat saw Roger crawl under the partly open door, then Wade went in. Less than a minute later the big door came open and Roger waved them inside.

One terrorist wearing black shirt and pants lay on the floor, blood had gushed from his throat and now puddled on the floor.

"Only one terr here," Wade said. "Looks like our boys wear all black. Watch for them. Take them prisoner if possible. If not, waste them and be sure you're silent."

They were on the Plaza Deck, the lowest one that held passenger cabins. Two corridors led off the small lobby area near stairs and an elevator just ahead. Wade checked his watch. It was almost midnight.

He looked up to see the elevator open and two couples come out. The men jumped in front of the women when they saw the military-type uniforms. All four passengers were in their sixties.

Kat hurried forward.

"No, don't be afraid. We're the good guys. We're going to take the ship back. Are all the terrorists dressed in black shirts and pants?"

"Yes," the shorter man said. "We're glad you're here."

A steward came around the corridor corner pushing a small cart. He stopped, frowned, then came forward.

"Young man, do you speak English?" Wade asked.

He nodded. "Some."

"Can you show us where the bridge is and the captain's cabin? We're here to rescue you and take back your ship."

The steward's face broke into a delighted smile and he nodded. "Yes, yes, this way. I take you where no bad guys are patrolling. Come, come."

"Wait. Where are the patrols?"

"On each deck. Men walking, with machine guns."

"Two of you take this deck, two the one above," Wade said. "Watch for the black outfits. How many terrorists on board?"

"Maybe thirty. Come quickly."

Wade pointed to Hershel and they sprinted down the corridor. Wade was lost within five minutes. They had been in elevators, through doors marked "crew only" and down past supplies and now they came out on a deck high over the others.

Wade and their guide peered around a corner. Clear. The three stepped out and headed for a door marked "Off limits to passengers. Bridge." At the same time, a man carrying an Uzi and wearing black pants and shirt came around a corner not twenty feet away. The terrorist shouted something in Arabic and pulled up the submachine gun.

The fraction of a second after Wade saw the terrorist, he slammed the steward out of the way with his left hand, lifted the MP-5 with his right and jolted off a three-round silenced burst. The three slugs made a line upward from the terrorist's chest to his throat and the third one punched into his forehead.

He stumbled backwards from the force of the rounds, slanting off the bulkhead and pivoting onto his back and side, dead in half a heartbeat. The Uzi dropped soundlessly against his chest.

Wade jerked the steward back and pointed to Hershel and they darted back around the corner. After ten seconds, Wade looked around the wall from the deck level. Nothing had changed. The door to the bridge was still closed.

Wade and Hershel ran down to the dead terr and pushed him into a storage room. Hershel put the Uzi over his back on the sling and they hurried to the bridge door.

"I've got the right," Wade said. They tensed, then the two Specialists pushed open the door and surged inside. They were in a section of the bridge to one side of the operation center. No one was there, only two desks and some readout screens. They continued across ten feet of open space and jolted through the next door and found only one terr and two ship's officers on the bridge. The terrorist scowled as he stared at the two MP-5 subguns aimed at his body. He slowly lowered the Uzi he carried.

"Don't kill me," he shouted in Arabic. Hershel knew the language and ordered him to lie facedown on the floor. They tied him with plastic riot cuffs.

"Ask him where the head man, Abdul is," Wade said.

The Arab shrugged. Hershel kicked him hard in the side just above his kidney and tears came to the terrorist's eyes. He spat out a dozen words. Hershel kicked him again, this time alongside the head just hard enough to knock him out but not to kill him.

"The little bastard called us some nasty names."

The two Norwegians in the bridge talked excitedly a moment. Then one looked at Wade. "You are to help us?" he said in accented English.

"Yes. We need to find Abdul. Is he in the captain's cabin?"

"He was," the same man said. "I take you."

He pointed to the door on the other side of the bridge.

They went out it and down a corridor and one flight of steps to a pair of double doors with a crest over them.

"Here," the Norwegian said.

Wade tried the doorknob. Open.

"Right," he said.

"Left," Hershel said.

Wade kicked the door open and charged inside, his MP-5 sweeping the right-hand side of the room. One man lifted off a couch and clawed for an Uzi beside him. Wade shot him with three quiet rounds in the chest and he collapsed back on the couch.

Hershel had one target but he dove off the bed, hiding behind it. Hershel sent three rounds under the bed then jumped forward and fired twice more at a figure on the floor behind, who was bringing up an Uzi. He sagged to the floor out of the fight.

"Abdul?" Wade asked the Norwegian.

"No. Both no."

"Where is he?"

"Radio maybe?" Hershel asked.

"Take us to the Radio Room."

The Norwegian nodded and led the way down one flight of steps and then on an elevator to the communications center. Wade looked around a corner in the companionway at the windows on the room to see if there was any activity. Nothing moved. He heard someone coming. Two men evidently talking and laughing. Both wore black pants and shirts and carried Uzi's.

"Tell them to surrender," Wade said.

Both Specialists pushed their MP-5 muzzles around the corner and Hershel shouted to the two terrorists in Arabic to put down their weapons.

One went flat on the deck and fired. The other one stood, with his mouth open frowning. Hershel slanted three silent rounds into the terr on the floor, ripping two into his skull, spraying the wall with blood and bone fragments.

The second man lowered his weapon, shock sliding across his face, leaving it hollow, dark, and lost. He dropped the Uzi and put both hands over his head.

Wade grabbed him and pushed him toward the commo room. The door was not locked. Wade opened it and shoved the terr inside. One man in a white shirt looked up from a desk filled with a radio, cable TV screens, and switches. He pointed to a terrorist who snored softly in a chair nearby, his Uzi propped up on his lap so the muzzle aimed at the radio man.

Hershel drew his pistol, reversed it and slammed the butt down hard on the terr's head. He slumped in the chair.

"Great, who are you guys?" the operator asked.

"Some friends helping you take back the ship. You know where there are any more of the terrorists?"

"No. They've had me boxed in here. Even brought in my meals. Want me to tell the home office what's going on?"

"Yes. We have the bridge, but not engineering. Our friend here needs to show us where that is."

Meanwhile, Kat and Duncan took the Emerald deck. They were about midship at the hatch. Both continued to move cautiously along the narrow passageway. They met two couples heading for their cabins. The people seemed frightened and didn't make any conversation.

They had moved up a hundred feet when they came to another lobby with two elevators. Just as they came into the lobby, a black-shirted terr sent two rounds at them from his Uzi, jumped into an elevator and closed the door before they could get off a shot. His shots missed but Kat frowned.

She took the Motorola radio out of the waterproof pouch and turned it on.

"Wade, Kat here. Trouble."

The speaker in her ear came alive at once. "What trouble, Kat?"

"We just flushed one terr out but he got on an elevator going up before we could nail him. Surprised both of us. So Abdul will know soon that somebody is coming after him."

"No sweat. We have the bridge and communications. Heading for engineering. Keep clearing decks. There are ten decks if I count right. My Norwegian guide tells me they killed at least six of the officers on the ship and two passengers. Down and dead is the play of the day."

"That's a Roger. We'll finish this deck. Corridors on both sides of the ship to patrol. When it's clear, we'll move up a deck or two."

Kat and Duncan found another lobby near the stern of the ship, made the crossover and began moving back the other way. They cautiously approached the elevator lobby where they had seen the terr go up. Kat bent low and looked around the bend in the corridor.

Four terrorists stood talking. It looked to her like they had just come off the elevator. They grouped for a moment, then they split up, two heading for Kat's side of the ship. Six passengers came off the second elevator and flowed through and past the terrorists, trying to ignore them.

"I've got the left," Duncan said. The Specialists brought up their weapons and waited for a clear shot past the civilians.

The civilians parted on the Emerald Deck and Kat got off a single suppressed shot that knocked down a terr. Three more passengers on the floor ran for the corridor. Duncan cut down two terrorists with a three-shot burst. The fourth one darted into the corridor behind some of the passengers. They could hear him running down past the cabins.

Duncan darted out and checked the three downed men. Two were dead, the third one was badly hit in the chest. Duncan saw one passenger staring at him and waved him over.

"You a cop?" Duncan asked.

"No, want to be one."

"Good. Stay with this terrorist and don't let him move. If he doesn't die in ten minutes, put these riot cuffs on his ankles and wrists binding them together. Then call the ship's doctor. Got that?"

"Yes, sir. Who are you guys?"

"Friends. Now take care of this one."

The man bobbed his head and sat cross-legged watching the man. He picked up the Uzi and lay it across his legs.

Duncan and Kat hurried down the corridor where the

other terr had vanished. "We don't stand a chance to find him," Kat said. Duncan nodded. They had to try.

Wade, Hershel, and the Norwegian officer came up to the engineering section quietly. They saw the door blown off its hinges.

"The terrorists did that," the Norwegian said.

Wade moved so he could see inside. He saw monitors and instruments and screens. He didn't locate any people.

"Go check it out," Wade told the Norwegian. "If anybody's there tell them you had some trouble on the bridge and didn't want it to get repeated down here."

The officer nodded and marched forward. He hesitated before he went to the door, then slipped through. He came out quickly.

"One of our officers is dead. One of the terrorists is dead from what looks like a knife wound to the chest. Our man must have stabbed him and then was shot before he could get away."

"Shouldn't somebody be there on the controls?"

"It's almost automatic when we're standing still. I'll get somebody to go in and take over."

"Where are the rest of the terrorists? A steward told us there were about thirty of them."

"I have no idea. I need to get back to the bridge and contact our home office with a report."

"We don't have control of the ship back in your hands yet. Some ships' officers were killed. Exactly who?"

"The Captain and first officer and this engineer. I'm not sure who else. Four more, I believe. We're down to our second officer to be in command."

"I understand. Do you have any ideas how we can dig out the rest of the terrorists?"

"Not a one. I'm concerned about the ship." The Norwegian hesitated. "You might ask them to leave, on the Public Address system, say at seven-thirty in the morning. Let them have that small boat they came on board from."

"That doesn't sound . . ."

"The alternative is to do a cabin-by-cabin search, which could take a dozen men and probably two days.

Wade scowled. "Yes, I see what you mean. Then after we let them go, it's a long way to shore, and some of our Navy planes could come in and greet them."

"Precisely, with air-to-ground missiles."

Wade took out his Motorola. "All Specialists, listen up. We have a situation here. We might not be able to dig out all of these terrorists. More than a thousand cubbyholes they could crawl into. I'm thinking of inviting them to leave. Give them back the Boghammar. We have any kind of a kill-and-capture count so far?"

The count came in at twelve. "Still leaves eighteen of them. I'll be making a call to Abdul at 0730 on the ship's PA system. In the meantime we get radio contact with the closest F-18's and see if we can get some air cover over this old scow. I'm on my way to communications if anyone wants me. In the meantime, work those decks and let's see if we can flush out a few more. Eighteen is far, far too many to let get away."